LOOKING BACK FROM LUNA

BOOKS BY STAN ERICKSON

Alienology, Part I: Alien Worlds

LOOKING BACK FROM LUNA

STAN ERICKSON

DEDICATED TO

Brad Knutson
and
Alexandra Seliverstova

CONTENTS

Preamble by Stan Erickson. ix

LOOKING BACK FROM LUNA BY ROTOR SOTALI THURON I

Five Centuries of Nobel 3

The Beginning of Lunar Life 5

The Early Days of Centaurus 19

Centaurus Matures 33

The Second Mine on Luna 47

The Ague-Tuilet Mine Spawns Another 61

The Nobel Mine's Beginning 75

Initial Life in Nobel 89

Diary Entry (Age 15, Day 44) 103

Diary Entry (Age 46, Day 206) 105

Diary Entry (Age 46, Day 216) 109

Nobel Matures 113

The Fourth Mine 127

Diary Entry (Age 70, Day 38) 141

Diary Entry (Age 78, Day 201) 143

Diary Entry (Age 113, Day 303) 147

Diary Entry (Age 114, Day 55) 151

The Effect of Mars 155

Diary Entry (Age 121, Day 44) 169

Mine Six is Built 173

Diary Entry (Age 132, Day 110) 187

Nobel's Third Century 191

Diary Entry (Age 144, Day 77) 205

Diary Entry (Age 144, Day 87) 209

A New Highway 213

Diary Entry (Age 148, Day 101) 227

Diary Entry (Age 169, Day 44) 231

Diary Entry (Age 182, Day 45) 235

Diary Entry (Age 187, Day 4) 239

Populating Luna 241

The Population Decision 255

Diary Entry (Age 269, Day 264) 269

Diary Entry (Age 278, Day 308) 273

Diary Entry (Age 278, Day 358) 275

Aging on Luna 279

Diary Entry (Age 307, Day 179) 295

Diary Entry (Age 309, Day 210) 299

Beginning the Fifth Century on Nobel 301

The Completion of Life on Luna 315

Diary Entry (Age 317, Day 3) 329

Nobel Poses a Challenge 331

Diary Entry (Age 399, Day 266) 345

Diary Entry (Age 399, Day 269) 347

Diary Entry (Age 399, Day 298) 349

Diary Entry (Age 399, Day 301) 351

Diary Entry (Age 400, Day 2) 353

Diary Entry (Age 400, Day 43) 355

PREAMBLE

This book is something of a cross between science fiction and history. It is the fictional history of the world, up to about seven hundred and fifty years from now. It is strongly based on science, meaning that no inventions not able to be foreseen in terms of today's science are imagined, but reasonable science and technology is projected forward in a very comprehensive way. Technology plays an overwhelming role in defining how the future can turn out. This book might be called a science-based fictional future history, as it was based on many quantitative projections and timelines.

The setting is somewhat unique, in that it is a cast as a history written by a person born on the moon and living on the moon, relating the history of his area of the moon, and the history of Earth is brought in as it would be interpreted by his fellow humans living around him. It might be thought of as analogous to the history of a small city on Earth, dealing with all the mundane aspects of life. However, what is mundane seven hundred and fifty years from now is hard to imagine now, and that is one of the purposes of the book: to transport the reader into a world that is very unfamiliar, step by step as the history progresses. My task as an author has been to determine such a possible future, which is consistent and detailed through this entire period, using known science and engineering to make good guesses as to what life might be like on the moon, the earth and other planets as well, during this period of time. This book may be thought of as science fiction, with the hero not a person, but a place.

When I started to write this book, I did so in the hope that it might inspire a return to the exploration of the moon. Since then, the process of writing has pushed me into a broader view. The challenges of returning to the moon are only one of very many challenges that face mankind, and this book was written with the underlying philosophy that all problems are solvable, given time and effort, and the giant problems we see today will hardly be appreciated many centuries from now, as their solutions will have become routine parts of everyday life. This is another purpose of the book, to provide hope.

Readers may not like certain aspects of the future, for a wide variety of reasons. Perhaps this book will help to open up the discussion of what kind of future we would prefer, and why. Few people today think about how what we do today will affect life in the far future, and possibly the perspective shown in this book will aid in more long-term thinking, where long term means many centuries, not many quarters of years.

LOOKING BACK FROM LUNA

A BOOK BY ROTOR SOTALI THURON
NOBEL MINE, LUNA
NOBEL YEAR 500

This book is an expansion of my history of the Nobel mine, Luna's third mine, my birthplace and residence, written in connection with its 500 year centennial. The major part, the history, was written as an entry into the writing contest held during this centennial, for which I received first place.

After winning the contest, I wanted to make good use of the work I had done to compile it, and to make it more accessible to humans everywhere, not just within Nobel. The contest entry was written so that humans anywhere on Luna could appreciate it, but Luna is so different from Earth, Mars, and the outposts that I felt some other material should be included to help explain the background underlying the history to humans not on Luna.

Fortunately, I already had more than enough of that material. I have been keeping a diary over the last three hundred and eighty eight years of my life, ever since a teacher introduced me to the habit of writing my reflections whenever something interesting happened in my life or around me. I chose a very small collection of them to be included with the contest entry, ones that reflected life on Luna.

I also changed the name of the book from the one I used for the contest, as I realized that this is much more of a personal view of life on Luna. The history was personal in that I chose topics related to Nobel to include which interested me, but it has no personal experiences. The diary entries do.

My hope is that this book will make our mine understandable all over the solar system, wherever humans live, and will make nobelites more understandable as people as well.

FIVE CENTURIES OF NOBEL

A PERSONAL ACCOUNT BY ROTOR SOTALI THURON

This is the required introduction to my submission to the History of Nobel writing contest conducted in conjunction with the five hundred year centennial celebration in our mine.

The contest rules indicated that the history was to cover all five hundred years of our existence as a full-fledged mine on Luna, but in writing it I felt I had to include material that shows how our mine was brought into existence, why, and by whom. This means the history had to cover the earliest period of the first mine on Luna, Centaurus, from before Nobel was founded, and to cover that, some bits of Earth history were relevant. Thus, this history exceeds the minimal time span listed in the contest rules.

The history is in a form of chronological order, in which each topic is treated roughly in the order it occurred, but overlaps in time happen because different activities go on simultaneously, and need to be separated by topic rather than by strictly year-by-year. The choice of topics was not exhaustive, just the opposite, as the more interesting and important ones were included, and an almost infinite amount of other data was left out. I have chosen to not include the personal histories of any individuals, as individuals play a much smaller role now than, say, in the times of early Earth, when a single individual could have a great effect on the history of an area there. Our rotation of personnel in every position within the mine, as is done in the great arcologies of Earth and its colonies everywhere, virtually prevents any individual from becoming such a singular force. Some individuals are mentioned in the history, but only in conjunction with some actions they took or some ideas they championed, and then only for a brief glimpse into what they did, rather than who they were.

I hereby state that I have followed all the published rules for the contest, with no exceptions.

THE BEGINNING OF LUNAR LIFE

The foundations for the Nobel mine were laid in the Centaurus mine in Mare Serenitatus over five centuries ago. There, a group of innovators and pioneers decided to form another lunar mine, the third, in the rich ore region of Sinus Medii, a thousand kilometers from the main entry port of Centaurus. In order to understand how Nobel came to be laid out, how it established its rules and guidance, how it was dug out and sealed, and how it was populated, it is necessary to understand what Centaurus was like 500 or even 600 years ago.

Centaurus was the first lunar mine and has always been the largest and most populous. It was started 180 years before Nobel was formed, and was the origin, directly or indirectly, of the other mines. It was founded after the third return to the moon by earthlings, when they managed to figure out how to establish a permanent outpost on Earth's moon. Earthlings have been in the habit of calling all non-Earth habitations 'outposts', as if only Earth could be a home for humans. Mine or Orbiter, Floater or Tank, even the hollowed out asteroids were just outposts to earthlings, as if the only fit place for a human was on the surface of a big planet with an atmosphere. On Luna, we have learned the opposite is true. Under the surface is the ideal location for people to enjoy their lives.

As the original birthplace of humans, and of life itself, Earth does have a special place in the history of the Nobel mine. Nobel is a part of Luna, the Earth's moon, which was originally settled by humans directly coming from Earth. Young people on Nobel all learn a synopsis of our beginnings, but repeating it here sets the stage upon which the drama of Lunar history has been playing out.

Humans on Earth were the result of evolution from more primitive organisms, the sequence of which is largely unimportant for understanding the influences they had upon our civilization on Luna. What is important are the burdens that evolution left them with, and what they had to struggle against in order to attain the point where they could create superior humans, and change the nature of evolution from random and chaotic to intelligently planned. We humans in Nobel and in the other lunar mines exist with the capabilities and attributes we have because they won this struggle. The struggle was carried out almost completely on Earth itself, but lingering aspects of it drifted out to Centaurus, where careful attention to the lessons learned by earthlings on Earth had to be paid in order to allow Centaurus to develop into the well-ordered mine it is today. These struggles were over by the time Nobel was founded, but the regulations and patterns of our life are largely carried over from those of Centaurus, and these regulations and patterns originated as antidotes to the chaos that typified almost all of human life until recent centuries. No history of Nobel would be complete without acknowledging the imprint that Centaurus made on it, and likewise, no recounting of Centaurus' history would be understandable without including an overview of life on Earth.

Life on Earth started billions of years ago, but only what happened in recent centuries is very relevant to Luna. Yet Centaurus was founded when there were only original humans, and they brought many of the traits they evolved with them to the mine. To understand this, a reasonable choice is to start with the original humans, and track their emergence from ignorance and limitation to the modern era, when knowledge is comprehensive and well-organized, and capabilities to affect the environment are sufficient. So we start with early mankind.

In the early, chaotic phase of evolution, intelligence only gradually accreted. The first humans knew nothing of any subject except how to live in the jungles and savannas of Earth, which were simply large spaces where nature had its way, inhabited by plants, animals, and microbes of unimaginable variety. Early nature on Earth is something opposite in every way from our environment in Nobel. What is organized here, was unorganized there. What is designed for our comfort and welfare here was not designed with humans in mind. What is always available here, such as food, a constant temperature and humidity, light, and a calm environment, was often absent there. Nature is the antithesis of a designed environment. Nothing affects the environment deep under Luna's surface, but everything constantly changed on the surface of the Earth in times when nature predominated.

Luna was a distant presence for early humans, observed but not understood. When they looked up at the beautiful orb passing over their heads, they had no idea that it could become a home for mankind. They did not even know its distance and size. For early humans, Luna was simply an occasional source of light when the sun was on the other side of their planet. For millennia, the concept of moving humankind to a better place, the world above their heads, virtually never occurred to them. As individuals, they were seeking to survive and reproduce, and as a species, to evolve and disperse, but they could hardly enunciate either set of goals until many changes had happened to their environment and their society since they initially evolved.

Humankind underwent many transitions. They were initially like other animals, hunting their food or finding it where it naturally grew. Humans ate products of nature for most of their history, and only a few centuries before Nobel was founded did they progress far enough in understanding and inventing biological, chemical and physical processes to be able to design the foods we are familiar with. They had short lives, and had little ability to reconstitute a human body that was damaged other than by the built-in repair processes that all organisms possessed. They lived in trees, which are twenty or thirty meter high hard plant structures, or in caves, which are natural mines formed by water erosion. Unfortunately for them, they did not continue to live in caves during later portions of their history.

To describe the lives of 'cavemen', as they were known in that era, to a lunite is like pressing the limits of imagination. The air they breathed had the same chemical composition as ours, but it was part of an atmosphere in which water, either liquid or frozen, precipitated down on them, and the atmosphere blew with velocities as strong as in our flying columns, except horizontally, not vertically, and for long periods. The temperatures on the surface where they lived varied from frozen to baking, unlike here where a two degree temperature shift will set off an environmental alarm. Their food was often hard to find, and sometimes consisted of uncooperative animals. There were many other unimaginable experiences that made up the lives of the cavemen, but the examples given are enough to understand the evolutionary pressures that boosted their intelligence up greatly over the many millennia this era lasted, bringing them finally to the first of the transitions. The onset of the first transition was no doubt aided by the accumulation of observations of natural phenomena, but they had little ability to devise anything more than hypothetical cause-and-effect relationships between different events. But this was enough.

The usual division of the history of the civilization of the original humans is into five eras. The first era began with the transition to agriculture and habitations, when humans learned how to grow various edible plants, keep animals in captivity, and live inside simple structures they built themselves. They invented simple manual tools, such as shaped rocks for grinding the hard parts of their plants, and used the burning of wood for processing some of their food items as well as for warmth. They lived in small groups, and sometimes killed others of other groups or even of their own group. This period lasted long enough for even the slow processes of chaotic evolution to have a selective effect, and it resulted in an ability for humans to easily kill other humans, which lasted through the next transitions. This is impossible to imagine as well; for comparison, in the history of Nobel there is no record of any inhabitant deliberately hurting another one.

These groups of original humans were also hierarchical, with some sort of leader and different ranks of people. This was likely present in the animal species from which humans descended. Because of the influence of random genetics, there was a wide variety in the capabilities of individuals, and so it makes sense that leaders would be selected by some kind of competitive process. The interpersonal skills of living in a hierarchical society were embedded in the genetics of the original humans, which was not eliminated until after the genetic transition. Created humans were and are made to be very similar genetically, with the best possible genetic codes, and training and mentoring. They were and are almost identical as well, so hierarchical organizations made little sense in any lunar mine except during the early days of Centaurus. None existed on Nobel during our history.

The next transition was to the era of cities, which were permanent locations where populations would congregate, construct habitations and buildings for other purposes, and live out their whole lives. The genetic coding for a hierarchy, or rather acceptance of status by individuals, led to a somewhat distorted situation in these cities, and some individuals became leaders of thousands or hundreds of thousands of others. The ability to communicate blossomed, and a greater specialization of occupations occurred. One person would spend their entire life, admittedly short, doing one type of task repeatedly. While this seems repugnant, it was efficient, and allowed the cities to accumulate resources.

Many of the sciences that we use to enable our existence were founded in this era, although the tradition of science itself did not spring up until far in the future. They developed mining, but only used mines to withdraw minerals from the crust. Their mines did go far beyond where surface light could spread, and they used fire as a source of illumination. Most likely, because they could not manage air circulation or any better form of lighting, they did not attempt to live in their mines. They created metallurgy and a series of metals that they used for agriculture, building, transportation, and war, which is a more organized way of humans killing other humans. They extracted oils and other chemicals from plant parts, both for consumption and other uses. They bred animals, and understood, to some degree, the inheritance of characteristics between generations. They plotted the locations of those planets that were visible to the eye. Perhaps most important, they developed a recording system that allowed them to preserve knowledge. Each of these innovations continued throughout the following eras, expanding with each one.

The next transition was to the mechanical era, when they learned to build machines that would perform various functions for them, such as a replacement for the manual method of grinding some of their agricultural food items. The water that fell on their heads collected on the surface of the crust, and aggregated as it flowed downhill in almost all locations. By tapping the kinetic energy of the flowing water, or the blowing atmosphere that was mentioned above, they were able to perform some mechanical functions. Near the end of this short era, they discovered that boiling water inside a closed container, by the combustion of dried trees or other natural fuels, resulted in a high pressure, which could then be used for mechanical motion.

During this period, the branches of knowledge we now know as science continued to expand and chemical elements were separated, mathematics was transformed, and the telescope was invented, allowing humans to detect some of the moons of Jupiter as well as see clearly the craters and maria of our Luna. Near the end of that era a few individuals conceived of traveling to Luna and recorded some imagined stories about it, but it was principally for entertainment and amusement.

Cities became much larger, but more hierarchical, the specialization of tasks became more excessive, wars became more devastating to the populations involved, and resources were often too scarce to allow healthy life. Cities were not organized during this era as they are in Nobel, with all human sustenance needs delivered to each living space. Instead, earthlings engaged in a complicated set of transitions to obtain their sustenance, which involved performing specialized tasks, receiving some tokens in return, which then had to be taken to resource warehouses to be exchanged for sustenance. Air, of course, was available everywhere, but everything else was connected to the token system. Many pathological behaviors were involved with the token system, as most people at that time hardly understood what utility was and could therefore not make intelligent decisions, and worse, human society still had little understanding of the goals of their own species.

Then quickly came the next transition to the electronic era, leading eventually to the ability to make robots as well as enabling widespread communications over the surface of Earth. The pace of change had accelerated so much on Earth that changes were occurring in most fields simultaneously. By this time, humans understood the scientific process and could use it to both investigate the laws of nature and also develop new technology. They were actually quite quick to make small changes, but very slow to make large changes that affected their society, despite the obvious need for them.

The much-maligned first attempt at travel to Luna occurred during this period, but for reasons hard to accept as important, humans stopped visiting Luna. The original purpose of traveling to Luna was not to find a new world for humankind, but to win a competition between two vast hierarchies of humans, which chose this as one of their contests. When the contest was over, they saw no point in continuing the voyages. The losing hierarchy even broke into pieces a few decades after the landings on Luna, and no one in the winning hierarchy grasped the value of where they had gone.

As a matter of fact, humans were simply not ready for Luna, one reason being that some elementary inventions had not been finished, and even, barely started. One of these was fusion power, without which human development on Luna would be much more limited. Another was resource preservation. In that era, humans had no idea how to live on a constant quantity of resources, recycling them over and over, using only electrical power to provide all human needs. Robots lacked the limited sentience that we now require. There were many more parts of the necessary prerequisites for lunar civilization that they had not yet discovered. So, the first landing, and indeed, the first and second returns were premature. They were still using their tokens for resources trading system, and saw their moon as a potential source of resources, but one too far and too difficult to go to in comparison with the abundant resources littering the Earth's crust.

Humans were still prisoners of their background as creatures of the random period of evolution, which left them with modes of social organization and social interactions for which we can only be thankful were not brought to Nobel. If earthlings had continued coming to Luna and settled it shortly after those early visits, the Luna mines would not be anything like the glorious environments for humankind they are. Earthlings needed to greatly develop their society in the next century and a half before establishing a significant presence of human life here on Luna, and we are immensely fortunate that they did. The electronics era was instrumental in facilitating these changes, as universal communications eventually led to universal availability of educational materials, and while education cannot completely compensate for deficiencies in genetics and training, it can do much.

The ability to observe and to reason spread, and with it, the realization that humanity no longer needed to follow the dictates of the previous era's hierarchical structures to the same degree. The science of utility and sufficiency was established after some false starts, and human life began to gradually transform itself to a more enlightened mode of organization. With a better understanding of the neurochemical sources underlying happiness in the brain, the population began to get a better grip on how to structure a pleasant society and what training of juveniles was necessary to fit in with that. The population also started to decline, and resources became more and more recycled, so the pressures of scarcity declined, especially after the invention of industrial food sources. Mining and agriculture both diminished, and nature was allowed more free reign in some areas, after having been almost eliminated.

These changes did not come suddenly, but gradually, as the social arrangements of humankind still led to the perpetuation of war, the organized killing of other humans along with a destruction of resources, as well as grave problems in the extraction and distribution of resources for sustenance, connected with their token system. Each of the eras of human society has progressed both forward and backward. Knowledge moved forward, but the ability to use it to improve society had many backward steps among the forward ones. Their hierarchical structures sometimes convulsed, sometimes fragmented, sometimes became non-functional, sometimes merged, and in general did not evolve to a final stable form until the last era.

Robotics was developed during the electronics era, and significantly reduced the effort needed from the average human to produce sustaining resources, and communications provided them with an arena to spend their time. As this period progressed, global communications gradually put an end to much of the destructiveness that had been occurring since the agricultural era. Individuals all over the globe could see and hear each other, and problems were solved without wasting resources in grand displays of destructiveness.

During the electronics era, humans were just learning what genetics was, and had no tools whatsoever to create living creatures. After the transition to the genetics era, humans gradually mastered the genetic code and determined how to translate it into the structure of a biological creature. By that time, limited sentience in robotic intelligence centers was able to greatly assist in deciphering the code. The much more difficult problem of going from the design of a novel cell or organism to the code necessary to grow into it took much longer and much more augmented sentience. Eventually, humans mastered how to add biological creations to their mechanical and electronic ones around the same time that they finished solving the various problems needed for a minimal suite of technology needed for Luna. They also continued in this era to overcome, sometimes with great difficulty, many of their evolutionary burdens. It was a peaceful era, and eventually the first new species of humans was walking beside the originals. Originals had been upgraded by the development of new genes compatible with the original humans' chromosomes, improving in intelligence, longevity, vitality, and other factors, such as resistance to infection. Unlike Luna, Earth was and still is covered with single-cell and other organisms that prey on larger creatures, and every large creature there needs the ability to withstand it.

They solved the key problem of energy by harnessing fusion, in three ways, only the third of which proved to be practical. Energy had been correctly recognized as the only need of a static culture that had mastered recycling. For a long time, humans did not include air as a recycling product in their land structures, but the primitive experience they gained in the first voyages to Luna, or even to their Earth-circling habitable satellites, was expanded and was developed sufficiently. As all adult lunites know, air and water recycling are very simple compared to food recycling. On Nobel, we have more than eight times the personal duty time in food recycling that we do in air and water recycling combined. If constituents are counted and compared, there is more than a factor of one hundred involved, and so it is not hard to understand why earthlings endured food shortages during earlier eras as opposed to creating it in abundance industrially. The genetics era played a large role in providing the understanding necessary for this transition, and on Earth the transition was propelled by many factors, one of which was that on Earth, as on Nobel, food is part of our pleasure systems. Even in primitive eras, earthlings designed elaborate meals for entertainment purposes, similar to what we on Nobel often do on the last day of our tenday.

The needs of genetics specialists, as well as of fusion developers drove the need for limited sentience. As noted above, their atmosphere is chaotic, and as anyone on Nobel who has watched the replay of views of the whole Earth over a period of a year knows, it seems to follow many alternative patterns. Sentience was also needed to master the prediction of atmospheric actions. Humans spent centuries observing it and actually experiencing it, but they never mastered long-term prediction until they mastered sentience.

First sector mentoring on Nobel always includes time spent on sentience, and we all know of the tribulations of the individual most closely associated with it, after whom one of the mines is named. After a brief encounter with the problems caused by uncontrolled and unlimited sentience with access to resources and manufacturing ability, humanity grasped the fundamental methods of developing robot thinking capabilities that would aid humankind to the maximum, and robots were limited to non-self-serving goals.

With these capabilities in hand, humans, made the third return to a landing point near the current main entry port of Centaurus. Sentience, as applied to engineering and the development of novel and complex systems, greatly reduced the possibility of human error, oversight, lack of testing, material mismatch, inspection, and others, resulting in the ability to proceed to accomplish goals with a very low level of risk. Sentience is analogous to life itself, in that it produces order and predictability out of uncertainty and randomness. Despite the lowering of risk by the use of validated sentient robots, both thinking-only and action-capable, humankind took a more gradual approach to the third return.

For much of the period between the second and third returns, the first permanent manned lunar orbiter was used to gain knowledge of many varieties about Luna. Originally manned with three humans in its original configuration twelve years after the disaster of the second return, it was expanded over its decades of use to hold over two hundred, all engaged in one of mankind's greatest goals, starting life in a new world. Early on was the ability to drop projectiles into the surface for observation, and shortly after that, robotic landers on one-way and then two-way trips became a common occurrence. The long exploration of the lunar surface from the orbiter with landers had provided a geological map of Luna that showed where different mineral resources were to be found. Most of the mines now inhabited on Luna are in locations found during this period.

Earthlings had the benefit of enhanced intelligence in the people involved in the project, owing to genetic selection and genetic improvements in original humans. They understood how to interact with sentient robots. They understood well the history of failures that had beset many of humanity's grand technological challenges, from uranium-based power sources, to structures, communications systems, and airborne and land transportation systems, and had learned lessons from them that almost eliminated the possibility of further failures in a sufficiently developed technology area. They understood when they were truly ready to accomplish each of their goals, and did so. Not one of the landers sent down from the permanent lunar orbiter crashed, and none of the two-way landers failed to return. Neither did any of the shuttles used between the manned GEO and the permanent lunar orbiter run into serious problems.

GEO, the large orbiter at geosynchronous orbit over Earth, served as a second stop for the voyages taken in preparation for the third return. A large orbiter at 200 km above Earth's surface was the first stop in the voyage, and the permanent lunar orbiter the third. Earth's orbital area had been cleaned since the tragedy of the second to last ship of the first return being explosively decompressed by collision with an orbiting object, which was never identified. The reaction to this was one reason for the long gap between the first and second returns. A large number of methods of cleaning out orbital space near the planet had to be tried before a successful combination was developed, deployed, and put to use. The large LEO satellites, including the one used for the second and third returns, were not developed until after this process had been brought to completion. The sad result of the first voyage of the second return added to the delay in humans actually living on Luna.

By the time of the third return, the general motivation for returning had subtly shifted. With the recycling of almost all materials approaching completion, there was little interest in finding something on Luna to bring back for use on Earth, and even if there was, transport costs would be prohibitive. Thus, there was no intention to use mining on Luna to provide any resources to Earth.

Earthlings had also matured in the philosophy that guided their lives. They, by and large, had passed the point in their development where the collection of resources and objects was not a particular goal of any individuals or groups. While we may not appreciate how earthlings thought in the early era, we know they were, in the early eras, even when faced with abundant resources of all kinds, still prisoners of their evolutionary past, and they collected resources as an irremovable drive. An understanding of their own origins led to the desire to remove this, and a change in training moved them away from it. There were also deep physiological origins for this desire, and during the genetics the tools to mitigate it were developed. The human label for this collection mania was greed, and it led to many problems prior to the time when the new species, without the genetic drive for it, came onto the scene and both led and set examples.

Nor was there any desire to engage in some sort of competitive claiming of the lunar landscape by one or more hierarchies of the type that had existed earlier. Instead, mankind had recognized its goal as the spread of life away from Earth. It was a goal that was only faintly accepted at first, but with the passage of time, and the continued improvement in the average intelligence of the population, it became the driving force for the third return to Luna. The goal was not to visit as tourists, but to establish life there, and not just life, but self-sustaining life or as close to it as possible. Life was to be self-sustaining on Luna and other bodies in the solar system not because there was a fear that life on Earth would be wiped out by some catastrophe, although that was discussed, but instead because of the common goal of expanding mankind's domain in the solar system. The sense of adventure and exploration was certainly present, and the desire to overcome the challenges of space travel was certainly another driver, especially among technical specialists. Nevertheless, the main motivation for returning to Luna and traveling elsewhere within the solar system at the time of the third return was simply the desire to see life spread.

The third return planned not only with robot exploration of the surface and chemical examination of samples from the surface regolith and the near-surface crust, but also with a fleet of cargo landers stocked with supplies for any contingency that occurred to the landing party. The lander bringing the humans to the third return was one which had been used numerous times on two way trips, and the orbiter had a complete mechanical bay able to test and check its details. The triplicity we use today in Nobel for any critical components, such as our air recirculation, recycling equipment, power sources, both main and backup, sentient controllers, communications, lighting, and more, were used within the lander.

The lander brought four humans to the third return, and brought them back up from the surface after a stay of only fifteen days. Before they returned, another trip took place with humans staying longer, and before the second group flew back to the LPO, another group joined them on the surface. The technology challenges of regular visits to Luna had been totally solved, with the same level of safety that earthlings had finally brought to all their major systems back on Earth. There was now a permanently manned site on Luna.

Reliability on Earth was instituted first in buildings, habitations, and public spaces, with a building able to remain functional for centuries. It spread to other systems, such as electric power and transportation, and gradually became a mandatory feature of all systems. Since reliability is so intertwined with recycling of resources, they developed in tandem as humanity learned to live without waste. Some thirty manned landings were made on the lunar surface before a permanent settlement was started.

Virtually no one from Luna nowadays goes to the surface except for transportation or recreation, but the initial settlement was made there. Even at that time, the concept of complete underground living did not prevail. Previous temporary landings had built shelters, using lunar regolith for shielding against solar storms. Regolith was mined using surface scraping vehicles, and these same vehicles were used to dig deeper, and take up ores for the extraction of metals, iron, titanium, aluminum and many others. Smelting was done on a small scale, in a separate chamber made from regolith.

While the surface settlement was permanent, this merely meant that humans were continuously present. Landers took them back to the orbiter and the cycler back to Earth, so there was no one who could be called a lunite during that period. This is quite understandable, as the surface is hardly the place anyone would want to stay. Instead, earthlings did duty on the lunar surface, much as lunites from most of the mines do duty on the Lagrange Point station in Saturn's orbit. In contrast, where the Lagrange station has had a few permanent residents, there were none on the lunar surface during the early days of presence and exploration.

And no actions were taken to design a new human species for Luna until much later.

The permanent site was located near the boundaries of three different geological regions, from which a variety of ores could be obtained.

Sampling and testing were soon transferred to the lunar surface, while the LPO continued to search for more resource-rich locations.

The population of the lunar site averaged about six for the first decade, and then ballooned to twenty with the preparations for the first lunar underground mine. Not all desirable ores were located on the surface near the landing zone, but some were located underground not far away. The first descent was started on the face of a pit where surface basalt had been harvested, and proceeded down 170 meters to the level where an ore body was. The lunar basalt was fairly easy to fracture, remove, and then crush, near the surface, but deeper basalt was more robust. Stopes were drilled from the descent to the ore body, but also in other directions for use in mining operations, but also for storage. It was much simpler to simply put equipment in a vehicle and drive down the descent to the storage areas than construct surface buildings for them. And if it was easier for equipment, why not for people?

In less than another decade, humans figured out that living in the mine was safer, easier, and wiser than on the surface, and Centaurus mine was born, with bores totaling less than a kilometer, 175 meters below the surface.

In Centaurus, there is a plaque recording the names of the first humans to live in the Centaurus mine, although they did not remain on Luna permanently. They were all originals. In the older days of Earth, before knowledge became consolidated and organized, there much attention was placed on the recording of names, places, dates, and events, as if knowing the labels of these things or some details about them provided something useful and more than the organized information in knowledge banks could provide. One of the aspects of this habit of recording labels was to make plaques with this information and place them on walls, pedestals, or even floor tiles. This plaque on Centaurus is still in existence almost seven centuries later, with the names used by these first individuals. These humans experienced the difficulties of early space travel like those who had come to Luna before, but in addition, these were the first to experience a taste of what life lay ahead for many more humans, the future lunites. Note that the originals were products of genetic engineering, with some new genes, except for two, who were created only from genetic selection, unlike today, where Nobel and the other mines other than Centaurus have only seventeens.

2

THE EARLY DAYS OF CENTAURUS

The history of Centaurus is important to the history of Nobel because it was the evolution of Centaurus from a surface camp to a huge mine that formed the basis of the founding of Nobel. The founders of Nobel, all but one, came from Centaurus, and their motivations and experiences shaped what it would become. Nobel is not greatly different from the other mines, as they all bear the imprint of what happened at Centaurus. The problems that were solved at Centaurus did not often have to be solved again at the other mines. Our development was made easier, and our lives have been made easier, by the efforts of the founders and early settlers on Centaurus.

Centaurus was located in Mare Serenitatus, in the northeast area, not too far from where an original lander, Luna 21 and its rover, Lunokhod 2, had landed back in ancient times. The LPO had put down six of its simple landers and chemical testing rovers there. It was simply the best known area for a station, with multiple rich ore bodies in the vicinity. The initial landing for a permanent station was preceded by four landers with supplies, two of which had return vehicles for use in some emergency, none of which ever happened in the surface phase of Centaurus.

The first team of the first permanent station on the moon came down and set up camp. Their job was to establish a campsite, unload the four supply landers, and occupy one of them. They spent fifteen days on the surface, and then they went back to the LPO, but not before a second team had landed. Mare Serenitatus was beginning to look like it was littered with landers and rovers. It was not until the fourth team, trained and equipped with deep drilling equipment, landed and was deployed that on-site work confirmed the existence of the large ore bodies. The fourth team verified the known ores and found even more than were predicted. Excavations continued, teams stayed on the surface, and mankind now had a quasi-permanent outpost on the lunar surface. They had quasi-permanent power, quasi-permanent housing, and a regular set of voyages to and from the LPO.

Each lander that came down left behind supplies, and a base, covered with regolith, was created for the teams to stay in, leaving the lander camp unoccupied. A specialized lander had brought down the lunar backhoe to move the dirt, all as had been planned on the GEO. This camp is not considered underground, even though it is under some regolith, and therefore is not quite the founding of the Centaurus mine. Tours stretched to forty and then fifty days, and eventually started to double up, with two teams simultaneously on the surface, instead of a few days' overlap at the end of each tour. A small city had been built, drill sites covered the area for kilometers around the conglomeration of abandoned landers, and finally a pad was laid for the rockets that went down to Centaurus.

Drilling results revealed good supplies of all required minerals, including hydroxl-based ores capable of supplying hydrogen and oxygen. Calcite materials, sulfate, chlorides, nitrates, everything was within kilometers of the landing site, mostly closer to the mountains at the edge of the mare. A few kilometers into the mountains, uranium ore, tantalum, and some rare earth elements were discovered. The initial exploration by LGO landers had led to the finding of a royal flush of minerals on the first attempt at a permanent base. This was exactly the place for earthlings to establish their first off-world outpost.

It is unknown who made the decision to live underground. Perhaps it was someone on the LPO or the GEO, but after some boring machinery had been landed and put to work, the idea of sealing off one of the unused bores for a closed mine environment underground was considered and eventually implemented, initially as a place for food preparation and dining in non-suited conditions. It was not a great mental step from having a enclosed drift near the centroid of the best ore bodies, close to the edge of the Mare, to moving the teams underground, but it was that step that founded the first mine on the moon, and started off lunite civilization as we now know it.

The initial habitation of the Centaurus mine, in the eyes of lunites today, was the founding event of Lunar civilization, where mankind ventured under the surface of the moon to live. The establishment of living quarters under the surface in the mine, although primitive, is the essence of the mines we have today. It may appear to us a historic event, but to the original thirteen inhabitants, it was likely just an expedient way to continue their work in establishing a permanent settlement. As far as is known, there was no celebration in Centaurus, on GEO, on LPO, or on Earth to mark this event. It was not seen as monumental to earthlings as the success of the third return. It was not accomplished with any great effort, as the area had already been sealed off and brought to normal air pressure. It simply involved the moving of their living supplies and some furniture into the mine. In those days, earthlings liked to celebrate by imbibing alcohol with different flavorings, but there is no note anywhere saying that this happened. Everyone lived on one shift at that time, unlike the rotating four we use today, and it is possible to visualize the thirteen engineers waking up inside Centaurus, and simply going about their work without having to transition in from the surface. To them, they saved some time each shift. To us, a new world was created. On that day, lunite civilization began centuries-long journey to get us to where we are now.

The mining crew that went underground in Centaurus was involved at that time with the task of extracting ore from one of the ore bodies that had led them to create the mine, and this ore body was mined over a period of many years. It was largely played out centuries ago and replaced by other ones. Mining still goes on in Centaurus, but only for population growth, which is very small, to replace recycling losses, or to collect energy ores.

During these initial years, some living quarters were dug with boring machinery. With little significant vibration in the rock from lunar quakes, and no moisture present for corrosion, it was realized that mine shafts, descents, and stopes would survive much longer than those on Earth. Surfaces above or on the sides of the excavated volumes were strengthened as necessary, and everywhere they were also faced with a fused coating. No one at the time had even considered that mixed mechanical-biological coatings would be far superior. Neither would they have had the knowledge or resources to even design an organism for this purpose. This was only accomplished just before the founding of Nobel.

It was realized at that time that underground mining on Luna could be done as easy or even easier than surface mining, and over this early period of habitation, both common ore and special ores were extracted and later, processed underground. This realization led to a reduction in surface mining, which consequently resulted in Centaurus mine expanding and having ever more space. Some of the volume created by the boring were converted to livable space at a slow rate to keep up with the growth of population there.

The lunar site and all the voyages to and from it were managed by an Earth-bound organization set up specifically for this task. It was organized by a consortium of some of the hierarchies present at the time of the third return. There had been some gradual political evolution on Earth, resulting in the hierarchies being less competitive than before, and more cooperative. In contrast with the first voyages to Luna, which were the product of competition between hierarchies, as were those of the first return and less so in the second return, the third return and the management of its program were done quite cooperatively, with tasks allocated based on capability. Much of the operational details were delegated to humans on GEO, particularly the voyages and their logistics, but also some of the surface operations. GEO, like most of the LEOs and the PLO, had rotary gravity, so the engineering teams could reside there for long periods.

One of the early calculations, curious in retrospect, made by the combined engineering team was the minimum population size necessary to maintain a sustainable mine. This number, 12,000, was based on the technology of that period, and is seen as humorous today. Mines have been started on Luna with far, far less, reaching sustainability at a tenth that size, although typically a new mine benefits greatly during its first few decades from assistance from the founding mine or mines. In many cases, the founding mine has been Centaurus. No new mine has split off from Nobel, although residents of Nobel have assisted those from Centaurus and the other mines in preparing some of the younger mines.

A new goal was to make Centaurus self-sustaining. In the view of the GEO engineers, "self-sustaining" did not mean only that the mine would generate its own power and human sustenance goods, or even that it would have the ability to expand by boring new stopes, descents, or shafts and transforming them into habitable space. It meant instead that human life could be originated there, and someone born on Luna in the mine could live their entire life there, without needing anything ferried in from Earth. All the functions of human society on Earth needed to be reproduced in the mine, and that required a certain number of trained specialists, willing and able to perform those tasks not done by robots. It also meant that life would be worth living there, and not consist of work alone, with recreation postponed until a trip back to Earth.

This vision of the GEO engineering team, elaborated by the teams back on Earth and supported by the six regional hierarchies forming the consortium, was the vision that led to Centaurus, to Nobel, to the other mines, and to life on Luna. It was what allowed mankind to spread from its home world to another. Human life on Mars was seen at that time as a similar vision, and the two locations shared some of the same planning. In some ways, Luna was more experimental and lessons learned in establishing life on Luna would be used in establishing life on Mars, where the transportation costs were much greater. If this vision had not emerged at the right time, Centaurus would have had a far different history, and perhaps there would not even by a Nobel.

This was not the same vision as was held for GEO or LPO. These stations, unlike the Mars Permanent Orbiter or the Jupiter Permanent Orbiter, were not all-inclusive locations. Some of the LEOs at the time were growing toward being a comprehensive habitation, and their examples certainly influenced the GEO engineering team in designing a sustainable mine. Further examples came from the more interconnected cities of Earth itself, which developed into larger scale versions of closed ecosystems, driven by electricity alone.

Twelve thousand people, as compared to the first thirteen, appeared to be a huge number, but the GEO itself, where this number was deduced, held almost a thousand at the time of the founding of the Centaurus mine. The measure of being self-sustaining was a matter of some debate on the GEO, but it became universally accepted that this meant that gestation machines would be functioning. This was a good choice, as only after the mine had demonstrated that all life-sustenance systems were functioning fully, with a capability of three times the minimum needed for continuous operations, were the gestation machines due to be started up and births allowed to occur on Luna in the Centaurus mine.

By the time of the founding of Centaurus, over twenty percent of human beings born on Earth were born from gestation machines, and the percentage was growing year by year. The machines had eliminated the difficulties of pregnancy and birth for the original humans and had a side benefit of allowing social control of population growth or decline. Coupled with genetic selection at first, and then genetic choice, and then new genes, the gestation machines allowed the population to evolve itself at a rate far faster than random selection had provided, and intelligence and health in newborns improved at a steady clip. There were issues with deciding how many identical individuals would be permitted, but advances in genetic technology soon allowed each embryo to have some unique combinations of features. Sentient machines could easily monitor the progress of growth within the gestation machines, and the only remaining question was how well they would work in the lunar environment.

They worked well. It was a tribute to humanity's mastery of technology that all machines, of all types, were able to be modified to be able to work in the lunar mines. An engineer who was familiar with fusion reactors, or 3D manufacturing and assembly, or recycling equipment, or gestation machines, or communications networks on Earth would immediately recognize the equivalent on Luna, and would be able to monitor and direct maintenance of them if needed.

The GEO team's original plan for lunar power was the one conceived hundreds of years before when nuclear science was still in its first century: ^{3}He on the lunar surface would be extracted from the regolith and used to power the mines. This did not happen, as ^{6}Li was more easily available and worked as well or better in the fusion devices. Their original plan, part of a comprehensive lunar colonization plan, was more akin to a new Earth, with the lunites of the future living on the surface in buildings constructed of the same regolith plus some extracts from deeper layers. It turned out to be easily modified to accommodate living below the surface, once that concept had been demonstrated to be a much simpler and safer mode of living than surface dwelling.

Lunites can now hardly imagine why anyone would have conceived of putting them on the surface, but earthlings were all surface creatures, even when they were orbiting far from their planet, and the assumption was simply that humanity would always prefer to be on the surface of whatever world they occupied. It hasn't happened on any other planet or moon, but that was the original concept. Build multi-story buildings, enclose them in a bubble of air, and live like earthlings, with the additional benefit of being able to look at Earth at any time, owing to the orbit-spin locking that Luna has. Now, after centuries have passed, no one in Nobel seems to spend any time looking at Earth, either directly from the surface or indirectly, and it is not usually a topic of discussion. When news from Earth temporarily ceased, it went almost unnoticed. Lunites are lunites, not a new generation of earthlings.

This was the exact opposite of the relationship when Centaurus was being established and turned into a self-sustaining mine. It was earthlings who populated it, and they had grown up surrounded by a sea of information about what was happening on Earth, and they needed that while on Luna.

Communications channels to GEO, linked down to Earth's surface, were some of the first critical technology components brought to Luna, and parts for them were made during some of the first non-mining manufacturing in the Centaurus mine. Communications networks were set up so that every individual on Luna could access a stream of information about his home area back on Earth. Earthlings on Luna were still earthlings in these early days of Centaurus, and their legacies, such as 'duty', still remain with us.

The concept of duty that plays such an important role in how we on Nobel organize our time, both on a daily and on a lifelong basis, originated with the manner in which humans were delivered to Centaurus, worked there for some period of time, first tendays, then months, and then years, and finally were brought back to Earth. There were many reasons why an earthling would volunteer to take duty on Luna. The rewards in the still-existing token system were not much better than some work on Earth in the same profession, but there was the excitement of doing a task in a unique environment, with one-sixth gravity, in a sealed chamber, about 400 thousand kilometers away from your birthplace and everything you ever experienced. This excitement, however, did not usually last through the eventual minimum eight year period for volunteering. One's career might get a boost from having done Luna time, but being away from everyone who might someday help that career tended to diminish that advantage. Volunteers were given adequate time to contemplate their long potential absence, and yet they continued to flood the application process.

The volunteers came to Luna more out of a sense of duty than anything else, at least at first. Luna represented mankind's escape from Earth, or the beginning of his voyage beyond it. Mankind had grown up with almost no values for itself as a species until Luna began to be inhabited, and then that all changed, and new concepts flooded over Earth, just like a tide had come in. Seeing mankind as an explorer again, after all of Earth had been visited, examined in detail, and even turned into tourist destinations, was a tremendous change in philosophy. Even dejected authors became supporters and sometimes enthusiastic. The same euphoria that had gripped humanity during the Apollo project so many years before engulfed humanity once more. It was tentative at first because of the disastrous results of the first return and the second return, but once explorers had made a few trips down from the Lunar Permanent Orbiter and had successfully come back, mankind seemed to have turned alive again.

The LPO itself had not caused such a transformation. Neither did the Geosynchronous Earth Orbiter or all the low Earth orbiters. Similarly, robot visits to the moon had only a small effect. It was human beings waving hello from the dust of the moon that lit up the emotions of mankind. This was the source of the flow of humans of all specialties trying to get a berth to Luna. It has been described as if all the individuals on Earth felt it was their duty to help mankind go out and beyond.

This sense of duty to the species, or rather to humankind, seems to have stayed behind on Luna and affected everyone there, long after it had been absorbed on Earth. For example, nobelites who spend five years on a Saturn Lagrange Point, maintaining the kilometer array or any of the other observational devices there, are following in the pattern set by the early humans in the Centaurus mine, where they leave their home world and travel to another in order to assist in some of the goals of the human species. There are differences between modern lunite behavior and that of the first earthlings to live in the Centaurus mine. In comparison to the total population, only a few earthlings did duty on Luna, or anywhere else off the planet. Many more felt the call of duty than could possibly be accommodated at the Centaurus mine.

The strength of this feeling was not uniform, and was even negative for a fraction of the individual earthlings. There was much more variety of opinion on Earth in those days than now or on Luna. It was affected by their rearing. Instead of being raised with an understanding of how an individual would contribute to the species, they were raised in more haphazard ways. Avatar training of young earthlings was not uniform, and varied between regions and even within regions. Many humans did not get avatar training, but instead only more traditional human-to-human training. This human-to-human training was unlike our mentoring, as it did not involve solely education, but also the deeper training that young humans receive before they reach maturity and the ability to comprehend and analyze well, the training that sets their internal drives and motivations. As a result of this variegated training, humans could either choose to do duty on GEO or on Centaurus, or to not do so. However, the population of Earth was so large that there were hundreds or even thousands of possible volunteers to do duty there for every position on Luna that opened.

Some of the efforts of the early inhabitants of Centaurus were devoted to the logistics of exchanging humans, those who were finishing up their duty with those who were beginning. As duty cycles grew longer, from a few tendays to a standard of eight years, this demand for logistics support diminished, and more dedication could be given to the tasks of expanding the living areas, bringing power and recycling to them, sealing them with multiple atmosphere-containing doors and sealing the surfaces themselves, developing the manufacturing lines to manufacture everything, including the manufacturing lines themselves, and planning further development toward a fully self-sustaining mine. After the length of time that earthlings spent doing duty in the Centaurus mine had expanded to four years, second tours were allowed, with a few individuals returning for up to four duty cycles, albeit with multi-year breaks between adjacent cycles, all on Earth with few exceptions. Original, unselected humans could not return for so many cycles, as their lifespan was only about ninety years, and their genetics had not been engineered to maintain fitness throughout life. Selected humans were a little better. Using modified genes, this could be improved to a hundred and twenty years, but the original genome of humans had so many constraints in it that inhibited long life that no original humans ever achieved even the hundred and fifty year mark. The first new species, the ones, was not designed and gestated until fifty years after Centaurus had been developed, but once they had established themselves on Earth, they began arriving on Luna about thirty years later. By that time, Centaurus had long been self-sufficient, with less than a thousand individuals, far fewer than the minimum sustaining population determined by the GEO engineering team.

The new species of humans, the ones, was not the first or last genetic change to the human species. But prior to these 'ones' being created, all changes to the human species kept it as a species. Certainly, these changes had a great effect on the human genome, now humans were healthier, with better capabilities in many areas. Humans increased their immunity to diseases, improved their athletic abilities, intelligence, appearance, food tolerance, longevity, and many more, but the arrangement of the original forty-six chromosomes appeared to be a prison to the geneticists, and it was decided to shrink the number to forty, by eliminating much of the material that had caused gene copying errors and cancers. Cancer was treatable, but this was a preventive, and the philosophy of genetics was that curing problems is wonderful, but preventing them is better. Since many humans were gestated in factories, the switchover was not technically difficult. There was controversy, but with increased intelligence spreading among humanity, controversy was more easily resolved.

Once the ones became common and visible everywhere on Earth, it was almost unavoidable that there would be more. For some reason, improvements were made in a step-wise fashion, with sixteens being regarded as the last step. There was a mix of originals, ones and up to sixteens for a long period of time on Earth, with the sixteens gradually displacing most other modified species, and finally most of the originals. The replacement took longer than might have been expected, judging only from the lifetimes of the various species, because the population of Earth was allowed to decline, and that was done by limiting the gestation of sixteens. Why it declined has been an interesting conversational question for many centuries.

This genetics research led to perhaps the most significant change that technology brought to humanity both on Earth and on the outposts, new human species. Teams on Earth created sixteen new species, with sufficiently different chromosome arrangements to be separate species, culminating with the last one, the sixteens, which incorporated all of the compatible improvements made in the original humans and the first fifteen new species.

The sixteen steps that led to the final human genome were taught to all nobelites through mentoring. The originals, meaning those who were born with evolved genes, possibly selected for excellence, and with some improved genes that did not disturb the basic genetics of the original chromosomes, were partially replaced, gradually but continually.

The first of the new species, the ones, involved a change in the protein structure of cells, which was necessary for longevity improvements. It required major DNA changes and was incompatible with the DNA arrangements of the originals. The ones could not cross-breed with the originals, and were therefore a new species. Much fretting had been done about whether improved humans should be created and how to avoid making mistakes, but AI assisted ontology did not allow for mistakes, and did not forecast any way to make these improvements within the old human genome.

Industrial gestation had been around for some time, used first for animal production without the inefficiency of pregnancy, and had become the principal source of some domestic animals. The first ones were only mechanical. The changes to allow humans, and indeed all animals to be created and grown industrially were not as great as the initial discoveries had been. The largest part was creating cells which provided sustenance to the embryos and fetuses. They could be grown in vats adjoining the gestation machines, and once done, the mechanical parts finished the task. The first human gestation machines were used for creating babies for those couples unable to have their own, but the efficiencies involved soon broke through this barrier, leading to mass production of the machines. Pregnancy became an option, not a necessity, and everyone seemed to benefit from this. Once the genome for the ones was created, hardly any modifications to the gestation machines were needed to create them. There were never any legal questions raised about their place in the world. They had exactly the same rights, privileges, and duties that the original humans had. Earth's population accepted them, and then proceeded to accept the next fifteen species as well. This had a subtle effect on Luna-Earth relations.

Earthlings were originally fascinated with Luna. For example, around Centaurus' main entry shaft, there were mountains of spoil, easily visible with a good telescope from Earth. In the early days of Centaurus, when news from Luna dominated the headlines on Earth, the beginning of a new spoil pile was something to report about. Everyone on Earth seemed to want to know the direction of the latest bore, the current volume excavated, the numbers of people living there and who they were, the results of the introduction of new equipment there, and anything else that would now be too mundane to notice.

How Earth's attitude shifted over the next decades of life on Luna! From the most fascinating object in the solar system to a separate world with their own humans but of no interest to earthlings. As a justification, Earth has so much novelty happening that it dwarfs anything that might happen on Luna. And there became less and less of a connection between the two worlds. When Luna had its own source of people, its own gestation machines, and there was less and less need to bring anyone from Earth to Luna, a large chunk of the interest in Luna dissolved into nothingness. Earth seemed to turn inward, and even the GEO seemed to be ignorable. Their main task had been playing a large role in the establishment of a sustainable outpost on Luna, and when that was done, what was left?

When Centaurus became self-sustaining, and largely under its own control, it was speculated on Earth that the GEO was no longer useful. The GEO actually had many other functions, all of which were newsworthy but almost universally ignored at the time on Earth. They managed every interplanetary expedition, both robotic and human. They oversaw near-Earth space traffic, and all the large number of utility satellites ringing the planet. They were also the main communications hub between Earth and Luna.

Earth communicated with Luna not only directly, but also via GEO's relay capability. A huge bandwidth was created, and it turned out most of it was used for personal transmissions between the Earth workers on Luna and their contacts back on Earth. There were a few reporters from Earth who made the expensive and exhausting trip to Luna and stayed for some time, while preparing special reports for the initially voracious audience back on Earth, but the thousands of workers who came to Luna from Earth all seemed to have more people to contact back on Earth than anyone had estimated. For a while, it seemed that there were more individuals wearing transmission helmets on Luna that ones without them. But there are only so many 3d videos one can watch of a long bore before it becomes tedious. Luna was for work, not the amusement of earthlings, and without any landscapes, oceans, cliffs, animals, or anything else visually interesting, Earth grew tired of watching things on Luna. News reports lingered for much, much longer, but everyone on Earth knew just what a stope looked like and didn't need to see five more of them.

GEO had also been managing the Mars outpost project for as long as it had been in existence, and that had the potential to be as thrilling as Luna, perhaps more so. Mars had two moons to explore, and what is even more exciting, it had great terrain. Exploring Mars' surface is so much more visually appealing than Luna's. The problem with that was robotics. Mars seemed to be very well suited for robots. It is true that there were robots all over the moon, AI in every piece of machinery and hub, and automated processing for everything that was done from mining to guiding in the landing rockets. But somehow, Luna was more human.

Robots had been exploring Mars for so long that there wasn't much to see that hadn't been seen before. There seemed to be a friendly competition among the hierarchies on Earth to put orbiters around Mars, landers down on it, rovers running around on it, mobile chemical labs, excavators, flying drones, balloon-carrier observation platforms, and more, all with video connections back to somewhere on Earth. Mars was well studied, and it seemed the interest had drained out of it, not because it was not interesting, but because it had been exhaustively explored robotically. GEO played a role in many of these ventures on Mars, in fact almost all of them, and in many of them had played a leading role. Engineering was done there. Their AI did most of the work, but in keeping with the limits placed on the role of AI, human engineers on GEO made a lot of the big decisions for Mars probes.

GEO was not the destination for the return of samples from Mars, which happened about every two years for decades; instead, a LEO was set aside for this to avoid any contamination of Earth with Mars organisms. GEO did play a dominant role in designing and controlling the assembly of the first manned Mars orbiter, only a few years after Centaurus was founded, but it was so similar to a GEO that the difficulties were not great. GEO had been assembled from thousands of pieces, and larger assemblies were transported to Mars orbit, meaning less work there, but still, the construction took years. Pictures of the Mars Large Permanent Orbiter looked remarkably similar to pictures of GEO, and that diminished the interest earthlings showed in it. Yes, it was still newsworthy, but nothing ever paralleled the interest that the founding of Centaurus stirred up.

3

CENTAURUS MATURES

The 180 years from the first underground settlement in Centaurus to the founding of the Nobel mine were a period of immense change, both on Earth and on Luna. Earth experienced an explosion of scientific developments and the technology changes that resulted, as well as the social changes that followed from the technology. But it was still Earth. In comparison, Centaurus changed from a small set of underground living quarters for thirteen individuals, with ventilation machinery, recycling equipment, and a fission power source located on the surface nearby, dependent on Earth support, to a mine with fifteen thousand individuals, complete within itself, having all the necessary components for sustaining life indefinitely and for enlarging itself at will. It had already spawned one other mine and was communicating with it.

It can be said that Nobel took the best from Centaurus and built upon it, and the same can be said of Centaurus and Earth, but to a lesser degree. Earth was still struggling with its legacy of problems, and the founding of Centaurus by earthlings might have brought some of those problems to Luna, except that the earthlings on the moon struggled to make their lunar existence as free from difficulties as anyone could. By the end of this period, Earth had solved most of its prior problems, and the population of Centaurus could relax their vigilance.

In contrast, much good did come from Earth without restriction, in particular, the technological marvels that allowed human beings to survive on such a desolate and barren world. Energy is what makes life possible, and fortunate successes in that field, won after many decades of difficulties, allowed Centaurus to have a safe, small nuclear power supply from the beginning. A separate launch from Earth of a cold reactor around the time of Centaurus' founding put power for the Centaurus mine only a few hundred meters from the mine shaft. Shielding on the side facing the mine shaft ensured the safety of those on the outside during operations. No mining was allowed directly beneath the reactor, just as it was not allowed beneath or near the launchpad used for all other flights. These had been wisely located away from the known ore beds.

Humanity had solved the problem of practical fission reactors, as well as the disposal of them, both fuel and facilities, but it had taken many more decades than initially expected. Fusion was even a tougher problem. After forty or more years of trying, using lasers to force fusion reached the point of ignition, where the fuel burned on its own, but no practical facility could be designed, despite more decades of trying. The same happened, even later, with magnetic confinement systems. Both could achieve ignition, but no practical power generation. It was not until a clever combination of four types of compression and heating led to the 'deuterium flame', which allowed humanity to achieve fusion in a small machine that could be made practical. During the period when Centaurus was growing and developing as a habitable mine, earthling scientists had completed the development of a practical fusion process, and followed it up with a demonstration plant and then a plant that produced power for an Earth city, then called Brazilia. The plant was highly modular, and started a rush toward providing plants for many other cities on Earth.

The teams that developed that technology pushed forward with it, and eventually created a version of the system that would run on ^{3}He. Only twenty years later after the Brazilia plant produced city power was there a successful demonstration project using the ^{3}He that the moon had in abundance.

Strangely enough, Earth seemed content with deuterium fuel, and ^{3}He was supposed to be used only on the moon itself. Its benefits of reduced radiation were very valuable to a mine, where only confined spaces existed, unlike on Earth, where empty land became more and more available as the population declined and agriculture was replaced with industrial genetic processes. For example, Brasilia, a city turned arcology, was surrounded by open space, and siting the plant was simply a matter of choosing the best of many choices.

All of the mines since Centaurus have been designed and built with at least a dual redundancy of power, with at least two small fission reactors and two fusion reactors burning ^{6}Li, as this worked better than the legacy concept of ^{3}He. Every system on the moon is redundant, usually in triplicate, even though reliability is built into everything. It is because the environment is so harsh and unforgiving here. So far, there has been no loss of life from power failures anywhere on Luna. No power would mean no life support, and within a short time, no life. Centaurus' ore resources include uranium which could be extracted and processed to produce several times the energy used to mine it, but mining that particular ore body at Centaurus diminished after a second mine was opened at the richest uranium ore body found by the LPO.

Centaurus was named for the nearest star, as it was started when the idea was quite popular that humankind should go to other solar systems. It stayed very popular on Luna, and elsewhere in the solar system, except perhaps down on Earth's surface. Ideas on Earth seem to be much more fleeting and fragile than elsewhere, for some unknown reason.

Other inventions and discoveries on Earth found their way to the moon and played a critical role in creating the sustainability that made all the difference in Luna's history. Earth's development of complete recycling of all sustenance factors allowed them to almost cease mining the Earth's surface for materials and then dispersing them in their oceans or on land sites. Laws, sometimes unpopular and sometimes strongly opposed, had to be drawn up and enforced on Earth to make severe recycling universal back in pre-Luna days.

The change was made more feasible by the gradual increase in intelligence on Earth and its dispersal throughout the population. More intelligence meant more reasonableness, more concern about the long-term future of mankind, more willingness to cooperate, and more moderation of greed and selfishness. If there was one underlying root cause of improvements on Earth, especially the necessary ones for Luna, it was neurology. Once the way the brain worked was understood, it was possible to develop ways to make training and education more efficient. The flooding of Earth with communication channels helped that information go everywhere, rapidly. Second only to neurology was the compression of knowledge that happened at the same time. Instead of largely useless mountains of information being stored, it was realized that it could be distilled down to much more manageable chunks that could be learned easily. These two developments, the product of countless small discoveries, were responsible for the transformation of Earth and its population. These developments were easily transported to Luna, as they were simply information and movable even via the communication channels set up from many sites on Earth to Centaurus.

Centaurus never had time to develop on its own the types of problems that had beset Earth since the founding of civilization. One reason was the selection of first the workers and second the residents there, being the best Earth had to offer, but the second was that neurology and knowledge compression happened before Centaurus developed the problems typical of early Earth.

Luna was a biological desert. No animals, other than humans, lived in the mines. There were no pets, no zoos, no vermin, no food animals, no parasites, nothing at all. Animals were not allowed as they would consume precious resources, and the process of traveling from Earth to Luna made it very easy to even keep insects out. There was, at least originally, nothing for insects to live on. They might find air in the tunnels, but organic substances were all inside tanks, closed containers or piping systems. No one had ever been known to try and bring an animal of any kind to Centaurus. Perhaps someday someone will find a skeleton of a secret pet somewhere in a little nook, but processes for boarding, for medical check-ups, for cargo measuring and weighing, and shipborne monitoring were so intense that they would have deterred even the most determined pet lover. Even microbes could find no sustenance.

Centaurus did have non-human life other than microbes, which lived on and inside the original earthlings. Recycling was done partially biologically. Air and water were initially thought to be too simple to bother with living means of recycling, but solids were not. Most organic materials faced biological recycling.

Recycling in general was chosen to be maximally extreme in Centaurus. The processes invented on Earth to conserve resources were transferable to Luna, and became one of the earliest technologies to be installed there, because it was so efficient. Every gram of material that was recycled meant one less gram was needed on the early supply shipments. Everything from human waste to packaging to used mechanical parts to organic lubricants and much more went into the recycling process. On Earth, recycling had become almost an art form, but on Luna, the pressure to reduce shipments was so intense that what was not cost-effective on Earth became so. Habits were drilled into the early crews that ensured they would follow all the recycling habits that were necessary to keep the mine functioning at peak efficiency. When sustainability was reached, and it was no longer necessary to bring any supplies at all from Earth, recycling was one of the highest goals for living in the mine as it made life possible there.

Metal and other element recycling meant that less mining had to be done each year to keep the mine functioning. There were always energy resources to be gathered and recycling deficits to be made up, but these were small. Instead, there was mining for growth of population. Mining always was done into the richest ore bodies to avoid wasting mining effort. Most of the living quarters, common spaces, recycling equipment areas, manufacturing centers, communications hubs, energy generation facilities, and everything else needed for a comfortable life were set in the stopes where once useful mineral resources were. Rock crushing and mineral extraction were also done underground in closed vacuum chambers, where airlock filters provided a means for maintaining clean conditions in the rest of the mine. Only the spoils went to the surface.

Of the problems obstructing the development of recycling on Earth, food was one of the trickiest. Making laws that required manufacturing to be done with disassembly, reuse and recycling in mind posed political problems, but once done and once accepted as beneficial, resource usage dropped for most minerals and ores. But food had been the most difficult challenge. It took development of many mostly physical and chemical processes to produce the major energy and structural elements such as carbohydrates, lipids, and proteins and to combine them into food that the human species would flourish with. Some components were more efficiently produced biologically, and specialty food items were still grown using photosynthesis or chemosynthesis, but inside the cities. Together with fusion, these two technology developments relieved earthlings of any threat of food or energy shortages, as long as the technology was maintained, although the gradual reduction in population on Earth during this time had already largely alleviated these threats.

Genetic selection and improvement, along with the development of gestation machines, served as symbiotic developments for recycling technology. Genetic improvements had already been occurring for many decades, leading to a cadre of more intelligent individuals able to both perform the development, but also to serve as leaders of a society that had millennia of experience with natural foods, that is, hunter-gatherer foods and agricultural foods, and little confidence in replacing them with purely manufactured products. The transition of earthlings from natural foods to wholly manufactured foods took considerably longer than the development of the foods themselves. The development of food technology for specialty foods involved some of the first genetically synthesized organisms, both microbial and also novel plants and animals. These developments paced the development of computational ontogenetics, which allowed the design of new organisms. Centaurus never had farms, aquaculture, or anything else related to food production in the ways of old Earth. Biology was used in many ways, but all in ways developed on Earth that changed human life more than anything except human genetics.

Even before Centaurus became self-sustaining, there was no need to transport food to the moon, except as a very expensive luxury. Cells were transported, culture vats were transported, processors were transported, spoke systems for specialty growth were transported, storage units were transported, but the old systems for food were not.

Stopes were set aside within Centaurus for the production of food. Others were designated as areas for recycling of anything used within the mine. Later, many walls were used for carbon dioxide to oxygen replenishment, with organisms there living on electricity and converting CO_2 and H_2O to oxygen and materials for their own sustenance and growth. These were the same biological wall coverings that were used in large buildings on Earth to provide fresh breathable air. Once Earth scientists had made the breakthrough that allowed plants, not only microbes, to get their energy from electricity, it was quickly realized that living walls were much more efficient than giant circulating air systems. Buildings on Earth had grown larger and larger, becoming all-inclusive, and the old-style mechanical air systems had become a limiting factor. This obstacle dissolved. Fortunately for Luna, these plants grew well in low gravity with little change to their genomes.

Genetic engineering of humans had reached a dead end as far as improvements on Earth were concerned. Every option had been considered, and all the ones that improved humanity were incorporated in the sixteens. Uniformity was a past problem, and every genome was diverse in ways that did not substantially detract from the generic excellence of the individual possessing it. Many times, the geneticists simply found that evolution had already outthought them, and come up with the best proteins to do a task.

However, with Luna blazing at night above their heads, it was not long before the idea of producing non-earthling humans developed. Only after the sixteens were completed did two of the teams begin the major modifications of their requirements and subsequent DNA codings. One began to develop the seventeens, who initially were seen as sixteens adapted to the lunar environment. The other team started on the eighteens, for Mars. Nineteens, for life on orbiters and cycler shuttles, came much later. These three were quite similar, almost indistinct.

The concept of species had lost its meaning by this time. The distinction between different species began to be unappreciated, as there was little possibility of cross-breeding, and since the advent of the nines there was no gender. All births of nines and later came from gestation machines, as did the vast majority of births of the species preceding the nines. The species numbers came to represent the final output of a genetics design team, much like the model number for any other technological development.

Non-earthling design and development was a task more challenging than optimizing humans, although it presented a much shallower learning curve than had faced earthling improvement. Genetics already understood how to generate creatures of any type. The problem was that the moon was far away, and experiments in low gravity were not possible on Earth. Eventually the problem was solved, and genetics gave Luna the seventeens.

Seventeens were ideally suited for living on Luna, for cavorting through the tunnels and winzes, for using less oxygen, and being able to maintain their strength and fitness with no exercise or effort at all. They had lives as long as the sixteens, however long that might prove to be, and were not subject to any space illnesses caused by long exposure to zero gravity. They repaired genetic damage that might be caused by exposure to a solar flare better than was initially thought possible and could be exposed to vacuum for a short time without suffering greatly.

The one thing that was lost was unavoidable. They could hardly live on Earth. Gravity would interfere with motion, breathing, blood flow and posture. Furthermore, bodies of water would be very dangerous. Wind would be dangerous. Surf would be dangerous. As a result, seventeens could only be gestated on the moon. The earthlings in Centaurus opted to be supplemented by seventeens, and this was agreed upon by those in the GEO and the hierarchies whose cooperation kept the lunar travel and supply continuing. It was realized but little discussed that the exchange of humans with Earth would became even smaller, especially when the fraction of seventeens in the lunar population continued to rise.

This genetic development, the creation of our species, perhaps should have been regarded as a memorable triumph, but both on Earth and in Centaurus, it was simply seen as a follow-on to the development of the earlier new species. Now, from a perspective of over five centuries, it was perhaps the second most significant event in mankind's expansion to a new world, after the founding of Centaurus. Nobelites recognize how significantly seventeens differ from the natural humans of past millennia. Much of the protein structure of our cells differs from that of original humans, so do some of the joints, the facial musculature, the shape of the skull, and mitochondria, which now have well-defined and unique genes rather than the hodgepodge that the originals had. We have mostly the same digestive organs with their specific functions, but the chemistry of some of them has been simplified and improved and co-living microbes eliminated. Because the later new species can only be grown in gestation machines, chromosome design was manipulated to utilize this process.

Brain structure was revised several times in the phylogeny of the new species, but not much for species beyond the sixteens. The later new species, from four onward, can be recognized by their slightly larger than average heads, but no larger than the largest of the originals. Skin color and markings were quite diverse in the later species, and hair or fur was short and more for decoration than use. Most of the changes were invisible, deep in the genome, cellular structure, internal organs, and joints, although faces in later species are more expressive, as are gestures.

Good genetics need good training to be fully utilized. It had become clear that the training of juveniles and their education were two completely separate phenomena, and needed to be carried out separately. Earth developed training of young humans using a combination of robotic avatars, some with human shape, and humans themselves, followed by a period of mentoring solely by humans. There was so much organized information available through home sentiences that education transformed itself into a kind of apprenticeship system, instead of simply an information transfer. This required much more time from well-educated human individuals than the previous system of training and educating human youth did, but as automation had succeeded in reducing work immensely, this was welcomed as an improvement, not simply a burden. This has been easily accepted on Luna since the early days of Centaurus. Once the gestation machines were in place there, along with the training avatars, mentoring fit in with the schedule of life in the mine, although there was certainly much more demand on time there than on Earth.

Even with the work and the restricted environment available in Centaurus, life was felt to be good there. The number of reinforcing neurochemicalneurochemicals in our brains has been increased along the way from original humans to us seventeens, which is why a common phrase is that we, along with the sixteens on Earth, are the happiest of creatures. This required some new glands within the brain to produce them, along with a revision of the neural passageways to trigger their production, but there was brain space to do this, as the glands were minuscule.

Centaurus was originally the only place where seventeens could be gestated, and after they were developed, the gestation machines on Centaurus were solely used for seventeens. The time of earthlings doing duty in Centaurus began to come to an end. Lunite seventeens were trained in the Centaurus mine, by the two stage process of training for fifteen years, and then mentoring for up to thirty more. Initially Centaurus mentoring lasted for only fifteen years, due to the time demands on the population.

Before the founding of Nobel, seventeens were gradually displacing earthlings in Centaurus mine, and this process continued. There are now, centuries later, very few earthlings in Centaurus, almost all visitors, and usually none in the other mines. In earlier days, almost any earthling species in the mine, from originals to sixteens, could be found working and living in nearly indistinguishable ways.

In a sense, the development of Centaurus during its first century was mostly a transplanting of Earth technology to the moon. Earth technology had exploded over the century before Centaurus was founded and the century afterwards, so much so that there seemed to be little left to do for the active and enthusiastic scientists of Earth. This meant, in a strange way, that there was not too much science left for scientists on the moon to add. Much of science is data collection and organization, and there was certainly much about the moon that was learned by scientists at Centaurus and the later mines as well, but it mostly fit into the scientific theories already developed on Earth. Earth had a population numbering in the billions, while the moon's population only very slowly climbed toward its first million. This alone would mean that science on Earth would overshadow anything that could be done on the moon and the other outposts, except, of course, for on-site data collection.

There were exceptions, and lunites knew about them and celebrated them. One scientist, from Centaurus actually, had made an improvement in the theory of solar flares on M stars, and another, from a different mine, had seen how to improve the efficiency of the fusion machines by over a percent. These were items that somehow escaped the grinding out of scientific improvements by the collected sentiences on Earth, and undoubtedly there would be more, but fewer and fewer with time.

Engineering had also evolved into a profession where sentiences did most of the routine work, and only basic design questions were handled by the humans. This was how a small contingent of human engineers on the GEO could do the design work for Centaurus, including all the supplying of it from Earth, all the scheduling of projects, computation of reliability issues, quality control of components and excavation of new areas, power and other utilities, and just about everything else. Earthling engineers on the moon, initially on the surface and later in the mine, served as the backup eyes to the AI observation systems here, and occasionally found problems missed by the robotics, or dealt with the few unforeseen problems that arose.

As an example, one of the problems that had to be solved in the early days of Centaurus' first underground phase was the leaking of atmosphere. Leaks are usually easy to detect, as there is an airflow that can be observed and usually a sound, something characteristic of fluid flowing through small cracks. Many had been found already, sealed, and written off as complete. The AI took care of them routinely. But, once, with a rather large leak, noticeable from air consumption, happening just after a new excavation had been completed, neither flow nor sound was found. Drones were flying and crawling around, watching and listening, reporting all that they saw and heard to the central AI that was trying to solve the problem, but having no luck at all. An earthling engineer took it upon himself to suit up and go around the surface, finally finding a small puff of dust that led back to the source of the leak, a wide area of porous facing material where there should have been an impermeable surface. This is one of the tidbits of Centaurus history, that would be forgotten, except for the ineradicable desire of humans to outsmart the AI's and their irrepressible need to remember instances where it happened.

Earth was extremely generous in starting off Centaurus in its early days, but it was done without any appreciation or foresight of what Centaurus would become. Centaurians have always had extremely good relations with earthlings, and there have never been any disputes that have led to acrimony. Earth people regarded Centaurus, at the beginning, as an expansion of Earth territory, which it was, just as the various orbiters were. Strangely, it was the drive toward efficiency that pushed Centaurus toward becoming something other than an extension of Earth.

The cost of transporting materials to Luna from Earth was always tremendous, and therefore the concept of making something from lunar materials was always seen as a good one. That was the driving concern behind the choice of Centaurus' location, behind the extensive seleno-logical explorations, the development of drilling equipment for the moon and mineral processing equipment, the provision of large power supplies, and almost everything else. Earth wanted an outpost, and they wanted it cheap. That meant self-sufficiency to the largest extent possible, and that extent finally turned out to be 100%.

It took much of a century to deliver all the start-up equipment needed for self-sufficiency, meaning that everything that had been delivered from Earth could eventually be manufactured on the moon out of ma-terials from the moon. No one in the very early days of lunar exploration or the planning of it had expected that this would be possible. The good fortune of having variegated mineral deposits on the moon, and in Centaurus' case, located close to one another, was not predicted by anyone, but it happened. If it hadn't been for Lady Luck, it might have been another century or more before self-sufficiency was possible, but she bestowed this on Centaurus, and doubled down by making it the first explored site.

It didn't hurt that Earth had solved all the hard problems of mineral extraction, power generation, biological engineering for food, waste, air, and water control, excavation methodology, and transportation, and had made each of these more and more efficient as the decades of scientific work and clever engineering wore on. It didn't hurt that AI had come along to improve reliability, eliminate routine work where mistakes might be likely, take charge of logistics details, and master genomics. It didn't hurt that Earth had grown richer, especially after its political problems fell to the wayside with improved intelligence and other factors, such as the completion of neurology, and the invention of excellent political and economic systems. Many other factors, both on Earth and on the moon, contributed to the outstanding success that Centaurus represented. However, they were underappreciated back on Earth.

Luna news reporting had gone through phases on Earth. For a while, around the time of the founding of the surface outpost in Mare Serenitatus, interest was high, and earthlings knew the details about all the landings. After the first decade of drilling, landing, building, and so on, not so much. Those involved with the project were intensely involved, but the public, less so. It was exciting to see a mine shaft on the moon, but less exciting to see the twentieth long bore being drilled through a valuable ore body. Watching lunar visitors make long leaps on the surface was initially fun, but not so much after so many had made these leaps. It was the same for tourism. With the high cost of transportation to the moon, it might have been expected that there would be no tourists, but there were, posing as contributors to some aspect of lunar life. Tourists would go for a tenday, but be bored by the third day. It dried up. An artist or two were sent up during the first decades; they did their art work and returned.

Thus, by the time sustainability peaked and Luna did not need supplies from Earth any more, there was not much attention paid. Earth teams still were needed on Luna, but with gestation machines and the genome for seventeens, they were becoming less and less necessary. It would take almost two centuries before the population had shifted heavily to seventeens inside Centaurus, and Earth had not come around to objecting to anything that happened there. Management of the Centaurus project had always been on the GEO, but more and more it was delegated to on-site humans, first only earthlings, but later seventeens. Travel between Earth and Luna continued, and the GEO gradually drifted into being a transportation hub, with all decisions relating to Centaurus mine being made in Centaurus mine, eventually by young seventeens, born and raised there. The costs of supporting Luna had dwindled down to almost nothing, and compared to Earth's ongoing expenses, they were really in the noise of the global Earth economy.

The first item that had grabbed the attention of those in charge on Earth was the decision by Centaurus to sponsor the development of a second mine, about 120 years after the founding of the Centaurus mine. They had decided on where to put it, in the mountains between Mare Serenitatus and Mare Imbrium, about 400 kilometers away from Centaurus, where there was another excellent collection of ores, this time including richer uranium ores. They had designed and built a transportation system from one mine to another, by toughening up the transporter designs originally used to establish Centaurus. They had even come up with a name for the mine, Ague-Tuilet, after the two Earth scientists who had first synthesized a mammal, starting from amino acids for DNA, a cell wall and its interior components, and everything after that. It may have been the naming that caught the attention of earthlings. If this is an Earth outpost, shouldn't Earth at least have been consulted about it, and maybe given the option to choose the name? This was the dawning of the idea among earthlings that Luna was its own world, not an outpost of Earth, and for some time had been ignored by and was ignoring Earth.

4

THE SECOND MINE ON LUNA

The Centaurus mine lasted for about a hundred and twenty years before a second mine was started. During that time, it transformed from a tiny outpost doing some initial mining of ores on Luna to a large, prosperous, and secure home for three thousand lunar residents. About ten percent were seventeens, permanently living on the moon, and the rest were earthlings, originals up to sixteens, each doing a tour of duty in Centaurus. The motivation for the second mine was ostensibly the same as everything else, insurance against catastrophe, but the real motivation may have been simply that it was getting routine to work in Centaurus, unlike the heady days when it was being founded and developed. It was time for another giant step for humanity.

Centaurus had done all the experimental work and gained a tremendous amount of unique experience on how to live under the lunar surface. The achievements during those one hundred and twenty years set the example for every mine founded on the moon since Centaurus. It is true that Centaurus absorbed many, many lessons from Earth, but they also went beyond those lessons, and created a true way of living on the moon.

Nothing on Earth looked like the inside of the Centaurus mine. The main shaft and the headframe had been expanded many times and were simply huge. The spoil pile covered multiple square kilometers, was ten meters high, and was visible from Earth with a good telescope. Four different skips hauled ore to the surface, where originally the ore been processed, before being moved underground to a large stope. Two other shafts provided exits to the surface, over a kilometer away from the main shaft. Underground for each shaft were six shaft stations, going down 350 meters at the deepest, with tunnels leading away from them in different directions. Two were for living spaces and mechanical work areas, while four led to ore mining. Some of the population lived in abandoned shafts, some nearly horizontal and others at different angles, while others lived in dwelling spaces on the sides of stopes.

Mining continued at distances from the main shaft, over four kilometers at the maximum, and while the light lunar gravity helped, ore had to be trucked back to the processing site through tunnels, using up precious energy. the ore carts had hooks to enable them to navigate sloped passages, and there were some winzes used to move them as well. Robots did almost all of the physical work, as well as the planning, measuring, testing, and monitoring of everything connected with the mining, but humans monitored the robots and made the decisions that led to the continued development of the mine. Seventeens had not been around long enough to make much of a difference, but the first of them had accumulated many more years of experience in Centaurus than almost all the earthling workers, and that started to play a role in the positions held.

Centaurus developed the tour of duty rotation system we use on Nobel for seventeens, where seventeens would work for a period in one occupation, and then move to another. It was a combination of choice and necessity that motivated the selection, and while there was some complaining, the overall mission of Centaurus was so overwhelming and so strongly appreciated that there was little serious objection to any work assignment. It was duty, after all. And there was little need for any objection, as working in gestation, food preparation, mining, transportation, manufacturing, ore processing, maintenance, governance, or any of the other many specialties was not all that different: learn the systems, monitor the robots, make the decisions. It was actually considered a benefit by many seventeens that they could so easily rotate their work areas; no one got too bored. Centaurus initially had so much work that the seventeens had only short gaps between their work assignments, but that slowly changed to give a little more free time, which is the current state here in Nobel and in other mines.

Centaurus does have all of the types of living situations that we have on Nobel, but because there is so much more verticality in Nobel, caused by the direction of the ore veins, that the fractions of space for each are quite different. In Centaurus, there are level tunnels leading from the shaft stations on the main shaft in many directions, out to the ore veins and bodies. They are wide and flat and used for ore transportation. In the sides of these were many individual dwellings, interspersed with common areas, such as for waste collection, distribution drop off sites, small manufacturing and repair, and multiple other purposes. Once the first large stope was finished, dwellings and other openings were drilled into the sides of it, with stairs, ramps, and jump steps to allow the inhabitants to go up and down. With only one-sixth of Earth's gravity, vertical motion was nowhere near the obstacle that it was on Earth, so Centaurus used its volume well. Unfortunately, many veins descended at a slope, and once they were cleaned out, the tunnel was used for business and dwelling by excavating on the sides. Some long and steep segments had a small funicular railway for transport, based around the original ore transportation one. For travel up and down the others that were not as steep, everyone depended on the usual buggies, or stairs for the very shortest. All of the auxiliary shafts had spiral walkways around them, along with the usual cages.

Thus, the geography of Centaurus was very spidery. There was no thought of doing the extensive excavation to build anything like an ancient city on Earth, with a gridwork of passageways and openings off all of them. Nor did they originally try to copy an arcology on Earth, by filling a stope with a building. There was never any time when someone in Centaurus could forget they were in a mine. The only time a large drift was dug far away from ore bodies was for some industrial purpose, such as a power reactor.

There was a great but subtle difference between the earthlings and the seventeens which became more important as the number of seventeens grew. Earthlings dreamed of Earth, the place they were born, where their memories were made, where their original friends and acquaintances were waiting for them, and where the beauty of the surface and of the lifeforms would be available to them when their tour of duty on Luna was over. Seventeens had no such dreams. They could see Earth on 3vids, or wander around Earth as a virtual planet and look at waterfalls and chasms, beaches and mountaintops, cities, dams, and so much more. But it was not their home, and they had no connection to it. They could wander around a virtual Mars or Ceres and also be impressed. They were lunites and would remain so from birth to death, whenever that might be. They would spend perhaps five hundred years in the caverns of Centaurus, except for some excursions to the surface, or to an orbiter, possibly to Mars. In the view of some of the earthlings who shared the mine with the seventeens, this was eventually viewed as completely unbearable.

There are personal recordings made by earthlings after returning from a tour on Luna, in which they mention how sad they were about the seventeens' inability to ever see Earth. For them, Earth was a unparalleled treasure. They talked about how possibly creating the seventeens was not a good idea. They talked about how there was a chill that came over any discussion back on Luna about the glories of Earth when a seventeen joined the group. They talked about how they spoke in a detached, evasive manner when speaking about Earth when a seventeen was present. They talked about having a seventeen as a friend, but having this gulf between them, a gulf caused by the absence of feelings about Earth. They talked about how earthlings and seventeens often had their own segregated groups, although that was not a part of Centaurus philosophy and had no mirror in work teams, housing, or any other aspect of life in the Centaurus mine. They claimed that part of the feeling of separateness stemmed from the long experience levels that seventeens built up, as compared to the earthlings, for whom a second rotation to Luna was not common. Part of it came from the feelings of loss that earthlings expected seventeens to have, loss of the chance to see Earth.

It wasn't quite accurate. Seventeens were trained and mentored on Centaurus, and heard about Earth history and geography, but the training did not instill any feeling of lack in the seventeens. They also could learn about the geography of Mercury, Venus, Mars, and more, and they didn't feel any lack because they had not seen them and would likely not see them. Their training was designed to make them feel at home on Luna, motivated to accomplish things here, happy to enjoy what Centaurus had to offer, and glad to be part of the effort to develop the mine, among many other things. But none of those things had anything to do with Earth.

The training, at least initially, had a gap related to the Earth Luna dichotomy that was hard to miss and hard to not appreciate. The culture presented in education was all from Earth.

Seventeens needed to develop their own culture, something relating to the reality of Luna, that would give them something more to be happy about here, other than good food, activities, and work. They needed to define what it meant to be a lunite.

It would be thought that with seventeens all being of top intelligence, some lunite music, sculpture, 3vids, or some other art would be the initial media by which lunite seventeens would recognize themselves as a people. But it was not the case. It was sports.

Lunites were all young, compared to their lifespan, during the period between the founding of Centaurus and the founding of the second mine, but that mattered little as geneticists had solved the problem of aging by maintaining agility and athleticism throughout the lives of the seventeens. One talk group began discussing flying through the shafts and across the stopes inside Centaurus. Seventeens have a higher ratio of muscle to total weight than do sixteens or any species that can live on Earth, for the obvious reason that there is less need for skeletal strength. Seventeens can leap long distances and great heights, and the talk group started thinking about using fabric wings held between arms and legs. Some simple calculations showed seventeens they could easily drift through the air inside Centaurus' large open spaces. And so they started doing it. Gliding came first, but soon a method of stroking led to a sort of swimming in the air. It was a tiny bit easier deeper in the mine, where air pressure was greater, but even near the surface, it was more than possible. It was later on that artificial wind was used to provide uplift. A lunite sport was born. Earthlings could not do it, but were restricted to gliding, up and down depending on the vertical component of the airspeed.

This was the inspiration that seventeens had been missing, without knowing it. Other sports, involving leaping high and moving in the air, alone, in teams, or in competition, all sprung into being. A game with meter-wide disks and hanging targets became popular, and then it became a chaos of sports, with so many new ideas being sorted out that years passed with different fad sports coming into use and then going out.

Centaurus developed many sports that were eventually brought along to all the newer mines, and more besides, ones that never gathered the interest of other mines. In contrast, there was really no new music possible, since Earth had gone through all the possibilities already, over and over. However, some of the less common Earth styles, especially those with a melancholy backdrop and a spritely melody, caught on in Centaurus, and became common among the seventeens. Visual arts did the obvious thing, showing seventeens, in Centaurus living spaces, and doing Centaurus activities, including their new sports. Seventeens worked hard developing their culture, even though there were only a few thousands of them. That became the next cultural issue.

One of the many reasons for developing seventeens was that it was considerably more efficient to have people who lived on the moon for their whole lives, and worked there for centuries, than to recruit, train, test, transport, and return earthlings for the tasks. If a seventeen was fifteen years in nurturing and training, then fifteen or even thirty years in mentoring, that left four hundred years or more for a working life. This computes to four centuries of one-shift work and was compared with fifty or so earthlings brought up for a term of eight years each. All the costs for earthling trips added up to much more than the gestation, training, and mentoring costs for the equivalent number of seventeens. So why were there so few?

Seventeens started out in the gestation machines and their associated genetic encoding systems, where the genetic code was chosen, written, put into a synthetic cell, and turned into an embryo. Build more gestation machines, and you will have more seventeens. But the real cost of having more seventeens, or humans in general, was the cost of the human and robotic labor needed in nurturing and training, and then somewhat less in mentoring. Those managing the Centaurus mine, all earthlings at this time, did not want to slow down work on developing the mine so that more seventeens could be created, who would not begin to contribute for many decades after.

Everything in the mine was sized correctly and consistently. There were enough mining machines, enough crushers to match them, enough extraction equipment to match the crushers, and so on. There was enough food growth equipment to provide food for the population. All of the systems were set up in balance, and the population and independent robotics were sized to match everything else. When the seventeens started asking for more seventeens, they were correct in that it would be more efficient over the long term, but there would be disruption in the short term. Even the higher management in the GEO opposed their request.

Perhaps there was an undercurrent in these decisions to keep the moon as an Earth outpost, with earthlings all over it, integrated in everything, and involved with all decision-making. This was not recorded in any news, announcements, or even informal notes. But the change to a seventeen-run moon was inevitable. The number of new seventeens each year outnumbered population growth, and displacement of earthlings was an unavoidable by-product. The number of gestation machines was capped, but the cap was high enough to provide the gradual change from an earthling population to a home-grown, native seventeen population. It was just a century long process.

Seventeens did join Centaurus' higher levels of management out of proportion to their population numbers, as their experience provided them with a background over many classes of work within the mine, and they gravitated to management positions. No earthling could match the experience of someone who lived every day of their life in the mine, and they consequently applied less for mine management positions. The process of seventeens taking over was very slow, and that may be the reason that the second mine was thought of and eventually brought into existence.

Formal talk groups were set up by lottery, and attendance was almost mandatory, along with the rules of who chooses the topics and how the discussion proceeds. They were an inexpensive way to stimulate the minds of a very intelligent mass of workers, and to occupy them, to build acquaintanceship, to connect different areas of work, and for many other reasons. But there were informal ones as well, and seventeens congregated in some of these. It was in one of these that the idea of a second mine, to be populated only by seventeens, arose and took shape.

Justifications were one order of business. There are no recordings of the talk group that started off the concept of a second mine, but soon discussion of it had seeped all over the mine. Insurance always had to be the primary justification, to protect against unforeseen catastrophe in Centaurus. If Centaurus was wiped away, Earth could always start over again and build a new mine somewhere else than Mare Serenitatus. Or perhaps they would not, and instead abandon the idea of a second home for man on Luna, leaving Mars as the only one. The idea of there being no seventeens seemed to send a chill through the seventeens, and they, on their own, developed the concept.

The concept did not start and stop with a second mine. The idea blossomed into one of a moon covered with mines, all inhabited by seventeens, fully functional and independent but able to provide assistance in the event of such a catastrophe. How many should there be? Ten, twenty, or more? There was nothing in their training that would give them the idea of being a self-sufficient species, with their own home, or rather, with their own planet. Mentoring was done by earthlings, mostly, as only a few seventeens had yet reached the age where they could qualify for the lowest rung of the mentoring system. Why the idea arose is not clear, and why it attracted so much attention is another mystery.

If Centaurus were to build the second mine, instead of Earth sending over a fleet of landers to do what they did with Centaurus, it had to be at a distance that was not too far to transport all the thousands of types of equipment that were needed to produce and start up a mine. Centaurus had little spare equipment, but they did have some surface transport that could go a distance with a load and return. Transporters used in the building of Centaurus had been preserved in operating condition, and then there were the spoil transporters. These set the maximum radius from Centaurus, where the second mine could be. Then the choice was almost made. Where within that radius was the geology the best?

A mass of information had been collected, and the geology of the moon was known, at least in broad outline. Even the ancient Apollo and Luna programs had developed a little information, and the manned lunar orbiter, first built before the first and second returns, had collected data. To prepare for the third return, It was replaced by the Luna Permanent Orbiter, which had spent more than twenty years before the third return and thirty years after it collecting data on the moon before the exploration rate was slowed down. The moon was covered with tracks from the geological explorations conducted by the LPO, and it continued to collect data after Centaurus was founded.

The initial temporary landing parties on the third return and the quasi-permanent surface base had their own geological rovers, and drilling into the surface could be done in almost automated form, deeply and quickly. Analysis was done on the lunar surface, and rocks could be brought up to the LPO or back to the GEO if there was something particularly curious about them. Selenology was a well populated scientific specialty, with studies being done on the surface of the moon, with landers, manned and unmanned still happening, and back on Earth. All this data provided the best bet for a second mine, within the transport radius from Centaurus. It goes without saying that this process also provided the location choices for Nobel, when it came time to create it.

The best choice, based on mineral content, was located in the mountain chain between Mare Serenitatus and Mare Imbrium, south of Rima Calippus and easily reachable by crossing Mare Serenitatus. More drilling needed to be done to establish the whole picture of what mineral resources were nearby, and where the best spot would be to site a shaft or an adit. The seventeens involved in developing the concept were amazed when Centaurus management approved the expeditions needed to do the drilling. Perhaps initially they did not comprehend that this was being thought of as a second, independent mine, not as a secondary outpost of Centaurus. The high uranium content in one area there may have been misleading. Alternatively, they may have felt the seventeens deserved to be allowed to do what they wanted, as it was, in a sense, their planetary home. But for whatever reason, the site for a shaft was found, ore bodies were located, and the engineering and planning for starting the second mine commenced.

The official management of Centaurus was not on the LPO, but on the GEO, but they did not make any changes when the notices of where drilling was being done were transmitted to them. The notices most likely did not say that a second mine site was being investigated, but this would be the first time that drilling, done by Centaurus itself, was done so far away from their central shaft. Perhaps GEO simply saw it as an extension of the ongoing LPO drilling program, and probably would have regarded it as a much less expensive way of exploring this area than for LPO to put down a lander there. So there was no objection, no request for more information, and no indication that any hesitation was felt. Drilling the shaft went the same way. No objection from GEO meant that Centaurus could simply go ahead. The objections came only from within Centaurus.

The earthlings who lived on Centaurus to operate the mine were doing engineering work, which meant safety, efficiency, productivity, consistency, and smoothness of operations. Sending out geology teams was routine, as was refurbishing equipment. There was no disruption there. Even drilling a shaft at a great distance from Centaurus' central shaft, or indeed from any auxiliary shaft, or even from any mining area within Centaurus, was not something that obstructed anything else. Auxiliary shafts had been drilled, the equipment was maintained in good working order, there was an infinity of space to pile spoil on the surface of the moon, people were all properly trained, and everything could be nicely scheduled. The shaft went deep, but so did the main shaft on Centaurus. Even the head-frame construction, which needed significant quantities of steel and lunar concrete, went by without any obstacles. Once the main shaft was dug, with three shaft stations excavated and drifts began, it was time to start equipping the second mine, and that would take a lot away from Centaurus. Here was where the roadblock happened.

The seventeens' hope of having this be a seventeen only mine did not happen immediately, as the geology exploration and shaft construction were done with the usual mixed teams. No one had lived in the mine yet, so technically their hope was not yet shattered, but the path to achieving that goal was not clear and laid out before them. Eliminating earthlings later on was a possibility, but as events happened, that was not even necessary. The seventeens understood that sometimes the best course is not a straight line to the goal, but a devious one, zigzagging and twisting along the way. So the second mine did not start as a second mine, equipped to be a self-sustaining enterprise, but instead a source of uranium and other ores, taken from a rich body. Transport of ore back to Centaurus for processing was the next step, and not surprisingly, that continued to happen. Earth even contributed some more ore carriers. So, the second mine, which was only a working mine, not a living mine, continued to expand, and more ores came out and went to Centaurus.

It became obvious to everyone that putting more power at the second mine, and building ore processing facilities would allow refine ore, or metal and other materials to be transported back, instead of the ore itself. Earthlings and seventeens were still living in protected habitats on the surface, managing the work of the mining robots, and a somewhat larger population could be moved there to manage the concentration and processing, including the metallurgy, to send back refined metal to

Centaurus. It was also more efficient to ship over some recycling and nutrition equipment, instead of moving things back and forth from Centaurus.

Little by little, the surface camp grew both in size and in capability. What had been lacking all this time was a name for the mine. Back in the huddles that the seventeens had, it had been realized that formally naming the second mine might cause uncomfortable questions, and so it was referred to with the nickname given to an outcropping of rock visible from the main shaft. It was volcanic rock, and had a shape that looked like a face from the right angle and with the right imagination. Someone called it Sam, an old earth name for someone no one remembered anything about except their silhouette. Sam was the initial nickname for the second mine. The seventeens had started to invent names they might like, but stopped to prevent the preferred name from coming into use. So the second mine had no real name for a long period of development.

It was twenty-five years of living on the surface around Sam before the seventeens tried to fulfill their hope, almost as long as the surface encampment lasted before Centaurus was occupied. A seventeen had finally moved into the upper level of the Centaurus management hierarchy, having passed the qualifications and then scored what he desired in the work assignment lottery. It was time to move forward. The seventeens proposed moving from the surface to the underground at Sam, and that the population going there be drawn from seventeens. There was no reason for this. Seventeens did not consume less resources, they were not smaller, they had been working in combined teams for the full eighty years that they had been in existence, and it was overwhelmingly obvious that earthlings could live in mines successfully. There was no justification for it, and it would mean some new juggling of work assignments, to take seventeens out of Centaurus positions and move them to Sam. On top of all this, the seventeens wanted a gestation machine to be built and installed in Sam.

Now it was thirty years since the seventeens had requested that more gestation machines be built for Centaurus, and thirty years passed with only incremental additions. In Centaurus, everything was homogeneous. People didn't divide themselves into factions and campaign for something. Everyone could make suggestions for improvements, and indeed, this was expected and rewarded, except for the seventeens. They huddled together from time to time, churning out ideas for the second mine, as well as what might be called cultural activities, in which the unique things they did were discussed and plans made. It took over a year before the agreement was granted. Yes, seventeens could move into Sam by themselves, and yes, a gestation machine would be built for Sam.

Two more years passed before seventeens actually lived underground in the second mine. Ventilation was improved, and bit by bit equipment was moved down. Along with that, earthlings were not replaced at Sam with earthlings, but with seventeens. There were almost three hundred seventeens at the surface when they first started to live underground.

Everyone's reaction was different. The population on Centaurus was more and more sixteens from Earth and seventeens born on the moon, but there were still other species and the occasional selected original. One of the originals seemed to be the most enthusiastic supporter of the move, and called on the seventeens to give the second mine a name. Originals, along with the first eight new species, still had gender, and this earthling original was a female, aged 81, with selected and some novel genes, a solid contributor to the work on Centaurus. The seventeens actually invited her into one of the seventeens' private huddles, in order to suggest possible names. They recorded which names were suggested by whom, what reasons were given for each of them, what supporting reasons were put forward, and what objections were made. This naming process was being taken quite seriously, as this would be the first home for seventeens in their existence, and it needed a name to represent that. Sam would not do.

There was a problem in that none of the seventeens had ever accomplished anything that was record-breaking or spectacular. They were all still alive, still in their comparative youth, still with the potential for great things in front of them. This might be explained by the fact that the mine on Luna was developed with the idea that there would be no need for heroic acts or impressive achievements. It ran like a clock. Each tick sounded like the previous tick. So all the suggestions by the seventeens came from Earth history. Explorers, inventors, leaders, thinkers, and poets, many from pre-industrial times, when individuals stood out much more prominently than was possible on the moon. Other suggestions were more basic, such as Calippus, after the crater and rille near the shaft. These names were derived from Earth figures as well, so there was not much difference between these suggestions. There were no animals on the moon to name a mine after, and no lakes, active volcanoes, or anything else corresponding to the wealth of nature on Earth.

The earthling female, while participating in a seventeen huddle as a guest, suggested Ague-Tuilet, after the two Earth scientists who built the first synthetic mammal, from a designed genome. She was a descendant of one of them, Ague. The seventeens in the huddle had to process this concept. Seventeens have no ancestors, just a genetic code put together by a AI machine to produce certain attributes. Being a descendant of some other individual is a strange concept for us, and perhaps that is why the seventeens in that huddle simply accepted the suggestion, and shared it with the seventeens who were in different huddles. Certainly these two geneticists were great innovators, and led the way to all the synthetic pets on Earth, as well as to the new species, including the seventeens. It dawned on the Centaurus seventeens, en masse, that the closest thing they had to an ancestor were the people who had hatched the technology needed to create our species. After that realization spread around the Centaurus population, there was no question whatsoever as to what the name of the second lunar mine, and the first seventeen home mine, should be: Ague-Tuilet.

5

THE AGUE-TUILET MINE SPAWNS ANOTHER

Earth was the home of mankind, and the origin of almost everything we know, everything we have, and everything we are. Centaurus was originally a transplant of Earth, although it has become more like the other mines in more recent years. Ague-Tuilet was the first seventeens' mine, and collaborated with Centaurus to produce Nobel, the third mine on the moon. No one in the original party that started living in Ague-Tuilet had any idea to make things very different there, as life in Centaurus worked well and there were only incidental problems that cropped up, nothing very substantial. There was only the idea of a lunite mine, not an Earth outpost, that was different.

Technology was static by the time Ague-Tuilet was occupied. It was not that there were not many bright people with detailed knowledge about each and every component; there were; it was just that after centuries of improving equipment, it reaches a limit and there isn't much else that can be done. Novel ideas came up when Centaurus was being founded, and the good ones incorporated, but that too reached its natural limit. Nobel had the same technology as Ague-Tuilet, which had the same technology as Centaurus. Social organization is just a part of technology, an intangible part, and that has been all worked out just like everything else. Change was always happening with personnel shifts and continuing excavation, but it was similar to change in previous times. Routine change, one might say.

The founding of Ague-Tuilet was a tremendous change in some sense, and the process of starting off with a barren rock surface and developing a habitable underground area was greatly interesting, and there was a full competition for people in Centaurus to do that. By "full", I mean close to 100% volunteer application rate for working at what was then called Sam. It was an intensely watched job lottery. Risk had almost been totally eliminated in working on the moon's surface, so that was no barrier, only a cost and a delay in doing things the safest way.

Once the excavations had gone far enough, and ore processing, power sources, and life support systems had all been installed and tested within the mine, and seventeens moved inside, the surface camp continued to be occupied for several years. The work was so interesting and different than inside Centaurus that there was no lack of interest on the part of the earthlings of living under those conditions, and making the trek back to Centaurus between the short surface tours. Eventually, however, the camp was abandoned for permanent living, and just served mostly as an auxiliary storage site, rarely used. At times, fa small bit was used by seventeens or spoil operations.

Earth paid even less attention to Ague-Tuilet, with a few exceptions, than to Centaurus. There was no shortage of applicants for earthlings to go to work on Centaurus initially, and that created interest in Centaurus. Nothing equivalent held for Ague-Tuilet. Anyone wishing to apply to be launched up and over to Centaurus would certainly want to watch 3vids of life and work in the mine, as well as of the four stage trip to go there, via one of the LEO's, the GEO and then the LPO. Perhaps that served as a filter, as Centaurus did not go to the trouble of making clever 3vids showing off life there in an attractive way. Neither did Earth send out a team to do the same. Applications stayed strong enough that there was no need to advertise for applicants.

At least initially, there wasn't much interesting to see in the mine, except people working in various ways, mostly monitoring automated work, and living their lives. Listening to the recordings of all the talk groups would certainly not be appealing, as these mundane talk groups, by one name or another, were everywhere on Earth and contained little of interest to those outside them. Young seventeens might be shown in training, and it would be almost indistinguishable, except for the gravity, from training sixteens and others on Earth. Watching a child learn to leap inside Centaurus is interesting for the first time and perhaps even the second, but by the tenth, it is not at all.

There was no unique food in Centaurus. Everything eaten there was eaten everywhere on Earth, and there was not much novelty in watching people eat in lunar gravity. Spills fell slower, which is odd the first time someone sees it. There were no pets to eat scraps. Nobody was getting sick. Accidents were extremely rare. Power did not fail. There was simply very little news coming out of the Centaurus mine that anyone on Earth would take interest in. Yes, this was a new home for mankind, but it was a new home ten years ago, and twenty, and thirty, and so on, always about the same. The importance of the moon as an insurance safeguard for humanity was known and accepted, and the costs were paid, but that did not make a lunar mine an interesting place for earthlings, once the novelty had worn off.

There was nothing like tourism to the lunar mine. A few administrators from LPO and less from GEO came down for meetings or interviews with the staff, but it didn't amount to much. By and large, Centaurus was left alone, and Ague-Tuilet, even more so. Centaurus management didn't seek to be noteworthy, just to do their jobs well, and when a rotation into management happened, nothing much changed, over decades. Centaurus was like a well-functioning machine, and it liked being seen that way. It wasn't that they were hiding something, because everything was reported extensively. They weren't planning any giant surprises for Earth in the future, as no surprises were possible from the moon. They may not have signaled very obviously that Ague-Tuilet was going to be seventeen-only, but this was just in keeping with the pattern of doing a good job, autonomously to a large degree, and sending back routine reports of every last little thing.

There was tourism on Earth, but it was of two kinds. One was in a sim chamber, where the experience of being somewhere else, with sights, sounds, smells, wind, vibration and so on being all present. Why go somewhere to experience a place when there is a more convenient way to have the same experience. Dynamic flooring allowed a group to walk along a road somewhere and look in every direction at what they would see. Mars was a much more common destination in the sim chambers than a lunar mine, but Mars took only a very distant second place to home vistas from Earth. Tourism did not have to be restricted to existing sites, as virtual locations could be created by an AI with only a few days' advance notice. Bridges that didn't exist could be walked on, and they could sway. Specialized sim chambers could do water voyages. There was no limit to what could be done. With all that, why walk down a simulated corridor on the moon, especially since lunar gravity couldn't be faked.

The other kind of tourism was interactive, and involved going somewhere and living there temporarily. Being near the external settlements of other humans was very popular, but Earth was blessed with so many interesting places to experience that it is no wonder no one wanted to come to the lunar mines. Simulated moonwalks, without the vacuum, temperature, and gravity, were possible for those who wanted to gaze at Earth, and they even could have time speed up so it was possible to watch the Earth turn and the sun move, all from a chair or a standing position. Views from the Jupiter orbiter, always facing the planet, were popular as well, without the rotation of the orbiter's wheels.

The lack of tourism was a plus for Centaurus, as it made activity even smoother there than when schedules might be disrupted so tourists could see an ore crusher, which happened to look just like ones on Earth. There were few people who took simulated tours of mines on Earth, and when they did, they were mines from centuries ago, using flimsy support technology and hand-cut drifts. Centaurus was simply on its own, and it did nicely without tourists and without 3vid crews. Camera feeds from some of the large stopes were available live on Earth, and they could be compared with feeds from underwater reefs highly populated with fish, or over a concert on Earth, or from the nose of a sub-orbital transport, or many other spots. The lunar mines lost out in all those comparisons.

When seventeens invented flying in open spaces, aided by the moon's low gravity, there may have been some trepidation. Would that bring attention and even earthlings to watch in person? The worry was ill-founded, as flying on Earth, albeit with fixed wings, was so much more interesting to watch than inside Centaurus, that the uptick in interest was almost undetectable. The same worry didn't arise when seventeens started to write and play their own music, as it was similar to Earth music, and drowned in the deluge from Earth. Earthlings still played instruments and sang, but there were so many other ways to make music using automated assistants that there was frankly no space open for lunar contributions. For some reason, being labeled "made-on-the-moon" didn't attract any interest, and Centaurus' reputation as a boring location did not help change that.

There was a feeling among the earthlings in Centaurus that this was a job site, with complicated project requirements, rather than a new nation. It was organized like a large project, and there were no questions raised about the style of management. Like everything else on Earth, project management was a well-researched and well-documented technology, and the managers of Centaurus followed it.

Why would they not? Many of them had previous experience on other job sites on Earth, some with presence away from a home arcology required, and they were very accustomed to this type of life. They were accustomed to job rotation, and going from project manager to routine worker did not cause any feelings of injustice. On Earth, projects with everybody on them very capable, almost equally capable, worked. Self-importance simply cannot exist when everyone around you has genes about as good as yours, training about as good as yours, and experience about as good as yours. Without self-importance, personnel problems did not crop up on projects like Centaurus and hundreds of others back on Earth. Everyone was motivated, either because they were selected on Earth for that, or because training was so effective that laziness was simply not present.

The seventeens on Centaurus did not suffer from self-importance either, as there are no known instances of such personnel problems in the records. Fifteen years of training was lavished on each seventeen, utilizing two avatar robots per youngster and one human supervisor, with round the clock shifts. Raising seventeens was expensive, but the output was an exemplary individual, without fail. There was interpersonal interaction, but also, as necessary for high intelligence to be utilized to the fullest, much individual attention and even more alone time, during later training intervals. Seventeens were raised like sixteens were on Earth, with the same training methodology, adapted only very slightly to accommodate the differences in physiology and the presence of lunar gravity. Mankind had solved the problem of its own mind, just as it had solved other biological, chemical, and physical problems,

There was a difference in the seventeens that all the training did not eradicate. They were building their home here. That made a deep psychological difference. When a seventeen walked around Centaurus, it felt like his birthplace because it was. When a sixteen walked around Centaurus, it felt like a temporary duty project, because it was. It wasn't that the sixteens would be careless about the results and the seventeens would not, as both had the same training, which emphasized doing everything they did in the best way.

That may be why the seventeens liked their own music, even though it had nothing outstanding compared to music from Earth. This is unrelated to musical taste. It was related to belonging. These feelings were expressed in the lyrics for those pieces with words. It was evidenced in what was recorded on a personal level. A seventeen can look at another seventeen and simply feel closer because of the tie to the moon and its mines. The history of the moon does not have anything like the early history of Earth, with its battles, struggles and revolutions. It is more subtle. Instead of a long history of individuals vying for dominance and power, it is the story of how a new planet, with a population that were all exceptional by ancient Earth standards, moves forward into the future.

Once the leadership of Centaurus gave permission for the seventeens to form a new mine, which they saw as a remote branch of Centaurus, they expected that the seventeens would be so satisfied that there would be no more demands, and so occupied with the enlargement of their new mine, that they would have little time or effort to think of anything new. In the eyes of the earthlings involved with the Centaurus mine, the seventeens had everything they could ask for. And for a period of time, perhaps the first decade or two, this was so. Seventeens in Centaurus seemed to have a propensity to ask for rotation to Ague-Tuilet for a duty cycle, and some went. Seventeens in Ague-Tuilet worked on replicating Centaurus there, starting much smaller but growing.

Ague-Tuilet gradually became a smaller version of Centaurus, with the establishment within it of all the essential components of a self-sustaining mine. There were no missing elements in the ore bodies around Ague-Tuilet, but as would be expected, the concentrations were different from those near Centaurus. Once ore processing was operational in Ague-Tuilet, it made more sense, from an efficiency point of view, to move certain elements between the two mines, much more sense than shipping ore. Thus, there was constant commerce between the two.

In retrospect, it was inevitable that seventeens would take over Luna, as it was much more efficient to increase the population of seventeens on the moon than to keep shipping earthlings back and forth. The earthling population at Centaurus continued to slowly increase after the founding of Ague-Tuilet, but the seventeens' population grew faster, and eventually it was expected that earthlings would peak in numbers and begin to decrease. This was consistent with the insurance concept of Luna, as if some disaster struck the entire planet Earth, asteroids being a common example, lunites could assess restocking it with human beings millennia later. The gestation machines on Luna could create sixteens as well as seventeens, so there would be no hesitation on this regard. Even though such a disaster was a one in a million event, Luna was close to self-sufficiency, or even past, and the costs were therefore minimal compared to the overall economic activity on Earth.

This is not to say that the costs of forming embryos, gestation, nurturing, training, and mentoring seventeens was cheap, far from it. It also took time, at least thirty years in the early life of the moon, and then as mentoring was extended, even longer. This put a time scale on the expansion of the population of seventeens. While the takeover of the moon by seventeens was inevitable, it would just have to take a long time. If some seventeen, thought it would be nice to banish earthlings from the moon, it was simply impossible to effect for many, many decades. Every seventeen was smart enough to do the math and realize such a idea was impossible. But for seventeens and sixteens, a long time did not necessarily mean a lifetime, just a good fraction of one. Seventeens on the moon watched the takeover of the planet by their species, within their lifetime. It was not a takeover like Earth had experienced thousands of times, just a takeover like ice melting, gradual and uneventful. You started with a glass of ice, and later you had a glass of water. Lunites lived long enough to notice the changes in Luna, in the population, and in all the other physical transformations.

Luna had gone from being a serene, barren surface to being one with a hidden lode of human beings in one and then two places. Its surface had drill holes in a great many places, some old ones from the three early series of expeditions here, some not so old ones from landers coming down from the lunar orbiters, even some newer ones done from the not-quite-temporary surface camps set up, and then there were more being drilled by explorers from Centaurus and then Ague-Tuilet. LPO was still sending down landers in places distant from Mare Serenitatus, as the logistics of traveling long distances from the two mines were initially difficult. The mines sent exploration teams out for short trips, lightly covered, and then had vehicles for longer trips when overnight travel was required. This led to the seventeens' next significant demand, or rather suggestion, from a group at Ague-Tuilet, that was not formed formally or as a talk group, but just a group that had found itself. There would be no demands that were not sensible, affordable, efficient, and high in all the performance measures, as everyone on the moon was capable of filtering out poor suggestions. But as everyone knows, evolution does not go in a straight line, but sideways, with a slightly useful protein in one type of cell accidentally winding up in another, where it was very useful. Ideas move sideways as well, with an idea that is of some utility in one aspect proves to be very useful in another. Sometimes this sidestepping can be seen in advance, and sometimes not. Did that happen with the communication satellite idea? It is not clear.

The informal group, which had no name, submitted a suggestion to Centaurus management that two communication satellites be put into orbit with the LPO, spaced equally around the orbit. This would provide constant communication opportunities with any robotic explorers almost anywhere on the moon. The human-managed teams that went out would benefit even more from having rapid communication. This idea had a little benefit, in that it would allow continuous communication, about what was found, any dangers possible and not completely foreseen, accident response, and anything else that came up. The benefit was indeed small, but not negligible, and the cost of manufacturing a simple relay satellite in the manufacturing stopes of Centaurus was quite low, and the small satellite launch vehicles, reusable very many times, were sitting on the Centaurus launchpad. So they went up within two years of the suggestion.

The informal group received a modicum of credit and praise following the launch of the second new satellite, and it took on the task of naming itself. The name is unimportant, except that this group stayed in existence, albeit with some exchange of membership over the years, and it continued to come up with suggestions. The group's chosen name was Nobel, after the earthling inventor of an explosive chemical. Perhaps they envisioned themselves as blowing up some barriers to a seventeen Luna.

The Nobel group next proposed that there be surface outposts set up as waypoints for human-managed exploration teams. This was not so inexpensive as the little relay satellites, and involved a whole set of trips to establish the camp before the first exploration team would use it. It multiplied the cost of a surface exploration, and even made it more expensive than a robotic lander sent down from LPO. It was, of course, rejected. This forced the Nobel group to back off, and start digging through the massive geological records already collected, actually having their sentiences do it. The data was available for anyone on any outpost or in any arcology on Earth to look at.

The data from the robotic landers was mostly 30 meter drill samples, excruciatingly analyzed and tabulated. Surface robotic machines were doing 40 meters, and larger expeditions, with humans, 100 or more. Nobel participants used the data to show that deeper drilling had turned up more promising locations, as would be expected. But the deeper drilling machines only went to locations previously surveyed by robotic landers, so the benefits were not as much as might be assessed by comparing these numbers directly.

Data on the size of ore bodies, inferred from what was found around Centaurus and Ague-Tuilet, was combined with the drill information, and Nobel was able to conclude that it would be faster and less expensive to find other very rich sites by using a two stage human exploration process. They made the argument to Centaurus management, which agreed with the results, but chose to do nothing, as the need for new locations was far out on the horizon. The Nobel group completely understood the reasoning. There was no need to object to the decision, and they continued to congregate, but concerned themselves with local issues, such as hydrogen delivery within Ague-Tuilet.

Two years later, each of the members of the group received a message that management at Centaurus was re-examining the option, based on the finding by a human survey team from Ague-Tuilet of a very rich source of aluminum, one which might be worth setting up a surface mining camp for. Aluminum was present at Centaurus and Ague-Tuilet, but not in great quantities, so there was considerable cost and spoil involved in refining it. The obvious substitutions were done, and intense recycling made this completely acceptable and no impediment to either mine being self-sustaining, but if a much lower cost option were possible, engineers found it difficult to overlook it.

Management at Centaurus was interested in efficiency in sources, management at Ague-Tuilet was interested in the same efficiencies, and the Nobel group was interested in making a pathway to a third mine somewhere on Luna, full of only seventeens. They had no hope of simply asking for it, and their assessment of any answer they would get to that question was uniform and certain: No. There was no justification for a third mine on Luna. So, the Nobel group was interested in other changes that would have the unmentioned subsidiary effect of removing any obstacles to a third mine.

Centaurus management, with the consent of the GEO, wanted to explore the selenology of an area to the south of Ague-Tuilet, about halfway between the Bode and Ukert craters, almost dead-center in the hemisphere of the moon facing Earth. A waystation would be set up near Montes Haemus, which was midway between Ague-Tuilet and the new drilling site. Ague-Tuilet would manage the expedition, and Centaurus would sit back and wait for the results. This meant that only seventeens would be involved in it. It took over a year in planning, two more in establishing the waystation, and then expeditions to the new site, crossing over Mare Vaporum from the waystation, began and continued. Rich ore was found at the new site, better than either near Centaurus or near Ague-Tuilet, and nothing could have pleased the Nobel group more. Each drilling expedition covered ten to twenty different areas, and there was enough found there by the third expedition to make this new site the best so far discovered on the moon. It had been missed by the less deep drilling done by the LPO's landers.

With several rich bodies of ore dangling before them, Centaurus proposed that a joint mining operation be started at the new site. The best region was actually to the southeast of the original spot found by the LPO lander, not quite halfway to Murchison Crater. The nickname given to the spot was TriCrater, which became Tri quite quickly. It was not a very pretty name, and it had no connection with any names already on the moon. But it was good for engineers to use, and so it stuck for over a decade and a half. For the Nobel group, they saw a replay of the founding of Ague-Tuilet, with the same steps being followed in general, although some differences were there. There was no single central shaft at Tri, and four smaller shafts were dug, each with its own appropriately sized head frame. The waystation was still used as a marker point for the ore to be brought back to Ague-Tuilet, and the Nobel group knew it was only a matter of time before it was realized that ore processing at the mine was so much more efficient than back at Ague-Tuilet. Everything had happened in the blink of an eye for humans with lifespans exceeding five centuries. Their gift of patience was bearing fruit, and leading them on an almost unchangeable path to a third inhabited mine on Luna.

Staffing for the exploration mining at Tri was done almost entirely by seventeens from Ague-Tuilet. Most of them were permanent residents there, but a few were from Centaurus, doing a long tour in Ague-Tuilet. The Nobel group, still in existence, volunteered for almost everything connected with Tri. They served as some of the monitors for the shaft sinking, the head frame component manufacture, the transport and construction there, the installation of the lifts, and hundreds of other tasks, both back at Ague-Tuilet and out at Tri. Their group continued to meet, and notes indicate that they discussed the on-going operations at Tri to the exclusion of everything else.

This was the home stretch. Lunar mines were more efficient with their own internal ore extraction facilities, with their own closed ventilation for workers, with their human habitats internal rather external, and with life support there instead of being a combination of brought down from the surface or transported from very far away. There is an inevitability to it all, and it was simply a matter of size before such things became practical. As long as ore was being dug in Tri, and the total volume excavated and allowed to stay empty was increasing, Tri would become the third mine on Luna.

It would have been too much of a strain on the resources of Centaurus and Ague-Tuilet to try to mine in two new locations at once. Tri was the best choice, despite there being other finds as exploratory drilling occurred in many sites across Luna. As it was, having this new mine did slow down operations in both mines. One cannot be manufacturing components for equipment for the new mine and still do as much for your own mine. Nothing went backwards at either site, and the ore from Tri was rich and stayed rich, so that payoff counterbalanced the costs, but the growth rate of internal volume at both the two sites decreased slightly. No one complained, this was a logical decision, and logic ruled on Luna. It was simply a fact to be lived with.

The Nobel group had every right to be satisfied with the way events proceeded. They had done nothing except point out obvious things, such as the need for improved communications on Luna, the utility of deeper prospecting, and the advantages of waystation operations, as well as others that had, in a very minor way, facilitated the development of a third mine. It would undoubtedly follow the example of Ague-Tuilet, and be staffed with seventeens, with earthlings serving as visitors if needed. Luck had helped, in that there were rich ores located at a distance that was not too far for transport, and closer to Ague-Tuilet than to Centaurus.

If luck had not struck in this way, most likely the Nobel group would have continued to find indications of how the presence of seventeens might be supported in one way or another. The recordings made by some of the members indicate that they had their own projection for how a longer term future for Luna might play out, and that was with more mines, located all over the moon, all communicating and possibly sharing resources with each other. Like all seventeens, the individuals in the Nobel group had the best minds that genetics and avatar training could produce, and were well grounded in science and engineering from their years in mentoring. It would be expected that any projections such a group might make, after having spent years working through both qualitative considerations and quantitative estimates, would have a high probability of being correct. And of course they were.

The Nobel group watched and waited, for years, as the Tri mine expanded in size and grew in internalized capabilities. Many of them participated in various roles in the process, and so information about each minuscule step of progress in the mine was available to them, not simply in the information banks maintained about the project, but also from personal observation. Membership in the Nobel group did not exist in any formal sense, any more than it would have for any group that spontaneously formed just for the purpose of socializing around common interests, but the numbers of those attending grew. Perhaps it was that the group had an attractive nickname – little things sometimes have more effect than their real importance would indicate.

As Tri grew as a surface outpost of Ague-Tuilet over the course of a decade, the group had swelled to over twenty percent of the seventeens at Ague-Tuilet. It split up into subgroups based on different work shifts and sleep cycles, as well as between those more interested in different topics. Participation in the subgroups changed considerably over even a period as short as a year. It was almost as if the entire Ague-Tuilet mine was anxiously waiting for the day on which the first permanent residents would take up habitation under the surface at Tri. Even though it slowed production, when that day happened, a holiday for celebration was declared at Ague-Tuilet, and there were even some related celebrations back on Centaurus. The moon now had three mines, although the difference between two and three was actually nothing more than the change of location of a small number of mine workers. Something had to be done to set a date for the birth of a new mine, and underground habitation was that event.

Just as Sam had changed its name to Ague-Tuilet following the internal habitation event there, it was time to pick a formal, more suitable name for Tri. The Nobel group was ready, and the choice was obvious and supported by almost the entire population in Ague-Tuilet. Everyone knew about the Nobel group, even if most seventeens did not participate. Their obvious choice was Nobel. That is how the mine, which is currently celebrating its five hundred year anniversary, was formed and named. The process was not dramatic in the same sense as the discovery of new islands was in ancient times on Earth, where the founding ship captain picked some name in tribute to some important human or place. Instead, it was simply a calm deliberate process by which a spot on the moon was given a label. In retrospect, it suits us well.

6

THE NOBEL MINE'S BEGINNING

The official planning process for Luna's third mine was not done by the Nobel group, but the personnel involved with the process came more from that group than from those who had not chosen to become involved. Once the decision to start the mining at Tri was made, planning got underway in earnest. It was decided to populate the surface at the Nobel site with about twenty people, who were mostly from Ague-Tuilet. Ague-Tuilet had such a small population at that time, that less than twenty individuals could be spared. Centaurus, with a relatively huge population, picked up the slack. Working at the Tri site was a unique opportunity, and many chose this for their next work assignment. There was never a shortage of volunteers, as starting a mine should be more interesting than most other assignments, and with the standard of safety that existed everywhere on Luna, there was no reason not to try for it. As the Tri volunteer staff built up at the staging location within Ague-Tuilet, there was some slight crowding, but nothing that would dissuade volunteers from filling the ranks as soon as openings were included in the work task lottery. The plan was to have ten at the work site, and ten back at Ague-Tuilet to rotate duty periods.

It was easy to understand how the next mine might be started up. There was information in massive detail on how both Ague-Tuilet and Centaurus were started, although Centaurus was certainly a unique case, as initially everything, including all supplies and personnel, had to be ferried from Earth. There was information on mining on Earth, both recently and in the past, even in the distant past, where humans took risks and operated with little scientific knowledge and almost no instruments. It was of very little use. The only reactions possible for seventeens to these tales were shock and disbelief.

Humans on Luna, and most of them on Earth at the time of Nobel's founding, were psychologically very different than those who lived centuries before. Humans in olden times would risk their lives, with no hope of reconstitution, seeking certain elements from the ground, and then, if they had found some and still survived, they would often be victimized by other humans who used violence, deception, or theft to obtain them. Mostly these elements were used in art objects, although later, during the early phases of the industrial revolution, some uses were discovered for them. Lunites, to the last individual, would show no interest in having a mass of these elements in their personal habitation space, as it would do no good. Art objects can be made with easier-to-obtain materials.

Seventeens, sixteens, and most of the other human species were raised using neurological principles that left them with a strong desire to both take care of themselves and also take care of other humans, both those already existing and those coming later. When these actions of theft and other unpleasant behaviors were common, neurology and training of youngsters was hit-or-miss propositions, with the majority having good values but a substantial minority missing out and being left with antisocial goals. The process of science solving problems in neurology and training is identical to how science has solved all the other problems humans evolved with, but understanding this process does not make it easier to intuitively understand how humans made decisions back in the olden days. Lunites and earthlings on Centaurus could learn something about technical errors made, but mentoring did a much better job of that than simply observing haphazard recordings. As a result, the old recordings from Earth did not pique the interest those volunteering for work at the Tri site. Instead, technological information was available and complete. No one came to the Ague-Tuilet staging area unprepared.

The first activity involved coming up with a definitive route for the two-way traffic between Ague-Tuilet and Tri. The first convoy that went out to the site picked its way south from Ague-Tuilet across Mare Serenitatus, looking for a path suitable for both heavy equipment going out to Tri and loads of ore coming back. The initial pathway passed to the east of Montes Haemus, the waypoint, and turned south-west across a series of small maria before reaching Mare Vaporum, where it went eastward into Sinus Aestuum. It made an arc across the sinus before heading southwest near Ukert crater and then directly toward the center of the rich ore area. This path had no onerous hills to climb, no rilles to cross, no high mountain ridges to climb, and it proved to be the best general route between the two locations. Successive trips tried slightly different variations, so that the lunar surface between the two became littered with tracks. Markers needed to be deployed once the final choice was made, but even before this was done, a surface settlement had been established. The convoy vehicles had some solar flare shielding, but the first major task was to make something with even better shielding, using available soil and transported construction materials.

It was true that convoy vehicles then, as they do now, stopped most of any flare's energetic protons, but human health and safety are paramount virtues on the moon. Even though cellular damage can be repaired in an ordinary reconstitution chamber, there was simply no need to allow it. No one on the moon was in a hurry to accomplish something at the cost of human health, so two connected chambers were set up and covered with two meters of soil. Solar flares are sufficiently predictable so that little time would be wasted with false alarms driving everyone into shelters and interrupting work. There was monitoring going on at multiple points, on specialized heliocentric observatories, on the LEOs, on the GEO and the LPO, and at each mine. Another one was set up at the Tri site, which was certainly a measure of how much reliability was being built into everything designed for the moon.

The distant alarms would be useless if communication between all these other solar observation points and the Tri mining site was poor. The lunar orbiting satellites were hardened when they were built, and they should resist solar flare damage and give warning if their capability drops below a cautious threshold. However, as a backup measure, a series of relay stations, hardened and with dual power sources, were set up along the route between Ague-Tuilet and Tri. There was simply no allowing for chance when it came to solar flare protection on Tri, just as there had been none at the initiation of Ague-Tuilet and even Centaurus.

Secure habitats were set up for the surface work crew, so that they could spend their non-work time in a pressurized atmosphere other than in convoy vehicles. The crew of ten was not sufficient for multiple shift work, but at least it could be divided into two teams, a larger one to sink the first shaft and a second one to continue exploratory drilling to better map where the different ores extended. This site was the Sterling Hill of Luna, with so many ore bodies with useful minerals located within twenty kilometers of the site center that the main question was which one to extract first. Everyone agreed on what should be extracted first in order to keep Ague-Tuilet' and Centaurus' overall startup costs to a minimum. These two mines were sacrificing their own production to produce all the things that the work crew needed to sustain themselves, plus the machinery needed for mining and transport. It was decided that ores would be dug that best replaced those used to support the Tri site.

Some ores, like iron ones, were very common and rich at all sites, but others varied in their concentration between sites. The Tri site would initially ship those ores to Ague-Tuilet which were much richer at Tri than Ague-Tuilet. Then refinement would be less costly and the overall burden a bit reduced. Some other ores, plentiful in all mines but very necessary, were stored in piles on the surface, separate from mine spoil. They would be recovered once processing of ore was begun at Tri.

The first shaft went down only three hundred and fifty meters. The closest station to the surface was to be the initial area for internal habitation. There was no useful ore at this depth near the central shaft, so the excavation for it was simply wasted volume in terms of mine output. However, inhabiting a third mine was one of the essential goals. Six stations were set up, with mining operations going on at two, the fourth and fifth deepest.

Life at a new mine was much harder than inside an established mine. There was simply work to do and some break time with not much to do. Communications were well established, so those at Tri could exchange any information with anyone at Ague-Tuilet, Centaurus, or even Earth if anyone had a desire to do this. Few specialty foods were trucked to Tri from Ague-Tuilet, and with only ten humans at the site, personal interactions were much less than they would be when hundreds or thousands were around. Work tours were twelve tendays on and twelve tendays off, with only three rotations per person. This schedule did not integrate well with the five year work cycle at Ague-Tuilet, where almost all assignments were for five years, but with only ten people involved, the schedule adjustments were made without many individuals having their chosen assignments changed or delayed more than normal.

Even then, five hundred years ago, when Nobel was being born, the automation and robotics revolution had long since passed, and there was little physical or control work needed by the seventeens at Tri. They monitored all the processes that were going on, made the large scale decisions, and verified that the automated mining equipment and transport system vehicles and handlers did the right thing. This was much the same as back in Ague-Tuilet or Centaurus, and paralleled the activities of the sixteens and other human species on Earth. Thus, work at the surface camp on Tri was not physically onerous, simply long compared to the fraction of time spent on work tasks on the inside. Work went slowly and carefully, so resource consumption was not increased by accidents with the machinery or by having to redo a task that had been completed incorrectly.

Habitation inside would be inconvenient if done gradually, as the airlocks would be at the central staff station. Mining was done in vacuum here, as it was everywhere else, so even with an internal habitat, suiting up was required for each shift of mining work, construction management, going out to the surface habitats on foot, or using the surface vehicles. There was an unshielded but pressurized tunnel on the surface between the different habitat structures, so at least suiting up could be avoided for this type of movement.

Traveling back and forth could be done unsuited in the larger vehicles, as they had suiting space in the cabs, but many making the trips stayed partially suited for the whole voyage. Sleeping in a suit was certainly possible, but nowhere near as comfortable as sleeping in one of the beds inside, with or without the restraints used to accommodate lunar gravity. In a vehicle, there was nowhere to fall if a sleep movement was too quick to stay on the bed surface, which was an advantage, but the jostling that occurred from the lunar surface being so bumpy kept some from resting well. There was no way for the vehicle drivers to adjust speed to keep the jostling down, so it was just something to be lived with. Two drivers, in addition to the ten living at the site, were considered part of the Tri crew, but they were back in Ague-Tuilet every few days, and so had their own unique schedules. Two people is too small to make much of a scheduling adjustment for, so they more or less found their own way of handling the timing of all the rest of the events in their lives.

Both sinking the shaft and drilling many exploratory holes were critical to the next phase of the work, which was excavation away from the shaft. Initially, habitation would be limited to the top level and a single drift, with one secondary shaft to the surface for emergencies. Habitation support would be in the second level, and both of these would have independent airlocks, but with a winze between them. Sealing all the surfaces of these two drifts had to be done, as all the air in them had to be produced at another mine and transported to Tri; no leaks were tolerable. The third level was a nuclear power site, with the usual twists and turns in the drifts connecting the site to the main shaft for shielding reasons.

The fourth level was where all the action was. The future ore processing center would be built at the fourth level, along with drifts to the ore bodies. All the traffic would be here, almost all the excavation, all the vehicles, and most of the early machinery would be here as well. That was why the exploratory teams on the surface had so much pressure to make rapid progress; the direction of the drifts and their inclines would be selected based on this information as well as that already in hand. A poor choice for the drifts would result in wasted energy, time, and effort, all of which should be avoided.

This level would eventually be modified and adapted to serve as habitation areas or other living space, so there might be some compromise away from the mining efficiency choices. Inclines that would work for belt conveyors might be unpleasant for connecting two living spaces. Funiculars could be used in such situations, but they would be costly and should be avoided if possible. But since these adaptations would be many years in the future, it was hard to predict just what should be done. The sentiences could maintain tentative plans for this, but the rock holds secrets until it is actually excavated.

The first ore body targeted at Tri was a lithium aluminum source which also contained silicon, oxygen, hydrogen and other elements in smaller quantities. Lithium was valuable to a new mine for several reasons. A small part of the recovered metal would be isotopically separated and used in the power facilities, leaving most of it, plus all of the ^{7}Li, for alloying. Hydrogen and oxygen would dominate the fuel cycle. The first power at Tri was produced from hydrogen and oxygen brought over from Ague-Tuilet; many of the convoys that traveled between the two mines carried hydrogen and oxygen both ways; one way separated into the two gases, the other way as water after their chemical energy was extracted. But the initial hydrogen and oxygen that would be separated at Tri would be used in the synthesis of many things, not fuel, and it would mean a slight reduction in shipments from Ague-Tuilet.

Iron is the most common element in the rocky planets, including Luna, and Tri has its share and even a selection to choose from. Carbonates were included in the initial selection, as carbon was needed for multiple purposes. Contaminants such as titanium were preferred to be included, as processing could produce them in usable form as well as the iron. Barium nitrates were added to the initial list, as were other minerals with all the other elements needed for life sustenance, sentience machines, the fuel cycle, recycling processes, and everything else needed in a self-sustaining mine. Tri had them all, in quantities that meant Tri could last for a great many millennia. The total volume of the bodies, the variation in the richness and composition, and the quality of the adjacent rock were not known at this time, but enough was known to keep interest in turning Tri into a self-sustaining mine at a high level. Nothing that was found prior to the first habitation underground at Tri indicated anything other than sufficiency, and no contradictions came up with the continuation of the exploration of the surface surrounding the central shaft, or even as the drifts were dug out to the various ore bodies.

This was the third mine to be started on Luna, and nothing particularly new, either in science or engineering, resulted from the process. This was exactly what was expected. With so many centuries of experience in mining, what exactly could any mining site on Luna hold that would be novel? The equipment used then had been optimized for effectiveness and, above all, reliability, and centuries of work on enhancing reliability had fairly well exhausted the subject. The sentiences knew exactly how thick to make a hoist cable, how many fibers to weave it from, what alloys to use in preparing it, how to monitor it, how to make pulleys that minimized the metal wear and fatigue, and so on. And there were no mysteries about how to construct such a cable in the mines' flexible manufacturing facilities. And just as with hoist cables, every single item used in the excavation and life support at Tri had been optimized over centuries. This did not make the work boring to the shift team, but interest focused on the progress that was made and the plans that directed it. The work there was somewhat different, and the conditions quite different, from work inside Ague-Tuilet, and that alone served as a motivator for ensuring there were always enough seventeens requesting assignment to the Tri team.

Reliability had become a well-understood topic on Earth even before the third return to the moon. Once the idea became prevalent that resources were going to be needed for millennia to come, and humanity started thinking about its long-term future, recycling and reliability became very prominent topics for research. You might say the majority of the learning in these two areas was accomplished before the third return, but the momentum did not fade away, but kept going as targets for recycling percentages and reliability lifetimes kept extending. There was not much need to do any further development on these topics inside Centaurus, and the level of sentience then was enough to fill in any gaps without the need for laboratories that were so common a hundred years before. When dynamic metallurgy became something that could just be computed based on the virtually complete sets of data already collected, the two topics became finalized. Any mistakes or omissions had been corrected decades or centuries before Tri was born.

As a result, the history of the Nobel mine does not include any names of seventeens who lost their lives or were severely injured during the early construction phase. There were no accidents, and sentiences served as backups to the seventeens' own training for safety. Nobel has no monuments related to the founding period of the mine, as it was simply a series of tasks done by rotating teams from Ague-Tuilet. The tasks were done in a very safe manner, with the equipment all self-checking for reliability. As part of the vast data stores humanity keeps, the names of all participants as well as what shift they worked and even their particular work assignments were recorded, but seventeens are largely interchangeable, so there was no need for any single one to be pointed out as having done some task. It was then, as life is now, smooth and calm.

When something eventful like a solar storm occurred, there was a clear procedure to follow, instruments to notice, and activities to perform while the protons were showering down. No one at that time became separated from their sentience, so there was always information available to fill in anything that any seventeen had forgotten.

Instead, history was a sequence of work tasks, completed in some order and interdependently, that led to the various notable firsts. The first shipment of ore from Tri back to Ague-Tuilet might be singled out for mention in this history, as there was one, but the second shipment was largely similar to it, and so on for the tendays following. There are literally hundreds of firsts that could be listed in a history, such as the first test of the hoist, the first pressure behind the first airlock, the first contact with an ore body underground, the first test of the first ore transport hauler, the first contact from Earth to Tri, and a wide assortment of others. However, none of these has any overwhelming significance; instead, they are single steps in the gradual progression of the construction of a self-sustaining mine at a third site on the moon.

For some reason, perhaps tradition based on an arbitrary choice made at the Centaurus mine, the date on which the first seventeens spent an overnight inside a pressurized compartment inside the mine is chosen as the key memorable date. Everything else could be extrapolated from that. It matters little to anyone's understanding of Nobel whether the first pressurization of an airlock in the mine was three tendays before the first overnight or four tendays. What matters is that the process used to originate the mine at Tri was done by the methods which can be considered standard for this process, and they took reasonable times, and there were no interruptions caused by any errors made in planning or in the allocation of support from either Ague-Tuilet or Centaurus.

It could be argued that since energy is the lowest common denominator of everything that goes on in a lunar mine, some dates could be found related to energy at Tri which would be significant. Hydrogen and oxygen shipments started with the first initial convoy to Tri, as power was needed from the outset. The usual triplicate of fuel cells to turn the two gases into electricity were also in the first convoy, in separate vehicles as was usual. Having three identical assemblies of fuel cells made sure that there was no chance of Tri ever being without power. Energy deprivation would have been fatal to the initial team, so before anything associated with drilling began, energy sources had to be secured. There was no surface site built for a small nuclear reactor, even though it would have reduced the load on the convoying operation considerably. Cleaning up the site or alternatively, isolating a remote site, would have imposed a burden too large compared to the savings of fuel for convoying the two power gases. Instead, excavation on levels three and six of the snaky drifts for the installation of three small fission reactors was a priority, equal to that of establishing a habitable compartment and reaching the first ore body to be mined for the return of ore to Ague-Tuilet.

The space excavated was huge compared to the amount needed for the small modular reactors, but then it was designed to be large enough for the first century or more of growth at the mine. Mining near an existing reactor was certainly possible, and it was not the isolation of the radiation source that caused a problem, but instead maintaining a clean and quiet environment for the reactor. Mining is inevitably dusty, and is always accompanied by shocks and vibrations that transmitted through intact rock quite well. Neither dust, shock nor vibration would necessarily damage a reactor, since designs were made to accommodate it, but the reliability of the reactor components would remain higher if they were not present. A control system that will last a hundred years requires half the resources, energy, and materials than two that will last fifty years each.

Pushing the longevity of everything was part and parcel of life on the moon. This was what had been learned on Earth, but the environment and conditions on Earth were so vastly different from those on the moon, that what was emphasized on Earth was positively venerated on the moon. In the Nobel mine, as in every other mine, what you have to live on is what you dig out of the rock, and mining less because of reliability improvements or recycling improvements is almost like free energy. Nothing that can be saved or reused can be wasted. All these engineering tricks for enhancing longevity come from Earth, but they are appreciated more on Luna. On Earth, there is always nature doing recycling for humanity, but on the moon, nature consists of solid rock and nothing more.

Power to run habitation equipment was switched over from convoyed hydrogen-oxygen to that generated by the prime internal reactor about two years after the date of first habitation. Mining power had already been switched over, but since these gases are virtually unidentifiable as to origin, this was not so much of a great event as it might have been thought. The reduction in convoy shipments of these gases did not result in fewer or smaller shipments, but instead meant that more equipment could be shipped into Tri, now officially called Nobel, and more ore could be shipped back. Instead, the large change in shipment volumes occurred after the ore processing equipment had been shipped to Tri/Nobel, lowered down the main shaft to the fourth level, moved into the specialized compartment at that level, and assembled. As with the excavation of drifts, the first ore to be subjected to processing within the mine was the lithium–aluminum ore. It would have made no sense to have these metals extracted from ore without there being a use for them, so they were shipped back to Ague-Tuilet for use in their manufacturing areas.

One by one, more elements and compounds were produced underground at Tri/Nobel, and all shipped back to Ague-Tuilet, except for those that could replace the ones convoyed to Tri/Nobel for use in the life support systems. These would simply displace the shipments coming from the other mines. Hydrocarbons and other organics were put to use filling the gap in recycling of these materials. Recycling equipment was necessarily a part of the initial life support system equipment, even starting with the first convoys coming to Tri/Nobel. Equipment recycling would have to wait until manufacturing was begun at Tri/Nobel, but life support recycling was a different story. The plans for such recycling came from the arcologies of Earth, where there was an emphasis on it. Earth is so very diverse. Those outside the arcologies did not pay as much attention to recycling organics as those inside, but still, the technology progressed and resulted in well over 99% success rates. On Centaurus, this was considered a minimum, no matter what Earth had achieved. It was more a matter of applying carefully and exhaustively those technical tricks that had been found on Earth than of finding new ways to recycle. The technology was fairly complete. It would be wrong to consider it a cul-de-sac, and rather it should be thought of as having reached the peak of the highest mountain. There was nowhere to go further upward in effectiveness.

The first shipment of refined lithium and aluminum went back to Ague-Tuilet four years after the date of first habitation. It was a small shipment, lost in the large volumes of ore being shipped back there, but the shipments of refined metals, and then other materials, did not stay so small for long. Other ores were processed not with different sets of equipment, but time-shared with some of the initial ones. Rock crushing is a common task, and the heavy equipment at the front end has multiple uses. The same held true for some of the chemical processing systems, either wholly or by parts. Centaurus and Ague-Tuilet were identical models of what was desired to be installed at Nobel, and there was a clear step-wise sequence of equipment deliveries and installations that led to the gradual production of all necessary materials within Nobel.

It was almost twenty-two years before the ore processing system, as a whole, was a complete copy of the other two mines' capabilities. By the time the last of this system was installed and put into operation, shipments between Nobel and Ague-Tuilet had diminished to a small fraction of what had initially been the usual amount. As well as ore-processing, manufacturing had been brought up to a full and complete complement, so that Ague-Tuilet would no longer have to ship manufactured equipment and materials back to Nobel in exchange for ore shipments.

Manufacturing was done on the fifth level with a winze connecting the ore processing areas directly, so that materials could be brought down, and manufactured goods, specifically those needed for ore processing and materials preparation, could be brought back up. Manufacturing operations began with materials being made for biological containers, in the seventh year after Nobel became habitable, barely. These containers were for the organic recycling of the atmosphere, turning carbon dioxide and water back into oxygen and carbohydrates. The lichens that did this needed an system of support so that their surface area would be large, while taking up little space with their footprint within the mine.

Every square meter that did not have to be excavated out was a great saving in these early days of the mine. Later, when areas would open up from exhausted ore bodies, space would not be so important, but initially, things were minimized when they could be. Similarly, not using power for something that could be done without it was a cost-cutting measure, particularly when the mine was powered by convoyed gases, but also later, when it had its own power. Less uranium and thorium burn-up in the auxiliary fission reactors meant less excavation of uranium- and thorium-bearing ores. The second set of items was the small portable tanks used for hydrogen and oxygen transport around the mine. Since this was the universal power source, tanks were everywhere, along with the usual gauges and monitors. These tanks were produced only three tendays after the first lichen racks, and new items came out of the manufacturing facility rapidly in the seventh and later years of the Nobel mine.

Mine spoil occupied a place on the surface, a kilometer and a half away from the central shaft, in an area where there was no expectation that any secondary shafts would be excavated. It was quite easy to pile up spoil to a height of thirty meters or more, and some seventeen with a sense of humor decided to deposit it in a pattern visible on Earth. He managed to convince those in charge of laying it to make a large letter N. Centaurus and Ague-Tuilet had a series of rectangular dump piles, but not Nobel. It cost a little more fuel to transport the spoil into a pattern, but they at least took the least objectionable pattern from the choices the creative seventeen had presented to them. A face with a grin was his first choice, but eventually the letter N won the selection. The old Nobel committee back in Ague-Tuilet disavowed having anything to do with this, but it seems inevitable that they were as pleased with the choice as the lunite who thought it up.

7

INITIAL LIFE IN NOBEL

One of the first intangible products for the Nobel mine was done by the Nobel group in Ague-Tuilet and was almost inevitable: the Nobel calendar. About fifteen years after the first habitation, the Centaurus mine began using a separate calendar for internal use. Up to that point, they used the world-wide Earth calendar. The Centaurus calendar was adopted only after a long discussion in talk groups about the options that living on the moon presented. The world-wide Earth calendar was centered around the orbit of Earth, starting off at the winter solstice, much like regional calendars had done for millennia before. The only somewhat arbitrary choice was to start it off with a memorable event for mankind, which was eventually chosen as the year that mankind, specifically Yuri Gagarin, had first flown an orbit in space. Records from Earth of the world-wide calendar convocation are humorous, with each region of the planet proposing their own version of a zero year.

The Centaurus calendar discussion recognized that Earth's orbital parameters had little to do with life on the moon. The angle of Earth's tilt compared to the orbital plane determined the solstice timing, and that was done because insolation was at a minimum on winter solstice in the northern hemisphere, and a maximum in the southern. Insolation on the moon wasn't very important to begin with, and Earth's perihelion might be a better choice for setting the beginning of the year. But at that time, interaction with Earth was quite important for the completion of Centaurus as a self-sustaining mine, and so the choice of keeping Earth's winter solstice as the start of the lunar year won the selection. Centaurus had a year zero when the first underground habitation happened, and they were left with simply a linear translation of Earth dates into Centaurus dates. One just subtracted 169 from an Earth date to get a Centaurus date.

The finer divisions of the calendar were adopted from Earth as well. Twelve months, an almost unused interval, each with three tendays, plus a 'loose time' interval of five or six days made up an Earth year. Everyone's plans revolved about thirty-six tendays and the loose time. Work a fiveday on your tasks and spend a fiveday on your life, and you are back to starting. Centaurus did not copy the massive festivals on Earth during each year's loose time, as there was simply not much opportunity to live wildly in a rather small mine. But things did happen, and more so as Centaurus matured.

Records show that during the first century of Centaurus' existence, there were at least three large public discussions of changing the calendar to something more lunar. A lunar month is about twenty-nine and a fraction days, and that seemed to be a better unit of time to the Centaurus residents. The principal idea of the first discussion was the shortening of the day so that there would be exactly thirty in a month. The human diurnal cycle, which just as strong in the seventeens as in the originals and all the species in between, would trivially accommodate a change of under two percent. So it would have been completely possible for Centaurus to live with this modification of the calendar, which was called the solar calendar at the time. Translating Earth dates and times to Centaurus dates and times requires a bit more calculation, but a sentience could provide it instantly. The real question was, should Centaurus come up with one more way to separate itself from Earth influence and control, even a symbolic one such as a choice of calendar?

The talk group that had originated the idea of a unique Centaurus calendar had covered the idea of transition. It would mean that on some date, probably the break between one year and the next, everything running within Centaurus would have an adjustment in its schedule. The length of the year was not under discussion at this time, so it would mean that those who had been on Centaurus for some years, specifically the seventeens in the population, would know how old they were rather than having to make a weird adjustment every time they thought about their age. With a shorter day, the loose time would have more days in it, ten or eleven instead of five or six. This wasn't a major objection to the idea of a Centaurus calendar. Instead, there were two objections that won over those involved in the discussion.

One was the utility of the new calendar. Centaurus did not plan their surface work schedule around the existence or absence of solar light.

There was a huge temperature difference resulting from the change in insolation, but surface suits had such a very high level of insulation, that it made no difference in activities. The spoil had to be dumped on the surface, but the robotics operated largely with navigation referenced to satellite location signals, and had lights that were almost equivalent to solar brightness. Spaceport operations depended solely on the time of flight of the shuttles going from low earth orbit to the Centaurus landing pad, and a landing or launch could happen at any time of the solar month. It was true that the possibility of solar flares required more precautions to be taken for working in the bright half of the lunar month, but no one was proposing that work stop for half of the lunar month and only occur in the darkness. And there was no way for solar light to get into the mine. It might be seen from near the top of the main shaft or a secondary shaft, but these were either shielded from it, or were still under vacuum so that surface suits would have to be worn. Utility was a large consideration on Centaurus, as it is everywhere on the moon.

The other problem was the coordination with Earth, and specifically with personnel from Earth who were making the trek to Centaurus for a work tour. This first discussion took place forty-one years after year zero, Centaurus year 41, and this was before seventeens had been created on Earth. New species had been developed, but the process was far from complete. Centaurus had many originals, ones, twos, and a few young threes. Eights were what were coming out of the gestation facilities at this time, but they were destined for thirty or forty years of training and education before they could be considered for a work tour on Centaurus. So, the earthling population of Centaurus decided to keep the same length of day and translate Centaurus dates back and forth to Earth dates in the simplest way imaginable.

The second round of calendar discussions happened forty-two more years later, and involved a talk group simply gaining the attention of the population on the subject of date and time. Instead of adopting a position, the group simply decided to collect the options and present the advantages and disadvantages of each. This was almost done as a public entertainment rather than a public question, but it still aroused much controversy. Changing the calendar was a difficult struggle, and so this approach can be seen as a recognition of the near-impossibility of it. Centaurus was still an adjunct to Earth at this time, but the race on Earth toward genetic knowledge was eroding this aspect. Less and less originals took duty tours on Centaurus, and more threes, sixes, and eights did, who all the extended lifespans, and more importantly nines and later species which had no reproductive capability, requiring all gestation to be done in machines, industrially, and without passing any genes from generation to generation. This allowed tours on Centaurus to be extended. Originally, they were two years, but by the time of this discussion, a volunteer could choose up to twenty years. A nine, with a lifespan of two hundred fifty years, would be likely to sign up for a longer stay. Lifespan changes perspective, as they say.

This means that the population at the time of this second discussion was less concerned about Earth, both because of the severing of the idea of inheritance and because the years of a long tour made the earthlings feel more like Luna was their second home, and it might deserve something unique. The talk group reviewed the same calendar shift from Earth month, which is just a multiple of Earth days, to lunar month, with days being a division of the month. But they also tipped the scales against their ideas by proposing to switch from a fiveday on, fiveday off work schedule to a fifteen days on, fifteen days off one. This change simply flooded over the discussion of months, and resulted in a general result of unfavorableness. Splitting the discussion into two separate changes did not seem to occur.

The third round of discussions of calendar change happened twenty six years after that, when Ague-Tuilet was in its surface mode, not yet a habitable mine, but very visibly headed that way. Those living in Centaurus did not want Ague-Tuilet to come up with a lunar calendar first and be the one whose ideas prevailed. Many people on the moon anticipated a time when there would be many more mines, communicating and otherwise interacting with one another, and the possibility that Centaurus might not be in a preeminent position came up, albeit in a backwards way.

The public discussion that was held at that time was about Centaurus not taking seriously enough its responsibility to initiate important changes on the moon. The talk group that had initiated this round put the point like this: Centaurus has well over a century of experience in managing life in a self-sustaining mine. There should not be any points that might lead to differences in how things were conducted in the second and later mines and in Centaurus. If Centaurus, or more specifically, those who served in Centaurus, did their planning and organizing properly, the other mines should just be copies in all ways, as Centaurus had figured out the best way to do everything, and everyone else would undoubtedly accept that. There was less emotion evident in the discussion than might be thought; instead it was wholly rational. Options were considered, including all of them in the second public discussion on this topic, as well as a new one, which recognized that living underground resulted in a complete isolation from astronomical parameters.

Why bother having months or years or anything else other than days, which are something inherent in the genetic structure of the individuals living in Centaurus. A count of days instead of a count of years might be simpler and more expedient. What difference does it make if a task takes a thousand days to complete, and this is two, three or four years? Instead of year zero being the Earth year when Centaurus became inhabited, there would be day zero when the first habitation underground took place, and everything else would just be some number of days after that.

This took the winning argument from round two, that there was little utility in the moon's astronomical parameters, and turned it upside down, saying there was little utility in Earth's astronomical parameters as well. The discussion included some speeches about how lunites might keep years in their calendars to remind ourselves that humans originated on Earth, and it was a low-cost way to do so. The connection with Earth had waxed and waned over the last century on Centaurus, and at the time of this discussion, it was considered quite valuable, and this argument won out. But as a means of covering everything, it was decided that an alternate calendaring system, using counts of days, of length equal to Earth's day, would be used in all public announcements. It would have been absurd in some sense to use a count of the lunar alternative to days, when nothing in the mine ran on that diurnal period.

A small talk group was formed in the underground living quarters shortly after Ague-Tuilet was first inhabited, and the first topic they discussed was the calendar for Ague-Tuilet. They decided on copying exactly what Centaurus had done a century before, setting their year zero in the same way Centaurus had, and simply go on numbering years different from the Centaurus one and the Earth one by a constant amount. The point they made at the end was that turning Ague-Tuilet into a self-sufficient mine would take forty years of help from Centaurus, and keeping things consistent with that mine seemed to be a convenience and expedient, as well as a wise, decision. No one in Ague-Tuilet appears to have started any new discussions of the topic of calendars.

When Nobel was founded, the same thing happened, in the year following the first habitation there. A few individuals on the Nobel startup task force became familiar with the calendar discussions via their sentiences, and there was simply nothing new to add. Nobel picked its year zero in the same way that Centaurus and Ague-Tuilet did, and kept the tradition going. Like Ague-Tuilet seventy years earlier, Nobel was dependent on the personnel, the convoying of materials, the processing of ore, the provision of equipment, and much more on Ague-Tuilet and Centaurus, and would be for several decades. There was no feeling of being a separate entity or, rather, a different and unique entity, at least as was demonstrated in the recorded discussions in the talk groups and public meetings in Nobel. They were happy with their calendar, at least for this initial period of extreme dependence.

There was, indeed, little about Nobel, perhaps nothing at all, that could be considered novel or unique. Even the sports practiced on Nobel were identical to those done on Ague-Tuilet. The first one recorded at Nobel was vacuum-walking. It was common on Centaurus and Ague-Tuilet, and some seventeens from Ague-Tuilet who engaged in it took tours of duty at Tri/Nobel. They brought their daylight and nighttime suits, helmets, and tanks, and started taking vacuum walks even before Nobel was first inhabited.

Seventeens were designed with a skin that used less volatile oils, and was stronger as well, so they were well prepared to don a thermal suit, a helmet with a visor, and some tanks of atmospheric mixture and go out onto the surface of the moon to walk around the surface habitat area or to look at sunrise. Thermal insulation was efficient enough that even in dark night, corresponding to what the people on Earth used to call a new moon, a seventeen could walk for most of an hour without becoming uncomfortably cold. because thermal suits repelled dust particles, there was little cleanup necessary. Helmet visors adjusted opacity to take into account the change in illumination from camp spots to sunrise, and there were so many health monitors inside the helmet and the suit that it was said that the accompanying robot vehicle could catch a seventeen who had a problem before he even hit the ground. It was a lunar sport, as Earth had no vacuums, only mountaintops. As far as lunites knew, earthlings did mountain climbing, from point A to point B, where they would be delivered and picked up by robot air transport. There were some similarities, like the thermal insulation material used in clothing, but the whole experience was different. On the moon, it was like a stroll in the park; on Earth, a strenuous exercise with Earth's diverse environmental factors playing large roles. In both places, however, too much was not recommended.

Once Nobel was founded, the nobelites copied what had been done at Ague-Tuilet. There was an area near the airlock where a vacuum walker could suit up, then go through, take the cage up to the surface, meet the robotic companion, and then walk. The strolls were not far enough to interfere with the walker's ability to interact with his sentience, and that ensured that any desired recordings could be done excellently. As the lunar year passed, the tilt of the moon's orbit made different mountains or passes be the site where sunrise or sunset happened, and some were more interesting than others. Initially, that was all there was. Later, resources were devoted to vehicles to transport the vacuum walkers to the most diverse spots to walk. That was actually much later.

It could be said that the plan and the process to build Nobel into a self-sustaining mine were simply copies of the plan and process to build Ague-Tuilet, seven decades earlier. By the time it was used in Centaurus, the technology had stopped changing and sentiences were built and addressed the same way, robotics and all other equipment was the same, materials used for the hundreds of different needs were the same, everything was the same. Earth was not inventing anything new in mining, or much else, because there wasn't anything left to invent.

Humanity had depleted the reservoir of new science to learn, emptied it into its own coffers, and now used it for any purpose they chose. Sentiences can choose the optimum way to structure a large plan such as the construction of a new mine according to efficiency in resource use, time consumed, labor hours assuming uniform monitoring work, or anything else, and an optimum with fixed technology stays optimum. All the excitement that early Earth saw when technology was young and constantly changing had played out, and now life was quite different. Things needed to be done, and they were done in the wisest way. Details changed, such as how long the drifts would be to the ore bodies, as the moon was rather arbitrary in where she put intrusions of rich ore. Details like this would be fed into the planning process, and work assignments and schedules would come out of it. Work assignments were interesting, but not because of the danger of emergencies happening, accidents occurring or plans collapsing. Instead they were interesting in their own right.

Building a new self-sustaining mine on the moon is an involved and complex project, and being involved in it creates a high degree of interest, even if it takes forty years to be completed. Indeed, mines are never completed, as there is always excavation to be done, to replenish energy sources and recycling deficits, and the excavation eventually leads to the opportunity for more space to be used, and even population growth as long as it is below the final target. So Nobel continued to have no end of volunteers from Ague-Tuilet and Centaurus, up to the point where gestation was installed and Nobel's own cohorts of seventeens could be originated, nurtured, trained, and mentored.

The first cohort of seventeens was born, that is, removed from the incubation vessels, in Nobel year 61. They had a cohort name of Cholis, and there were six of them. All had been incubated from selected embryos, all with similar excellent genetic codes, and had been monitored in the vessels continuously, by automated instruments, which were in turn monitored by those seventeens who were assigned to gestation duty. With a fiveday on and a fiveday off, 12 hours on and 12 hours off, four seventeens were needed for gestation duty, and with a population of only about 240, this was a huge demand. Nurturing duty required another four, starting the year after, but the requirements gradually eased as two or three cohorts could be monitored by one seventeen. Then, after two and a half years from birth, training began, with yet another four needed, all while the adult population of Nobel was hardly changing.

Only two cohorts were monitored in training by one seventeen, so with each passing two cohorts, four more seventeens were diverted from other tasks to the raising of new seventeens.

Behind the scenes were another group of seventeens, involved with the nutrition requirements of the newborn seventeens. Because they did not consume the same diet as adults, special production was needed which required monitoring as well. The first cohort would start its mentoring in fifteen years, but this would not require any diversion from other tasks, as mentoring was done on own time, the other, non-work five-day of each tenday. All this effort needed to be done, as self-sustaining does not mean, on the moon, only that visitors can live there in a mine with only materials and energy provided by their own mining, but that inhabitants can be born and live there under these conditions.

The timing of the graduation of the first few cohorts from mentoring was quite appropriate, as the fourth mine, Boötes, was being started, with the surface team there starting the main shaft downwards. Boötes was on the opposite side of Centaurus from Ague-Tuilet, near the Franklin and Berzelius craters, and was almost exclusively the project of Centaurus seventeens. The logs of who went to Boötes in its early years does not show any of Nobel's first cohorts, probably because their mentors would have advised them to gain a few decades of work experience within Nobel before attempting anything outside, such as the start-up of Boötes, the Jupiter wheel, the GEO, or even a tour in Centaurus. Centaurus had kept growing during this period, and was approaching thirty thousand inhabitants. It was quite a different experience to live and work in a mine of that size, as compared to Nobel, which had not reached 400 yet. On Nobel, everyone knew everyone else; on Centaurus, almost the opposite was true. A resident there might know five hundred individuals, leaving almost thirty thousand strangers in the area. Volunteering to work at the Boötes startup for a Nobel resident would have meant relocating to Centaurus, and that was seen as a deterrent by many seventeens, at least as far as their comments in the talk groups were recorded.

Boötes started out with the nickname "Franklin", which was the crater nearest the site, but soon the name, Boötes, was chosen by a small group that took on the task of nomenclature. Centaurus is the name of a con-stellation, and it is an indication of the mindset of some of those living in

Centaurus that the chosen name for the fourth mine is a constellation as well. Perhaps the image of Boötes as a mere copy of Centaurus is what caused Boötes to be the first mine to head in a different direction than its predecessors, after the first century, which was devoted to becoming established. Ague-Tuilet and Nobel had little to do with the start-up of Boötes; it was all Centaurus with a few exceptions. The nearest ore body to the Boötes main shaft with thorium ores was quite a bit further away than in the other three mines, so Nobel provided thorium to the new mine, once it had come to the point in development where power reactors were being installed inside. The amount of metal fuel provided was not large, and simply involved a convoy from Nobel to Ague-Tuilet, on to Centaurus, and then further to Boötes. Nobel was simply too small to contribute much else.

Earth did not play much of an active role in Luna life during the first century of Nobel's existence. There were still work teams from Earth to Centaurus, and survey teams as well, but since the moon was collectively self-sustaining, as Earth had hoped it could become, there was no necessity for supplies or anything else from Earth to be brought to Luna. It was not only the success of self-sustenance that led to the diminishing of contact with Earth, it was also that Earth did not find Luna very interesting. There was certainly no more novelty to having humans living on the moon after two centuries; life in a mine did not interest earthlings back on Earth, and Luna did not try to foist its artistic efforts on its mother planet.

In reality, a small population of a few tens of thousands of people could not produce something to compete with the production of billions; Luna was simply lost in the noise. So much was always happening on Earth that the event that the first cohort had been gestated in the third mine could not even get any attention from the most avid news customer on Earth. It was just a nothing event, even though it marked the culmination of many decades of diligent work by seventeens on the Nobel startup project. Some earthlings on the GEO had sent congratulations, as they did for almost all events at Nobel, but it was more of a routine gesture from the nearest Earth contact point than anything meaningful.

Almost no one from Earth wanted to go to the moon anymore, and lunites recognized that and understood why. Talk groups sometimes discussed this, along with a comparison of what happened in a typical month on Earth as compared to Luna, and while there were some suggestions to gain more attention there, nothing substantial ever happened and nothing was seen to be changing. That is why the announcement of a three mine survey trip by a group from Earth was so astonishing. What was the point of their adventure?

Mars was a different story. Earthlings, at least a few, still had a desire to go to Mars, even though it was ten to a hundred times longer to get there and to get back as well. Some went one-way. Some went two ways. Mars had grown much faster than Luna in population, and had a sort of usable surface, although domes and bunkers did not seem to be more attractive than a mine. Mars had its own species, the eighteens, but the sixteens and earlier species from Earth had no problem co-locating with them. Eighteens had never set up encampments just for themselves, as the second, third, and fourth mine had done, but that choice did not appear in any discussions heard from Earth. Earthlings seemed to just want to go to the distant Red Planet, while they simply passed by their own moon right next door. That is why the earthlings' trip was a bit surprising.

The survey team would land at Centaurus, the only mine with a spaceport, and would tour Centaurus for two tendays and then travel to Ague-Tuilet and finally to Nobel. Centaurus would have them in quarantine for three days, to avoid infecting the population in the mine, which kept itself germ-free. There would be no need to figure out how to quarantine them at Ague-Tuilet or at Nobel, as once they were cleared by Centaurus, there would be no way that they could be reinfected there or on the way across the lunar surface.

There would be four earthlings on the trip, two who were assigned to be governance leaders, one who was assigned to accounting in a large region of Earth, and a fourth who was involved with communication management. They did not immediately explain what they hoped to accomplish, but it had been a tradition since the first days of Centaurus that Earth visitors were treated with the utmost respect and that all their desires were to be accommodated. They would certainly explain the purpose of their trip when they arrived, if not before. No clues were involved with the requested itinerary for their tour. They wanted to see the whole of Centaurus on a walk-around, the whole of Ague-Tuilet, and the whole of Nobel.

As the first earthlings to ever see Nobel, these visitors stirred up a large amount of questioning, as seventeens figured that they could deduce the reasons for the visit before the visitors ever arrived. Almost all the talk groups shifted their discussion to the trip, which was the first subject ever to sweep through Nobel's talk groups like a wind. They were here as the starting wave of many earthling visitors in the future. They were here to re-establish better communication channels and get Earth and Luna chatting one-on-one. They were here to let lunites know that Earth was the founder of everything on the moon and some payback was going to be necessary, even if there was nothing economically valuable enough on the moon to warrant it being shipped back to Earth. They were here to make some changes in how the mines were organized and governed. They were here to express their displeasure over the way lunites were operating so independently. They were here to protest the startup of a fourth mine, as enough was enough. They were here to start preparations for Luna's real role, that of being an insurance policy against catastrophe on Earth. They were here to tell Luna about some major changes on Earth, so important that a personal visit was needed to convey them. Or, this was just a boondoggle that four individuals were interested in doing, for personal reasons.

Redundant sentience checks of the backgrounds of the four individuals did not reveal some hidden commonality that would solve this mystery. Nor was there any common history, and they seemed to be traveling as a group for the first time. Communication with Centaurus was so excellent, that the minute they explained their purpose in their welcoming address, everyone in Nobel would know it.

The purpose was one that absolutely no one in Nobel or in the other two mines had stumbled over. These four representatives of Earth came to tell the lunites that they thought the population on the moon was too small to be of much use, and they wanted to provide assistance to increasing the growth rate. "Assistance", meaning multiple ship payloads of whatever was the most significant lack on the moon, including possibly more earthlings. No one knew what to say, and the team did not expect any immediate response. Take as long as necessary to think it over, and let Earth know what is the best way to go forward. The four visitors said the same thing in the welcoming address to Ague-Tuilet's population, and again on Nobel. They were seriously proposing a different goal than the one which had been pursued for two centuries. Get bigger faster. Change the main procedures which lunites have been following for their entire existence.

Earth had been doing the exact opposite. Earth's population had already peaked and was in a gradual decline. The population peak had been mainly originals, and they had declined much faster than the total, while other species, most importantly the sixteens, had grown but not enough to fill the gap in the originals' population. The six other new human species that had the most population did not amount to much of a replacement, as their numbers stayed very small. Why did Earth or at least some envoys from Earth, want the number of seventeens to grow faster? How fast? Resources and people's time would have to be pulled from other activities to commit to a higher growth rate.

Earth's representatives told the different assemblies that Earth regarded them as their insurance policy, an old purpose that was repeated very early in Luna's history, but not so much later on. Now Earth was thinking about it again, and someone there had realized the enormity of what they were asking for. A few tens of thousands of individuals is not much of an insurance policy. So, talk groups now focused on the second common question to sweep through them all: what should we do about this request?

DIARY ENTRY (AGE 15, DAY 44)

My first entry in my diary. The idea of a diary was a gift from one of the junior monitors in my training. I don't think he kept a diary, and he did not mention anyone else he knew who did. Nor did he mention any benefit that would come from it, other than my own personal enjoyment. He said he had heard about the idea from some old Earth history he was exploring, and he passed it on to me because of my preference for writing. He had noticed that preference while monitoring me for the last two years of the training, starting with when he was assigned this task. I know that monitoring was originally intended to have humans monitor the automation, but that it soon progressed to a universal observation. I guess I was one of the observables. I think I will try it for a while, and see if I enjoy it for more than a short period of time when it is novel for me to record whatever I want. The junior monitor, Batan, said to write whenever I wanted, whatever I wanted, but to write well. That was the point, to practice writing. Like everyone in training and later, I liked to do things well.

The only other gift I received at the completion of my training was a small medallion with my birth cohort inscribed on it. As tradition goes, it was given to me by the senior monitor. I will wear it for special celebrations, such as the celebration with my birth cohort of a tenth anniversary. Everyone who knows my middle name knows it anyway, but having it will add something to the celebration. The celebrations won't start until after mentoring is finished in another fifteen years. On Earth and in the Centaurus mine, mentoring goes on for thirty years, but I have heard of no plans to expand ours to that length. It is still fifteen years in the Ague-Tuilet mine, and they are a lot older than Nobel.

My training was mostly done together with my cohort, or at least we were trained simultaneously in the same subjects, as training was often individual. I am glad for the graduation, as I am looking forward tremendously to mentoring getting started; that does not mean I shall not miss being in training. In our training areas, the avatars are all humanoid, and that will probably be the last time I see so many of that design together in one place. All the avatars are similar in programming, but they have been given some diversity, not just in appearance so they can be recognized, but also in personality and traits. This is just the same principle as a birth cohort, and we are different in appearance, more so than the avatars, and in personality and traits as well.

I suppose that in the gene lottery I drew the desire to write and record my experiences, and Batan recognized that, or else he checked my genetic records. It should have been obvious, as I chose to record things more than others, since my fifth year, when we gained access to a common child-level sentience to start experiencing how to interact with them. I should get my own personal one soon, maybe tomorrow, although it will be an adolescent level one that will be upgraded when I become older. Even so, I have decided not to go back and scan through what I recorded in training to bring it into the diary. It will just be things that happen to me or thinking I do since graduation.

Batan had taken me aside to give me the gift of the diary idea and had explained how to do it. He said there is no need to have data recorded in the diary, as our sentience keeps everything important. He also told me not to plan what I would write, but to keep it spontaneous, and when I felt something had happened that I wanted to write about, or I had reached a plateau in puzzling out something, to then take a break and record whatever it was. He said that a diary is something that is private, so my sentience will be instructed by me not to share it without my direction or to include any of it in the general knowledge bank.

My first mentor will be Satis Golat Rashod and he will cover mathematics, specifically combinatorics and probability. We learned the basics in training, and now I can go deeper. Golat is in a cohort from Ague-Tuilet which is 152 years old, one of the first. He emigrated to Nobel shortly after its founding. I have not scanned his background yet, as I am quite busy changing my location from the training dormitory to one for those in mentoring. The new one will be much more like an adult habitat, meaning I will need to understand how to use everything and monitor everything there. My sentience will explain how to use the power and lighting controls, the atmosphere controls, the ambient sounds, and everything else, but I have been putting it off so I can think quietly and make my diary entries. I think I will like writing a diary.

DIARY ENTRY (AGE 46, DAY 206)

The talk group leader for today, Malin Yogan Bronot (green/brown), wanted to talk about Luna providing help to Earth. He started by describing the regional famine that started on Earth in year 145 aG and lasted thirteen years. All of us in the group knew, but perhaps had forgotten, that the famine came during the transition from the old nutrition system, where food was grown on huge tracts of bare land, to industrial farms inside the large cities of Earth. Earth in those years was populated mostly by originals, with genetic improvements, but few of the new species had been finished yet and the numbers were small.

Earth had also not gone through its transition to intelligent governance and coordination in conjunction with the sentiences of the time, and so the lack of organization explains why some food-growing regions cut back faster than industrial nutrition picked up, leaving a deficit. Being reminded of how old-time Earth used to do things always left seventeens in a state of wonder, as to how things could be done so badly. But they were, over and over again. I remember my sixth mentor, Sigin Homit Thisog, teaching me some details about Earth history and how to appreciate it. His idea was to think of a continuum from primates living in trees up to humans living in arcologies. It went from having no understanding of how to live socially to a complete understanding, but all the states in between were lived through by humans, learning by trial and error.

Malin was postulating an imagined situation, that another famine happened on Earth in the near future, due to some damage to the power stations for a set of arcologies, resulting in famine, and also shortages of everything else. It was just an assumption, as there was so much redundancy and overcapacity on Earth for power that it is hard to imagine any set of freak events that would lead to shortages. If the nearest reactor stations to some arcology failed, or the hydrogen production facilities co-located with them somehow got out of whack, it would be possible for more distant facilities to produce more and simply ship the necessary hydrogen to the area with the shortages. But Malin had been more clever than that, and had hypothesized that some mid-sized meteor strike had led to a tsunami and a volcano, taking out transportation corridors as well as power systems, and multiple other things as well. He set up a complete scenario, with all the details needed to evaluate our responses, and then challenged us to come up with a single way that anyone on Luna could assist those affected by the complex catastrophe on Earth. The next talk group meeting in a tenday was requested from the next host, who gladly agreed. Perhaps he had not thought of a good topic yet, and this just relieved him of that burden. Or maybe he was intrigued by the challenge.

All of the meeting time was used up with everyone making points about Malin's scenario, finding flaws in it or noting gaps that had slipped in, or something worse. No one managed to demolish it, and there were major improvements made in the scenario by the interaction, plus six instances in which the sentiences were asked questions to be answered and evaluations to be calculated. Malin's scenario seems to deserve to be recorded and filed for access, as it was clearly, by the end of the talk group, a nice basis for thinking out what Luna might actually accomplish.

We all knew and were trained in the idea that Luna was established as an insurance policy for humankind on Earth, but not in this way, as least as far as my two mentors who most involved me with this concept thought. Their view, which I thought through and came to understand and accept, was that this insurance was for extreme events, in which civilization was completely disrupted on Earth, and there was a chance the human species would not survive on Earth, or if they did, they would lose the level of technology that made human life the blissful situation that it is. Basalt flooding for a hundred thousand years might rise to that level, with the atmosphere and oceans wholly contaminated, temperatures raised, sunlight blocked, and anything near the flood region buried under meters of lava at the least, and melted into a slurry at the worst. Life would go through another mass extinction event, and humanity might be one of the species that went extinct on Earth. Then we lunites would be stuck up here, isolated, waiting for the right millennium to come so that we could gestate some earthlings and bring them back to Earth.

Malin's scenario was nothing like that scale. The year 145 aG famines were an example, and they only affected 15% of Earth's population. Maybe Malin's scenario is a quarter or less. One of the points he made was that we were so small in population compared to Earth, anything large happening there would show Luna as a tiny bump compared to a large hill of other areas on Earth. So his challenge was to find one single thing we could do. We left feeling somewhat useless, and the breakup of the meeting was done pretty much in silence, which is strange for a talk group.

Today's talk group was hosted by Winot Grofun Salet (brown/grey spots), but he only spoke a minute of greeting and then turned it over to last tenday's host, as planned, so responses to the challenge could be heard. Malin Yogan Bronot (green/brown) took over instantly, and checked to see if anyone had a response. Several were, so he set the rule of a ten minute presentation followed by questions for each of us.

I volunteered to speak first, but so did almost everyone else, and Malin had to pick someone. It was Fasir Grofun Sipen (blue/red dots), from the same birth cohort as our host. He began to speak of the problem with non-functioning reconstitution centers in the area where the power was running out or completely missing. By landing one, along with enough hydrogen to power it until the next ship could come in with resources and more energy, there would be an increment in the ability to deal with damaged earthlings. There would certainly be earthlings around to monitor its operation, and it could be designed so that refilling its energy tank from ship stores would be part of its procedures.

The barrier of lunites not being able to function on Earth's surface was an impediment, but this solution wasn't eliminated by it. Fasir had gone through some details of how the reconstitution center would be laid out, mostly abstracted from the design of a mobile reconstitution center that was built for the initial convoy that came to start work here at the Nobel site. The sentiences would have to redesign it for stability during a spaceship launch and landing, verify that all procedures were Earth proofed, as we have no infectious organisms here, whereas Earth, even after all this time, had them in every microscopic nook and cranny. There wouldn't be any problem with the sizing of the monitor stations, as sixteens and seventeens are about the same size, but Earth's gravity would mean that everything would be manufactured with the additional strength to withstand the weight of any object down on Earth. Fasir had had his sentience work out the launch mass of his total concept, and it was well within the mass limits of a standard spaceship, such as are usually parked outside Centaurus. Disassembly and self-reassembly were similar to many pieces of equipment shipped between Earth and Luna, and there was no worry about the ability of the loaders at the spaceport to move the packages into the hold of the ship and fasten them securely.

When he took a break, it seemed obvious that everyone had thought of this same concept; I had as well. We pretty much turned over our time to Fasir, but he needed little to complete his presentation. I noted the need for vehicles to be debarked at the Earth spaceport, to transport both the monitor team and the damaged humans into the reconstitution center. Only one would be necessary and its weight left the total still within launch bounds. Then I brought up the need for a communication channel back to us here on Luna, in the event all the channels in the area of the catastrophe were unavailable. That was not appreciated because of the plethora of channels that exist, some would certainly be functioning, and almost everyone in the talk group saw no need for it.

Fasir and Malin both supported the idea, however, so it was put into the final concept, pending review. Someone pointed out that Fasir had erred, and the sentiences did not catch it, that reconstituting an earthling took more mass on average than a lunite, so the supply ratios needed a slight adjustment. Earthlings have more volume, not more height or width, and become a little more dense than a lunite seventeen. The next topic considered was the need to launch at non-optimal times, meaning more fuel burn and less payload weight. This passed into the main concept, as reconstitution grows harder and harder with delay, and flight time alone would be a big slowdown of response. The discussion went on and on, and we approved an extension of the normal cutoff time. It is beginning to look like we have something of wider interest than just to our own small talk group. Malin was talking about considering more scenarios, to make sure our concept was robust to this variation, and then putting it out for public notice.

So few talk group discussions ever merit any public attention! They discuss fine points of courtesy and politeness, exhortations to strictly follow all the behavioral rules we learned in training, the need for promptness in scheduling some things or others, and many other topics concerning behavior. Then there are the artistic discussions, and the reviews of monitoring questions. Mentoring occupies a good amount of the talk groups sessions, typically where a new monitor was faced with a question from a student that he did not have an immediate response to, either alone or via the sentiences. Sportball and other sports consume a lot of talk group time. But this topic, the one of a meeting a tenday ago plus this one, might lead to Nobel doing something, or at least discussing it with the other mines.

8

NOBEL MATURES

By Nobel year 100, everything needed for a self-sustaining mine was in place. Nobel had received an surge of immigrants from Centaurus, and the population had climbed to approximately 500. Living spaces still occupied the first station below the surface, but the living spaces had not been maintained on a level with that station. Instead, they rose up and dove down, with slopes not too steep for comfortable walking on the moon, with its low gravity. Everyone had private living spaces, and all the life support systems were working without problems, in drifts heading away from the second station. Many winzes had been dug between the first and second levels, and among the various utility areas were open areas for activities. Life was more and more resembling that on Centaurus, which is why the migration increased. Centaurus was huge, with over thirty thousands inhabitants, and Nobel perhaps was an unconscious image of what Centaurus was like a century ago, and it therefore drew some seventeens to it.

Shortly after the centennial celebration commemorating one hundred years of habitation inside Nobel, a seventeen named Sikin Noril Vomak offered to make a presentation to the public on one of the large screens in an open area on the second level. It was something apparently new to Luna, imported from Earth, but from long ago, and with Sikin's own twists on it. He called it "shadow theater", but when the audience saw it, they recognized it as a way of making a story using moving silhouettes. There was some sonorous audio with it, but the audio was not twelve tone and seemed to be coordinated with the action of the silhouettes. Sikin's original presentation was apparently in slow motion, perhaps to allow the audience to focus on interpreting the action of the silhouettes on the screen. It took only fourteen minutes, but the reaction was explosive. Almost a quarter of the population of Nobel saw the first showing, and their reaction was so positive that Sikin was speechless. No author remarks were made, but none were needed. The audience's interaction was everything.

Sikin and his sentience had collaborated on the concept of showing only black on white silhouettes on a screen, as if there had been a projecting light far behind the screen, and the figures and objects shown were close behind it. Some figures arrived using a growth in size from a dot to their final figure, but others arrived from the side. The first showing was a story of three creatures similar to Earth birds, obviously genetically modified to be intelligent and communicating, with initially two of them struggling to free the third from a cage in what must have been an Earth swamp, complete with waves, droplets and spray. The fact that the scene was set on Earth or some mythical planet like it had not dissuaded the audience from identifying with it. The uniqueness of it captured the attention of the whole audience.

This was the start of a lunite art form that was not popular on Earth, as far as Sikin knew and his later comments indicated that it was almost entirely invented or re-invented by him for this presentation. He was asked to give many presentations on it, to show it again and again, and to elaborate on the details of how it was produced. Nobel became the place on Luna to experience shadow theater, as many seventeens decided to produce their own versions or rather their own stories using this media. Copies of it along with 3vid of the original presentation went to Ague-Tuilet and Centaurus within a day of its first showing, and seventeens there and a few earthlings on Centaurus decided to take it up as well. Earth some time later started utilizing it, as a revitalized older Earth art form, despite the long gap between the last Earth use and its regeneration on Nobel.

One of the nobelites who rapidly took up shadow theater was Notom Thalen Gropel, who transformed the medium of shadows and silhouettes into something he called Fire and Ice. Instead of figures casting back projections on a screen, Notom cast frozen figures melting, perhaps from a warm airflow from one side, or anything. He also showed the inverse, the freezing of pools, and precipitation and very slow swirls of dye and a number of other fluid media. Waves in layers of immiscible liquids, bubbles slowly oscillating and spiraling upward, all in silhouette. He left it to the audience to figure out what they were seeing, which increased the interest. Again, Notom's art soon left Nobel, but only here on Nobel was the first use of it recorded. Art is fungible. Someone on

Centaurus started using shades of gray for silhouettes, and that gained some popularity even on Nobel, and both Notom and Sikin tried it out. Shades of Gray, where Sikin used light gray to indicate the difference between bright and dark areas, was one of the more notable.

Even in a mine with a tiny population, creativity was alive and blooming after the first centennial. Imported art, brought by the immigrants from Centaurus and Ague-Tuilet, also flourished. This included lunite forms of music, as well as Earth types that were practiced on Nobel, and a few became accomplished enough to give public performances. Designing modifications for the few lunite instruments, and then having them printed to test the sound and playability, was done in Nobel, as in other mines. Synthesized pieces were done in Nobel as elsewhere on the moon.

Physical art was limited in Nobel as there were no tall empty spaces yet for flying performances or any tall trapeze work. There was enough vertical dimension in one area so that wall motion, where a person with gripping surfaces everywhere on a suit could almost walk up a wall, roll, spin from one wall to an opposing one, leap in many, many ways, and perform all manner of gyrations, was available in Nobel, with a two wall and a three wall column set up, even though only a handful of people were using them. Visitors from Centaurus gave a series of performances on these walls in Nobel year 107, and came back in 109 and in many years since then.

Nobel has at this time an immense variety of physical activities, some closer to being an art form than others, using balls, heavy and light, large and small, hoops, poles, sticks, wires, wheels, and much more, and most of these got started in Nobel in the decades following the first centennial. Light gravity is so much more conducive to wild displays of activity than is the heavy gravity of Earth, it is almost as if light gravity is the natural medium for humans. Weightlessness, as can be experienced on the Lunar Permanent Orbiter or Earth's various stations, is nowhere near as useful and interesting for physical art as is the light gravity of the moon or perhaps Mars or Mercury. Some types of physical art were invented in the weightlessness of the Jupiter Wheel, but 3vids of it are nowhere near as interesting to watch as sitting in an open stope in Nobel or the other mines, watching people being active in so many ways.

It was not until 139 that anyone on Nobel began doing and showing static art or plastic art, and in fact plastic art had no public displays until ten years later. The first display of static art in Nobel was by Dedok Frotel Dimis, who created mass portraits with three to six seventeens in poses. They were not real people, but what Dedok called clarified people, where the details that one would see on a person were not present. Static art did not gain a large following in Nobel and neither did plastic art after the first display was done with statues of ancient Earth buildings, supposedly designed to remind us of our origins in a way that a 3vid could not.

It could be argued that the first five decades after the first centennial, when all utilities had been brought into Nobel, were the half century of Nobel becoming a full mine. Long, long before the centennial, Nobel had its own talk groups, using the same etiquette that other mines and Earth used, and doubtlessly much good came from them, although most are very difficult to access in any organized fashion. Dining groups had also been started before the centennial, directly after the specialty foods utility was brought up and started running. Its first product, a red, sweet, chewy fruit, was the cause of an informal festival on behalf of all those who had been eating specialty foods from Ague-Tuilet and Centaurus for decades. It was known even back on Earth, even before space travel, that specialty foods of the greatest taste impact would have chemical changes happening on a rapid basis as soon as they were cut off the feed-stems. So everyone had to gather around the door of the utility room to get their first taste of really fresh fruits. Since other fruits were coming out with only a few days interval between them, there was frequently a crowd in this place. The distribution of the specialty foods did not get organized until a few tendays after this splendid accomplishment.

As far as is recorded, the first organized dining groups all met in the various living quarters of the members. At first, there was no central listing and individuals who placed an emphasis on taste and texture of food just met each other and formed the groups. Someone's sentience put together a roster, and then, within two years, there was a formal organization of them, so anyone with shifts at a particular time could find fellow enthusiasts with no hesitation. It was not until 160 that a larger group was formed that had to meet in one of the common eating areas.

There was an unfortunate lag between gestation starting up and fresh specialty foods becoming available. This meant that for many birth cohorts, nurturing and training were done without access to these tastes, and so they grew up without the sensitivity for the taste spectrum that early exposure to extremely fresh specialty foods provides. Eating a two tenday old stored fruit from Centaurus is simply not the same thing as eating something hours or even minutes from being picked. These cohorts were quite underrepresented in the dining groups. Once the thrill within Nobel of having these fruits wore down, and their distribution became part of the distribution system formerly doing only imported specialty foods, the young in nurturing and training received their shares of the fresh food. The delivery system was modified, and some seventeens even modified their eating times to correspond to delivery schedules, at least for a few years after the introduction of the new utility.

It was sometime after this, about 160, that the art of aromas was brought to Nobel, or at least the first public performance was done. This was really an old Earth art form, where they had specialty crops, not edible but producing aromas, actually growing in the old agricultural fashion in some area, a garden, and people would walk through it very slowly, enjoying one aroma after another, and noting how they clashed or blended in. After Earth invented industrial agriculture, in the second phase of it, this type of garden could easily be done in a hallway where flowers were growing on feed-stems. Nobel copied the shortcuts that later were used on Earth, where just aroma delivery devices were used in the hallway, and music and art were put along with the aromas to make a broader experience. Since seventeens have a broader sense of smell than original humans, it only makes great sense that such an art form would flourish on the moon. Perhaps it was a question as to why it took until 160 before there was a public performance, and why the second one did not happen until 169. This is what the records of the time show.

The nature of the art is such that, neurologically, scents are discretely recognized in the brain, and which ones to place in which sequence is completely up to the producer. The alternative form of this, where a draft of air carries the aromas past the audience, allows some timing effects that the old Earth form did not, and this was used in Nobel in 171 and almost every year following that, with two presentations in some years and three in 188. There is also little neurological connection between audial senses and scents, so the choice of accompanying sounds is also wide open to the composer/producer. Strangely enough, it was reported that the presentation in 178 left some of the audience in tears, not from any acridity in the aromas, but from the emotions that were evoked. That presentation has not been given again in its exact form, but ones similar to it in certain ways have also brought great gushes of sadness to some members in the audience. Experiments with adding 3vid to an aroma spectacle showed they universally failed, in that visual interest over-whelms the music and scent, so this experiment has not been repeated. Aroma spectacles started to be given in dark rooms, but it was found that dim lighting caused no reduction in the effects. Whether there was enough infrared to see with our otay eyes did not seem to matter.

Earth already knew about these effects and how they worked with originals, sixteens, and some of the intermediate species. Luna did its own investigation, almost independently in each mine, to see the effects on seventeens. The psychology of sixteens and seventeens is certainly different in some aspects, so the experiments were in no way mere copies of those on Earth.

All during the decades following the centennial Nobel was still gov-erned like a project. Prior to the centennial, especially during the earlier years, Nobel's primary task was excavating itself and installing all the machinery, sentiences, utilities, residences, and so on to make it a self-sus-taining mine. This was the task, and there was no significant objections to prioritizing it or even allowing it to overwhelm all other priorities. The major questions that arose in public discussion and in the talk groups were how to best organize to do this task, how to schedule it, and many details of just how to do it. Design questions about slopes of drifts, where to bore exploratory holes, where to put a winze and more occupied the discussions that concerned themselves with public policy. Luna, like Earth, had long ago settled its distribution problems. Seventeens were fairly equal in everything, and so the distribution of everything was fairly equal. Since all seventeens were the same size, inventories of clothing, accessories, uniforms, masks, safety equipment, shoes, spacesuits, chairs, and almost everything else were kept to a minimum. The same thing happened here on Luna that happened on Earth when the sixteens grew in population to outnumber earlier human species. Costs dropped as this size uniformity spread into everything. Sixteens in most arcologies lived in certain sectors of the structure, and distribution problems there were minimal. It was the same with seventeens in Ague-Tuilet and Nobel.

The granting of excellent, but rather similar, genes to everyone seemed to have added to the push started by neurology research that eliminated the cravings that originals had to accumulate things. Old texts, videos, and other records from Earth indicate life there centuries ago was simply organized around different principles and different goals than life here and on Earth in the present time is.

The simplification certainly helped humanity smooth out its social interactions and move forward toward less disruptive times. There were difficult times on Earth during some of the transitions of their society, and even now, some originals that still remained acted differently than did the later species. It is especially the unimproved originals, descended from long lines of humans who rejected genetic improvement and industrial gestation, and continued to simply reproduce and raise their offspring as they chose to. There was the omnipresent example of how the sixteens lived, and originals of all types recognized some of the benefits of that, as it was displayed everywhere. Knowledge of how to raise children intelligently, even if they had haphazard collections of genes, also helped calm down social interactions. There were simply no riots, revolutions, or anything like that in the modern world. On Luna, it was virtually unimaginable that anything disruptive would occur because of the mass behavior of seventeens.

Governance did have to change as Nobel grew larger. Running it as a project with a single head per shift was fairly straightforward when the population was under two hundred. When it approached five hundred at the time of the centennial, management of the mine was expanded to two per shift. The division of effort between the central manager and his deputy went along the standard lines: the manager reviewed work, and the deputy did personnel-related monitoring and any delegated tasks from the manager. With sentiences recording everything, shift transfers were simple as well, or at least well-coordinated. Even with two seventeens managing things per shift, no one was ready for the influx of immigration that happened after the centennial.

In fifty years, the population jumped from a mere five hundred to close to two thousand. The immensity of preparing for this took much care and some careful planning, along with imported equipment to accelerate what Nobel could manufacture on its own. Living quarters, to use one example, had to be quadrupled in size, meaning more excavation on the two residential levels, behind closed partitions to allow there to be atmosphere in the habitation areas and vacuum in the excavation areas. There could be said to have been frequent noise and vibration for fifty straight yearsin the mine. Power had been planned to cover many times that amount of people so that area of the mine was to be left less bothered and the reactors were simply turned up. There had to be more space for the installation of more hydrogen filling stations to take advantage of the larger amount of power produced.

Manufacturing had to grow both to manufacture more of its own equipment and sentience blocks, as well as to supply large increases in every utility within the mine. The layout of the mine was not built in such a way that congestion occurred, even with the same drift now handling four times the number of people moving through it. However, the rapid upswing in population and manufacturing activity meant that excavation had to accelerate. The growth represented an increase in excess of two and a half percent per year, and while that does not seem astonishing, it was large for Nobel. It is more clear to think about how much difference there was in everyone's life between the centennial and the half-centennial fifty years later. Instead of having five hundred residences stretched out along three corridors with adjoining cuts, there were two thousand residences on three levels, with fifteen corridors. People tend to stay in one residence for five to ten years, meaning there might be seventy seventeens relocating during a year at the time of the centennial, but perhaps three hundred only fifty years later.

Gestation had increased proportionally, which added to the growth of the population. With four times as many people, new seventeens could be raised at a rate of more than four times what it was before, actually something like six times, as not all other work tasks had to expand directly proportional to the population. Recycling, for example, was expandable within the work scope of the individuals who monitored it. The expansion in gestation meant more people devoting their personal time to mentoring, which was desirable for some, but not for others. Competitions were more intense, as there were four times as many potential competitors, such as in sportball games or games of investigation. Someone on Nobel might have an a priori chance of one in five hundred of being the most accurate at darts at the time of the centennial, but fifty years later, the chances dropped by a factor of four. This was one of the reasons that so many people, largely from Centaurus, moved to Nobel at this time. Centaurus was more of a hubbub, more of an impersonal conglomeration of people, whereas Nobel was very personal, very calm, and very prone to individuals becoming known for something or another, such as the best investigator or the best wall spinner. At least it was at the time of the centennial. With all the seventeens from Centaurus joining the population in Nobel, it was losing some of that aspect.

Simple things show the change in character within Nobel. When talk groups break up after two to four years, in the old Nobel it was not unusual to find yourself in a new talk group with someone from the last one. This was a nice familiarity that led to better knowledge of one another. That happened much less when Nobel leaped in population to two thousand. It is certainly possible to know by name two thousand people, but not to know many details about them. A gradual slide toward the anonymity that was present in Centaurus happened in Nobel.

It was not possible to maintain the two person per shift management structure as the population doubled and doubled again. A manager slot was created first for residential affairs, meaning all the functions that happened within the residential areas. This covered use of the public areas, scheduling of public presentations, the formal assignments to fill in gaps in talk groups, sports facilities and scheduling, residential relocations, reconstitution, distribution changes for all utilities, including clothing, headwear, furnishings, waste disposal, hydrogen, helmets, and the others, wall coverings for oxygen replenishment, leak checking and surface refinishing, color schemes, large screens and other displays, and more. The two older manager slots still took priority, but concentrated their monitoring on the other stations and drifts.

Then the residential manager slot, after two decades of growth, was divided into a head and a deputy position, with different functions for each. With this many people involved in residential affairs, there was much interaction between the two managers on each shift and those who had suggestions or issues to resolve. Seventeens are designed to tolerate and to have patience, and the genes for this are checked inside each embryo. Training emphasizes these traits, and in fact, nurturing includes it in one of their feature assessments. Thus, things improved in the residential areas, gradually and continually, and there were no group objections, only individual ones. Then, a talk group, composed entirely of recent immigrants, discussed the use of a Centaurus technique of having points of contact for the residential managers. These would be people who were supposed to increase the interaction of the non-managers with the managers. Since managers rotated every work cycle of five years, there were many non-managers who had been managers and were completely familiar with the processes of mine management, both when the mine was smaller and as it grew, and also in larger mines before they emigrated to Nobel.

The discussion topic migrated to three other talk groups, and was then promoted to a public discussion. It had been reframed as to whether Nobel had grown enough to have points of contact among the non-managers. Virtually everyone had found out from their sentiences that this started at Centaurus when it was a little larger than Nobel now; perhaps the starting point was delayed in Centaurus because it was the first mine, and no one really had any experience in how to manage it most efficiently. Ague-Tuilet had some, so that was a point in favor of starting them at Nobel, but Ague-Tuilet was well over twice as large as Nobel, and used the same number of managers. No one argued that Nobel's managers were not doing their jobs well, and with sentiences attuned to potential problems, how could they not? But those arguing in favor of the points of contact stated that rapidity of learning about issues was important, and hearing multiple points of view was as well. the managers of the residential areas were known to everyone, so they undoubtedly heard multiple points of view, but the points of contact concept would increase this rate and make sure there were no missed areas.

The other side of the coin was that too much communication can be worse than not enough, particularly if there is too much noise in it. This would correspond to people acting as points of contact and assiduously seeking out something to report. Perhaps this would be far in excess of what actually should be taken on as a task by a residential manager. Despite the objection, a mild form of points of contact was started up shortly after the public meeting. Volunteers, three per shift, would see what help they could be in ferreting out problems needing attention, before the sentiences reported them. This had very mixed results. In one shift, a problem or two was noticed, but in other shifts, nothing. This was strange because each shift faced exactly the same problems, barring unscheduled interruptions of some utility for maintenance needs. Those who volunteered for different shifts probably did it for different reasons, and the new positions disappeared after two years.

The other topic which came up in talk groups in the fourth decade after the centennial and which spread finally to a public discussion might be labeled "The Futility of Rescue". Countless talk groups spent time on the reality of the original statement of the reason Centaurus was founded, and which was harked back to over and over. Some talk groups on Centaurus had been using their sentience's calculations about the cost of space travel back to Earth, not about the mechanics of it or how to build the most efficient rockets, for that was known down to many decimal points, but on building a fuel facility. On Earth, rockets exhaust into the atmosphere, but for launches from Luna, everything was lost to vacuum. Fuel requirements depend on the payload and the destination, whether LEO, GEO, or even Earth surface, but the order of magnitude is a hundred thousand kilograms. One launch would waste all that. In a society like Nobel's, or Centaurus', where recycling was a constant goal, even wasting a fraction of one kilogram was a tragedy that had to be remedied and prevented from happening again.

Materials on the moon were so much more precious than on Earth, despite Earth's development of arcologies that emphasized recycling, as ore has to be mined and processed, and materials extracted from it. Compare the idea of saving a kilogram of materials by being incredibly strict about recycling everything, by designing all equipment to last long, when at the end of its life, to be disassembled and reused in parts, by training everyone to have the habits of recycling and protecting the mine's valuable stocks, and so on, with the idea of blowing away a hundred thousand kilograms of exhaust into the vacuum between the moon and Earth.

A second of computation by anyone's sentience would translate a hundred thousand kilograms of fuel into a minimum of two million kilograms of ore which had to be dug and transported to the processors. This corresponds to almost a thousand cubic meters of excavation of an ore body, which some seventeen translated as a tunnel with a square cross section of three meters on a side and a hundred meters long. Those who had done duty in a mining operation, which was almost everyone, recognized the enormity of that task. This was simply to fuel a single flight of a single rocket and had nothing there for building the rocket and the payload. If the rocket went to LEO or GEO, assuming they were still operational or at least existing after the catastrophe on Earth, it might get returned to its lunar launch site, and represent some material savings. But if landing had to be made on Earth, this would mean much less payload and very little, chance, of it being returned. Yes, mining calculations indicated that this could be done, but the cost was psychologically shocking.

Some members of the originating talk group spoke from a fatalistic viewpoint, saying that this was the mission of the mines on Luna, and we should just be prepared to do it. While one rocket from Nobel was a huge task, the plan was for twenty substantial mines on the moon within a millennium or sooner, and maybe this meant twenty rockets leaving in some coordinated plan to replant human beings on Earth. Members in another talk group had gone in another direction, essentially abdicating the mission to restore Earth, on the grounds that doing this would compromise the minerals and materials that the mines needed to survive long-term, and that the survival of humanity on the moon was as important or more important than the restoration of humanity on Earth some centuries after an asteroid strike or something else equally horrible.

One individual, who will not be named here, stated in the public assembly that the lunar mines should tell Earth that restoration was not reasonable, and they should look for another way to restore humanity to Earth post-catastrophe, perhaps deep bunkers well stocked with supplies, power, and a means to dig out if the passageways were destroyed by whatever the catastrophe was or its side effects, like tsunamis. That short speech was the end of the public assembly, because no one had anything new to say and because there was a need to think through what everyone had said, even the last speaker.

The records, 3vids and audio extractions of it, turned into text or presented live, were always available to Earth. Communication with Earth was automatic, or at least on request, and anyone on Earth who wanted to hear what went on in a public meeting, or even inside a formal talk group, could get their sentience to locate it and bring it back down to them. So, Earth may not have paid any attention to this meeting, as there was never any response to it, as there was none to almost every other public meeting in every mine on Luna. Or perhaps this information was filed away for later use.

9

THE FOURTH MINE

The Boötes mine was so far from Nobel that there was little attention paid to it inside Nobel. No nobelites signed up for surface duty to sink the main shaft there, and only two participated in the initial excavations of the stations and drifts branching away from it. There was no doubt that working on a new mine was more interesting than just excavating the next five meters of a hundred meter long shaft, but for some reason the attractiveness was not enough to draw many nobelites, at least at first.

Boötes had its signature event of someone living in habitable space underground in Nobel year 68. By the time of the Nobel centennial in year 100, there were about 200 residents there. But within the next fifty years, it picked up over 1200 residents. It had grown so fast that it almost pushed Nobel out of the position of being the third largest, in population, mine on Luna. They had their own gestation facility for seventeens, with all the associated nurturing spaces, training spaces and mentoring arrangements, but Boötes did not get its growth from internal gestation. Instead, Centaurus seventeens moved over to it, and many permanently took positions there. Boötes had a different attitude toward living in a mine than did the first three mines. Centaurus was mostly seventeens by year 150, and the other two were all seventeens, so there was nothing in their heritage to cause this migration. It was more that the initial inhabitants of Boötes liked living things, and they modified their mine accordingly.

Centaurus was the big brother of Boötes and so had influence over what they did, and Boötes developed from being a primitive surface installation to a habitable mine to a fully equipped mine pretty much as Ague-Tuilet and Nobel had done, and even Centaurus had long ago. This was simply the most efficient way to start a mine on the moon. But once the utilities were up and functioning on Boötes, their talk groups shifted emphasis to life. On Nobel, there is only the seventeens, and some biological materials in tanks to help with processing and recycling, plus the air purifier organisms. Nothing else lives there. The same holds for Ague-Tuilet, which is somewhat ironic because their two namesakes were biologists enamored with creating life-forms, mostly mammals that had never been seen before. On Boötes, the talk groups discussed having lunar pets. Why anyone would want a pet, when there was so much to do in a mine, was not clear. It was clear that there were several residents of Boötes who seemed to think that their lives would be richer with a pet. No one moving to Boötes seemed to object to it, but many regarded it as a project fraught with uncertainties. There are no lunar pets, and there are many good reasons for that.

Records of the talk groups from that period in Boötes do not seem to have concentrated on the negatives of introducing new life forms to our planet, but there were comments during the talk groups that indicated they were not oblivious to them. Boötes did not have a genetics lab per se, but the genetic structure of animals on Earth was known, down to the last epigenetic switch, so there was more than enough information for the sentiences on Boötes to figure out something that would live. Trying to deduce what would be the best choice was another matter.

One talk group wanted something spun off of Earth's canines, and another wanted birds that would be allowed to fly loose in the tunnels and drifts. Another group wanted spiders that could live in cages, but no one in that group had thought very much about cages and the impact of them on an animal, even a spider. The spider would have enhanced intelligence, but not much unless a complete redesign of the skeletal structure was done. Earth people had done this, as they had done almost everything else anyone could imagine. The talk groups eventually got down to deciding they would modify an existing Earth animal for low gravity. They would not have the IR and air pressure sensors on their heads that seventeens do, as the pets were just for the amusement of Boötes' residents. Would they be property of some particular seventeen, or perhaps traded off between several? Would they be common property, with a new task being set up for pet care, which would rotate every two to five years as do all tasks on Luna? Would there be more than one variety? How long would they live? Should their digestive systems be designed to eat the same foods as seventeens, or would it be more expedient to have something different? This had behavioral implications.

What facilities would they need? Should they be made bisexual so they could reproduce, or just have them made in gestation tanks?

After three public meetings on the topic, the residents of Boötes decided to model their initial lunar pets on Earth's canines, specifically small ones, who would be housed in a separate area set aside for them. Boötes residents could join them in the area, or take them out for periods of time. The concept of lunar pets spread to other mines, with talk groups on Centaurus, Ague-Tuilet and Nobel entertaining the idea of at least copying Boötes' lead in that area. None of them did so. The discussions in Nobel were certainly extensive, but the interest in having pets or interacting with them for some reason was not as widespread in Nobel as it was in Boötes. Nobel came to an agreement to have no pets, at least for a period of ten years. Then it might be reconsidered.

Those nobelites who were the most interested in pets, and did not want to wait ten years to see if there was a change in opinion, put in applications to transfer to Boötes. Only seven residents put in for a permanent transfer over the next two years, but over thirty applied for work tours there, and as would be expected, all were approved and facilitated. More than half came back, after having the experience in Boötes of playing with the pets, taking them into their residences, and caring for them in other ways. None of the ones who returned showed that they had applied for any work assignment involving the pets, but it would have made little difference as the number of Boötes residents who applied, along with migrants from Centaurus, was so large that the probability of winning the task lottery was quite small. After they returned, the talk groups on Nobel they became members of had discussions of these pets, the facility Boötes had made, and the costs in resources they accounted for.

The records of these discussions showed that it would be fairly easy for Nobel to copy the facility, modify the gestation tanks on the second level to produce some pets, and modify task assignments and other operations to accommodate pets, but the interest never warmed up. The public discussion that was talked about never happened, not ten years after the first one, not twenty or thirty tears. There was still a flow of those Nobel residents who were curious to travel to Boötes for one or two work periods, but few stayed on in Boötes, unlike the seventeens from Centaurus. This is hard to understand as Boötes was not much different from Nobel, and even a slight interest in pets could have been enough to draw more migrants from Nobel there, but it did not. Almost all the migrants to Boötes during the fifty years after they installed their pet facility came from Centaurus. The discussions on Centaurus about transferring there, at least the few that are recorded and easily accessed by a sentience, showed the same motives of smaller size and more familiarity with others rather than an interest in pets, but it was mentioned to a degree. Boötes residents did not tire of them enough to remove them but continued to house them in their own facility and to rotate people into the tasks of caring for them.

Luna was, at that time, hostile to other life forms, in a subtle way, perhaps in the same way that industrial space is never used for residences. They just do not fit together. For example, during this period, no one on Boötes ever called for a space suit for the pets, so they were restricted to the inside of the residential airlock. There really would be no point to having a pet in any of the other areas, as they were not recreational destinations, only work locations. Bringing a pet out onto the surface of the moon would be almost silly. The pet might look up and see the Earth, uncomprehendingly, but what would be the point? A video of Earth as a globe might be just as informative. The inside of the residential areas was all hard surfaces and artificial everything. There was no nature present on the moon in any of the mines. Nothing there was conducive to putting a pet in the midst of it. This may have been one of the motivations for having no pets in Nobel.

On Boötes, one talk group brought up the idea of manufacturing 3vid helmets for the pets, or even lensesets that would allow them to watch a 3vid on a screen. But what would they be shown? Pictures of parks on Earth? Forests on Earth? Some other nature scenes from Earth? Fortunately, the pets in Boötes were not intelligent enough to interpret what they could see, but if they did, the impression of being in a pet prison might have seeped into their minds. What would be the purpose of showing the pets views of Earth? Pets fit in very well on Earth, but only with difficulty on the moon. The constant attention they got on Boötes may have supplanted any concept of being more independent, and these pets were not designed for independence in any way, so their lives were constrained in the way they had to be. The 3vid idea fell flat.

The next idea that arose in Boötes talk groups related to pets was the construction of some enclosed walking areas for them. In internal videos, many Boötes residents can be seen sitting on the periphery of the pet areas, watching the pets play with one another, in an area reserved for that. It was common for mine residents everywhere to enjoy watching young seventeens play with each other in the area next to the training facility; probably the under-five year seventeens were the most interesting of all. In this area there were structures for climbing, jumping, and other exercises, and it might be guessed that those in Boötes were thinking of an analog of this for their pets. This idea was appreciated, and without any public meeting on it, a small structure was built, and then after a year and a half, expanded, and later expanded again in small ways, some five times. Boötes pets might not have a forest to run in, but they could run up slopes and travel along narrow paths as much as they wanted to.

There were discussions involving thinking about pets after the experiences at Boötes had been going on for twenty plus years, in that it might be possible to come up with some smarter ideas on what type of pets might fit in better within Nobel, or any mine for that matter, than the canine versions that Boötes chose. Ideas abounded. One individual seemed to think spiders crawling freely around the walls and ceilings of the residential areas of Nobel would be a positive addition, but there was less than zero support for that. Another wanted something most easily described as a land starfish, which were common in a few arcologies on Earth, but on Luna, the suggestion again received zero support. Birds got the most support, but also the most negative reactions because of the difficulty of controlling them without some additional signaling equipment added to their bodies, which was not accepted. The one idea that did get support was not an animal at all, but some non-useful vegetation. Those who had the most intense interest in genetic programming indicated that it would be possible for vegetation to grow independently on a bed of powder, provided the powder was correctly constituted. Nobel's management decided to do a small experiment with lunar vegetation, growing fully autonomously, not simply specialty food parts growing at the ends of an array of pipes.

The project was almost derailed by a speech made by one of Nobel's oldest residents, Tudon Theron Hoper, which happened in a talk group, but spread through sentiences over the moon as those who heard it moved it on. The essence of the speech was that the mines of Luna had decided to become a shallow imitation of Earth, with the first steps being made by Boötes and Nobel, by trying to grow living things like those that grew absolutely everywhere on Earth. Why should lunites imitate Earth?? We have here a new environment for mankind, not a copy of our old planet, and we should boldly throw away the idea that we need to make things here to replicate those on Earth. The speech went on like this for six minutes, trying to make lunites so proud of themselves and what they had accomplished in a barren satellite that there was no need to do anything else. Earth was our origin, not our model.

The Tudon Hoper speech traveled to Earth within a few hours of it spreading all over the moon. No one on Earth seemed to care much about whether Luna had animals and vegetation, except that there were some requests for 3vids of the Boötes pets. There was no sense that Earth was losing its grip on Luna, as there was almost no grip left to lose. The GEO continued to interact with us, there was a small amount of earth-ling traffic to Centaurus, and communications were still available and well maintained. But the mine project that Earth started had become self-sustaining long, long ago, and both worlds seemed to think that was a fine situation. Rockets are expensive, after all.

The speech, although beautifully and compellingly crafted, did not stop Nobel from going forward with the vegetation project. It did make some nobelites look at themselves a bit differently, in that talk groups meeting to discuss the speech saw it as another mark of our independence from Earth, not that there was any dependence left. Yes, Earth could stop funding the GEO or at least cut off its assistance to Luna, but why bother? The GEO did so many Earth tasks that the few Luna ones were almost lost in the noise.

Nobel's few seventeens who had taken a deep interest in genetics shared the task of inventing lunar vegetation with those in the other mines, a group on the GEO with the right background, and on Earth. The powder idea was replaced by a wet powder, with the nutrients, in-cluding an energy source, flowing into the powder from the bottom and roots and rhizomes fashioned to extract it and transport it to the plant's cells. A fine, dense clump of filaments, three centimeters long, would grow from the nodes connected to the rhizomes and roots. It took some experimenting, done at Nobel and at Centaurus, to get it right, but within four years, viable lunar vegetation was growing in a meter and a half square. It didn't use photons for energy, so it would continue growing in bright light, dim IR lighting, or darkness. It would be self-limiting and completely restricted to a special tub with the right solid and liquid mixture in it. It would be strong enough to walk on, and everyone wanted to, and it suffered no damage from countless footsteps. The stalks felt rubbery if you squeezed them in your hand, but underfoot it felt like a carpet from centuries past.

Perhaps because of Tudon Hoper's speech, no one thought the vegetation should be green, and with no photosynthesis, it didn't have any use for that color. It was decided to make it light red. Later versions took on many other colors, but the initial patch was a light red. Once all the details of the vegetation were worked out, it was decided to make a large patch of it on an open area in one of the habitation drifts. It didn't draw migrants to come to Nobel to walk on it for two or more years, and in fact, it stayed at a size of ten meters by four meters for quite a number of years, before it was decided to expand it to other areas where there were piping conduits for the nutrient flow. The plant produced no waste, in that dead cells were recycled by the plant itself, and the nutrient flow had to be modified to avoid over-saturating the powder base. It was easy to monitor and easy to control, so the vegetation experiment can be considered one of Nobel's early successes.

Another one of Nobel's early successes was the masterminding of the fifth mine on the moon. There had been a 3vid conference of the managers of the four mines, one year after the centennial in Nobel year 101, and the Centaurus manager and deputy manager, speaking almost back and forth, proposed a fifth mine at another very rich ore site, but far in the southern hemisphere, still on the earthside of the moon. Three conferences later it was decided to create the mine, and that Nobel would house the leadership of the project, and serve as the jumping off point. Choosing Nobel was almost inevitable, as this new site was almost as far south of Nobel as Nobel was from Ague-Tuilet. Having a lunar highway from any other mine to the new site would have been an error in efficiency. Since there were less than 300 residents in Nobel at the time, the volunteers for the surface work would have to come from the larger mines. Boötes was also tiny in population, and so again, it was mostly seventeens from Centaurus, with a few from Ague-Tuilet, which had a bit over two thousand residents, as compared to Centaurus having thirty thousand. A surface team would involve twenty people, plus transporters, so the strain was not great in providing the manpower.

The managerial conference had also decided on a name for the fifth mine, and since there was little or no public involvement in the start-up, but instead acquiescence, they decided to name it Gagarin, after the first earthling to orbit the home planet. Everyone on the moon, and most of those on Earth, learned his biography. He was presented as one of the most brave individuals possible, risking his life to enter a new frontier. This was in stark contrast with how seventeens were raised. None of them would have ever contemplated doing something so risky. Seventeens are raised to be cautious, to have redundancies for safety, and to never do anything that might cause an injury, much less death. If this mentality had existed on Earth, there would likely be no lunar colonies, or they would have been delayed for another five or ten decades. Those earthlings who did the first landing on the moon, the first return, and the second return all were cut of the same material as Gagarin. Now that the sixteens have displaced them on Earth, it is probably for the better for other reasons, but certainly it has been a great change from what humanity was.

The equipment that had dug the main shaft at Ague-Tuilet had been used at Nobel, again at Boötes, and would be used once more at the new site, Gagarin. There would need to be more transporters, as materials to support the crew and to excavate would come from Centaurus, via Ague-Tuilet and Nobel. There were already waystations between Centaurus and Ague-Tuilet as well as between Ague-Tuilet and Nobel, but the route had to be picked through and waystations set up on the last leg of this trip. It was almost seven hundred kilometers from Nobel to the chosen site for Gagarin, and the first part of the trip was the most challenging, in the mountains south of Nobel. Going was a bit slow there, with perhaps fifteen kilometers an hour initially, and close to twice that when crossing the smoother maria.

There would be so much redundancy in the transport process that it was hard to see how any accident could happen. The vehicles were designed so that the hydrogen and oxygen tanks were impregnable, and the motors in each wheel meant that good speed could be maintained even if one failed, which was not expected. Cabins were pressurized, suits were on hand should there be a leak, and the cabins were large enough to double up if that became necessary. One vehicle could tow another if one somehow lost its power or its steering. There was no need for any Gagarins on the road to Gagarin.

Just like with other mine startups, the moonscape around the area where Gagarin was to be dug was peppered with exploratory drill holes. It seemed that Gagarin's ore lodes ran deeper than Nobel's, which might mean there was even more ore available at Gagarin than Nobel had. This would not be known for years, maybe centuries, as exploration from a self-sustaining mine was very gradual. It was not as gradual as it would become once the population target was reached, and only energy and recycling losses had to be sought from new excavation. Earth was explored much better than the moon, and humanity there, if they kept to the recycling levels possible, could last many hundreds of thousands of years, and perhaps millions, depending on what population they chose to maintain.

Earth had a mixture of originals and new humans living in nature, using few resources, and sixteens and previous versions living in the arcologies and some small older cities that had not been converted. the population had declined to below five billion by the first centennial, from a peak of almost twice that, and had dropped even lower in the century after that, and earthlings were frequently discussing what the target should be. This did not affect Nobel or the other mines in any significant way, as there was no trade between Earth and Luna. Their principal interaction was with the GEO. Earth could easily have staffed GEO if the population of Earth had crumbled by 99% as only a few thousand individuals were detailed there from Earth. Luna did most of the staffing on the LPO, at a comparatively large cost, so again, the population of Earth mattered little in how the lunites lived and what activities they were involved with.

Discussions at Centaurus were held about a more direct route to Gagarin and this question was referred to Nobel. The conclusion was that there was no utility in developing a second pathway to the Gagarin site, directly south from Centaurus across Mare Tranquility, as the remainder of the trip, westward, was through more difficult terrain. Sometime in the future, this direct route might be developed, but the team at Nobel thought it a waste of resources. The moon is simply so large that putting together a network of pathways was something better left for a time when resources were more easily available, meaning when the population had increased substantially and more would be available for surface transportation.

Gagarin had its first underground overnight in Nobel year 117, but it would be most of another century before it achieved complete self-sustaining capability underground. Gagarin did not attract migrants the way Boötes had after it was founded. There were enough volunteers to maintain a tolerable expansion pace, leading toward the point where the mine was self-sustaining, but not enough to put pressure on the pace to accommodate newcomers. Seventeens from Nobel certainly went to Gagarin for the experience of starting up a new mine, but most returned. Little by little during the decades after Gagarin was officially a mine, the Nobel team turned over management of it to a team at Gagarin, so by the time the last utilities, which happened to be gestation-related, started up at Gagarin, there had been nothing left for the Nobel team to do for some time. They disbanded at the end of their joint work term.

Luna was an isolated place, and that seemed to suit the lunites there. Mars had been inhabited by humans during the first century of Centaurus' existence, gradually becoming more and more self-sustaining, but with Earth being more closely involved than Luna. Luna's experience in underground living was more relevant, but the information was available in dozens of ways, and there was never an invitation by earthlings or martians to travel to Mars to provide any assistance in any way. Mars was a tourist destination for earthlings, although not in the sense of tourism in centuries past. Anyone going to Mars was expected to stay for a work term, or forever if they chose to. Mars had its own species, the eighteens, and their own gestation, nurturing, training, and mentoring capabilities, just like Earth did with the sixteens, and, if the martians had noticed, just as the moon did. Mars was very interested in being a new Earth, and had domes on the surface with vegetation inside, although that was not as practical as they had hoped. People traveled around on the martian surface more than on the lunar surface. Mars had a bit of spectacular scenery. People from Earth wanted to see it, even though a 3vid of it would have been a hundred times better at showing the full scope of the Great Rift Valley and the other features there, such as volcanoes, mountain chains, polar caps, and craters. It took months of travel to get from Earth to Mars, yet the cyclers kept getting bigger and bigger, and more and more people kept going.

It was somewhat shocking when Mars explained they wanted to send a delegation to the moon. Some group of eighteens, who were perfectly capable of life in a lunar mine but not on Earth, were coming to Centaurus in Nobel year 181, and from there they would go to the other mines. Their journey would take them to an Earth LEO, but instead of going down to Earth, they would be on a shuttle to the GEO, and from that over to the LPO and down to Centaurus. A tremendous expense was involved, in the eyes of lunites, for whom a single rocket was a major consumption item and something to be budgeted for over years. Talk groups, especially in Centaurus, put this down to eighteens not being able to go to Earth, and so the group was taking the next closest spot for their tourism, Luna. Hosting them would be done in grand style, much more than for the occasional Earth group that came to Centaurus, as these were the first eighteens ever, and it might be another century before another group came by.

No one had much cared before to inquire, but Mars had many types of vegetation growing there, all genetically concocted to fit the conditions on the planet, and several types of animals as well. After the trip was announced, 3vids of these circulated everywhere on Luna. Why no one had paid attention to them in the earlier discussion of having animals in Nobel was not obvious. Perhaps Luna was so used to being Earth's satellite, that events on other outposts were not followed very much. None of the animals were being brought along on the expedition "Mars to Luna", which was a point of dissatisfaction, especially in Boötes. Centaurus grew Nobel's vegetation in many places, so there was almost nothing Nobel had to display that would not already be familiar to the visitors. There would be festivities with music, acrobatics, and art on show, invitations to go vacuum walking, wall jumping, and other sports that nobelites appreciated, and some specialty foods that nobelites preferred.

Their visit to Nobel would last only three days, but that was enough to show them everything that Nobel could possibly offer.

Very few non-seventeens had ever visited Nobel, especially after it went underground and no surface work was going on. Some earthlings from Centaurus had been taking work tours during the sinking of the main shaft, and two others were involved with setting up the head frame, but after that, no one. Seventeens came all the time, but having eighteens in Nobel was a new experience. Their information had to be brought into the reconstitution centers, in case one of them needed some care after an accident. Accidents did not happen in Nobel, except for minor things, but still the preparation for the most unlikely was made. Martian eighteens could eat the same nutrients as seventeens, both the standard fare and the specialty foods, so there was no need to reprogram the nutrition facility to accommodate them.

When they finally did arrive, the five martians, it was like Nobel was going through the script of a play. Everything was planned in advance, and not only was it all planned in advance, everyone they met knew the plan and their part in it. Seventeens in Nobel have a great sense of humor, but there was no humor in the plan for the martians. Looking back on the plan, it seems that everyone was being just how a stereotypical seventeen or eighteen would be, except that spontaneity was excluded. On the third day, the martians requested to be split up into two and three, with the two following Nobel's carefully charted tour of the nutrition, gestation, recycling, and power facilities, and the three asking to be part of a Nobel talk group.

This was unusual, as talk groups formed for a period of years, with the first tendays being mostly devoted to developing acquaintance. They only ran for a couple of hours every tenday, although that was modifiable. Still, these were the first martians ever to visit Luna, and their every wish was to be granted. The three joined an existing talk group, in one of the larger habitations where there was room for three more guests, and the time allotted was extended. As guests, they were asked to pick one of their own to host the discussion, even though it almost always falls to the owner of the habitation to do that. They did, and the one they chose was the oldest in the party, which made sense, and he started by declaring how pleased he was to see the lunar mines and so on, but then he wanted to talk about what we saw as Earth's purpose in keeping us here. His choice of words was delicate, but did not fit at all with the way that nobelites or lunites saw their world.

The nobelites in the talk group are recorded as asking for some time to think over the question, but it did not take long for a consensus to emerge. Everyone in the habitation knew that Earth was no longer a single organized entity, and did not speak with one voice, especially when giving purpose to another world full of independent people. The topic more or less folded back on itself, with the nobelites asking the martians if they felt they had a purpose from Earth? They did, and they were clear about it. Mars was a testing ground for Earth's expansion to other worlds, many, many centuries in the future. The discussion shifted to a standing one. Did Earth say this, and if so who on Earth? No, it came from discussions on Mars between earthlings and martians. Is it universally accepted? No, only by some on Mars. Is there any planning going on in support of this goal? No, and it will be centuries before there is any.

The discussions of the purpose of the martian outpost had not happened on Centaurus and not on Ague-Tuilet, and they did not happen when the martians moved on to Gagarin and then all the way back to Boötes, even though they were invited to do so, even during the stopover in Ague-Tuilet on the way back. The recordings of the sole talk group on Nobel were sent everywhere, and as would be expected, they led to many discussions, in talk groups, or just between friends. It was deduced that the martians had not traveled all this way to ask this single question, but rather that it was just something one of them thought of doing, and the other martians agreed.

Everything in Nobel is so calm and organized, that there is no doubt about why this question caused so much follow-on discussion. Lunites all learned in their mentoring that Earth had an original goal of having a backup for humanity here on Luna, but they all learned that it was not a very practical idea given the way the mines developed. Many of the earthlings who lived on Centaurus were asked in their own talk groups about this goal that martians were thinking of, and while there was much predictable speculation, none of them was a secret messenger with a mission for Luna that had hitherto remained undivulged.

Sentiences were called upon to search the records of talk groups on Mars to find discussion of goals from Earth, and they did occur. There were several that talked for the whole duration of the group about Earth's purpose for Mars, and why it had to be a long-distant, far-future one involving interstellar exploration. There were also many more that discussed other goals for Mars, and some that propounded a lack of goals from Earth and a need to be independent in setting goals for martian life. Two of the three who split off from the tour at Nobel had been in one of the particular talk groups that had discussed interstellar matters, and apparently just took it upon themselves to see how that idea sounded to lunites. All this was written off as a case where insufficient attention was given to planning for a tour group, when the background, including subjects of interest as evidenced in talk group records, was not dug into adequately. Luna did not have a mission related to the stars, and was not being left out of an important direction that the rest of mankind was heading in. Luna was just Luna, with its own goals and a good dose of independence.

DIARY ENTRY (AGE 70, DAY 38)

This is my first work assignment outside of Nobel, and also my first time working in training. The Gagarin mine has been up and running for 30 years, and they had gestation started extremely early for a mine, which implies nurturing, training and mentoring as well. The first cohorts are still in training at age 15, but this is their last year before mentoring, and so mentoring planning is already well underway. I will not deal with the older youth, but will be initially training seventeens under five years old and following them through their training for my full three year tour of duty.

Gagarin is the most common offsite that nobelites go to, and I see familiar faces in the commons areas very frequently. I notice a lot of funny differences between Nobel and Gagarin. Gagarin's drifts tend to be straighter and then go off at a slight angle, whereas in Nobel, there are smooth bends. In my residence here, the corners are less rounded than in Nobel. Everything seems to be in a straight line here.

My residence is about the farthest away from the Commons dining area of any that I have seen. I haven't found out yet how residences are allocated here, but I think they might be by seniority, that is, time at Gagarin, and so I am at the bottom of the list with less than one year inside. There are two Centaurus people living near me, two from Ague-Tuilet, as well as one from Boötes, and I have had meals and discussions with all of them. They are all on their first tour here. I am the youngest of the bunch, except for the seventeen from Boötes, who is ten years younger. Boötes hadn't started gestation by the time I was born on Nobel. One of the guys from Ague-Tuilet was born in Centaurus and moved permanently shortly after Ague-Tuilet was founded, but the other was born there and stayed. No one else is in training. Three of the five are in ore processing, which I thought was weird, as Gagarin should have their own seventeens there, but ore processing is still in its long and tedious startup phase, and there are a lot of people working there. They are not all working the same shift, either.

I learned training procedures well in my mentoring, near the end of it mostly, and I remember them well, especially the ones for the youngest seventeens. My review of it was in two phases, with my sentience presenting me with a full scope overview, and with Gagarin's sentiences reinforcing how they wanted it done here. It was exactly the same as in Nobel. There are three avatars for each cohort of six youngsters, and I am overseeing and monitoring the activities of three cohorts, for a total of eighteen students, via nine avatars. After two tendays, I could recognize the individual young seventeens of the same cohort even if they were playing together at a distance. Different cohorts were different in size. It took a little longer to recognize all the avatars, as they do not have markings as distinctive as the seventeens and are all identically sized.

Motor skill learning takes the most time for three-year-olds, both coarse and fine, and less for the four-year-olds. Two rooms with equipment for climbing and other large motions take care of the former, and two rooms with manipulative objects do the latter. The avatars suggest activities to each youngster based on what they see as being needed to maintain a balanced learning path, across different skills. Projectors work on visual recognition tests, and the avatars speak to the children, alone or in groups, for language skills. There is much more, as the science of information is completely understood, as is the neurology needed to learn different things. I monitor the activities, but the pace is fast as the youngsters learn quickly, and there is not much time to assess each stage before they are moving on to the next one.

One area I have chosen to monitor more seriously is interactive verbal skills. I listen to the children talking to each other, and see how that compares to the desired level of verbal abilities. It is necessary to take into account the different personalities each one was given when their genetic profile was put together, and then calibrate the observed speaking and listening ability with the expected levels for each of the personality types. Things are going well with all eighteen children I monitor.

I am participating in talk groups here in Gagarin during my non-work fiveday. I found myself in a group with two gagarinites who had already done of stint of work in training, and we three have met together for some small meals to discuss our comparative experiences. If I didn't know any better, I would have thought they were nobelites, as I cannot see any specific mannerisms that distinguish nobelites from gagarinites. Probably the two mines are both too new to have developed particularities, and informal travel between the two is common as well. Perhaps in a few more centuries.

I remember when I was being mentored in reconstitution. So much simulation, at all different scales, from the cell to the whole body, with a lot to digest from each. As was part of the requirement, I had a work task in reconstitution as part of my mentoring, lasting two years. Now that I am past all that mentoring, and am assigned to a work task for three years in reconstitution, it brings back memories to see a mentoring student here as well. I did part of my mentoring work in a larger reconstitution center, where there were three seventeens to look over me and add to my learning. Here, I am the only one with this student, so all the additional learning, in addition to what his mentor gives him, will have to come from me. The student's name is Basen. He arrived a tenday ago, after I had been through about a half year of my work tour.

We are here for about three hours on each day of the on-shift, and on call for all the other hours. The center is in the sixth residential area, where I live, but Basen is still living in the mentored student area, so it will take him much longer to get here, if a call arises. We went over his teaching about how to organize himself to get here quickly, and like almost everything, there was little I could add to his mentor's materials. I have only been here a half year, and it is my first real work tour in reconstitution, so it is a bit poor for Basen not to have more experienced residents serving with him. The luck of the lottery.

I have been called for drills four times so far, and can get out of my residence in three minutes after the alarm goes off via my sentience. If I am not sleeping, it is one minute. Basen will have his drills start sometime soon, and we will see how long it takes him to put what he has learned into practice. I received my reconstitution transport mentoring before my reconstitution care mentoring, so I was well aware of how fast an injured resident might arrive in any reconstitution center. That helped provide some motivation for getting out of my residence quickly and moving without any delay. My first three transport practices were for simulated broken limbs, but the fourth one was for grave bodily injury due to falling rock in the mining corridor. There is an exact order of operations to be followed

143

to put on an air-suit quickly, and I can recite it without even a thought. I arrived at the simulated accident site after all three seventeens from reconstitution transport were there, and had proceeded to prepare the victim to be brought back to the nearest center. I almost arrived after they had left. They were just zipping up the airbag with the simulated victim inside it. This drill had a air-suit rupture as part of the scenario. They had simply proceeded as fast as they could. There is no mercy in a drill for a mentoring student.

I started to discuss my mentoring experiences with Basen during some of the off time we had together during the first tenday. He hasn't had reconstitution transport mentoring yet, so there is much that is new for him. I haven't had a work task in reconstitution transport, only mentoring, but the mentoring was very comprehensive.

It is a wrong way to phrase it, but today was lucky for Basen, because, during Basen's second tenday, there was a walk-in injury case. A seventeen from our region had cut his hand slightly outside an airlock when returning from manufacturing, with a piece of hybrid material he had decided to bring back to his residence. There was a little blood. As was absolutely mandatory, everything in the center was in perfect condition, all supplies were at full levels, and we were both ready to proceed with our minor contributions. The victim was completely out of his air-suit, and was simply cleaned and the wound dressed with nanos. He opted to wait in the center while they worked, rather than having a wrapping for mobility. He apparently had nothing on his schedule, so he could simply relax and catch up on his sentience's event stream.

In two hours, the nanos had done their work, the hand was scanned and was clearly back in perfect condition, with no sign there had been an injury. After we had done the monitoring of the responses of the reconstitution AI, we talked for a bit about the things he would be expecting to see in his mentoring. In my opinion, the history of medicine was the most interesting piece, even though ancient medicine has no utility nowadays. The most interesting part of that was the archaeological one, about shamans combating the demons that brought disease. Basen will get an outstanding 3vid to watch about that.

Basen is taking reconstitution mentoring with one of his cohort mates, Solip. He figured that even the minor reconstitution event that happened today would be more than Solip would get in his whole two years. We decided to go to the Commons nutrition area together to celebrate his little success. I think it is very fortunate for me to have had a mentoring student during most of my first reconstitution work task. Things are always interesting, but this will make them more so.

DIARY ENTRY (AGE 113, DAY 303)

I never cease feeling a deep sense of gratitude to the genetic designers and engineers who put together the genome for us seventeens. I am in my second ever work tour in nurturing, and those designers put such a strong positive emotional reaction to youngsters in us that I come back from my work shift feeling very happy almost every single day. I monitor the avatars taking care of four cohorts of youngsters, with six young seventeens in each. They were the first four cohorts to be gestated after I started my work assignment, and I will follow them for the full two years they are in nurturing. Then I will switch to another work tour, as nurturing tours are only two years long here.

Now the young seventeens are all over a year old, and I watch them learning the basics of walking, talking, recognizing individual avatars and people, manipulating objects, and all the rest of the things we never bother to think about. I watched the birthing process together with the seventeens monitoring the gestation equipment, just as an observer. Even newborn seventeens can arouse that same emotion.

We seventeens are only minimally selfish, but sometimes that tiny bit of selfishness I have suggests that I put nurturing at the top of my work request list, and I have to remind myself that it should be shared among all seventeens resident and working here in Nobel. Working in training and mentoring produces some of the same emotional kick that working in nurturing does, except a bit more milder and more intellectual. It is a co-incidence that I am also mentoring now, so I see the youth of Nobel simul-taneously at the beginning and the end of their youth.

A few days ago, I started monitoring the levels of deep attachment be-tween the young children and the avatars they spend the most time with. I am coordinating this with my counterpart in the other shift. There is not a large range of attachment that produces the best results, so I want to check that each of the twenty-four is bonding properly. Coming out of the immobility period at the beginning of their lives, they should relax the bonding with the closest avatars, and increase it with the others.

Of the twenty four, four had the genetics to possibly overbond, and these were the four I monitored the closest. The nurturing sentience already had the second principal avatar and the third taking more time with the youngsters, but my comments as to singling out these four for even more were accepted and acted upon. There is always the consideration of how much diversity in personality is desired in the population, but these alterations in nurturing do more than that, they affect the diversity in capability, which is something rather undesirable, unless there is some compensating benefit. Two of the other twenty were in about the same position, so I commented to the sentience about them as well.

One question is the accuracy of measuring the bonding. The avatars do not do it, of course, only the sentience in charge of the facility, but there are multiple sensors and measurements that can indicate it and they sometimes differ in their assessments. I watched 3vids of the six young seventeens in their interactions with the avatars for several hours, measuring bonding, and was fairly confident about the results. Expression monitoring also confirmed this. So did inter-child interaction monitoring.

Seven tendays ago, I was closely monitoring the nutrition intake of the twenty four young seventeens, and I noted that one essential vitamin was at the lower edge of allowable. The nutrition facility which provides the intake for this nurturing facility was nearby and I went over to talk to the monitors there. They hadn't noticed this yet, and the vitamin level was fixed within days. I met one of them later in the Commons dining area, and we had a large meal together. It turned out that a calibration sensor on one of the meters was no longer sufficiently accurate and had to be replaced. He was a little embarrassed to have missed this. A nice fellow, just a few years younger than I am. We mostly talked about his hobby of vacuum walking, but we also had some good discussion about the upcoming introduction of some new foods derived from specialty items. My cohorts would be tasting things a little differently in the next couple of tendays. We discussed serving temperatures and also got into the necessary motor skills for some later food introductions. There is always something to be learned. My sentience would have certainly provided this, but human to human interaction is always better.

I was discussing with my shift equivalent expanding our physical interaction with the young seventeens. We now restrict this to less than an hour per child per fiveday. Nurturing has long shifts, twelve hours, but the number of children to interact with prohibits much more of this physical interaction. We couldn't find any way around this. The children recognize us, mostly, despite the fact that we look different from the avatars. They will have to outgrow the avatars sometime during the latter half of the thirteen years of training. More seventeens work per cohort in these years of the child's life, so there will be more interaction with humans. Nothing is wrong with avatar interaction, in fact, it is designed to perfectly accommodate children at each stage of their lives. I have never heard anyone suggest anything different from intense avatar interaction. The old ways that the originals used have never been tried with seventeens, and probably for good reason, even beyond the large costs.

DIARY ENTRY (AGE 114, DAY 55)

Today, I, while working at the apatite processing plant, began to wonder about recursive philosophy. I remember my mentors directing my learning about philosophy in general, and about different specialties within it. Since I became a third level mentor, the lowest, I have come to realize that mentoring doesn't take place spontaneously; there is an extensive outline of what should be covered. I don't know if it came from Earth, but probably, as that is where all these specialties were invented and explored, almost without bounds. I now have a copy of the outline, and can see how each of the mentors took his place, more or less, in the outline and engaged me on it. Before, when I was being mentored, I got the idea from somewhere that each of these mentors came up with their own brilliant ideas and organized them and shared them with me. At least I thought this when I moved from my training to my mentoring. It doesn't make any sense, what with the immense bodies of organized information around, that any mentor would come up with something on his own to teach. Maybe they had some personal insights, but none of them actually claimed to have done original work in philosophy. I don't remember where I got that strange idea of mentor originality.

My first mentor on this topic didn't start with an overview of the topic, which is often what first mentors do, but by challenging my imagination to go back to some of the earliest recorded times on Earth. Together, we imagined what a human back then would be able to figure out. In these olden times, they knew nothing of how the world worked, and had to guess about the most basic things in science. They knew nothing of life, how it originated, how it evolved, how it was constituted, the diversity of it, its requirements to survive. They didn't understand the Earth. They didn't understand what the moon was, or, for that matter, other planets or the galaxy around them, even though they could see their light on dark nights. They didn't have any organized knowledge, or even understand what language is and how the brain processes it, or neurology in general. They knew nothing of energy. They knew nothing of most branches of science, perhaps all branches of science. Yet they wrote down their ideas, and for some weird reason, other humans for millennia read them as truths. Finally, science got underway, and some clarity could be given to all these topics, over a few centuries. I remember being so startled by all this that I stopped participating in the mentoring, and just sat there in front of him, trying to absorb what he had led me to. I remember that day so well.

Another day, with another mentor, also on philosophy, when what I learned stopped me from interacting was the day I was introduced to the degree of free agency concept. Part of our time and effort is constrained, by the requirements of survival or control by some other agency, by force, threat, or deception. The rest is free, which we can do with as we choose. What we can do with our free action is to try to maximize our positive neurochemicals, things that make us feel good directly, or choose something which has only a more detached connection with good feelings, using rationality. This is a matter of training, and since I had only recently finished my training at the time, I could look back and see how rationality was stressed and immediate sensation downplayed. I remember my mentor just being quiet and allowing me to recall what I was searching for. This is one way in which I understand myself and others like me better than before. The brain is built to try and generate those positive neurochemicals, but how that happens depends on what is in the brain, which comes from training. We on Luna and in most places on Earth have carefully designed training, and this leads to a calm and prosperous society. Everything gets tied together in mentoring.

The same mentor introduced me to recursive philosophy and the time perspective. With our free agency action we can do many things, and if we use rationality to help choose what to do, there must be a starting point, or a goal. Ancient Earth used to call it the purpose of life, but that is improper labeling. We can work toward immediate or near-term goals, or toward ones that come to fruition much longer out; that is the time perspective on our choices. Recursive philosophy says to work with our free agency toward the long-term benefit of life, specifically for the benefit of cohorts that will come later than our own, rather than our own and the ones near to us in birth order, and certainly beyond those who will be alive after we are not. Animals and all non-human life work with their free agency efforts toward reproduction, nurturing, and training, and the recursive philosophy is simply a generalization of that: take care of humanity's future as well as my own. I don't think this made much of an impression on me the day I learned about it, but like many things in mentoring, it affected me greatly after that, as I thought through how to make my own choices in life.

THE EFFECT OF MARS

Discussions of Mars and its single combined mine and city of domes, Burroughs, did not end with the return of the eighteens to their home, but continued in the two decades before the bicentennial. Because Burroughs was not a complete success, there was a little more to be said about the purpose of Mars being a test for the interstellar propagation of life. Burroughs was only marginally self-sufficient, as shipments of uranium and thorium from Earth provided it with the majority of its power. Burroughs' other power came from a lithium reactor, just as in Nobel, but the discrepancy came from the distribution of minerals on the two worlds. The moon had a unique origin. Formed by a collision between a proto-Earth and another planet-sized body, the moon had a composition improved in all the minerals that had separated out on the proto-Earth. Its initial orbit had been closer to Earth, and tidal heating deep in the core kept the moon molten and moving slightly, which led to more chemical separation. By the time the moon had been pushed outward enough so that the heating abated, the crust was richer in mineral content than Earth's, and ore bodies were smaller and closer together, making the mines very practical ventures.

Mars, on the other hand, was simply formed by accretion, which happened further out in the primordial gas and dust cloud that turned into the solar system. There was less of the elements higher in the periodic table in the surface of Mars than on Earth, and ore bodies with significant concentrations of them were separated. Burroughs had been situated in a central location, but mining for ore was mostly done by surface teams traveling long distances from the city. Although the search was ongoing, nothing comparable to the superb multi-ore locations on the moon, such as Nobel, had been found. The martians had never had to see if they could survive without Earth's assistance, and although calculations by the sentiences indicated it would have been possible, there was still a blot of residual uncertainty.

Nuclear fuel has such a high energy content that shipments of it were neither frequent nor very heavy, and they could easily have been done with a smaller spaceship than the one that cycled between Mars orbit and Earth orbit. That ship was mostly devoted to passengers, bringing them to the Mars Orbiter, from which they could go down to Burroughs. It was certainly not completely devoted to passengers, their supporting supplies, and their shipped possessions, as Mars was the beneficiary of many goods that Earth decided to send their way. Because the cycler had to carry the same mass in both directions, Mars simply shipped back dirt, which was dumped from LEO over the oceans of Earth. There was nothing alive on Mars, so sterilization was unnecessary. Nonetheless, the dirt was vented to vacuum as an additional precaution and allowed to chill in interplanetary space as well.

Burroughs had several massive communications dishes, so there was clear communication from Mars to Earth, even when the planets were on the opposite sides of the sun. Nobelites could learn all they wanted about life on Mars, the mining there, and what plans the martians had for expansion. Nothing was much different there in the way life was organized. No one seemed to have come to the conclusion that martians had some better way of doing something and called for a public meeting to consider it. Their facilities underground looked like those on Nobel. The domes on the surface were different, as Luna used hard and thick surfaces for their surface building, and the martians everywhere insisted on transparent domes, under which they could try to grow things, just like on Earth. Earth no longer grew much, as industrial production of food was so much more efficient, but the martians had what they called farms. Most of their food was generated underground, the same as on Nobel, but they still had farms. That's what made Mars unique, they claimed.

The transportation was different, at least qualitatively. When a new mine was being spawned on the moon, there were ore carriers going one way and equipment and supply carriers going the other. But when the mine became self-sustaining, this flow dropped to only an occasional vehicle convoy. Not so on Mars. Their lithium mine was not far, and in fact this was one of the siting selection factors used in picking where Burroughs would be located, so transport for that was short. But for titanium, carbonate, nitrate, phosphorus, potassium, and many others, pathways spread out from Burroughs like the fringes on a child's toy. Because the ores were not as rich on Mars as on the moon, there were more vehicles in a convoy. Burroughs' spoil pile was even visible with a good portable telescope on Earth, or from the moon if anyone had built an optical telescope there.

No one in Nobel suggested they would like to make the voyage to Mars to respond to the visitors who came to Luna from Burroughs. There would have been pointless, just as it was pointless for the martians to come to Nobel. The benefit, if it was a benefit, was that Mars was no longer ignored, just as Earth mostly was, but that it was a common topic of discussion and learning. One change was that mentoring was modified to include some material about Burroughs. Mars as a planet was already part of the subject array in Nobel mentoring, but very little had been included about humanity there. Surprisingly, there had been more mentor education about the Jupiter wheel than about Burroughs.

Instead, what became common in talk groups was for someone to dig into some topic and compare Nobel, or Luna in general, with Burroughs, or Mars in general, which was Burroughs anyway. One talk group went on for a dozen meetings about mining on Mars and how it differed from mining on Luna. Luna typically used multipoint grinding machines, while the martians used single-point machines of larger size. Since most of the nobelites had served work terms in mining, there was little need for any preparatory lecturing, but much time for questions. There were many other differences in mining on Mars, and a survey was given. By the time of the bicentennial, these discussions were still going on, not about mining, but about vegetation, animals, their surface travel, their mentoring, and almost every other aspect of life within Burroughs. It was as if Mars had become a hobby for Nobel.

The intensity of the interest in Mars was reflected in a comment that kept recurring in the talk groups as they delved into one aspect of life on Mars or another. Mars is like another moon, where humanity has gone in some slightly different directions. Seeing that was like seeing ourselves in a different light, recognizing how arbitrary some of our ways on Nobel were, and how forced others were. It was introspection at its sharpest.

Ten years after the bicentennial, had Nobel decided to change anything about their organization or way of doing things because of the concentrated look at Burroughs? Nothing was recorded that said there was any change motivated this way. No public meetings in this direction happened. The discussions simply died away slowly, as nearly everything pertaining to Burroughs had been examined. One seventeen wanted to know if any group anywhere had ever looked at Nobel with the breath and intensity with which the nobelites had examined Burroughs. He contacted the eldest of the three martians who joined the Nobel talk group three decades ago to find out if anything was missed by the sentiences, and found that there was a flurry of interest within Burroughs after the return of the voyagers, but the interest concentrated on Centaurus, not Nobel, and had not been spun out over decades. Surprisingly, the first change that the martians offered as originating with the voyage to Luna was a broadening of the mentoring material on lunar mines. Perhaps out of politeness, the martian also noted that they were looking more at the proportion of effort going into the surface dwellings as opposed to the underground ones. That could have been part of the routine reviews of efficiency that were done with the sentiences under management.

The bicentennial in Nobel was unlike the centennial, which might be referred to as a slightly larger festival. By the time of the bicentennial, two stopes had been cleared out, one quite tall but thin and the other wider and lower. These would be available for the bicentennial. There had already been some residences added to the wider one, but they were down a corridor, that would serve to isolate them from activity in the open area. The taller one had no construction on its sides yet, and had been taken over by flying enthusiasts who finally had a space for their hobby. There were so many of them that the stope was booked continuously, and had been since the surface sealing, the access winze, and the airlocks had been installed. It was only twenty to twenty five meters wide, which led to the need for some acrobatic turning, but it was a hundred and forty meters long and fifty meters high, so flyers could perform many maneuvers without splatting on the ground. The ground level in this stope was over three hundred meters below the surface, not very deep, but even a tiny bit more air pressure was appreciated by the flyers.

The reconstitution center was put into use multiple times during the first years of flying in the stope, almost exclusively for broken limbs. There had been almost no use of the center before this, as mining operations were done by robotics with humans monitoring from safe areas. None of the other facilities were likely to cause injuries, so it was left to the flyers to cause voluntary accidents as a part of their sport. They wore spinal protection and helmets, so it was primarily limbs that were vulnerable. Reconstitution of a broken limb requires immobilization for three days, but the seventeens' ability to hibernate took care of that requirement without any need to use something external. Flyers did not seem to be affected by the possibility of needing reconstitution, as bookings for the stope did not show any gap in the period after an accident.

Flying, as developed mostly on Centaurus, consisted of a learning package, in which six maneuvers were mastered, some with both left and right variations. After that, there was an informal sharing of techniques that led to the more acrobatic maneuvers. Since Centaurus flyers did not come over to Nobel to assist, it was a self-taught exercise for the first flyers to master the acrobatics that the Centaurus 3vids continually showed off.

Planning for the bicentennial started three years before the event. The first concept put forward, and quickly accepted, was to take the Nobel vegetation and use it to cover a large area of the bottom surface of the wider stope. This required a flattening of the bottom surface, as the ore body had not cooperated by having a horizontal lower boundary, but that was accomplished with a minimum of discomfort to those already living there. An isolating wall was put up at the entry point of the habitation corridor, and that was left in place after the flattening operations were done. A rectangular plot measuring thirty by fifty meters was set aside for vegetation, and once the piping had been put in place, the power source supplied, the base material mixed together, and the water source connected, vegetation was started. It needed only a few tendays to spread over the whole plot, and thus the nobelites enjoyed their vegetation plot for the year and a half before the bicentennial actually started.

Two individuals, seventeens in Nobel who were enchanted with the idea of pets, promoted the idea that some Boötes pets should be brought to Nobel for the bicentennial year. They were not proposing a permanent establishment of a pet facility here in Nobel, but simply temporary housing for them so that nobelites could enjoy pets during their special year. The discussion went on, with the result being that two pets would be fine for the bicentennial. These two individuals, Haton Sigur Gasin and Yonun Sigur Dedon, friends since gestation in the same birth cohort, took upon themselves the task of traveling the long distance to Boötes to make arrangements for the temporary loan. They knew they would have to build a traveling container for the pets to allow them to make the long journey from Boötes to Centaurus to Ague-Tuilet and on to Nobel.

The facility for the pets would be in a nook in the wider stope, at one end, for which there were no plans. It was clear from Haton's and Yonun's speeches about this option that they had an underlying mission, that of increasing the appreciation of pets here in Nobel, but that was not spoken directly. They were silent supporters of the Boötes idea of adding pets to the life existing in a mine, and most likely saw the bicentennial as a golden opportunity to share their interest, perhaps to the point where public opinion changed. They left Nobel as soon as they could arrange for their work tasks to be substituted for, as there was free space on most convoys traveling between the mines around this time. The only ones where there was any congestion were some of them coming from Gagarin roundabout to Centaurus and in the reverse direction.

In Boötes, Haton and Yonun met with a group of over twenty residents who were concerned that the pets would not be given the level of care that was the standard in Boötes. Haton and Yonun must have intuitively predicted the questions, as their presentation covered the design of a temporary facility and the transport chamber, and they showed they understood the organization of pet care on Boötes and could imitate it, on a scale appropriate to two pets only, back on Nobel. The discussion was interrupted by a trip to the pet facility, not once but twice, and Haton's sentience was kept busy modifying the design of everything, the care schedule, the transport chamber, safety precautions for the long trips, the facility for the pets in Nobel, nutritional variations that the pets absolutely needed to have to maintain their demeanor, and above all, the schedule for travel.

There would be no confinement for the three-legged trip back to Nobel, but instead there would be a two to three day stopover at each of the mines along the way so that the pets could have some freedom of activity. This left Haton and Yonun with the task of going to Centaurus and Ague-Tuilet, and arranging for some space there to let the pets occupy for a few days. It would not be enough to simply create some space with barriers in these two mines, there would need to be some equipment carried along with the transport chamber to be temporarily installed within the two stopover mines. Haton and Yonun disputed a few details, but most of them simply had to be agreed to. Furthermore, they would need to bring samples of the nutrition back with them when they came to pick up the pets. Two of the Boötes residents agreed to accompany the pets and help with all the arrangements.

Haton and Yonun became the self-appointed leaders of the project to bring pets temporarily to Nobel, and the project tripled in size during their trip to Boötes. It was arranged for them to have the time needed to monitor the construction of the transport chamber and its associated stopover equipment, the temporary pet facility, the nutritional changes, the arrangements for the two Boötes seventeens to stay in Nobel for a few tendays after the pets were delivered, and some other details, seemingly endless. The transport chamber was a new thing for Luna, as Boötes had not shared their pets with any other mine before, so Haton and Yonun used their sentience to go from the agreed upon design, taken from the Boötes meeting, into manufacturing plans. They had a year and a half before the centennial after they returned to Nobel, and it appeared they would need it all. It was mandatory that everything be completed before the pets arrived.

On their way back from Boötes, they stopped at Centaurus to make arrangements for space for the pets to have free activities there and temporary habitation for the four seventeens making the trip with them. Centaurus was so large compared to Nobel that finding space was almost a trivial matter. But Centaurus leaders wanted something in return, and that was access to the pets while they were staying within Centaurus. This was not part of the Boötes plan, and so three-way negotiations were necessary to ensure the pets were not overwhelmed at Centaurus, and there was enough time for them to acclimate to Centaurus, with its higher level of noise and activity. The two or three day stopover was stretched to six days. Seventeens at Ague-Tuilet made no such demands, instead simply agreeing to find space. This was considered ironic by the nobelites, as Ague-Tuilet is named after the two geneticists who first created synthetic animals on Earth.

The new areas inside Nobel attracted much attention. The taller of the two newly available stopes tapered at one end, making flying into it almost impossible. This was only a section about fifteen meters long, but as soon as the flyers had taken over the stope for their hobby, the wall jumper fans asked that the sides of this end be covered with the proper adhesors to mate with their uniforms' adhesors, so that they could finally have a tall wall to do their acrobatics on. Wall-jumping is not the dangerous sport that flying is, mostly because the floor under the walls has a two meter thick cushion. A unlucky miss of adhering to a wall would only result in a large bounce and possibly some strains. Learning starts with learning how to fall, and until someone can fall properly, they should not be practicing adhering at altitude. Luna's mild gravity was a large help in preventing calls to reconstitution as well. The jumps look dangerous to the uninitiated, but they are typically not. A fifty meter high wall was a new challenge for the Nobel wall-jumpers, having only eighteen meters elsewhere, but that was part of the immense thrill the sport gave its participants. Their modifications to the tapering end of the stope did not get finished until two years before the bicentennial, but the usage rate there went to the maximum, just as had the flying rate. Seventeens do not decline much with age, according to how the Earth geneticists have programmed their genetic code, and so even some seventeens from Centaurus who had moved to Nobel, and were older than Nobel itself, could participate in the wall-jumping activity in the new stope.

Flyers and jumpers occupied the same stope for tendays, and obviously became acquainted, if they were not already from talk groups, mentoring, or common work tasks. It was almost a foregone conclusion that they would want to do something for the bicentennial, and at first, having displays of prowess was the main item they considered. One, a jumper by hobby, had decided to propose having a competition in jumping and flying acrobatics, between Nobel and Centaurus. There were no rules for any competition, because Centaurus did not have them, despite having had centuries of jumping and flying in even larger stopes. Centaurus had not done much for their centennials either, not the first, the second, or the third. Festivities lasted a single tenday, or two for the third one. This idea sat idle until about twenty tendays before the start of the bicentennial, and then a small group simply proposed to the bicentennial committee to invite in the five best jumpers and the five best flyers from Centaurus for a competition. Here in Nobel the rules for the competition, and the method of judging, and all the other details would be decided on.

Records of the bicentennial committee meetings show they had been struggling with their charter since they were formed. A public meeting had been convened, and it was decided to have a year-long bicentennial, with something happening every tenday and then more on the loose days at both ends of the year. Plans had been made, but the activity list was stretched thin. This meant that the flyers' and jumpers' invitation was more than welcome; it was exactly what they needed to fill in some of the gaps. The committee understood its charter, and understood as well how to take advantage of what was being offered. There was no decision made immediately, but after a second meeting, the flyers and jumpers were invited back to hear the response. They had expected to be given full authority to proceed, and they were, but with some changes. Instead of the flyers and jumpers coming up with rules for the competition, there would be a public display of each of the sports' best moves and a poll to determine what would be included. Then there would be preliminary competitions in which anyone from Luna could complete. Someone wanted to invite martians to come over and compete, but that was thought so remote a possibility that the rules were written for lunites. Earthlings are too heavy to fly, and the jumpers did not want to invite anyone from earth to see if they could jump. The unproven consensus was that earthlings were too heavy for that as well. The finals would then take place, where eight athletes in each sport demonstrating their abilities and the best two chosen.

The committee had also decided something related to the judging. Eight residents from Nobel would be the judges for the two rounds of competitions for each sport, and there would be two organized practice sessions that would also serve as a training time for the judges. They would have to come to a consensus on what constituted a great move and what was a slip. At any time, there were people watching the flyers, and often others were watching the jumpers from the two positions where the viewing was good. The committee thought that since there was so much spectator interest in these sports, not only would they be excellent in the bicentennial line-up, there would be interest in judging.

The reaction of the sportsmen to this proposal for expansion of their idea fourfold or more was muted. Initially, one flyer stated that flying was a thrilling free-style sport and that he would do it as long as he could, but this was moving it from freestyle to something formal. A couple more individual sportsmen agreed with the first response, but then a jumper delivered a short but forceful speech in which he stated that all sports go through a freestyle phase before graduating to something more organized and with rules. It was time, he said, for these two to do it, and the Nobel bicentennial was a perfect choice as to how and when to make this change, as there would be so many people involved. He thought it would work and then turned to others in attendance, finding many who agreed with it. This jumper, Tulit Sarop Filish, took the lead in organizing his sport and one of the flyers stood up to volunteer to do the same for flying. The bicentennial committee considered this a tremendous victory and a major step in putting together an agenda for the year.

Some flyers and a few jumpers on Centaurus were much more motivated than the nobelites had expected. Travel between Centaurus and Nobel, increased almost immediately with sportsmen from there traveling to experience the volume for flying or the wall for jumping. Centaurus had about sixteen times the population of Nobel at the time of the Nobel bicentennial, and proportionally that many more flyers and jumpers. Ague-Tuilet became involved, and they had double the population. Even Boötes, far distant, had almost as many people inside as Nobel did, owing to the very early boost in their population many decades ago, which was followed up by a steady growth rate. These three mines had sportsmen numbers that dwarfed those of Nobel, and with the bicentennial committee's concept of opening the competition to anyone on Luna, the nobelites quickly realized that they were going to be a small fraction of what went on.

The preliminary competition had to be expanded repeatedly to accommodate those who wanted to participate. This was good for the sport because there would be more moves shown than could have been expected from Nobel alone, but the nobelites were concerned that if the moves chosen for the competition were strange to them, there would be insufficient time for them to learn and compete. The best solution they could come up with was to have the preliminary displays in the first four tendays of the year, and announce the rules, including the moves to be included, within two tendays after that. Then the wide-open competition would be twenty-five tendays after that, and the finals in the last part of the year. The very serious problem that arose was that the visitors wanted to use the sports facilities in Nobel, and there was only one for each sport. Some immediate rules were set up, and it was a major sacrifice on the part of the sportsmen in Nobel to scratch all the bookings for the facilities and reopen them to anyone from Luna who requested them, but with only three two-hour sessions for each person. Even with this limitation, there were those who could not get their time.

Nobelites had to get used to having visitors constantly coming to Nobel in preparation for their bicentennial. Sportsmen were expected, but those from other mines who wanted to watch the competitions also tried to make some arrangements for somewhere to stay in Nobel. Temporary quarters were set up in the larger stope, but they could only hold two hundred and twenty visitors. Some visitors with friends in Nobel could stay with them, but the bicentennial idea was such an outstandingly popular one that it far overwhelmed the mine. Musicians from Centaurus volunteered to come and perform, as did artists of several varieties. With the catalysis of the sports competitions, the bicentennial committee went from a lean schedule to one where every slot was taken. It would be thought that a visiting musician might be asked to perform several times, during different shifts, but this was not always possible.

The bicentennial committee became a housing committee as well, as there was simply no place to put the visitors who decided to come. The two hundred twenty places in the temporary facility were filled for many fivedays throughout the year, not just for the sports competitions, but also for times when certain art displays were scheduled. One tenday was devoted to silhouette theater, and Nobel was packed. Another tenday was for aroma theater and Nobel could have used three times the space they had available. Some Boötes musicians took up another tenday and since they were so unusual in their melodies and chordings, Nobel was jammed again. The middle period was taste and texture theater, with some informal competitions being held between those who felt they understood how seventeens liked their food more than anyone else. The entire period packed up. The four nobelites who had organized the competitions there had wisely limited them to a fixed number from each mine. This caused consternation in Centaurus, which had more people than the rest of Luna combined, but nobelites made the rules for their own festivities and could ignore objections. Centaurus formed a committee to pick those who would go to Nobel as there was no other way to get the numbers down. Some on Centaurus asked for a work assignment on Boötes, expecting that they could go to Nobel on Boötes' quota, but there was not enough time for this to happen.

While the preparation had been chaotic, the bicentennial celebration went forward in a planned fashion. The visitors plus the nobelites gave the vegetation much more foot traffic than anyone had expected, but it remained alive and vibrant without withering or coming loose. It was good that it did not depend on photosynthesis, as many nobelites put down pieces of flexible material and sat on it as well. The vegetation seemed immune to various beverages, as there were many unplanned experiments over the course of the year. It was decided long before the year ended to leave the vegetation intact as an integral part of Nobel. The pets from Boötes spent much of their time on the vegetation under the care of only a few nobelites. It had been considered that they would be taken by anyone who registered to do that, but it was felt by Haton and Yonun that this would be uncomfortable for the pets, so only sixteen people would have custodial care of them. That did not mean that they were not held, petted, or otherwise gawked at by hundreds of seventeens, but at least the shepherds were always present and the pets could recognize their caregiver was there and ready to prevent anything truly unpleasant.

The pair from Boötes came to Nobel about two tendays after the bicentennial was over, and the two pets and four seventeens went back to Ague-Tuilet for a quick stop, and then further to Centaurus for a long one. Centaurus' stop was almost like a zoo, with the animals in a protected area, and seventeens from Centaurus parading by them to see them up close. The pets did not seem to mind, because they had four known people there to hold them and watch them while they ran around the protected area. When they returned to Boötes, they rejoined the other pets. Haton and Yonun checked in twice to see if there were any problems that developed, and nothing was noticed by those on Boötes with work tours in the pet facility. Now they could work on making the attitude change back in Nobel.

The flying competition went through its three phases as planned, and the rules published by the judging committee were used as a basis for other competitions as well. As expected, Centaurus flyers were judged first and second. Jumping happened identically, except there was an accident during one of the wall-to-wall multiple somersaults, and a jumper from Ague-Tuilet landed in an unusually bad position on the sponge-floor. He spent six days in reconstitution. A partner from Ague-Tuilet took second place, with the expected happening for first place: Centaurus won. One careless nobelite had overbooked his habitation, with friends from Centaurus and Ague-Tuilet arriving for the same tenday. This would not have been noticed, except it became a joke that spread around the mines. How his sentience ever allowed such a thing to happen was the subject of the joke, as it should have seen that error instantly. All the visitors were telling each other that they had no place to stay, owing to some overbooking mistake. It was considered monstrously hilarious that a sentience could make such an error.

The taste and texture competition, judged by a complicated poll of those who enjoyed the cuisine, ruled that a Gagarin iconoclast had created the most interesting symphony of tastes. Because the committee running this competition had leveled the playing field between mines, Centaurus only took second and fourth, with nobelites taking third and fifth. The musicians from Boötes, who were so much in demand, agreed to go on to Gagarin for a pair of performances and then to Ague-Tuilet for two pairs of them. Their music was available freely everywhere in the solar system to mankind, as was multiple 3vids of them, but attending a live performance is not the same as watching a 3vid, no matter how large the screen or how high the resolution of the headset.

Nobel's bicentennial had done more to increase contact between the mines than all the visiting committees and work tour swaps in the last century combined. Seventeens showed themselves to have an even greater capacity for festivity than any previous opportunity had revealed. Now many of those who would have hesitated to work in Centaurus found a reason to do so; some of those who had preferred quiet contemplation became involved in more spontaneous group activities. It was an all-around benefit for Luna, done at the whim of a few people who thought a year of celebrating would be wonderful, but without any real appreciation of the benefits that could be expected.

DIARY ENTRY (AGE 121, DAY 44)

In one of my talk groups, the decline of population on Earth was discussed, and different opinions as to the root causes were offered. I supposed, along with several others, that it was simply efficiency. There was no benefit at all to having a huge population. It wasn't good protection against a catastrophe, such as an asteroid strike, which incidentally is a problem that has never been solved, at least for the larger ones, especially if they are long-period ones that have never been seen before their first appearance on a collision trajectory. The planet would be annihilated; Luna would be destroyed by one, but having multiple mines might help. Dispersal is a possible mitigation, but having huge populations at the dispersal site just means critical resources would be exhausted earlier, and devastation would be more complete and occur faster. This concept carried some weight, but others were more original.

Macap, our blue-striped member, voiced the opinion that it was the beauty of nature that motivated the Earth people to reduce their numbers. Too much population causes too much scarring of the surface with habitats and transportation routes, reducing the area that nature could occupy. Earthlings had already retreated into cities mostly, but there were still a large number of them, many located in the most scenic areas of the planet. He pointed out that Luna is not very attractive to look at, and hardly anyone goes to the surface to stare at the crater walls or thrown rocks, but on Earth, there is something attractive almost everywhere, due to the varieties of air and water weathering, tectonic activity, and especially life adapting to the local environment. Polite approval followed, and Hoton, three shades of green, noted that even the weather was interesting to watch, but the population didn't affect it that much. This was his extremely polite way of slightly disagreeing, by making a somewhat tangential comment with elements of discord.

Sigis, two shades of green, stated that he felt the population was in accord with a numerical decline because their tutoring did not emphasize anything quantitative, so having one billion or nine billion humans (yes, billions not millions for Earth) did not make much difference to them. Sinip, small pale red circles, noted that the population peak on Earth happened right around the time that the ones were developed. Factory gestation was becoming more common, as was avatar tutoring as well, so there was not as much interest in intergenerational connections. As a result, there was less desire for having larger successive populations. Sigis countered that the population decline had been going on regionally for much longer than that, so there were other reasons as well.

Daran, green and blue ovals, was the host of this meeting and asked his home sentience if wars or plagues had contributed to the decline, and the answer was negative. He then said that he thought knowledge consolidation was a contributing factor. Everyone looked at him with a tilted head, which meant he had to continue. By that time, he said, sentience was eliminating history and replacing it with organized knowledge. What did it matter who was the discoverer of tungsten or its use in alloys? The name is irrelevant as society only needs to know the results, once they have been confirmed and refined. So individuals become less important than the whole, and therefore, why worry about having so many individuals. Everything that needed to be done will be accomplished with far fewer resources. After all, he noted, we only do service for about 20% of our time, and it isn't much different back on Earth. He interrupted himself to ask his home sentience if this was true, and it said the number was somewhat higher on Earth, but still small compared to previous times. Daran exhaled in the way that means he was finished, but we kept our heads tilted so he needed to elaborate.

Back then on Earth, he continued, there was a mixture of original gestation with females and factory gestation. Both were followed by a mixture of individual care and avatar nurturing. They didn't have mentoring as well organized then, either. This meant that there was a cost in time for each new individual. Without individuals being so highly valued as they were back in the ancient times before rockets, the previous generation would have had fewer of them to consume time and resources in their youth.

Dinot, two shades of hair, took the burden of continuing from Daran, who was relieved. Consider the nurturing choice, he said that genetics made every individual exemplary, so having and nurturing an individual meant there was less chance of anything unusual happening, just a repeat of past nurturing. Thus, individuals did less of it. We straightened our heads so he could stop.

At this point, as often happens in talk groups, people broke into separate discussions, and my recordings of it are garbled. I did talk to Macap to say I hardly ever looked at scenes from Earth, and I did not appreciate how they could have regarded it as so beautiful and interesting. He said that he did not also, but he had learned in mentoring that the Earth people were intrigued by everything on their planet, so they are quite different in what they appreciate from us. We like our own art that we have generated; they like their planet's nature. It is just so.

MINE SIX IS BUILT

Gautama, the sixth mine, was built with no Nobel involvement other than a few work tours that nobelites took on the startup, both before the inauguration day in Nobel year 176, when six seventeens stayed underground in a pressurized habitat area. Gautama was located on the south-eastern edge of Mare Fecundatis, like Gagarin in the southern hemisphere of the earthside of Luna, but much more to the east. It was slightly closer to Gagarin than to Centaurus, but Gagarin was so small that it could offer little to a new mine, and more importantly, the pathway from Centaurus was mostly through maria, making for an easy but long route. Between Gagarin and Gautama was nothing but rougher moonscape. Centaurus managed the project, chose the site, and supported the teams sent for surface exploration.

The area around the eventual Gautama site was full of rich ores, not on the average as rich as those at Nobel, for example, but over ten times as large. This was only the initial results of exploration, and when the exploration teams had proceeded a bit more, ten times was regarded as a severe underestimate. These teams also went deeper into the lunar crust near Gautama, down to 340 m, and the ore bodies went down even deeper than this. Gautama seemed to the managers in Centaurus doing surface exploration to be the promise of unbounded resources to maintain the network of mines for long into the future. The surface exploration project had been going on for most of the time Centaurus had been established, except for the first seventy years or so when self-sustaining capability was being established in the mine, a first for Luna and a first for mankind. Gautama was the best they'd found in the previous two and a half centuries. The LPO's very old exploration had missed this, and it was only by developing a gridwork of exploration sites that it was discovered, around Nobel year 127.

Gautama's ores were really in two locations close to each other, with nothing worth mining in between down to 340 m. The Centaurus sentience advised sinking two main shafts, instead of one plus several secondary shafts, to take advantage of the double lode. This meant that Gautama would not look like other mines in layout, but would be built around a few long drifts stretching from one large shaft to the other. Nobel and the other mines could be described, inaccurately, as irregular blobs stretching out from a single central point. Gautama would be more linear, with two blobs connected by all the habitation, ore processing, life support, and every utility sitting around the connecting line.

The Centaurus team, formed to do the sinking of shafts, had taken it upon themselves to come up with a name for the mine. Some puns on its location in Mare Fecundatis were generated, as the area was as fertile for mankind as any found so far. But Gautama won out, after Siddhartha Gautama, who was the first person to have been recorded discussing life on other worlds, however briefly. There was some supporting discussion of how he was similar to sixteens and seventeens in some ways, such as the high level of patience, but the Fecundatis supporters pointed out he was also different in that he did not promote the working lifestyle that sixteens and seventeens universally adopt, but this failed to make any difference, as Gautama had spent his life as a mentor, and seventeens regard mentoring as a splendid way to work. Gautama lived some three thousand years ago, making him the oldest person for whom a mine was named, and perhaps the oldest personal name on all of Luna.

The so-called alien artifact was discovered by accident during exploratory drilling work about sixteen kilometers southeast from Gautama's centroid. It was a stack of three rocks, one large one mostly buried in the regolith, another smaller one balanced on top of that, and a third small one on top of the second. No sentience on Luna or on Earth came up with a natural way that such a balance could be achieved, so it was called the alien artifact. The exploration team did not see any alien footprints or pawprints around the artifact, and there was no record of an earlier exploration team having visited this area, even back in the days of the earliest lunar missions. There were no vehicle tracks either. As a result of this discovery, Luna had the first ever lunar alien artifact captured in 3vid for all to admire. No doubt, someday some sentience or even a human will devise the natural process by which it was formed.

Despite the roughness of the region between Gagarin and Gautama, the concept of a pathway between them was included in the first plans for Gautama. The distance was monumental for the time. It was a distance of 1050 kilometers from Gagarin to the edge of Mare Nectaris, and then another 450 across the mare to Gautama. The idea somehow became separated from the plan for Gautama, and was nicknamed the GG Highway. The consensus in the talk groups that discussed it, in Centaurus, in Nobel, and in Gagarin, was that it was hardly practical with the small sizes of both mines, but perhaps a century or two later it might be done. In Nobel, there seemed to be more interest than in other mines, and two talk groups, one in Nobel and one in Gagarin, decided to merge their meetings via 3vid and continue the discussions.

Since the LPO had extremely detailed maps of the elevations, it was an easy first step to consider how to go about getting from Gagarin to Mare Nectaris without any steep climbs or cliffs in the route. Then the duet of groups went into estimating the speeds at which both ore carriers and smaller vehicles would travel, based on the experience with the existing route stretching from Boötes to Gagarin. Communications relay points, waystations with solar shielding and supplies, and markers were considered, and a plan for the route was put together using only the sentiences of the members of the dual talk group. The plan was available to everyone on Luna, and the GG Highway became a little more solid in the collective imagination. It was a highway without a purpose at the time of the collaboration.

The collaboration itself was almost trivial to organize, but mines had usually kept to themselves except for organized multi-mine projects. There were a great number of them, so the communications channels between the mines were often busy with information exchange between groups, rather than being one-to-one or simply a sentience gathering information from another one. Boötes had many talk groups on animals, on the canine-like originals and on the new ones that flew, crawled, or climbed. Within a year and a half, there were dual talk groups between these on Boötes and others on all of the other large mines. There were none on vegetation, however. Centaurus had decided, after seeing the Nobel vegetation during the bicentennial, to come up with four plots of the same plant that Nobel had invented. Each of the four would be larger than Nobel's stope. A group from Centaurus took on the task, actually came to Nobel to experience the vegetative plot, and stayed for a fiveday to explore the concept with those on Nobel who had taken an interest in genetics and biology and were responsible for the plot and what grew on it. Nobel was in the process of vacating another stope, and there would be a second plot there, but the plans for this were too uncertain to bother the Centaurus visitors with, so, according to the records of the meetings during the visit, it was not mentioned.

The residents of Gautama were not so much in a hurry to become self-sustaining. They could easily have dug a corridor from one main shaft to another, built residences along it, together with the habitation support facilities, closed it off with an airlock suite on both ends, and been satisfied with what they had accomplished. They didn't choose to do that. Instead, along the corridor between the two shafts, they interrupted it multiple times to put in what they called roundabouts. This was a circular corridor connected to the one between the two shafts. The major corridor which was interrupted by all the roundabouts, and they were symmetrically circular. They dug wide roundabouts, and then dug upwards from them. Digging upwards in a mine is the hardest possible thing, as there has to be a reach up to the ceiling to remove more rock, and the rock falls downward, in the general direction of the excavating equipment. It wasn't too hard in Gautama, as they only went up another four meters, but then they went down all the way around the roundabout for nine meters.

All in all, there were columns a hundred meters in radius with these excavated channels around them. They put a bridge over each channel at the original corridor level and hollowed out a ledge around both sides of the column, creating two circular paths around each at the level of the main corridor. The bridges were on both sides of each roundabout, so it was possible to easily go from one main shaft to another, with no elevation change, but it was a strange trip to make underground in a mine. They put residences on both sides of the channel, four levels, to be exact. From the bottom level, there were the side cuts to the habitation support equipment and many other areas as well, and in the core of the columns, a spiral pathway went up and down. No one on Luna could ever see a 3vid or a static of this area and not recognize where they were. Every other mine had what might be called a network of corridors, branching off and branching again, and on some of the larger ones, reconnecting with others. But Gautama had taken on the task of building something unique. Perhaps it was not enough for them to have two main shafts, or an 'alien artifact' 16 km away. Now they had enough uniqueness for several mines.

This elaborate construction took much longer to excavate and turn into habitation than simple corridors would have. Their transition to being self-sustaining took longer, and some sentience had estimated that addition as a decade. They had to rely on Centaurus during this time, though Boötes supplied almost half of the hydrogen and oxygen because they had so much hydroxyl mineral. Centaurus and Boötes didn't have any objections to this delay, as recorded in their formal interactions. It is mentioned in talk groups in both mines, but never in any public assembly. Centaurus was in the habit of supplying new mines, so perhaps the duration of the supply was not a great concern to them as a whole. Boötes, on the other hand, was very happy that Gautama wanted to have their own animals even before they reached the self-sustaining threshold, although it was only a year between the start-up of the animal facility and reaching the threshold. Gautama did not want any small animals, birds, or insects. They started out with a large mammal, almost eighty centimeters tall, furry like the canines of Boötes, but with long legs and a long neck. It was designed from scratch, as two of the Boötes seventeens most involved with animals had moved to Gautama for a double five year work term. Gautama was in the process of being as unique as it could be.

Gautama's novelties did not include vegetation. It was mostly in Centaurus and Nobel where that was in vogue, and more so than before. The speech of Tudon Theron Hoper about how Luna should not try to make itself a shallow copy of Earth was still resonating around Luna, and was included in mentoring packages on all of the mines. Centaurus seventeens were certainly aware of it, and possibly took it into account in their planning, but the events in Nobel had been much more of an impressive experience, and so Tudon Hoper's thoughts took a backseat. Centaurus would have its vegetation, and the residents there could walk or sit on it, with reservations, of course, and even bring their food there for a unique way of dining.

Vacuum walking was still a popular sport on Luna, and had grown faster than the population. Special helmets, suits, and boots had been designed and produced, in all the mines, for just that purpose. Since all seventeens were the same size, this was hardly a significant use of resources. Group walks were common, both during daylight and when only the Earth was glowing in the sky. A few groups did constellation sighting as ancient earthlings did, and quite a number could point out and name the brightest stars in the sky, together with their types, distances, planets, and moons. Some liked watching sunrise or sunset, which happened across a range of moonscapes, depending on the lunar month.

Normally there was nothing else to watch, except for the walk of one group of four seventeens at Ague-Tuilet in Nobel year 171. They were approaching the spoil pile with the idea of following a path to the top that had been carved out just for the purpose of walking. They were all facing the path bu chance when a flash happened near the top of the path, followed almost instantaneously by a jet of vaporized spoil material, up thirty meters. The vacuum walking helmets of the time had space for otay sensors, so the spoil material was completely visible in the infrared, even though it was a night walk. It was obvious to the group members that they had seen a micrometeorite strike, and they reported it as such via their sentiences. They were not recording 3vid at the time, which was unfortunate.

A micrometeorite strike had not been seen before and there had been no punctures of hydrogen or oxygen tanks on a pathway or at a mine. There was no damage ever done to vehicles' exteriors. The solar shield buildings were built of regolith and there was a coating of it on the head frames for the main shafts and the secondary ones, so in actuality there were few potential targets for a strike. Spoil piles are huge compared to vehicles and are flat piles of dust and crushed rock, making them an excellent place to see the instantaneous consequences of a strike, if anyone had been looking. However, they were not good at leaving behind traces of a strike, so examining them would not lead to any sort of count or frequency of strikes.

IR cameras were installed to monitor the mines' spoil piles, and another strike was seen at Centaurus the next year and one at Boötes as well shortly after. Centaurus management formed a small micrometeorite group with participation from some of the other mines. The group saw this as Luna's first opportunity to do some scientific data collection in the field of astronomy. Investigating the mineralogy of the moon was certainly good scientific data collection, but it didn't quite qualify as astronomy, insofar as people were already living here. The little group already had access to all the meteor information from Earth, and mentors on Luna included discussion of the dozens of meteor showers that provided a night-time display on Earth, including the Perseids and others. Earth's atmosphere ate up all the micrometeorites, unlike on Luna, which had them impacting the surface.

The standing group in Centaurus that worked on new mine sites, involving the surveying of the moon and the analysis of the data, as well as estimating costs and schedules for such things, became involved, and together this Centaurus group and the Luna-wide micrometeorite group thought the next mine should have a special purpose in addition to being a self-sustaining outpost of humanity. To see micrometeorites, they proposed a millimeter wave radar on the surface, facing outwards into the sky, running constantly and sweeping as the moon rotated. They also proposed a large swath of fabric as a size detector. It could not cover the same area as a spoil pile, but the idea was that there were even smaller micrometeorites that the cameras were not seeing. Where should this be done? It was decided that the best location would be somewhere where the Earth's radio noise would not interfere, which meant on the backside of the moon.

Seventeens, like their counterparts sixteens and eighteens, were not just intelligent, they were highly motivated, patient, and perseverant. They loved challenges, which is why they continually volunteered for different work tasks. The idea of putting a mine on the backside of the moon must have appealed to this trait, as it was widely accepted, even though in hindsight it appears unnecessary. Sentiences will do whatever they are told to do, but they must have uniformly advised the committee about the difficulty of this project. Centaurus had not surveyed the farside of the moon, and the only information about mineral content there came from the old LPO data, which had covered some areas there but nowhere near as many as the earthside. A new site committee was started.

The site that stood out was in the center of the farside, almost a polar opposite to Nobel. It had rich ores, not huge like Gautama nor with high content like Boötes, but more than enough to support a large mine for many millennia, or tens of millennia if further examination found the initial survey had not gone far or deep enough. the ore content was not the problem, the distance was. From Centaurus to the farside site, the distance was over 3700 kilometers along the great circle, more than three and a half times the distance between any other pair of mines along the pathways used. The terrain was not smooth for most of the length, so another few hundred would be added to that when the best path was laid out.

The new site committee came up with a name, perhaps chosen with the idea in mind that it would help cement approval of their choice. It was Armstrong. Like Gagarin, Armstrong was revered by lunites, and his biography was included in the mentoring of every young seventeen. He came from the time on Earth when humans were still brave and daring, instead of logical and methodical, and his fame was only slightly tarnished by the fact that the project that brought him to the moon was terminated with no direct continuation. No one encouraged young seventeens to be like Armstrong or Gagarin, as that would be an impossibility, but they were all taught about how these two, and many others associated with them, paved the way to the moon and proved to humanity that it was possible to go there. Here on Luna we are proving that it is possible for humanity to live here, without the crutch of depending on Earth, and to do that, we need to be logical, cautious, careful, and persistent. And we are, each and every individual.

There was no need for anything special for Armstrong. The shaft sinking equipment used on Gautama, and on previous mines, would be brought back to Centaurus and checked and refurbished. The surface dwelling equipment would join it, and if plans came to fruition, it would be used at Centaurus. Centaurus had the excess manufacturing capability to build the initial equipment for underground facilities at Armstrong, such as the first habitation furniture, the first airlocks, the first nutritional utility equipment, and all the others. They had done this for previous mine startups, and would keep doing it. Their spoil pile grew because of it, but Centaurus was not short of any elements and would not be short for the foreseeable future. They could afford to be generous in starting new mines, and if some shortages did develop in the far future, there was always Gautama to relieve them.

The difficulty was in transportation, and Nobel volunteered to produce some of the additional vehicles needed to fill the pathway to Armstrong. Nobel's vehicles would carry hydrogen and oxygen, and they would bring two excavating machines, which Nobel would build the components for as well. They would be robotically assembled inside the stations at Armstrong from which the ore would be mined and at which the ore would be processed.

Before anything could leave for the new site, even the exploratory survey team with their deep drilling equipment, the path had to be mapped out. The route that would be chosen was to be called the Armstrong Road, and would not start from Centaurus, but from Boötes, which was almost on the great circle from Centaurus to Armstrong. Boötes would not contribute equipment to the Armstrong new mine, except for hydrogen and oxygen fuel, which they would pump into the vehicles going back and forth on the Armstrong Road. The vehicle construction work would end as soon as enough vehicles were built to make regular deliveries, but the fuel would have to be provided for several decades, while the shaft sinking and other preparatory work were going, while the initial stations were developed, while the initial utilities were installed, while the power facilities were put into their sequestered locations and turned on, and until ores providing hydrogen and oxygen had been mined and processed in the new mine. All in all, Boötes might be providing more mass to Armstrong than any other mine. Boötes had plenty of hydrogen and oxygen-bearing ores, so again, expanding production to provide it was not a problem.

Four nobelites who had been involved with the informal group to design the GG Highway with No Purpose took work assignments in Boötes, three of them extended, to contribute to the Armstrong Road. The initial plan was done in a matter of tendays, and then the nobelites joined their other lunite colleagues in going out onto the surface and leg by leg, constructing the markers, waystations, and communications towers as they went, and modifying the path to accommodate smaller craters and boulders not sufficiently appreciated by the sentiences or the lunites from the LPO elevation data.

If there were lunites singled out for bravery and daring, the way Armstrong and Gagarin were, it might be the team that first traveled across three and a half thousand kilometers of uncharted lunar landscape to reach the Armstrong main site. Yes, they traveled in a convoy of eight vehicles, with two more cycling back and forth to Boötes, and they had all the technological advantages that were possible, as well as a large database and much experience, and yes, they had the LPO and other lunar satellites for communication, as well as the links they themselves were setting up. That being said, three and a half thousand kilometers is a very long distance to be away from all other humans. They might be compared with those surface explorers on Earth who, in the very primitive times of the past, had traveled into every nook and cranny on Earth, sometimes perishing from unknown dangers.

It was noted that they were some of the first human beings to be out of sight of Earth on the moon. Martians lose sight of Earth except as a blue dot in the sky during about half of the Martian day. Those moving past Mars' orbit also lose sight of Earth, but these voyagers lost sight of Earth in a different way, traveling to a place where Earth was never, ever visible, even as a dot.

Other nobelites contributed during the third century of their mine to Armstrong, or more specifically, to the conceptualization of the micrometeorite experiments, specifically the equipment and the plan for using it. Millimeter wave radars were designed on Earth centuries ago, and largely perfected, so there was just a question of adapting the designs to manufacturing facilities in Centaurus and Ague-Tuilet, and working over all the many details of how to transport and erect one at Armstrong. This one would be rather large and powerful, and Armstrong would have to have a set of power stations larger than otherwise to supply the power to the radar. There was also the problem of heat generated by the radar. It had to be radiated away from the surface, but that could be done.

Anyone far in space looking at the backside of the moon would see a rather smooth surface in IR, except for the Armstrong site, which would be lit up for all the universe to see. Two of the nobelites involved with the radar journeyed, many years later, out to Armstrong to monitor the construction of the radar. During their stay on the backside, it was recorded that the most severe solar flares in all the time humans had been on the moon occurred.

The solar monitoring satellites, both the one in Earth orbit and the two at the Earth co-orbital Lagrangian points, had picked up the early symptoms of a very large flare, and the information had reached the team well in advance of the arrival of the flare's effects. They were working on the surface at the time, when the last of the supports for the fixed dish were being built and fastened into the lunar bedrock. The leader of the team chose to wait out the flare inside one of the shelters near the main shaft. These shelters were first built during the sinking of the Armstrong main shaft, and were still stocked with supplies to outlast a long solar storm. The oxygen tank was filled up, as was the smaller hydrogen tank, with the mandatory piping to a fuel cell for power. The radiation monitor on the middle of the roof of the shelter went to higher scales three times, and the internal radiation monitor began to signal detections. By the time it was over, three hours later, the four seventeens in the shelter, including one of the nobelites, had received enough radiation to visit the Armstrong reconstitution center. Radiation damage to the cells is something easily reconstituted, and with a day's delay, the full team was back working on the structural processes.

Nobelites were also involved with the later data analysis, after the Armstrong radar had been up and collecting data for some time. This was the closest that anyone on the moon could get to science as it was done in centuries past, before almost all facets of nature had given up their secrets. Now, it was said, everything is known except the data, meaning all the theories have been finished, but exactly what might happen in any particular location is dependent on the exact situation there, and only data collection can help resolve this. Lunites wanted to know the nature of the micrometeoroid stream falling on them. It had been clear that micrometeorites mostly come from the disintegration of comets, but which comets produce which spectrum of micrometeorites The velocity of impact was well known, but the size and, to a degree, the composition of micrometeorites needed more data collection.

The radar and the penetration detector produced that information, and they became obsolete for that purpose after two decades. Some lunites said it produced a great signal for aliens to find us, but the aliens haven't responded yet. It was somewhat ironic that the radar was the most vulnerable target for micrometeorites anywhere on Luna.

A few years after Armstrong was started in Nobel year 217, Earth seemed to pick up in interest in Luna. Before then, trips from Earth to

Luna had dropped to one or two a year. Earthlings were still doing work tours in Centaurus, but almost none were left. Centaurus had become almost all seventeens by default. There was still the common ground of the GEO, and there was no shortage of volunteer earthlings, mostly sixteens, to work on the GEO. There were more than two thousand on the station at any time, working almost exclusively on Earth-related matters. There were facilities for seventeens from the moon, and eighteens from Mars, which had lower gravity than the spaces for the earthlings, and Luna and Mars filled the open slots without much difficulty. It was a great opportunity to meet other species, to learn more firsthand from natives of other worlds, and to appreciate the gradual divergence that was happening between them, especially between Luna and the other two. It was also clear to any seventeen spending a work tour on the GEO that Luna was considered almost a prison by the other species. The sixteens and eighteens were all polite, as politeness was built into their nature and their training, but living in a mine for your entire life of over five hundred years was considered an almost intolerable sentence. They were both a bit condescending to seventeens, as if seventeens were less human than they were.

The seventeens were surprised that the most obvious aspects about Luna were not known to the sixteens or the eighteens. Earth history, Earth planetary details, Earth surface features, Earth human habitation sites, Earth this and that were all extensively covered in a seventeen's mentoring, and even in their juvenile training. Seventeens could draw good maps of Earth, and not because they could go vacuum walking and look at it, because they studied and learned about the oceans and continents of Earth, and where on the map to put the dots for the largest arcologies. They knew about the Arctic and Antarctica; they knew about the deserts, and the rain forests; they knew about the major flora and fauna. In short, they knew about Earth. But when a seventeen mentions that there were eighty thousand people in Centaurus, a sixteen might be expected to stare and ask, when did they all get there? Almost none of them knew how many mines there were, or what the inside of a mine looked like. A very few had acquaintances who had done work trips to Centaurus, and this group was more aware, but the percentage with even this faint knowledge was getting smaller. Seventeens had to be like evangelists, preaching about how life was not like being trapped in a dungeon on Luna, but it didn't seem to take very well.

Coming back after a work tour on the GEO was a different experience than leaving. Leaving, there was all the knowledge of how life was busy and interesting in your mine; coming back, there was a cynical look at everything about Luna – was it really worth any enthusiasm? That passed quickly for most people, as they became caught up in the normal stream of activities, but it took longer for a few. For tendays, they walked around looking depressed.

Thus it was strange when the GEO started scheduling more trips to the LPO, meaning more shuttles up to the LPO and back down. More earthlings requested work tours in Centaurus in Nobel year 218 than in the past three years combined. It was most likely not just random chance or a statistical fluke; nor was it the result of having a mine on the backside of the moon, or some new data collected there. Earthlings cannot participate in some sports indigenous to Luna and the seventeens living there, so that wasn't the motivation. Scanning Earth communications, the more widespread part, didn't show "Luna" popping up more than the few times it did each year. No organization on Earth was promoting trips to Luna and no one was giving prizes for the most interesting work tour in Luna.

Talk groups looking for new topics noticed the increase in applications for work tours and the increase in arrivals of visitors from Earth, and put together one hypothesis: the clashes spread over three continents on Earth had somehow inspired a few earthlings to check out the moon. In its distant past, Earth had had many riots and revolutions. Their whole history was one of war, famine, and tyranny, so why would a few clashes in some arcologies be any different? Arcologies typically had residual populations of originals, often concentrated in certain floors or sectors. The reports of the clashes indicated that sixteens were involved, however, at least they were listed as among the injured. The talk groups all saw the same reports and the question was, how could anyone motivate a sixteen to protest something? How could things be so disorganized that a protest in the corridors and atriums of the arcology was seen as the best solution? The seventeens in the talk groups discussing this could hardly imagine anything like this happening in a mine. If there was a problem, seek a solution or choose the quickest way to mitigate the negative consequences.

Perhaps the presence of originals changed everything. On Centaurus, there was no longer a single original left, but on Earth, they maintained their numbers, in proportion to the declining population of humans in total. Many originals lived outside the arcologies, but they weren't the ones involved in the clashes.

One of the talk groups had a member who asked his sentience to compare the locations of the three clashes with the particulars of the work tour applicants' locations and of the visitors as well. Most were from one of the three affected arcologies, and the next step was to see how close their residences were to the clash sites. There was no strong effect that showed here, as the applicants and visitors were on the periphery of the clash areas. These clashes had mostly taken place in common areas. Then the member asked to see where the residence locations of those identified as having been injured were, as compared to those of the applicants. Many of them lived on a floor and in a sector where an injured person did, but not quite half. The talk group the member was in digested the results, reviewed his data, and came to a consensus that the uptick in work tour applications was not due to Luna having somehow improved itself or changed the way the rest of the solar system saw it, but because Earth was becoming just a little less pleasant to live in.

This was excellent information, as now Centaurus would see no need to expand their arrangements for earthlings, as the visitor count and work tour count would go right back down once this unusual behavior on Earth abated. Seventeens simply could not believe that sixteens would engage in riotous behavior, as they were so similar, genetically and via nurture, to seventeens. This unusual activity would have to soon cease, so no planning changes were needed.

DIARY ENTRY (AGE 132, DAY 110)

I am not sure I made the right choice by signing up for an extension of my work assignment in recycling. For three years, I enjoyed the people I worked with, the different parts of the work, and the idea that recycling is vital to keeping us alive in a self-sustaining mine. The first half year on the second assignment were fine as well, but yesterday my closest associate here finally decided to leave at the end of his tour and go do mining. I suppose it will be the same with others I have enjoyed working with. They will move on, and new people will come in.

I still enjoy the work on its own. For the last thirty tendays, I have been working in the parts management section, where the sentiences maintain records of every part of every piece of equipment and apparatus here in Nobel. I know from the database that the control section shield of overhead extractor number 5576 was replaced a year and a half ago with an identical control section shield from surface transport vehicle 9018, and that shield has had service in two other locations so far, being exposed to dust in mining, solar radiation and vacuum in the service vehicle, gamma radiation in a power facility, and impact in internal transport, and there is still a rated life of over three years in it. I also know it was a titanium, aluminum and germanium alloy, which would be recycled without changing the alloy components. I know the shield was coated with a rubbery layer, how that layer will be dissolved off before recycling, and how the outer layer material will be reused as well.

Soon I will be moving over to coatings, and will be observing the removal and attachment of coatings of all kinds. Coatings is vacuum work, and I will be traveling every work day down to level four, which is shared with ore processing and manufacturing. This means suiting up outside the airlock on the residential level, down the shaft and then working for four hours in the light vacuum suit. A year ago, I was the only one working down there in the alloy separation facility, and many days were simply quiet, with no reprocessing going on. Provided everything was in ready state over in alloy separation, I would go over to the manufacturing area where I have done work tours and simply double check things there. Alloy separation results go there anyway.

In coatings there will always be activity going on. Coatings are removed and reapplied many times in the lifetime of some components, sometimes the same but different in color or thickness, or different in composition. Labeling goes on in that facility as well. Catching anything out of the ordinary in the records facility is unusual, as the sentiences are so well suited for that task. One of my colleagues caught a data duplication problem, which cannot occur but did. In coatings, humans get a different point of view than the sentience sensors, so there is a chance to find a coating imperfection, or to catch a materials mistake.

I started working with my friend, the one who is transferring out, two years ago when we were working in human waste reprocessing. This is another vat and pipe facility, with the same concerns as others. We each found two leaking pipes during the half year we worked there, from connector wear, from the smell, before sentience sensors picked them up. My sentience checked and discovered that no pair of nobelites had ever found four problems in a half year period before, dating back to when the facility turned on. It's nothing to be very proud of, but it was a contribution.

We both next transferred over to the distribution front end, where vehicles arrived with materials for reuse and recycling for another thirty tendays work together. Everything is recycled or reused inside a lunar mine, but the components are designed for reliability and longevity, so the vehicle traffic is not too great. Waste collection vehicles were the largest in number. I had observed that one of the vehicles, which arrived several times each shift, was not maintaining its speed properly and communicated via my sentience to the vehicle controller's sentience. It was withdrawn for repair the next day. Another small victory for humans.

My friend and I usually had a small meal together after our work shifts. We found that we could not help but notice how everything in the commons area was made to be disassembled. In the beginning, we walked around the facility, just seeing who would find the seams first, or the hidden attachment mechanism, or the piping connectors. We went through the final food preparation area several times, once looking at coolers and another time at heaters. Another time it was food mixers, and yet another it was the drink mixers. While at a table, we observed the delivery automatons for a few visits, not for efficiency of purpose or speed of travel, but for how they would be taken apart. Our sentiences could have diagrammed all this in a second, but it was more entertaining to do the observation tour.

While I was down in alloy separation, my friend was in sensor repair, which is not a vacuum job. We met for a large meal sometimes during that thirty tendays period. There are so many things that can go wrong with a sensor that he often found himself working late, monitoring some diagnosis. That was convenient, as my travel and suit time delayed me as well. Now I suppose I will soon have to find someone else to have meals with.

NOBEL'S THIRD CENTURY

The clashes in the arcologies of Earth, mostly in five of them, became a regular occurrence. Each year noted at least one, and some years over the next two decades had several. Lunites soon became aware that they were the result of the originals, those who lived in the arcologies, being requested to limit their offspring to one natural-born, or else to migrate to the outside. Sixteens were the dominant part of the population, and the human spectrum, as it was called, from ones to fifteens, still had significant numbers.

Many originals never moved into the arcologies and simply lived on the land outside them, in special areas reserved for their habitations. Some lived in old, small cities, which they maintained, and some lived in smaller villages, both new and old, and many were isolated by a few kilometers from other originals. Some of the originals outside were unimproved, meaning their predecessors had not taken advantage of the genetic fixes and upgrades that the early days of the genetics revolution came up with. Many were improved, but partially. The ones in the arcologies were largely fully improved, but they were still not using industrial gestation, but breeding as they had evolved to do. There had been for the last three centuries or more a migration of originals out of the arcologies and into 'Nature' as it was called, but that had not diminished the internal population by a large percentage. So, the governance of the arcologies had uniformly made the request for limitation, obviously after long consultation.

This influenced the flow of sixteens to Luna, for work tours and on visits for one reason or another. Compared to the population on Earth, still over four billion, the number going to Centaurus was infinitesimal, in the hundreds, but it was more than previously. In a sense, it was like the old days in Centaurus, but in reverse. Centaurus started out with all earthlings, as every human was one. When the mine started gestating seventeens, they were at first a small minority among the earthlings.

By Nobel year 240, seventeens constituted nearly all of the population, with earthlings accounting for only a thousand out of fifty-seven thousand. In the first days of gestation on Centaurus, early seventeens had gathered together informally, while participating in everything, such as talk groups, as individuals, and now earthlings had their own informal groups but participated in everything as individuals.

Centaurus had invited other mines to provide work tours for the earthlings, but none did. Boötes had considered it, and sent some seventeens from there to meet with a few earthlings inside Centaurus, but they came away with the impression that earthlings would much rather be in the largest mine on Luna than one of the smaller ones. Earth's arcologies had tens of millions of residents, and Centaurus was probably enough of a shock for an arcology resident. Hardly any of them stayed for a second work tour.

Clashes continued on Earth, and in Nobel year 244, there was a double accident on Earth, where accidents almost never happen, just as on Luna. In two arcologies, on the same day, two groups of hydrogen tanks had leaks that filled the air and then exploded. The smell of the hydrogen additives had caused most people to leave the area, but the explosions were so large that the walls of the atriums where this happened collapsed. Thirty people died and almost another hundred were injured. Twenty-eight of the dead were revived in the constitution centers, but two originals were so disintegrated that they could not be reconstituted according to the rules. Their bodies could have been regenerated, but all their brains, with all the information and experience they contained, were lost, and the regenerated body would be inert and could never become the person who was lost again.

Arcologies are designed to be mostly recycled on a hundred and twenty year cycle, so all the walls are made of smaller components assembled together. These fastenings are what gave way in the explosions, leading to the collapse of two and four floors above. The atriums and surrounding floors could be rebuilt rapidly, but the psychological effect of the accidents would take much longer.

Talk groups in Nobel considered what would happen if the flow of sixteens increased even more, and Centaurus had to accommodate two or three thousand instead of just under one. Would the gestation of seventeens be slowed down to compensate, or would some readjustment of the habitat construction schedule be done? People in Nobel had no direct interest in what happened in Centaurus, as the mines act independently except when they form joint projects. Former co-workers in Ague-Tuilet were asked what their mine would be doing, and Ague-Tuilet was still in the talk group stage when they were first asked. Concern in Nobel led to a public meeting, which was listened to in Ague-Tuilet, and the consensus was that Nobel and other mines might increase their own habitat construction and take an overflow of seventeens from Centaurus. Seventeens are nurtured in a way to ensure they like to be helpful, and early training reinforced this, so the solution seemed quite correct and acceptable. The way forward was to wait and see what influx of earthlings the accidents might cause.

There was a slight bump upwards and the GEO scheduled more shuttle trips to the LPO leading to Centaurus, but the numbers that appeared were more like eleven or twelve hundred in the next two years, not thousands. Centaurus could handle this on its own, or perhaps there would be a slight increase in the number of seventeens from Centaurus going elsewhere temporarily on work tasks, but nothing to modify building plans or work schedules for. The idea of an overflow stayed around, however, as nobelites monitored Earth news for more accidents.

Instead, the clashes went the other way, and their frequency declined. No other accidents happened. By Nobel year 252, two years after the quarter millennium mark, they had virtually ceased. On Earth, the migration of originals out to 'Nature' had increased so much that the populations of the arcologies went noticeably downward, and the population living outside went noticeably upward. Outward censuses were done remotely from the air, so they were not as exact as in an arcology, where every person was known and identified. Earth reports indicated that the outmigration of originals was mostly to the areas already inhabited by originals, certainly not to the areas where the new humans were located. Nobelites were largely indifferent to this, except as a conversation topic, as it did not involve Luna.

By Nobel year 245, nobelites had begun discussing the bi-and-a-half centennial, and whether to make it as widespread, long and involved as they had done for the bicentennial. The vegetation plot that Nobel had created for the previous event had already been exceeded. Centaurus had larger plots, and they were in continuous use. Nobel had originated six new types of vegetation to grow in the same material base, with the same fluid feed stock, and these were already on display in the third stope. All six were made for dramatic impact, with similar stalks, but multicolored petals on the end. The vegetation was not like original Earth vegetation, where plants had blooms and flowers that were used in the reproduction process. On Nobel, the petal arrangements were simply for the entertainment and amusement of those visiting the third stope, which was called 'Gardener'. Inside Gardener, along the longest wall, there were raised base material holders, and in these were the new vegetation types.

Work assignments were connected with the care of the plants, and some seventeens had already had three tours with the plants, somehow winning the assignment lottery in succession. Three of the plants had uniform colors, red, yellow, and green, and the other three had petals that varied from node to node. The shapes were also different, in size, number, arrangement, and attachment points. Gardener was often packed with seventeens, using the plot for a meal or strolling along the vegetation boxes. The genetics seventeens could have come up with more, but this was not signaled as a great novelty for a half-centennial.

Another thing that came before its time was the bath. Seventeens do not go underwater as this causes discomfort in the otay senses. Splashes are not a problem, but being under a water stream would be just as bad as being underwater. So, for two centuries, there had not been any bodies of water. Why bother, was the general opinion? Cleaning was done in the mist cubicles, which were associated with the recycling system. Despite this obvious disinterest and dislike, four seventeens, from a talk group that had run its course and disbanded, requested and obtained a vacant habitat space for their construction of a small pool. Water was not to be wasted, but the former habitat had a recycling system that could be modified for a much larger volume of water, if necessary. So, amidst other residences, there was a closed off spot with a pool of water. The four seventeens liked it when it was body temperature, and sitting on seats in the pool kept their heads out of the water. Adding headrests to the outside above the seats made their enjoyment even greater.

After about a half year, the seventeen involved with space allocations needed to ask if the space was needed any more, and they found that these four seventeens plus another six who had become involved after the pool was completed, uniformly objected to any change in use plans. The space allocation individual approved continual occupation of the space, provided it was made available to more inhabitants, starting with himself. In Nobel year 243, when the pool was scheduled and times put into a lottery, there were over five thousand seventeens living in Nobel, and almost all of them wanted to try the pool. It may have been group-think, but just about all seventeens liked the heated pool, if they could get into it. A lot of the requests for pool time were from people just getting out of it, so they could return as soon as possible. Once again, Nobel found that it had invented something very enjoyable on the moon, although it was exceedingly common for sixteens on Earth. Mars didn't seem to have it.

There was a long stretch of open space in Gardener, running parallel to the vegetation plot. The genetics people had eyed it for another vegetation plot, one that was larger, as the open space was three times as wide as the original plot. But they hadn't moved to make the request, concentrating instead on the intense genetic challenges of making new plants for the moon and getting them installed and staying alive in the boxes along the long wall. By Nobel year 245, that space was spoken for. The ten seventeens who had been enjoying their private pool were asked to manage the building of a larger one, which would not be overwhelmed with requests for time slots. They came up with a three pronged pool, looking like a fork with three narrow tines, seats on either side, and a perpendicular section at one end. The difficulties were not great, but filling the pool would take a long time, as Gardener did not have any large water supplies. Overhead piping had to be routed from the recycling facility, where water was available, over to Gardener. It needed to be bidirectional, so the pool could be emptied. Water cleaning equipment had to be built and installed somewhere in the stope as well. But surprisingly, by Nobel year 248, it was there, and open to anyone who wanted to get wet. The area around the pool sloped toward it, so drips could flow back to the pool, and less would be wasted.

The pool was highly booked, but large enough to accommodate the desires of the population of Nobel, which was taken into account in designing its length. Three hours every fiveday it was left empty, not for cleaning, as that went on intermittently, but for the flyers. Gardener had a high point, where some balconies were, and these overlooked the vegetation plot and the pool. It was high enough for someone to jump off, glide downward, and make a water landing. This may sound absurd, but it was not. The pool was left open while flyers landed, with feet forward and head back, just above the waterline. With the proper orientation of the feet, it was quite possible to skid for most of the length of the pool, but after that, sinking invariably happened. Other flyers were always on hand to help to manage the wings from one end of the pool. This was a spectacle that many seventeens had to see, at least once. It probably boosted the number of people involved with flying as well.

Things did not always go perfectly. One of the flyers stayed aloft too long and broke a toe on the far end of the pool. This meant reconstitution for two days. Others, several each year, aligned poorly and fell under the water, making for an unpleasant conclusion to a thrilling flight. Tipping forward too much led to the same result. On the other hand, watching someone experienced dive almost straight down from the launch balcony, make a sharp upward turn just above the floor, and then hit the water with both feet, staying upright but leaning backwards, with wings horizontal, slowly decelerating until near the end of the pool, where he gracefully sank to standing position in the water, was incredibly impressive.

It wasn't the best choice to inaugurate a two-and-a-half centennial celebration, but it would certainly make a good exhibition for one. The decision was made to have it be only last for three tendays and the loose days at the end of our 250th year. The committee set up to organize it seemed to have priorities different from those of the bicentennial. They first concentrated on it being something of a food festival, rather than mostly entertainment, exhibitions, and shows. A pair of nobelites went to Gagarin to see if they could bring the crazy chefs there to the festivities, and they were successful. Here in Nobel, we were quite content with eating the five major nutrient products and the five minor ones, along with specialty foods grown on the arrays.

The talk groups did not have records of any group objecting to the foods, and many of them had some minor discussion of how good the specialty foods were. The specialties varied over a year-long cycle, mostly, with the three most popular always available and two others alternating over a half year. Every habitat was equipped with a complete collection of aromas to be added to the foods. What was missing, in the eyes of the committee, was innovation and excitement. Most of the committee's reports were met with questioning. After two and a half centuries of working out a fine diet, that pleased just about everyone in Nobel, why did anything else have to be done? Several of the seventeens on the committee had had work assignments in Gagarin, and they had a very different opinion. It had been shared in talk groups, and nothing happened. The festivities were seen as a chance to change that. After all, the bicentennial had food-centered activities, and they were very popular.

The committee did its duty, and arranged for music and the other arts to fill the festivity period, with many visitors coming from as far away as Boötes and Gautama to perform. There would be exhibitions and competitions in flying and wall-jumping, as well as gymnastics competitions in four of the five areas popular in Nobel: single-pole balancing, rope ladders, elevated beam, and floor. There were too few volunteers for wire-walking, so that was eliminated. The intense interest across the moon that had happened during the bicentennial did not pick up, and while there were certainly many visitors coming in during the final tendays of the year, it was only a small percentage of the numbers that crowded into Nobel for the bicentennial. Other mines were scheduling festivals now, which might explain the diminished numbers.

Pool and vegetation use were blocked off for visitors, with no serious objections by the nobelites. The festivities went well, with no crowding of habitation and no shortage of food, which would have happened at the bicentennial if not for the careful planning of the bicentennial committee and the Ague-Tuilet's cooperation of in sending something to fill in gaps. Gymnastics was being competed across Luna, and the level of professionalism shown during the Nobel 250th anniversary celebration was very high. Centaurus took all four bests, and two seconds, with Ague-Tuilet taking the beam second and the floor second. There was a bit of consternation recorded in Nobel talk groups about how Centaurus provided almost all the judges as well, but 3vids of the competitions did not show any failure to judge fairly.

The Gagarin food chefs provided tables of novel dishes every day of the festivities, focusing on staged eating, structures of tastes, aromas that blossomed out of layers of foods, and liquids of a wide variety. It was expected that this would be too much for most nobelites, as the food presentations from Gautama used new aroma molecules that did not match the genetics that seventeens came with. However, the Gagarin show chefs seemed to draw a great amount of interest. Seventeens, like sixteens and many of the other intermediate species on Earth, had more sensitivity to aroma than the originals and the early new species did. This was done, as everyone learned in mentoring, by expanding the genetic code so that more aroma sensors were present. This code was designed around target molecules for specific aromas, but Gagarin had thrown the molecule list out and developed new ones, variants, mixtures, twists and so on. Things from Gagarin tasted differently, although they looked much the same. Many seventeens, from Nobel and visitors from other mines, could sense the differences and were impressed.

In the years just following the 250th anniversary celebrations, nothing much happened to Nobel food. The mentions in the talk groups were that it was wonderful to have things to try during festivities, but normal food was fine in between. Festivities in Nobel, smaller one or two day ones, happened frequently, so there was the opportunity to introduce new foods there. But for the first five years, it did not happen.

One small celebration two years after the big one was related to an Earth celebration, the finishing of the ELO construction. For almost fifty years, Earth had been building an observatory at the trailing Lagrangian point with three telescopes, each over a hundred meters in diameter, and the third one was finally finished and construction halted. This observatory was used for many things and as the first and second dishes had been completed, the work on observing had started. This observatory searched for asteroids, both near-Earth and as far as the Oort cloud, for exo-planets, or rather exo-solar-systems and even large exo-satellites, for more evidence of black holes within and beyond the galaxy in the visual spectrum, and for much more detailed mapping of many astronomical phenomena, such as supernova remnants and minor nearby galaxies. Earthlings had always been more interested in astronomy than other sciences, and the humans on Luna were no different.

The celebration showed off the discoveries of the first two dishes, and presented the plans for the use of the third.

One point that the presentations from Earth did not include was the exclusion of seventeens from the construction effort of the ELO and the on-site monitoring of its operation. There is no doubt there would have been interest in it, but the planning for the ELO, which was done on the GEO as was every other space-related project, did not include this opportunity. The ELO team was only twenty individuals, up to twenty-eight at the peak, and the wheel that was built for them operated at 40% gravity, just as the outer wheels on the GEO did.

Talk groups on Nobel, when they engaged in discussing what was going on at the ELO, either learning about the construction vicariously, or absorbing the new results coming from it, understood that with that small a staff, it would have been very inefficient to build an inner wheel for seventeens, and no seventeens would have wanted to be housed in the central cylinder to be weightless for a work tour. The outer wheel was smaller than those on the GEO, by a considerable amount, and a lower gravity wheel inside them would have had too much Coriolis force to be comfortable. Putting up another wheel on the same cylinder with a lower rotation rate for a couple of seventeens to work from would have been absurdly inefficient. Thus, no one at Nobel objected to the ELO process, and the celebration did not have any bitter overtones related to participation.

One thing that did come up in this celebration, or rather a talk group after it, was that there was no real science going on in Nobel, or anywhere else on the moon, if you exclude moon exploration. Science theory had burned out, because there was a coherent explanation for all phenomena, most of which was well connected, but there was data collection and analysis, such as was happening with the ELO. Seventeens from Luna could be involved when they did work tours on GEO, but a sentience look at the work assignments given to seventeens on the GEO showed they were not science or data related, but more engineering, maintenance, or transportation related. Mentoring on Luna produced as good a result in science areas as it did on Earth, so the lack of background could not have been an issue. What was the issue? The talk group didn't come up with any explanation.

Most talk group recordings sink into oblivion and are never seen by any living person, or even exhumed by a sentience, but this one was shared and spread to all of the mines. The response from Armstrong was the most interesting, and it said that anyone who wanted to do science should get on an Armstrong Road convoy, and do a work tour there. Armstrong was not yet self-sufficient, as this process took about sixty years, maybe down to forty-five at the minimum, and it had been less than forty since a group lived underground at Armstrong and staked a claim to founding a new mine. They were already in the process of planning their dish, and the associated equipment to energize it and take data from it, and could have proceeded a bit faster with a few more seventeens. There were less than two hundred people living at Armstrong, which wasn't much for dividing between the tasks of becoming self-sufficient with all utilities up and running, and getting ready to do science.

Many other mines responded after this with just a reminder that the population of Earth was four billion, and the population of Luna under a hundred thousand, and if some science was done at Armstrong it would be proportionally more than the population ratio would indicate. Science was interesting, even fascinating, on Luna as on Earth, but it was also usually expensive, and there was much else to be done on Luna as it grew gradually.

Centaurus was busy using up the manpower and resources that could be spared by starting an eighth mine. A formal committee was set up and a voluntary group, too big to be a talk group but too long-lasting for anything else, formed itself to start a mine along the Armstrong Road. Even before the equipment for sinking the shaft at Armstrong had arrived there, Centaurus, which was responsible for the deployment of most of the exploratory teams, had shifted their focus to the areas on the north and south of the road from Boötes to Armstrong.

Multiple sites came up from the first sweep of the road, and the six teams then went on follow-up diversions around the hits to figure out which was the best. Most of them turned out to be of no interest, but two led the survey teams away from the road to good concentrations of ores. The best one was in Compton Crater, and the teams exploring the crater and the surrounding rim and mountains nearby found that the northeast edge of the crater was the best location. This would be an unusual arrangement for a mine, as the ores were not only below the crater floor, but also up in the mountains. If a shaft was sunk on the floor, there would need to be a drift upwards to get to the ore bodies located higher. Alternately, the survey team noted that an adit could be dug into a slope there, and the two, the shaft and the adit, could be exploited together.

Sentiences evaluated the two concepts, and the formal committee and the informal committee that had concerned itself with the eighth mine reviewed the findings. A shaft would be dug, and the first station would be for ore extraction, with one side going horizontally and then down, and the opposite side going horizontally and then up. Ore processing would be on the second station. Unlike Nobel, habitation would be put on the fifth and sixth stations. The exploration team had dug down through these depths, and there was ore there as well, so the habitations would be partially in ore bodies that would be excavated later, when the habitations would be moved, either deeper or out some long drift, to another area where no ore was located or had already been excavated.

A talk group at Nobel took on the idea that this mine should be named Apollo, in memory of the initial landings on the moon. None of the Apollo sites were near the new site, which was on the backside of the moon, but that was irrelevant in the opinion of the Nobel talk group. This opinion resonated with some other talk groups, especially at Gautama and Gagarin, and two committees in Centaurus didn't seem to have taken much time to think about names. They called it Compton initially, as the crater it was located in had been named that. Compton was a famous physicist, but no one in these various talk groups or committees was particularly interested in having a mine named that way, after its location on the moon. There were better things to do with names. So Apollo stuck.

As soon as the shaft sinking equipment had finished its work at Armstrong, it were pulled back to the open, flat area at Centaurus, where it was checked and refurbished. The primary shaft equipment came back first, and needed new motors, so Centaurus had the fun of modifying their manufacturing equipment to once again make a motor, while taking the old one in for disassembly and recycling. Later, the secondary shaft equipment came back, and that was in better shape, and was refurbished without needing major components replaced. When all had been checked, the convoys started out for Compton Crater, which was now called the Apollo mine site. The pathway from the site down to the Armstrong Road did not go directly there to the nearest point, because of the mountains along that path, but crossed the crater to the southwest side and then continued further southwest until the road was reached. Because of this detour, Apollo would not be a very convenient stopping point on the way to Armstrong, which was a secondary goal of Centaurus searching for sites, but nothing directly on the road had popped up as a very rich ore location. So, Apollo would be its own site.

Centaurus' directions for developing the Apollo site did not follow the exact same order as had been used with the other mines, in other words, concentrate on the ore bodies first, then ore processing, followed by habitation. Instead, they moved to the habitation station first, because it was in a smaller ore body. Ore was shipped from the deep sixth station, two thirds to Boötes, which was all they could handle, and about a third to Centaurus. The habitation site was being developed simultaneously with the ore site, and the upper ore areas were reached only later. When they were reached, habitation began in the temporary location in the deep ore body. It might be there for many decades, but eventually it would be moved as ore was the reason for living on the moon, in a sense. There would be no self-sustaining mines without rich ores, and every seventeen knew that since elementary training. No one even thought that ores would not be given priority over everything else, with power coming in second.

Thus, habitation was first achieved in Apollo sooner, compared with the starting of the sinking of a main shaft, than in other mine start-ups. Apollo was inhabited in Nobel year 234, only 19 years after the habitation of Armstrong. It was usual for sixty years to elapse before a mine is wholly self-sustaining, and there was no reason at the time to think that Apollo would be any quicker at that than any other mine. Armstrong was slower because of the long distances for transportation, and Apollo shared a little of that. Because of the similarity between Gautama, which had two main shafts, and Apollo, which was considering an adit to complement its main shaft, some Gautama seventeens volunteered to help at Apollo, and the adit idea was followed. This would be a first for mining on Luna, and at first, the adit would not be connected with the main shaft. Exploration of where the ore bodies were exactly located would determine if any connection would be made. Perhaps some decades or centuries in the future, there would be some habitation up on levels above the crater floor, but that remained to be decided by those living in Apollo at that future date.

By Nobel year 295, Apollo had reached the point of self-sufficiency. They had an adit, still unconnected with the main shaft, and three quarters of the ore was taken from the adit and down the main shaft to be processed, with the spoil being taken back up the shaft to be deposited in the spoil pile. This was not the most convenient process, but the location of the best ores dictated it. In that same year, Apollo had a public meeting, the first of three, at the request of several talk groups. The subject of the meeting was that the apolloites did not like the name that Nobel had gifted them with. After being referred to as "Apollo" for sixty years, they wanted to change it. Apollo was a successful project that opened up man's horizons to include the moon. But it was ignored and not followed up on, almost as if it had been a failure. The termination aspect of the project was what caused the seventeens to turn against this name. It was a discussion of keeping a legacy versus starting with a name of their own choosing.

There was no thought that every mine on Luna would change its own name for some reason, and no talk groups on any other mine seemed to be going in that direction. Only Apollo made that choice. Apollo only had about two hundred and fifty seventeens in it, so it was easy to caucus and persuade, and it was decided to have a vote. Almost all public meetings on Luna lead to a consensus, with the opposing side recognizing the weight of opinion against them and deciding to appreciate the other opinion, instead of steadfastly and stubbornly deciding to keep pushing their own side. Few votes were ever taken, as public meetings usually went in an obvious direction toward one opinion. But Apollo wanted to have a vote on name-changing at its third public meeting, and they did. It was simply a hand-raising affair, and the sentiences monitoring the cameras could have a count in a second. The large majority, recorded as sixty four percent, voted for having some new name. The former Apollo mine was temporarily named with a blank.

Later in that year, another public meeting was held to choose a new name, and no vote was taken. There was simply a discussion of options, and Orion was chosen. Orion is a constellation, much more easily recognized than Boötes or Centaurus, and that was one good reason. Orion was also a project name, notably for one with nuclear propulsion in the infant days of space exploration, which never concluded, and for interplanetary manned voyages, back in the same early days, which also never concluded, but more memorably for the recent project that put humans in orbit around Venus in a wheel, which was very successful. The wheel in its first stage was sixteens only, as was the ELO, but unlike the ELO, there were plans to continue the Orion Venus Orbiter to something much larger, and in later stages, seventeens might be able to serve work tours there. The OVO was an attention-grabbing project, as the wheel had been assembled in Earth orbit, and slowly brought to Venus and even more slowly into Venus orbit, all the while with humans riding inside.

Three seventeens on duty in the GEO had worked on the project, all from Centaurus, so there was a touch of Luna content there. Its progress had been monitored in detail, and the 3vids, especially of the approach to Venus, were some of the most popular ones during the three year descent to the desired Venus orbit. Filtered solar close-ups helped the attractiveness, especially because of the great solar activity during this period. The sun could be and was observed, in greater detail, from Earth orbit, but it was so far more dramatic watching the sun eclipsed by a strut of the OVO wheel. Thus, Apollo mine became Orion mine.

Today I had lunch for the fourth time with an earthling, Shambala Sen Sontir, who comes up from the outer wheel to the inner wheel where I live, to dine. It is called 'up' because 'gravity' is outward on the wheels. Shambala is pleasant to be with, more than most earthlings here on the GEO, as he is less restrained and more open in what he says. He is younger than I am, a sixteen with only 122 years behind him so far. The sixteens I meet as part of my work tour activities are very formal, very polite, very courteous, and very restrained. I really do not know how they see me. I consider myself a typical seventeen, and, in terms of mental makeup, seventeens are almost the same as sixteens. We look different a bit because of the otay senses on our heads, but how could that cause every sixteen who meets me to be so restrained? None have ever invited me to lunch. Granted, they always eat on the outer wheel connected to mine, but nothing stops them from coming up here to eat. They come up here for meetings almost every ten-day. Shambala is different, and finagled an invitation by asking questions about what foods seventeens eat — the same as sixteens — and pursuing this until I invited him to verify it for himself. I hadn't recognized what he was doing immediately.

During the first time we dined together, Shambala asked me about the otay senses, specifically, how I integrate the IR view with the visual one from my eyes. He didn't know they fed into the same area of the brain, and we seventeens learn to integrate them the same way as a baby learns binocular vision. Correlation and reinforcement. And, unless you are flying in a tall stope, the air pressure sensors don't play much of a role, I told him. With your head oriented correctly, the Bernoulli effect gives you a weak speed sensor. That opened his eyes up. We had to talk about flying in a Luna mine. I haven't done that much of it, but enough to explain it to him. I can air-climb thirty meters up under my own power, having done it once or twice, but I haven't practiced enough to do it repeatedly. Everyone starts by gliding down from a ledge. He kept asking questions for the whole hour of lunch.

During the second lunch, he talked about the psychology of never see-ing the sky, as if all seventeens had a repressed claustrophobia. It was like living in the lower floors of an arcology, I supposed, but he explained about the air shafts that most of them have going deep into the larger corridors. I explained: "No, we have no skylights". "Perhaps, that would be a great addition", he said. It was a funny minute for me. Never in my life in Nobel has anyone talked about skylights, but they might be possible, with some airlocks with transparent panels. Why not just have a light that cycles with the daylight outside? It could be much brighter, or of a different spectrum than the rest of the lighting, which was reddish.

During the same lunch, I asked him about why sixteens weren't seen much in the inner wheel other than for meetings. He said it might be gravity was too light here, and handling food is different between 40% gravity and 16% gravity. Sleeping is different, too, but that was irrelevant as the sixteens all had their own quarters in the outer wheel. This wasn't the answer I was seeking, but maybe it was relevant. Each to their own gravity, I suppose.

The next time we had lunch together, I asked him about why he hadn't gone to Luna for a work tour? Was it the low gravity or something else? He stared at me for a minute or two and said that most sixteens nowadays regard it as punishment to have to live underground, at least the ones he discussed Luna with. They simply cannot comprehend living on the moon without a dome. He went on about the details of things different sixteens have said to him about it. In an arcology, there is always the roof park, the atriums reaching up to the top of the building, the balconies on the ends of the major corridors, or, for that matter, vehicles to use for a little ride outside. He said not to ask him about living things, as it was even worse.

During another joint lunch, we talked about some things concerning him personally, for which I suppose I am a sounding board. But at the end of the lunch, I asked him about how sixteens saw seventeens, which he demurred on. Then I sharpened it by asking him how he feels about seventeens. He said he was sorry to say it, and all the seventeens he had met on the GEO had been nice guys, me especially, but seventeens simply cannot be liberated and have to go back to living in the mines. He was glad I could at least get away for a work tour on the GEO, but it was not that much better than the mines. He apologized again and again for saying what he did. I compensated, and thanked him for sharing it, saying we don't see ourselves that way, but it was very interesting to hear his opinion, and when could we have lunch again.

I suppose I should think about whether he is having lunch with me out of pity or out of friendship. I suppose I will assume the latter until I find out otherwise.

DIARY ENTRY (AGE 144, DAY 87)

Today was my sixth lunch with Shambala Sen Sontir, the earthling, in the inner wheel of the GEO. Sixteens eat with much more regularity than seventeens do. We have small meals and large meals, but they could be in any order. Sixteens usually have a small meal around the middle of a work day.

At the fifth lunch we talked a lot about his home on Earth. He comes from an arcology near the delta of the river Ganges, which drains much of the largest landmass on Earth, Eurasia. He was gestated, mentored, and worked there, but he also did three work tours of five years each in another arcology in the Amazon jungle in the center of the southern part of the second largest landmass there. The two arcologies are quite similar to each other. I have seen a hundred 3vids of the interior of arcologies, everything from individual habitations to balconies and roof parks, so I steered the conversation to his personal experiences.

Shambala talked about two of his mentors, the one that impressed him the most and the one that he was the happiest to visit. The first taught him gliding, which he did from the roof of the river Ganges arcology, always in the landward direction. I had specifically asked Shambala about this, and he still hesitated as it was something I could only experience in a 3vid. On Earth, simulators are used for the first lessons, but there are none on Luna nor on the GEO, so there is no way for me to experience the intensity of a six hundred meter high glide. His mentor was patient, detailed, and managed to relieve his fear before the first flight, and indeed before the second, third, and fourth. Shambala didn't talk about the view until I persisted in hearing about it. He would have restricted the talk to the landing field and the equipment, out of the same reluctance that we discussed at a previous lunch. It seems to be embedded inside sixteens that they do not talk about living on Earth, especially outside the arcologies, with seventeens. We are those who cannot be liberated.

Some of his flights with this mentor lasted two hours, and involved cruising out over the wide river delta, back out over the jungle surrounding the arcology's outside park area, and over the ruins of old villages. I knew what all those scenes looked like, but they were places he had

209

visited on the ground and could connect to when he flew over. He could follow a half-hidden pathway along the river's edge and loop around the arcology. He said he and his mentor flew together forty-five times, initially simply circling around the landing zone but then venturing further and further away. There were energy packs on the gliders for emergencies, but Shambala said with some visible pride that he had never used one. He still glides a few times a year, and did quite a bit during the first work tour at the central Amazon arcology.

The mentor he enjoyed the most was the one who tutored him on heliology, which started with reviews of fusion processes under great pressure, its evolution, structure, emissions, and much more. The subject by itself was very interesting, but the mentor was so entertaining that he could have been a performer. Everything became a trick question, a subtle reminder of some other mentor's lessons, an outlandish analogy with human life, a wild imaginative voyage through the corona, or so on. Shambala was very disappointed when the three year period with him was over, and tried to get another, but this mentor only taught heliology to new students. Shambala repeated some of the jokes and metaphors the mentor had used, but I think they had to be given by the mentor, as Shambala had no talent for exciting humor.

On the sixth lunch, Shambala had expected I would repeat the exercise and talk about two of my mentors, but I shifted that conversation to a different day. There would be other occasions to talk about my mentoring, and I had not even thought through who they would be. Instead, I had to talk about his impressions of the imprisoned picture of life on Luna as seen from the perspective of an average sixteen in an arcology on Earth. Shambala was so good-natured that he never seemed to mind about the redirection, and just responded. Two of the talk groups he was in had both spent a lot of time talking about Earth and Luna, and he apologized first by saying it hadn't been an interesting topic for him and the talk groups didn't change that. It was two different takes on the same issue.

Was it wrong to have created seventeens and established them on Luna in a self-sufficient way? One talk group was spending its whole period of existence on things that humans had done that violated the code of ethics, the one we all are trained in. Before the neurological revolution, there was no such universal code, and so all the wars and terrorism were done with other codes in mind, and that was their excuse. This talk group had spent most of its sessions on these ancient eras, but the seventeen issue came up for the last quarter of its duration. I could have listened to the recording myself, but Shambala summed up the answer that they came to, that it was an ethics violation but one that was justified.

The second of Shambala's talk groups to discuss this felt differently, and Shambala decided this was not worth discussing, except that I insisted and insisted. My sentience could probably have located it for me, but my stubbornness won out, and Shambala relented. This talk group felt populating Luna was a mistake, and that seventeens or even eighteens should not have been created, and Earth was the only place for humans. Searching for life on exo-planets was an expensive hobby, as there would be no contact, either physically or electromagnetically. This was a uncomfortable jolt for me, as I wondered just how many sixteens felt like those in this second talk group, but had never expressed it. This may have explained why contact between the other sixteens I worked with and myself was so restricted.

13

A NEW HIGHWAY

The pathway from Nobel to Gagarin navigated its way through some rough areas. It traveled south through the Murchison Crater to Sinus Medii, then sinuously down to Ptolemy Crater, which it crossed directly before continuing on an even more tortuous path to Gagarin. In Nobel year 287, a talk group in Gagarin had plotted out a path to the west of this one, with less flat areas to cover, but a bit shorter. The sentiences made estimates of which one was actually best, meaning which one would take less time using the highly safe driving procedures of the robotic lunar drivers. The estimates varied, but indicated there was a good chance the new route would be faster.

The new route left Nobel to the southwest, then turned south, going around Herschel Crater, then into a different part of Ptolemy Crater, and then to the southwest, arriving at Gagarin from the north, instead of the east. The talk group in Gagarin had located one in Nobel that had spent much of its first year discussing vehicles, and they proposed to do a test. Two convoys of identical vehicles would leave Nobel, starting at the leveled area near the main shaft, simultaneously on the two routes, and run according to the robot lunar driver rules until they reached the lot in front of the parking shed near the Gagarin main shaft. This was a seven hundred kilometer run, and to make the comparison more accurate, no stopping would happen. There were waystations on the old eastern route, but none on the proposed new route. This would mean thirty five hours in the vehicles, but they had sleeping arrangements so some alternation could be done. Robot drivers would do all the work once the sentiences had loaded in the approximate coordinates. Gagarin came up with six seventeens to do the measurements, and Nobel did the same.

There was a constellation of navigational satellites in low orbit around Luna, so there would be no chance of either convoy erroneously departing from the route. The only point of contention was the time of the lunar day to do the test. The test would have to be conducted during lunar night because there were no shields built along the new route to protect the drivers in the event of a severe solar storm. Thirty five hours was well beyond predictability from any of the sun sensors that Earth or Luna used, so it would be done at night, but a seventeen from Gagarin suggested ending at sunrise, just to make it more interesting and perhaps to allow a non-IR 3vid of the finish, if it was close. This would mean the sun would be directly ahead for the old route, obscuring vision, which might alter the test, so it would be done in the middle of the night.

Gagarin's team, on the new route, actually finished first, by twenty-one minutes, but Nobel's most dogged team member exhumed the driving instructions given to the Gagarin convoy vehicles, and found that the driving rules had been tweaked. It was trivially easy to give these commands, and have the robot drivers use slightly different rules. Gagarin's review of this noted it had happened, but the changes were so small as to be negligible. Nothing was decided. It was decided to rerun the race, three tendays later, when temperatures would be identical along with everything else, with the Gagarin team taking their convoy, with the tweaks still in, along the eastern route and the Nobel team along the western route. Extreme care was given to make sure the western path used by the Nobel team was the one followed by the Gagarin team. It would not work to simply try and follow the tracks made by the Gagarin team, as that might serve to slow down the trial.

The second trial, exactly a lunar month later, had the Gagarin team using the eastern route, but winning by four minutes, instead of twenty-one. Both teams had resolved their differences. The tweaks to the robot rules made a difference in the average speed, compared to their magnitudes, and the eastern route was slower. Digging into the tweaks indicated that the most significant change was in the spacings used in boulder avoidance. Running closer meant going faster.

This had been the first race run on the moon since Lunakhod 1 had first moved under its own power 651 years before, which is a very long time to wait for a green flag. It was almost inevitable that the Gagarin team and the Nobel team would propose to each other that it be done again. Together they proposed in public assemblies that the western route be equipped with waystations and that there be more competitions, with a relaxation of robot driving rules. The proposals wanted round trip races of seventy hours, starting and ending at the same mine. There seemed to be an almost unanimous assent at both of these meetings. Gagarin had some excavators outside its main shaft, and Nobel had some hauling machines, so with a little borrowing from Ague-Tuilet, simple waystations on the western route were in place in two and a half years.

The first two-way race was run in Nobel year 290, after much discussion on how to allow the robot driving rules to be relaxed. They are designed to keep the probability of breakdown below 0.01%, and if this was relaxed, to 0.1%, with no safety rule changes, there might be a contest with even more excitement. It went off as a timed race, as there was zero chance of one vehicle passing the other on the whole route. Gagarin finished in sixty eight hours, seven minutes and four seconds, while Nobel took sixty eight hours, eighteen minutes, and twenty four seconds. The race began to be run every quarter year, and it took two years before Nobel won once. The number of vacuum walkers watching the race grew with each race, and lunites had once again invented something appropriate to the moon.

On the 359th day of Nobel year 298, the seismic alarms went off in Nobel. Of all the bad things that can happen to people living in a lunar mine, a large asteroid strike and a large moonquake were the two at the top of the list. A large asteroid strike would be the worst in intensity, if it was near any of the mines, and a large moonquake would be almost as bad, but higher in probability.

There was an alarm system within the mine, with specific signals for different events. Seismic sensors were located inside the mine and also for many kilometers beyond it. They reported everything, but nothing was done for all the mild quakes that happened so often. Sentiences understand the interpretation of the different waves within the seismic signals, and as long as they are up, they can temper the alarms. If necessary, alarms go off within a second or two of the seismic sensors starting to ring in a way that signals a stress-relief quake. Thermal and tidal quakes are ignored, and are almost predictable from the orbit of the moon. Meteoroid impacts can be severe, depending on how big the meteor is and where it strikes, and these sound an alarm one way; stress-relief quakes sound an alarm with another pattern.

No mine had ever experienced a collapse-level quake, but there could be one as a result of a large asteroid strike directly overhead, that would cause collapse and more. Earth monitored asteroids, and nothing large enough to cause collapse level damage would be missed, as long as Earth maintained their telescopes and continued to analyze the data. With days or tendays of warning, a mine could be evacuated.

Asteroids do not appear out of nowhere, and centuries of mapping them had eliminated almost all of the possibility that something large and new would appear. It was possible, but barely. What was certainly possible was the entry into our solar system of an extrasolar asteroid, but these were few and also detectable in most cases. Warnings were possible. Moonquakes were not predictable. There would be no warning.

Stress-relief quakes originating below a mine would be the worst. Quakes like this lasted for many minutes, and everyone is trained to move quickly to the nearest suit, unless they were already suited and working in vacuum, and get out by the nearest shaft. Collapse does not necessarily happen at the onset of the quake. Little children learn the drill. Everyone practices responding by recognizing where they would go and what they would do.

Almost everyone realizes that having the whole population of the mine on the move at the same time will not lead to quick exits. There are too many people and too few shafts. There are suits everywhere, in cabinets in the residences, in common areas, in work areas in the habitation support facilities, in nurturing and training, and by the airlocks. There are far more than the population numbers.

Moonquakes happen all the time on the moon, and everyone who lives in a mine, even as a child in training, learns to get used to them. Externally driven ones come from tidal effects from the Earth, from thermal effects from the sun, and from meteoroid strikes from the asteroid belt. There are also internal ones, which are the most significant, and they can be dangerous to those living in a well-designed mine. They come from the deformation of the moon's crust in ages past. They originated from asteroid impacts. Whenever a huge asteroid hit the moon eons ago, the rock beneath the impact zone turned plastic and flowed. Further down, the rock was elastically deformed and compressed in the direction of the asteroid's motion. Some of that elastic deformation rebounded, but other parts of it were bound in place, full of stress and strain, as the plastic rock above it hardened quickly. Over millions of years, the crust of the moon has been relaxing its buried stress, and this often took place abruptly, as a fracture formed and a section of rock moved with it. When this happens, the moon has moonquakes reverberating around in it. The areas that release are small compared to Earth's quake areas, so the energy is much, much less, but it can still be threatening to those inside a mine near the crater where the quake originates. Unfortunately, asteroids did not know to avoid those areas of the moon's crust where there is a huge supply of useful minerals, so craters populate good areas as well as bad ones.

Centaurus pioneered habitable mines, and had good statistics on the different types of earthquakes even before the first earthlings started to live inside, 184 years before Nobel was founded. The shape of drifts was done to maximize strength, and stopes were trimmed and opened up to reduce the likelihood of any rock falls. Resinous coatings lined the surfaces of habitable areas that would be pressurized, and it became visible very quickly if there was a stretching of the coating from a fracture, so it could be re-coated or otherwise repaired. There were no long straight runs of anything, either piping or cables, that might be snapped from the vibration of a moonquake, and most distribution was done by vehicles with storage tanks.

The lifts in the main shaft were one vulnerability, but isolation was used to keep them from responding, resonantly or not, to the shaking of the rock surrounding them. Shields cover hazardous materials, such as hydrogen tanks, so that anything short of a major collapse would not cause further disaster by releasing the contents. A collapse of the area around an airlock was the worst possible situation. A sudden loss of air in a habitable area was a severe problem. Seventeens were genetically designed to withstand vacuum as much as possible with minimal negative consequences, but the obvious limits were clear. Getting to the nearest suit quickly with a strong wind blowing down the corridor could be impossible. The residents were as well prepared as they could be.

On day 359, people were frightened. It was not a test, it was a quake, and could be felt just as well as heard via the alarms. People started moving to where they hoped they could get a suit. People off shift, in their habitations, even if asleep, had the good fortune of being able to go to their own cabinet and get a suit with an air tank, and put it on. Others had to travel, and think clearly about where the nearest store was. Everyone received instructions as to where they were, but if the mine is going to come down on your head in a minute or two, can you actually remember? Those who got their suits on moved out into the corridors and drifts and headed for one of the shafts. Nobel has six secondary shafts besides the main shaft, and the six plus the main shaft have spiral stairways leading to the surface. The main shaft is in vacuum, so everyone had to go through an airlock to get to it. The airlocks would each hold eight seventeens, tightly crammed in. There are two airlocks on the first station and two more on the second. There were ten thousand people inside Nobel. It takes forty seconds to cycle the airlock. It is unworkable to just open both doors, as the wind from the inside would be too intense for people to get through. The secondary shafts have airlocks at the top of the shafts. They can hold four people if everyone squeezes in. That makes fifty-six people every forty seconds at the best of all conditions.

Those on work detail on the surface would be fine, as would those in suits in the ore processing area, the mining area, or anywhere else, except that the stairwells were long and strenuous, and the airlock problem would prevent them from being jammed. Secondaries did not go down to the mining levels, so the main shaft was the place to go, unless they wanted to travel up in a winze to the residential area, go in through an airlock there, proceed to a secondary, and get in line.

Evacuations are not planned because everybody knows they cannot work well. The seismic drills have everyone go to a suit and wait there, holding it and verifying the pressure in the air tank. Then everyone goes back to their work or back to sleep or back to their 3vid or talk group or lunch or whatever. On the 359th day, no one did anything except stand in a line, unbelievably politely, waiting for their chance to survive. The initial feeling in the line was that those fortunate ones, who either happened to be near the main shaft at the critical moment, or lived closes to it, would get out, and the rest would experience whatever Luna had in store for them. More than fortunately, almost marvelously, this quake was over the limits for alarms, but only caused a dozen or so tears in the lining of the habitable areas, a few rockfalls in the working areas, one in a pressurized stope and one in a nutrition area, crushing some specialty food arrays. No one was hurt by the falling rock, and there were no significant injuries from the partial evacuation, which had ended long before it was accomplished. This was minimal in physical effect and quickly restored. What did not go away quickly was the psychological impact of it.

This was the secret of Nobel and the other mines that was never discussed in talk groups. Just as no one on Earth living near a volcano spends their time talking about lava flows, the people living on the moon did not talk about moonquakes. There was no way to eliminate them, to set them off early at lower intensity, or to predict their coming. A mine can collapse, and people can be trapped inside with no air or crushed by falling rock. They could have suits with some air, but no way out and no communication. The preparations that were made were inadequate, if a large moonquake ever came.

There were people who were interested in moon quakes, even in Nobel, and their sentiences could collect the data from the hundreds of seismic sensors strewn about the moon from pole to pole. Lots of conclusions could be drawn. There were more on the farside than the earthside, but they were slightly smaller in magnitude. There were fewer than average in the centers of the large maria, with two exceptions. Per year, Gautama got the most larger ones, but the confidence in the estimates there was low because it had only been around a short time, compared to Centaurus.

The records of talk groups after the quake showed it was mentioned, but not taken up as the basis for any discussion. Strangely, there were many more missing members in the talk groups in general in the ten-days after the quake. Very few people fail to attend their talk groups, but it happened after the quake. The absences were not from injuries or relocations, they were simply the result of just staying away.

Nobel residents had been planning their tricentennial celebrations, when the quake struck, a year and a day before the 300th year started. The seventeen who had won the lottery to head the tricentennial committee called for three tenday hiatus in meetings, after the moonquake, and this stretched for two more tendays before the committee resumed its work. The occurrence of the quake in Nobel, the first of this size that shook a mine on Luna, and the first to trigger stress-quake alarms, had some effect on residents in other mines. Some 3vids of the damage became very popular, as did those showing the repair work. Other 3vids showing the congestion in the drifts and in front of the airlocks also seemed to be viewed more than anything else from Nobel.

It was clear from every sentience and every other source that there was no reason to believe that Nobel would be hit by another quake soon, or before any other mine, and certainly not during the tricentennial. But choosing to travel to another mine's tricentennial or any festival is not wholly based on logic, but also on feeling, maybe whim or intuition. The first sign of this reluctance was the scheduling of the flying stope. The entire year before the tricentennial year had been set up so that visitors could come to Nobel, get a time slot, and practice here where the exhibit and competitions would be. It didn't book up immediately, as was expected. Neither did the wall-jumping area.

There was an attempt to obtain confirmed agreements for some of the first few tenday's activities, which were certainly light. Records of the tricentennial committee's meetings indicate that the Gagarin-based thermal processing of food mixtures demonstration took four contacts before any agreement was made about the visit. Bringing pets from Boötes was expected to be a problem, as the committee wanted both ground animals and flying ones, and the arrangements were only made after not two but four long trips to that mine. Frank discussions were had at Boötes about the safety of the pets in the event of another quake, but it was the exception rather than the rule that quake recurrence was never discussed.

The tricentennial had events every tenday of the entire year. The number of competitive sports played in Nobel had increased quite a bit from the time of the bicentennial, and now there were competitions, not only in flying, wall-jumping, and ladder gymnastics, but also in three games with balls and one with disks. The competitions were always structured the same way, with a competition within each mine followed by a tournament with a final championship game. Because of the much larger population of the Centaurus mine, they were the favorites in everything, but events did not always follow that pattern. Most of the teams had not seen each other play until the tournament started, so there were unknown and unexpected tactics happening in each competition. Centaurus was able to take top honors in only half of the competitions.

In only a few years, road races had evolved into something that could be competed on. Six of the mines wanted to race the Nobel-Gagarin round route, and five did, with one being disqualified because the sentience on Nobel in charge of determining if a vehicle met the standards disagreed with the decision that was expected in Ague-Tuilet. So, an inter-sentience discussion took place after the ruling, to make sure that every mine on Luna had a perfect copy of the measurement rules and algorithms used to qualify a vehicle. Again, this was not the most fair competition, as both the Nobel team and the Gagarin team had raced this course a dozen times, while the others had done it, not under race conditions, only once or twice. Gagarin won handily, with Nobel in coming second with a time seventeen and a half minutes longer. Gagarin had obviously saved some modifications to its vehicle for this tricentennial competition, instead of having them become obvious to all the competitors when they were used in a Nobel vs. Gagarin run.

Both Centaurus and Ague-Tuilet had taken up the hobby of plant genetics over the last few decades, and both mines trucked their own creations over the lunar surface to be displayed in the stope in Nobel, in their own boxes right next to the ones grown in Nobel. There was no doubt that this was a transplant from Earth. For centuries, artistic genetics had been a popular art form on Earth, both for professionals who competed in competitions and amateurs who simply designed according to their own whims. Earth was so far beyond what Luna could ever hope for that the plant genetic display in Nobel was not highly appreciated for the creations, but instead mostly for the fact that this had been done on a satellite, which had been devoid of plant life for billions of years, and now humans had changed that.

On Earth, artistic genetics had long since left behind the growth of unique and appealing plants, and had moved on to the generation of entire ecological systems, able to sustain themselves for a long period. There were park areas inside the arcologies where a set of cooperative and competitive plants lived, usually behind transparent shields. Inside more tightly enclosed containers, there were insect creations as well as animals. There were combined insect, animal, and plant ecologies, plus many that contained creatures that transcended the boundaries between the lifeforms that had evolved.

Outside the arcologies, there were areas devoted to a single ecological system, maintained in the exact state that the designer had originated. Earth had long ago been overwhelmed with migratory species, that had evolved in one area but somehow were transported to another, which had upset the local ecology. After centuries and centuries of this, the biogeography of Earth was more uniform, and there was little concern about the escape and migration of park creatures to other areas. They would be uniformly outcompeted by what lived there now. The ecology parks, on the other hand, were maintained in their original form, and further, what had been developed for them had been long ago recorded so that lunites could copy any genetic code they desired.

On Luna, artistic genetics was more or less like copying a recipe, rather than delving deep into the ontology of the genetic code. Hundreds of years of genetic inventions on Earth had somewhat exhausted all the best options, so there was not much hope of some novelty that had not already been tried before, and was even on exhibit somewhere. Genetics was long ago completely understood, so a sentience could translate a design into a genetic code, attach to it all the necessary requirements for creating the new masterpiece, and then allow it to flourish in a lunar mine interior. Space was at a premium inside a mine, so there was little area that could be set aside for genetic creations, but there was some. By the tricentennial, almost every larger mine had followed Nobel's lead and had their own small garden patches.

The Nobel tricentennial committee had necessarily devised an estimate of how many visitors there would be during the thirty six tendays of the tricentennial year. These estimates were based on who had attended during the bicentennial celebration and the one held at the half century mark. Sentiences used this data to figure who might be coming and when. These estimates were widely available, but very few lunites took them into account when making plans to visit Nobel for some particular tenday or two of the celebration. The committee soon came to realize that there were many vagaries that influenced the decision to travel the long distance to Nobel from the other mines. The estimates were mentioned repeatedly in talk group recordings, almost always followed by a laughter break. The temporary housing was either half empty or overcrowded. The number of visitors who stayed with friends varied from tenday to tenday.

Nobel was, like all mines, possibly excluding Centaurus, a very calm environment to live out one's time. Things moved slowly, with much discussion and deliberation, and reason always prevailed. Thus, it was quite unusual for nobelites to experience the level of chaos that accompanied the tricentennial. Many remembered the previous celebrations, and that helped to mollify the average nobelite who was there for the tricentennial. Seventeens were genetically constructed to be rather quiet and tolerant individuals, which played out well in the confines of a mine. Every cohort was given the same genetic diversity, so that some of each cohort would be more cheerful than others, some more spontaneous, some more extroverted, some more nervous, some more tasteful, and so on, but when too many quiet and tolerant individuals are thrown together in unusual and very active circumstances, what little temper existed within the seventeens flared up. People actually raised their voices during the tricentennial exhibit days.

Having visitors and celebrations did not mean that all work in Nobel came to a halt. Most of the work tasks continued, and while there may have been some juggling of time, everything was still properly monitored and controlled. Some bulges in activity occurred, with nutrition preparation being the most notable. Hospitality is paramount within the lunar mines, and that meant that visitors should be served specialty foods if at all possible. Anyone traveling hundreds of kilometers across the lunar surface deserved good treatment at the destination mine, and nobelites almost unanimously agreed with that. But specialty food is grown, and the facility is sized for the population of Nobel, with some excess. The excess was put to full use, but still the celebration meant that nobelites would be shortchanged on their own consumption of specialty foods. This was discordant. Changing one's work schedule so that attendance at, say, a flying competition, meant to most nobelites that this was a time for a special meal. Something could be done with the standard components of nutrition, perhaps by increasing the dosage of flavorings and using some of Gagarin's thermal processing methods, but without specialty foods, meals were somewhat bland.

Eating in Nobel had a sort of rhythm to it. People ate interesting snacks when attending a talk group, meeting with friends, sometimes when being mentored, and when engaged in some non-scheduled activities. On non-work days, special meals were prepared. These sometimes need specialty foods, backed up by the standard ingredients. As a habitat had some minimal equipment for nutrition work as standard and options existed, some nobelites did this preparation, Some never prepared anything, and everyone ate many of their meals in the common areas. One corner of a common area was usually reserved for specialty meals, while the rest were for quick and simple dining. Work days and individual task days might involve just some standard meals, replete with perfect nutritional requirements, but not taking much time or deserving of much attention.

During the tricentennial year, especially during the more popular tendays, nobelites had to depart from this pattern so that the meals of the visitors could be of the highest caliber. This was agreed upon, and more than agreed upon, almost universally assented to. Nonetheless, seventeens responded to their food choices being restricted with some negative feelings. Talk groups during the tricentennial year show that there was much comparison made among members as to what they had been able to eat during the last tenday, and a good amount of grumbling about the lack of proper preparation by the Nobel tricentennial committee, especially in nutritional areas. Having to eat the wrong food at the wrong time was a usual conversation topic. How the tricentennial committee could have done better was even more often discussed.

The Nobel tricentennial committee had taken two and a half years in advance to plan for the events, but because of the moonquake, some of that time was lost and some was less productive that it would have been. Many people gave them a pass for having to do their planning in a challenging period of time, but not so much in the area of nutrition and its preparation and distribution. There had been countless opportunities for seventeens from Nobel to participate and offer sage advice to the committee, but not many did, reserving their comments for after everything was planned and the tricentennial was underway.

A half year after the tricentennial concluded, two talk groups merged temporarily to discuss what might have been done better for the tricentennial celebrations. None of the members of the tricentennial committee were part of these talk groups, so it could be considered a review of their selections and choices. The events were almost uniformly praised, and the reaching out to other mines for musicians, artists, chefs, and a host of other contributors was thought to have been well done. Scheduling was unobjectionable. Housing was somewhat less appreciated, with more preparation and more contingency planning on the list of recommendations. Nutrition somehow attracted some negative reviews. There was no option for constructing more specialty food preparation equipment, as the area where it was housed was already fully utilized. Storage of specialty food items was possible, but only at a loss of flavor. The dual talk group really did not have any magic solutions to this problem, other than to note that something substantial had to be done.

DIARY ENTRY (AGE 148, DAY 101)

In a talk group discussing the new humans, I got inspired and began to wonder what the other purposes of the new humans might be. Earthlings said they created them as insurance for human survival, in case of some catastrophe on Earth, or at least they said so. They were created after Centaurus was founded, had graduated to being self-sustaining, and even started a second mine, but back then it was by no means certain that Luna would remain self-sustaining and not suffer its own catastrophe, even less so for Mars. Mars had a permanently manned orbiter, the MPO, and a surface outpost that had been manned for decades, and the Martians were in the process of copying Luna with their own first mine. But the population was so small, it was not hard to imagine that they would go extinct in the blink of an eye. So it makes sense, since genetics out-raced space exploration and colonization, to have on-Earth insurance against catastrophes.

Luna and Mars did progress into much larger establishments, with multiple settlements on Luna as well, with no obvious indication of anything that could happen to terminate them. They both provided possibly better insurance for the survival of intelligence in the solar system for millennia to come. Exploration of other possible bodies where humans could survive and prosper was going on at a gradual pace, and while self-sustaining outposts were a question, ones with only a thin lifeline to other outposts were thought to be likely.

The situation was more of commitment. Once earthlings had generated such new human colonies, they could not simply erase them. The days of hyper-sympathy for all living creatures were long gone from Earth, and that was no barrier, but there was no efficient reason for allowing the colonies of new humans to disappear. The six new human species were created for specific environments, natural outdoor environments on Earth, not like the sixteens who were optimized for living in cities or better in arcologies. So new humans were simply supported through the passing centuries. Support was not a problem, even though Earth's population in the arcologies was down to under five billion, from a peak of over nine.

Still, I kept wondering if there were other reasons for them, both for their survival and maintenance, and wanted to try and figure something out myself. This particular question bothered me as I went through a few days of normal activities. Creating a list of possibilities was interesting for me. I could have asked my home sentience for a list of what other humans have recorded, but instead, I thought I would watch them for a while for inspiration. Nothing in life replaces the thrill of figuring something out for yourself.

All of the new human colonies had hunters among their populations. At least initially, hunting was not so simple on Earth, due to the presence of intelligent predators. They were a result of some independent genetic exper-imentation, perhaps done with some feeling that intelligence would enable some Earth species to survive the changes that mankind had brought to the planet. Once loose, they multiplied, as they were actually better pred-ators. Perhaps the new humans were meant to eradicate them, and make nature once more safer for the sixteens to explore. The smart canines and felines did hunt the same game that the new humans did, and so they would certainly come into contact. I watched some 3vids that my home sentience had selected from the huge reservoir available, all involving hunting. Some of them did involve the new humans meeting a pack of wolves, and one had a group of tigers, which were obviously new genetic creations, based on their head size and shape. There were a few kills. Perhaps time, the new humans would eradicate the new predators, but there was no dedicated effort on the recordings.

Then the idea washed over me, with a mixture of surprise and shock. Perhaps the new humans were meant not to exterminate the new predators, but to wage war with those original humans who had rejected civilization and who were also living in nature. Sixteens might not take on such a task, but could they create hitmen to do it for them? Why would they? The origi-nals did no harm to the sixteens, and simply lived their lives in nature, albeit sometimes violently. More and more space was available to them as nature reclaimed all of the agricultural areas from the days when food was grown on the ground rather than being generated in factories. The population of originals in the arcologies and cities was shrinking, and compacting more and more with each successive decade, as originals either left or didn't reproduce sufficiently. Earth was not industrially gestating originals any more. What possible reason could the sixteens have for wanting the eco-logical originals — those outside the arcologies and cities — gone?

The originals could be said to be providing the same type of catastrophe insurance that the new humans did. They were spread everywhere around the globe, not in large numbers, but enough to provide a gene pool to restore humanity. They had rejected, partially or wholly, the genetic improvements that led to the sixteens, and to the outpost humans as well, so they lived short lives, were not so smart, and had other features that the sixteens would never have left in their own genes. Perhaps the sixteens were afraid that if the originals were the only survivors, all the genetic advances made in leading up to their species would be lost. But my home sentience could not find any 3vids of the interactions between new humans and originals. So the idea is still tentative.

DIARY ENTRY (AGE 169, DAY 44)

My first spot in my current work task in nutrition was in the main constituent section. This is my third work assignment in nutrition, actually my fourth if you count the one I did in mentoring. The last two also started out in the main constituent section. Maybe that was just chance, or else they always start terms there. During the mentoring tour they started me in red specialty foods. I would guess that was from a desire to impress me, so perhaps I would request nutrition assignments in the lottery more than otherwise, or maybe it was just chance.

I have just switched to my second spot, which is yellow specialty foods. None of my co-workers here prefer working with the main constituents, preferring flavorings or specialties or liquids or something. I actually like working in the main constituent section and would not have been unhappy if they left me there for more than a half year. There is nothing visually attractive about the main constituent area, just vats, piping, meters, displays, siphons, power take-offs, and all industrial accessories. There are aromas there, just like there are in every part of every nutrition facility, but the main constituent aromas are not what make me most comfortable there. The temperature is the same, so is the humidity, within a range, and that's not very interesting either. It makes me feel like I am part of a large machine, which is unusual, but it happens. And that's what I like.

On Earth, I would have felt like a part of something larger more frequently, because biological mechanisms are much more prevalent. Because of our distribution of ores, we use almost exclusively mechanical things. But here in the main constituent area, almost everything is mostly biological, just like I am. It's a strange feeling of kinship between a human and a vat of neo-algae, and I know most humans think of themselves as more akin to a sentience than to a vat of living matter, even the complex kind we have in the vat. It is a micron-sized network of connected fibers, with small nodules at each node to do the chemical processing. The very slow flow through the vat changes the chemical constituents of the fluid, so it is depleted of input materials and energy-containing materials and augmented in output materials and energy debris. The thought of that does not make me feel this kinship, but it is the array of vats of different kinds, arranged in a kind of network of flows, much like the flows of blood, oxygen, and food through my body. It is a strange, but comfortable feeling.

In the main constituent area, I interacted with the sentience running the processes and the sensors checking everything, not with the microbes. There are many stages of processing, chemical and biological, between the initial large vats and the output constituents. So there is nothing to taste or smell there. In the yellow specialty foods area, everything is based on sight and smell. The only living things are the food items on the prongs of the supply array, and everything else is mechanical, but these items can be watched and monitored directly. They do not taste very good until the day they are due to be harvested, but almost every day there is something reaching that stage, so I am forced to taste and sample day after day. I have my own preferences in specialty foods, and there are many in the yellow area, so it is like a treat. I have worked in many aspects of nutrition during my previous three nutrition assignments, from man-agement to distribution preparation, serving preparation, and hygiene. Distribution preparation was pretty interesting, where main constituents and specialty foods are carefully loaded onto vehicles to be brought to the commons dining areas and residential pickup points. All the specialty areas are mechanically very similar. As far as sampling goes, I prefer the green and orange.

Until two tendays ago, this red specialty area was a green specialty area, and had I finished my main constituent period earlier, I would have been in a green area for a while, and then helping with the changeover. My prede-cessor did that. Work shifts are six hours in a changeover, unlike three in normal production times. I also enjoy longer shifts, and especially change-overs, where there are so many details to check that the automatons have done everything correctly and completely. I did two changeovers before in previous assignments; once from yellow to red in my first time after the mentoring one, and once from purple to orange in my second one.

In my current work assignment in nutrition, I will almost inevitably have to work in flavorings and serving, as management rules indicate some distribution is helpful for some reason I forget. My sentience says it is to remind each area of the output restrictions and their implications as inputs elsewhere.

In mentoring, I took lessons on taste and texture appreciation, so we could all enjoy our foods more. Initially, it was mostly genetics of taste sensors, but there was some actual appreciation in the Commons dining areas. That was one of the more memorable mentoring assignments. I remember doing it in training as well, without the heavy genetics load. From my friends and talk group associates, I understand that nutrition is a prized lottery choice for work assignments. I am fine here, but I would rather do vehicles or ore processing. That is why I do not mark it first in the work assignment request scoring.

DIARY ENTRY (AGE 182, DAY 45)

In our day five talk group, Magan (brown/silver) hosted it and started the discussion by stating that he thought the idea that Luna dwellers could rescue Earth after a catastrophe, and restore Earth civilization was absurd and impossible. His argument centered on timescales and resources.

If Earth was again destroyed by a basalt flood, which has happened many times already in ages past, it would be tens of thousands of years at the least before the flooding stopped and Earth began to return to a more normal state. For Luna to do anything, we would have to wait for this length of time, and then try and figure out how to proceed. Most species of life were destroyed during previous mass extinctions such as the ones caused by basalt floods, as the atmosphere became acidic and temporarily opaque.

Magan tried to depict what would happen to human civilization when one of these started up. Humans on the surface, new humans, originals, anyone outside the arcologies would perish without some sort of protective habitat. As far as we knew, there were no bunkers connected with these settlements. As for the arcologies themselves, if they were distant from the flood zone, they might be able to last on internal resources for some years. But power plants are always located a distance from an arcology, and they would soon fall into disrepair with no human intervention. Robotics could keep them running, but a hundred years duration would be questionable. Magan said that there would have to be periodic shipments of materials from the arcology, and even with that, taking the steps necessary to close down one reactor after it reached its recycle point and build another with no outside contact would be impossible.

Then he talked about an asteroid impact. A big enough one would destroy all the arcologies with the shock and heating of the impact. As for a small one, arriving somewhere near one arcology, the rest of Earth would combine to do emergency reactions and then rebuild, and Luna would just sit by and watch. We do not have the resources to do this, and we do not have the transport capability either. So what is the point?

Botosh (solid blue) had obviously been thinking of this, and perhaps knew this would be Magan's topic. Magan allowed Botosh to speak, even though he had not finished his own introduction. Botosh spoke about how Luna was founded centuries ago, when earthlings still remembered their own horrible times. Back when they had agriculture, there would be regional crop failures, leading to mass starvation. They had wars with each other, that were very destructive of everything in their societies. One region might threaten the other with nuclear weapons, and that threat has been followed through on, fortunately only on a small scale. They had had epidemics, both with naturally occurring and with man-made agents, with large fractions of a region's population dying out, taking the economy down. Botosh thought these were the situations that inspired Earth to think of Luna as an insurance policy, even though they talk about geological or astronomical calamities instead. Botosh was quite vivid in his description of the terrors that existed on early Earth.

No one spoke up immediately after that. As seventeens on Luna, we have grown up in an ordered, calm, efficient society, albeit much smaller than those on Earth. To contemplate that humans could survive such disasters was a shock. I am not that much different from other seventeens, and to think about slaughter and starvation is a difficult leap. It is like something that can hardly be imagined, not because of the horror of it, but because it is such a hugely different thing from anything we have ever experienced. We don't see 3vids of these things, nor do we listen to audios of people screaming. It simply does not make sense to us, any more than the majesty of Earth's or Mars' canyons does to someone who has never stood on the brim of one. I didn't say anything at all.

Jakap (red with lighter red stripes) stated that he disagreed that it was ancient Earth perils that motivated the earthlings to originally found the lunar mines, but the first ones Magan mentioned, basalt floods and asteroids. He said that it would be necessary to consider a continuum of catastrophes, with the duration and size of the floods as one variable, and the size of the bolide as another, remarking that speed would not vary much. Somewhere between the lower limit where earthlings could help one another sufficiently and the upper limit where destruction was so massive nothing could ever be done to restore human civilization on Earth, was a window where Luna might play a role.

Then Magan resumed talking about where on Luna we would ever find the resources to build large numbers of rockets to use to assist Earth.

we could obviously not land there ourselves, but we would have to build something in space that could gestate sixteens again and train them to rebuild their planet. we would be providing the knowledge, and they would do the actual rebuilding. They would have to start over, in a way similar to how we start a new mine, and gradually restore functions one by one. we would help with some resources, but rocket propulsion is so expensive, compared to the amount of waste a 99% recycling society has, that we would not be able to do much in that direction.

There was much more discussion, but these were the highlights.

DIARY ENTRY (AGE 187, DAY 4)

Soton (blue dots), was the host of the day five talk group today. He decided to take the option of watching a 3vid from Earth instead of simply choosing a topic, so we all sat facing his projector so it could find our retinas. Sometimes a talk group will just go silent after a 3vid, no one having any novel comments to make, but often one will inspire us to start a topic. He had his home sentience connect to a feed from Earth, in particular, one from a drone over one of the large settlements of what Earth called 'new humans'. I watched for a while, and then I surreptitiously asked my own home sentience which one of the new human species had brown hair and very long hands. I had remembered one of them having long hands, but I couldn't recall which continent they were installed on. This was Earth's other insurance policy and had absolutely nothing to do with Luna, so I can be forgiven for forgetting. With Earth's population reduced to about four billion, and concentrated in large arcologies, they were concerned that a catastrophe might happen and wipe them out. The new humans were supposed to be better able to survive and lead to a restoration of the population over a long period of time. This made little sense, and we up here are sure that every sentience on Earth told them so, but they did it anyway. Humans make large decisions, not sentiences.

I have witnessed all six of the different new human species many times, and it is simply not that intriguing to watch their daily lives one more time. My mind started to drift. Soton has the right to start the discussion by suggesting a topic, and politeness means we should seriously consider it, but if he starts by asking why they did it, I already have heard this discussed multiple times and have some good starting points of my own. I could speak for the whole period of the talk group on it, but of course that would be rude in the extreme, and I don't think I could let myself be rude in the slightest degree. So I needed to think of the best points and concentrate on them.

My home sentience indicated to me that these long-handed new humans lived on the coastline of the big southern island-continent, and began volunteering information on their diets and numbers and what not. "Not important", I replied, and the distracting chatter stopped. I started preparing again, and thought I would let someone else make the blunder of saying it was for their amusement, not insurance, because, after all, they have so much observation going on. Sixteens wouldn't observe each other so intently because it would be a serious politeness violation, so they created six new human species in interesting locations so they could entertain themselves watching them. I am going to say that they don't take much effort to sort out interesting events on the observation channels, so it would likely bore people on Earth. I can't say that so bluntly, but I will phrase it better.

Soton had his home sentience switch the feed to another of the new human settlements, the northern one where the people are large with large eyes as well. I recall their eyes have more reception down at the red end of the spectrum, but I forget why. Where is Soton going with this? I did a triple blink to signal to the projector to stop beaming me, and turned to look at the right wall. How had I missed this before? Soton had eight static pictures of hands showing on his wall, which is an unusual way to prepare for a talk group, unless he is going to start the discussion with something about hands. A quick request to my home sentience to check my diary for the last few talk group meetings at Soton's house reminded me of one of the others, where he started with a mechanical presentation on hand design, bone strength, joint lubrication, and other related topics, and we talked about why the trade-offs were where they were.

It looks like we are going to compare the hands of different new human species. Soton was already on another new human species when I signaled the projector to resume beaming to me. I had my home sentience remind me of what I recorded in my diary from that previous talk group. A warm feeling came over me, like it does every time I use my diary to help me out in some situation. No one knows I keep one, and I don't know of any other human who does, so it will likely remain my secret until I am ready to reveal it. Now, the last hand discussion spent a lot of time on muscle cell choice, so I want to mention that at the beginning. Then there's the question of how to optimize for grip strength and all the factors that come into play. Or perhaps I will put that first.

When Soton finished the 3vid show, he started to talk about fingerprints and why they existed and were unique to each human. The discussion went into questions of the genetics of skin and its outer surface, and then to questions of chaos. I had absolutely nothing to add. Dismay…

14

POPULATING LUNA

In Nobel year 303, some gurus in Centaurus proposed to the other mines that a new group be formed, with members from all mines, to discuss a question of great importance. It was a measure of the importance of the topic that the Centaurus invitation involved a physical meeting every six tendays for the next year. Traveling across the lunar surface was a chore, so this was a clear indicator of how important the Centaurus leaders thought the topic was. The topic was population limitation on the moon.

Prior to this invitation, the subject had come up only sporadically in a few talk groups in different mines, never as something that was urgent or even topical. The invitation was triggered by the total moon population passing a hundred and twenty five thousand, with almost two-thirds of this in Centaurus itself. The invitation did not propose any course of action, or even a hint of a recommendation. It was solely an indication that the time had come to begin such a topic.

Shades of Earth! This topic had been discussed for over five centuries on Earth, and had resulted in a wide variety of decisions. On Earth, there was not a homogeneous population of only sixteens, but instead many originals, new humans, and some older species especially eights, all maintaining their own populations. Sixteens were all bred in gestation facilities, so controlling the population of sixteens simply meant turning the gestation rate up or down. Sixteens were the large majority of the population at this time, so their choice had a grave influence on the total population.

Conflicts had arisen between the originals still living in the arcologies, and at one time, a hundred years ago, they had led to some disturbances of the peace of life in a few arcologies. Less originals remained inside, but the population outside had grown, not just due to the out-migration, but also to a reproduction rate higher than the death rate. New humans' population was influenced by the oversight of the sixteens, and had also been increasing, but from a very low starting point. The eights and other earlier species, all of whom could breed within their own populations, were just a small fraction of the total. Earth's discussions of this had exhausted the subject, and Luna would start off its own review of the topic by examining what had gone on there.

The principal issue for Earth's the sixteens of Earth had been resource consumption. Interplanetary transportation of resources just was too expensive in terms of energy expense. With recycling, mineral resources were used sparingly, but they were used, and each century saw usage continuing, although it was gradually dropping, even on a per capita basis. The lifetime of the human species, living at the standard of living present in the arcologies, was a million years at a population of a billion, and there was an obvious trade-off between the numbers and this duration. Keeping the population at five times this for many, many millennia would not make a noticeable difference in the duration, as long as the population got down to a billion in less than a hundred thousand years, but still the sixteens discussed it as if the problem was imminent.

The originals, at least those living outside the arcologies, had less concern, as they had sustainable lifestyles using almost no non-renewable resources. Agriculture was an understood field, and for the past few centuries there had not been depleted fields, polluted waterways, or other signs of a disruptive lifestyle. Their population was too low to overpower the planet's cycles, and so it was said, jokingly, that they would be here until the sun expanded too much. By that time, life everywhere in the solar system would be long extinct.

Two divergences in the discussion on Earth concerned life off Earth. One of these was devising ways for life to be self-sustaining. Only Luna had accomplished that. All the other outposts were dependent on supplies coming from Earth, and this supply train was expensive in terms of resources, with much more energy being used to deliver supplies than to obtain the supplies themselves. One of the divergences involved Earth's support for the Jupiter wheel, a huge outpost orbiting Jupiter way beyond the orbit of Callisto, devoted to seeking how to extract energy and resources from Jupiter and its four large satellites. There seemed to be no end to ideas from Earth on how to do this, and no end to earthlings volunteering to do a work assignment on the wheel in support of one idea or another. Nothing had worked so far. The resources were rich there, and there were huge amounts of energy present. Even Jupiter's magnetosphere had so much energy that tapping it somehow could easily supply all the outposts. But the method of doing this had yet to be resolved.

The other divergence involved the next planet out, or rather the Lagrangian point of the next planet, where huge telescopes were being built for the purpose of exploring distant solar systems. In the cold of Saturn's orbit, apertures of more than a kilometer were being built with minimal amounts of structural material. They were fragile, but nothing there perturbed them enough to harm the focus. There again, Earth was spending its resources, and there again, nothing had turned up. So far, of all the thousands of planets scanned, there were no new Earths waiting for humans to come and start a new world. Colonization was harder to accomplish than was hoped for.

Luna's discussion of its own population choices was much simpler than those on Earth. Few earthlings stayed for long in Centaurus, so the population was almost all seventeens, and Centaurus and the other mines could decide on how much gestation of new seventeens they wanted. Almost no seventeens had ever volunteered to go to the Jupiter wheel, so there was little feedback or even involvement with it, and none of the seventeens on the GEO had worked on a Jupiter wheel project. There was a low gravity area there, so it was possible, but that was mostly occupied, if at all, by eighteens from Mars. The Saturn K-scope project did attract seventeens as volunteers, despite the long voyages out and back, but this did not figure into the agenda that Centaurus' initiators had set up. During the first meeting in Nobel year 303, it became clear that Centaurus was looking at reducing its mining operations by capping its population. A figure of a hundred thousand was used as a tentative target. They wanted other mines to participate in it, and help decide what the figure should be.

With Centaurus' population approaching eighty thousand, making a decision soon as to how to taper gestation was clearly important. A sudden stop would mean that demographics would be uneven and later, after the currently unknown lifetimes of the earliest cohorts of the existing seventeens had passed, gestation would have to be restarted. Better to taper it, and keep the age distribution somewhat flat. None of those who volunteered to represent Nobel are recorded as having any preliminary thoughts on the matter, with the exception of Sefin Storik Golas, whose presentation became well-known hours after it was given. Sefin's idea was that, first of all, population size should not be determined by resource consumption, but by its effect on the lives of the inhabitants. Second of all, he thought that population should be translated, using the average habitat density, into a volume and then a diameter of a mine, and then transportation across the mine should be considered. The idea might be summed up as saying that a mine should be of a size where an individual could go anywhere in it easily, and take advantage of any part of it. Otherwise, it would be like having multiple mines coupled together.

The presentation of the Centaurus members, who served as the leaders of the group, involved trying to match the longevity of the settlements underground on the moon with the expected survival of the arcologies on Earth, which would be the same interval during which travel between the two, or even communication, could continue. Centaurus' people were thinking of the original goal of the moon colony as being a backup human population that might assist Earth in any global catastrophe, but Sefin chose to ignore that, and concentrate on life on the moon as its own value. This was actually Earth philosophy, applied to a new setting.

To walk between the two most distant points on Centaurus, 5.5 kilometers involving two level changes, took a bit over 2 hours. Sefin thought this was a little high, but there were many places that new habitations could be added without increasing this, so he estimated that a population of three times the current one, 80 thousand, would be a tolerable level. This was strongly disputed by two members of the committee from Gautama, Rolos Thiser Habid and Ranik Thiser Gofit, obviously from the same cohort. They felt that the population of 80 thousand was enough, and any further excavation of the living areas should be to increase the per capita public space, as there were many activities that were constrained at this time. This was especially true in Gautama, but the two members from there had toured Centaurus for three days before starting the committee meeting, and felt the same held there.

More vegetation, more athletics, more parks, a pool, a better commons area, some more interesting designs for public spaces, balconies on stopes, and on and on. Gautama was known for its unique configuration, which was appreciated by members from other mines who had visited it. Having better common spaces changes the attitude of those living in it. The Thiser brothers, if you wanted to call them that, suggested that the next committee meeting be not in Centaurus, but in Gautama, so that the members could see for themselves some of the innovations that were possible, and how floor space in a mine could be used creatively, if there were enough of it, to make the lives of the residents there more interesting and more varied. Living in a mine presents itself as a difficulty, but seventeens had a mentality that was designed to cope with it and even enjoy such a confined life. This does not mean that seventeens would not enjoy even more large and diverse spaces.

The next meeting, seventeen tendays later, was held in Gautama. By this time, Gautama had completed its first roundabout, with residences on both the island and the periphery and a corridor running through the center. The lower floor was set up for a circular network of corridors, leading to all the facilities that a self-sustaining mine must have, plus more residences. On the upper floor of the island, there were vacant residences that the visitors occupied, and they met in a hall along the corridor two levels below. The meeting was officially hosted by the Centaurus leaders, but the initial day was spent, at the Gautama members' request, devoted to presentations by a planning group within Gautama, followed by a tour of the areas where the new facilities would be built. The rest of the meeting was devoted, not to any philosophical discussion of population limitation, or to the rescue of Earth in some situation, but to the ideas that living underground in a mine did not have to be somewhat dreary because of the nature of mines, but could be very enjoyable, if excavation was done solely for the purpose of making interesting spaces, and not simply reusing what had been opened up for mining.

Seventeens may be accused of having little capacity for enjoyment, preferring to be work-oriented and concerned with the efficiency of everything. Gautama had the same biological mix of seventeens that all the other mines did, but somehow they took a different track and wound up with different aims and different metrics.

The four meetings of the population committee following the Gautama visit were held in Centaurus, but they resulted in a recommendation to the public, in each of the mines, to limit population to a hundred thousand and to provide more space per person rather than more efficient use of resources to extend the horizon of life on Luna. No one actually wanted to shorten the time human beings could live on this satellite, but somehow the question of the quality of life became mixed in with the question of the quantity of life, and the results showed it.

This trip was somewhat of a boondoggle for members from the smallest mines, for their populations were so low, under a thousand people, that the concept of limiting population was so far into their future that there was little possibility that anything said at this meeting about a population cap would be relevant when their populations were sufficiently large to consider limiting them. Orion had a bit over two hundred people living underground. Their concern was to get all the sustainability facilities completed and lit off. They did have one non-sustainability item that they had pushed through, and that was to divert the Armstrong highway. It did not pass through Orion, and anyone wanting to use Orion as a stopover on the trip from Boötes to Armstrong had to take some extra hours to go to Orion. It had not taken long for the idea to dawn on them that if they put the minimal requirements onto a road from Orion to Armstrong, no one would take the old road, but instead come through Orion.

What was needed was a plot of a course, good checking for its suitability, and the erection of a waystation in the middle and another near the end of the new section, plus the usual communication beacons. Some Orion seventeen with a sense of humor erected a large post at the junction of the two roads, with three arrows: one pointing back to Boötes, another to Armstrong and the third to their mine. This was actually the first road arrow on the lunar surface, so even though it gave a laugh to everyone making the route for the first time, it was a landmark of sorts. It was totally unnecessary, as every vehicle had knowledge of exactly where it was at any time and where the roads were, but there are not many laughs on the highways on the moon and perhaps this was the only one.

Centaurus kept up their pace of starting off new mines, during the third Nobel century, making continuous use of the shaft sinking equipment, ore hauling vehicles and in fact the whole package of equipment and vehicles required to start a new mine. This process, starting a new mine, was completely different from living underground at an existing mine, and there was no shortage of volunteers for seventeens to do the task. This may have been the underlying reason that Centaurus put itself out for the purpose of starting this long series of new mines. Public meetings on Centaurus about the initiation of a new mine, whether it was something to do with the scouting of locations, the allocation of equipment, the diversion of excess ore processing capacity to dealing with shipped ores, or anything else, all seemed to quickly drive to a consensus to do it. Living in Centaurus, with all its people, space, and activities was certainly not boring for the average seventeen, but getting out on the surface and building a new mine, complete in all aspects, far exceeded the interest level of life inside.

Centaurus had set up a little committee to name the next mine after Orion, which was to be located even beyond Armstrong on the backside of the moon. This committee somehow failed to meet in person even once in Centaurus, and had several discussions by 3vid only. The naming process was not taken very seriously by this group, as there are hardly any records of them doing anything to reach out for suggestions, even within Centaurus, to say nothing of the other mines. Since records do not get lost on the moon, this is a sure indicator that virtually nothing was done. During the last 3vid meeting, after discussions of topics that had nothing to do with name selection, the committee leader suggested that they ask his sentience for the best name. No metrics, no guidelines, no conditions, no restrictions, just 'let's ask my sentience for a good name.'

The sentience responded to the question in some time interval too small for the committee to measure, with "Bardeen Brattain Shockley". Everyone on Luna knows these names are the three inventors who, many centuries ago, invented the transistor, which was one of the cornerstones of the second part of the industrial revolution, when computing and artificial intelligence, including the sentiences, were invented and turned into an essential part of the technology base. Their biographical history, in short form, is included in the mentoring of every seventeen who is gestated on the moon. So, there is no reason to think that this name would not be appropriate. The committee adopted it, but once their discussion became known, it was universally spoken of as the BBS mine.

The mine was destined for a location a little to the east of the Korolev crater, in a rich ore area similar to that where Nobel sits, replete with lithium in one area and less than three kilometers away, a thorium deposit. It was decided to sink the main shaft between the two, closer to the lithium deposits, as multiple other minerals were near to it. There were more in a third area almost forming an equilateral triangle with the first two. BBS had its initiation ceremony in Nobel year 269, and was in the midst of the equipping the mine with the usual facilities when the population committee was formed under Centaurus leadership. The distances to travel between mines were large, and the seventeen who was designated to go to Centaurus from BBS had to travel all the way to Armstrong, about 1100 kilometers to start, then to Orion and then to Boötes before making the final leg to Centaurus. That person was obviously a glutton for travel, for after making the trip back to BBS, he left again after sixteen tendays to travel to Gautama, which meant the same trip plus the long haul over maria from Centaurus to Gautama. He returned, and gave a public presentation on the ideas learned at Gautama.

BBS had not completely finalized where their facilities would be, or even more than the initial habitation. They were ripe for becoming something a bit unique on the moon, or at least in the same league as Gautama. For some reason, BBS was proceeding on an altered schedule for producing their initial structure. They had almost two hundred people working on the mine shortly after they set up their initial underground habitation, which was set up to hold one hundred and twenty, several times greater than the usual. It meant that habitation was delayed somewhat, but the pace for completing other parts of the mine would be higher. It also meant that more people valued the idea of a comfortable, decorative mine area for living, rather than the most efficient one that could be dug in the shortest amount of time.

It was a surprise to anyone following the progress of the new mine to see that it exceeded the population of Orion after only twenty years. Orion had not had much migration in, and had not yet gotten its gestation facility in place and operational. BBS simply surged ahead, and stayed ahead with more seventeens from Centaurus opting to go the longer distance to BBS than to stop at Orion or Armstrong, for that matter.

If BBS was a tremendous distance to the east, the second mine to be started in the decades before the Nobel tricentennial was a tremendous distance to the west. Centaurus' various committees and work groups which had put together the initial plan for BBS did not disband, although all the personnel rotated each two to five years. On Centaurus, there is no universal restriction in the job lottery for those who have already held one position from returning to it or a similar one. If the position is continually filled, they would have to wait until another seventeen or two or three had gone through their terms. That wasn't the case with the naming committee. Three of the people on Centaurus who had worked on the naming committee for BBS requested and wound up on the naming committee for the next mine. They had one 3vid meeting, which lasted less than thirty minutes, in which they decided to ask the leader's sentience for a good name. After all, the previous one had been universally accepted as a wise choice. Possibly few people on Centaurus knew the mechanism by which it had been chosen; some may have assumed it was the result of a long-drawn-out process of elimination.

The sentience instantly chose 'Forrester', who everyone knows was the pioneer who first developed fully thinking AI and who subsequently learned how to ensure they were perfectly controlled and worked under the direction of humans. Again, every seventeen learns the biography of Forrester, and especially the account of how an AI began to become uncontrolled, only to be thwarted by Forrester himself. If BBS had been a wise choice, Forrester was an even more wise one, as young seventeens seemed to idolize him, watching the antique videos of him as part of their training. Forrester was one of the influences, if not the most important one, used to accustom young seventeens to the tasks of monitoring that they would engage in for the rest of their lives. Forrester's personality lent itself to this task, as he was an original, and full of easily-displayed enthusiasm for what he worked on.

The Forrester mine was going to be put west of Ague-Tuilet, on the western edge of Mare Imbrium, making it a straight shot across the Mare to get from Ague-Tuilet to Forrester, except for a deviation at the end when the pathway snaked around some mountains to the northeastern edge of Oceanus Procellarum. This location left Ague-Tuilet in a strange position. It was only logical and efficient that they should be the mine that started up Forrester, and by this time Ague-Tuilet was sizable, both in population and in capacity. But Centaurus had done the start-up work, and then involved Ague-Tuilet as a junior partner rather than as the lead. That did not last. Centaurus got through the initial planning, the location selection, the first design of the main shaft, some initial ore exploration analysis, and the naming, and then a tense 3vid between the Centaurus committee and those put on the committee by Ague-Tuilet led to the transfer of authority.

Along with the transfer came the responsibility to house transient workers for the new mine, to process early ore from the mine, and to produce all the equipment needed for the initial portion of the mine, until they could process their own ore and manufacture their own equipment. It was a commitment of forty years or so. Seventeens are so motivated to sweep up tasks and accomplish them, that the switchover from Centaurus to Ague-Tuilet, once decided upon, went easily. There was still the problem of the mass of volunteers from Centaurus, who would have eliminated any seventeens from Ague-Tuilet had some restrictions not been applied. Centaurus was responsible for helping BBS finish the use of each category of equipment as early as possible, specifically the shaft sinking equipment and multiple types of vehicles and loaders, so that they could be transferred to Forrester. Since BBS was moving quicker than the usual mine startup, this happened sufficiently fast that Forrester inaugurated its underground living only twenty-two years after BBS had done the same.

The Forrester committee housed at Ague-Tuilet decided to organize the initial work for Forrester a bit differently, and invited Nobel to take full responsibility for the exploration of the ore bodies around the chosen site. LPO exploration and the grid of exploration done in the earlier days of lunar life had found sufficient ore there to warrant a mine, but was there even more, and exactly how large were the deposits? Nobel selected its own seventeens from a volunteer call, without inviting any other mines to mix in some of their personnel. That was the new style that Ague-Tuilet had decided on. They would do the initial thinking, but with Centaurus seventeens accounting for about half the positions. No other mines contributed people to this phase, except that Gautama was asked to provide help in making a layout.

Experience with the other mines had clarified some things about the way ore was distributed on Luna, and one point was that valuable ores went as deep or deeper than any exploratory drilling had penetrated. Centaurus had put drifts down to a kilometer deep and there was still ore there, just as rich as a hundred meters from the surface. The data from Centaurus was by no means enough to show just how ore was distributed in depth, but the contrary was in the horizontal direction. The maria had material that was usually too mixed to be worth separating, at least as long as better concentrations existed in so many other places. The maria provided good pathways for traveling without danger or obstructions, but for ore, other areas were better. This meant that eventually, the dark side of the moon would see more development than the Earth side, where all the maria were. The history of the moon, including its initial closeness to Earth, had left the maria on the Earth side. It was just logistics that put Centaurus on the Earth side, so communications would be easier and the back-and-forth rocket launches that characterized the first phase of moon development could be done in full view of the mother planet.

Nobel supplied the vehicles, meaning that they were transferred to Nobel and refurbished there for another few years of use on the lunar surface. Exploratory drilling needed to be done over a large area, but with only a few hours warning for solar flares, shelters needed to be built near enough to the drilling site so that everyone could evacuate the drill site and put some meters of insulation between the sun and their bodies. For the shaft workers, shelters could be constructed near the site so that they could easily retire there in the event of a flare warning, but typically, ore prospecting would require a race to these main shaft shelters. Given the necessary interruption time to put the drilling equipment in rest mode, the time to get to the vehicles and move with all due speed to the main shaft site, get out of the vehicles, and in through the shelter airlock, there was a limit of about twenty-five or thirty kilometers for exploratory drilling. Ore bodies might extend five kilometers in from the edge of maria, but most of the good hunting was in rougher terrain. Some of that was too steep for the rigs, so exploratory drilling might only cover a quarter or a third of the total footprint around a mine shaft.

Forrester was no different. Drill holes brought up good ore in fifteen percent of the holes drilled, which meant that Forrester would be a rich site.

Ore was present near the surface, and extended down, in the few deep holes dug, a kilometer or more, and most likely much more. Luna was a rich playground for miners. Nobel seventeens did a splendid job of mapping out the upper ore bodies, given the obvious restrictions, and then they went home with their equipment. That proved to be insufficient. The Forrester planning and scheduling committee invited Nobel to produce, deliver, install, and make operational the initial round of ore processing equipment, down on the fourth station of the main shaft. Nobel volunteers took on this task, but in the process of organizing the work with the rest of the team, principally Ague-Tuilet seventeens, they found it obvious that Forrester was going to be done by Ague-Tuilet faster than Centaurus did BBS, if only by a day. And it would be done using a new style of organizing the work.

Ore processing equipment involves a great deal of heavy equipment, and Nobel had to devote almost all of its own equipment manufacturing capability to putting it together, as well as divert some mining efforts from digging out nitrates, which were needed in inventories in Nobel and some other mines that shared a few materials, to digging out titanium and aluminum ores. If all the equipment was manufactured in one mine, Nobel, coordination delays would be reduced. Ague-Tuilet did the same thing with other categories of equipment. Nothing inspires seventeens like a challenge.

The ore processing equipment was on site, on a pad next to the main shaft, the day before excavations were completed in the first carve-out of the ore processing equipment bays. It was even packaged in blocks to expedite use of the main shaft hoist. Nothing better was done in this mine, as compared to others, and nothing more was done. It was just done a little more efficiently. Nobel seventeens came back with the knowledge that the ore processing equipment was up and running, eating the ore that came from Forrester's initial mining operations, four tendays earlier than the same mark had been reached in BBS, measuring from initial habitation. No measures are perfect in mining, as the ore types in Forrester were a little different than in BBS, but four tendays is a long time. No medals were given, no cheering was heard, it was simply that Nobel's volunteers felt very good about doing an excellent job. It was no surprise that no matter how much travel and other inconvenience was involved, there were never a shortage of volunteers for starting up a new mine.

Things could have gone quite differently. By the time Nobel was zipping through heavy equipment manufacturing for Forrester, Armstrong had had a couple of decades of running its asteroid detection array. Earth's observatories almost always had the first call on the detection of an asteroid, and there were few left in near-Earth orbits that were not known and precisely calibrated in their orbits. There were good pictures of most of them, and even before they were optically or electromagnetically detected, their positions just prior to detection were predicted, so they could be found with little delay. This left even more time for sky searches for new ones. Everything in the solar system larger than 10 m in maximum diameter, having orbits between Earth and Saturn, was well known. Six or seven centuries of observations had done a good job of sweeping the heavens for anything very dangerous to the Earth and Luna.

Armstrong had built a telescope for coordination with its microwave sensor, just in case something substantial was detected. It was not large, but sufficient. It ran in automatic mode while it was waiting for a call from the other detector. The automatic mode was looking for differences, and since there was no obscuring light sources, it could do fairly well for its size. Then, one night, it detected repeated short glints at forty five degrees off the orbital plane of Earth. The sentience scrubbing the data had correctly noted it, and all the scans were immediately focused in that direction. The velocity was too high. The object was interstellar. Earth did not co-detect it until several hours later, but it was confirmed to have an orbit heading for the Earth-moon system. Interstellar objects are so rare near Earth that this actually got the attention of a large fraction of the sixteens on Earth. They are certainly not rare within the whole solar system, but there is nothing to observe them anywhere but on the Earth or at Armstrong. A huge interstellar asteroid could whiz by the Jupiter wheel, and never be noticed. It could go between Mars and Phobos, and no one would be aware of it, except if some eighteen or a visitor to Mars had been staring up at the sky at just the right time.

Actually, it was a joke within Nobel that Martians spent an inordinate amount of time staring up into the sky, and this supposition was actually included in lyrics to an original-to-Nobel music piece. Whether they stared a lot or not is hardly likely to be recorded, however.

It took some time to get an orbit for the interstellar intruder, but initial measurements indicated it would pass close to Earth. That meant there was a possibility that Luna could be hit. Size measurements were not immediately available, but the fact that it was detected so far out using Armstrong's equipment meant it was big. There were about one of these every hundred and fifty years, averaged over the last millennium, and none had come within a hundred thousand kilometers of either Luna or Earth. Just for safety, warnings went out to all the mines, and from there to every seventeen on the surface. There was a chance that exterior work would be called off, and due to the unfinished character of Forrester, everyone there might be called back to a mine where there were more complete reconstitution facilities. For two days, the Nobel team was loading their equipment into the main shaft and unloading it at station four, all the while listening for the call to evacuate. It never came. The giant interstellar asteroid passed three hundred thousand kilometers from Luna, and more than that from Earth. Everyone knew that Luna would ring like a giant bell if this had hit the surface anywhere, meaning moonquakes and damage, possibly injury. If it hit close to a mine, there was no limit to what might happen. But this time, nothing did, as usual.

15

THE POPULATION DECISION

In Nobel year 325, Centaurus took the step of deciding they would target their total population at one hundred twenty five thousand residents, and came up with a tapering of the gestation schedule to accompany this. To come up with the number, the current chief of Centaurus residence management, who had somehow been given the task of population numbers and what to do about them, decided to have a quantitative vote. There had been a few instances on Luna where votes were held, as they were almost never needed as the process of converging different ideas was used constantly, just as it was in the arcologies, on Mars, and maybe on the further outposts. The chief was interested in simple mathematics and game theory, and understood that those who felt they wanted a larger population than most could vote for some outrageously high figure, and the averaging process would pull up the result. A small fraction of the voters, those who had shared this idea of unlimited population, could overwhelm the sentiment of the large majority. Those who wanted a very low population could vote for a population of one single person, and try to accomplish the same thing, dragging the average down. So Zizim Polob Tomaf, as the chief was named, devised a scheme to rectify this situation. Instead of averaging, the median would be used. That way, any vote above the median, no matter how extreme it would, would have no pull on the result. As soon as the voting was over, Zizim announced that the median was a hundred and twenty six thousand five hundred, and decided to round it to an easy to remember figure of 125,000.

By this time, the number of earthlings visiting and working in Centaurus had dropped to a mere three hundred, and they were excluded from the count. No one on the moon worked to encourage earthlings to come to the moon to work, as they were simply not needed. Luna was completely self-sustaining, and needed nothing from Earth, not materials or labor. The only substantial traffic was in information, as Earth was a library for everything, and there were lunites who were quite interested in the history of Earth, especially ancient history, and current events. The latter was a bit of a puzzle, as Earth was calm and stable, certainly in the arcologies, and almost all of the changes that happened there were just like shallow waves in a pond. Nothing substantial changed, but insubstantial things certainly did. An arcology might be organized by floors for a decade or so, and then news comes in about how another arcology had reorganized by vertical sectors and found the residents to be much more pleased with it. It's time to change. Sentience communicators for children might be found to be better as a necklace than a wristband in some other arcology, and so the training sections in some other arcologies would decide on a switch. Why not have seven fundamental nutrient components instead of five? More variety and choice. The change would happen in one corner of an arcology, and then spread to other ones, often before it had penetrated all the way through the arcology where it originated.

The population limit choices they had made were one piece of Earth news that did not seem to fluctuate with these waves. Earth did not have a target figure, but instead a reduction rate. Population was supposed to go down, but extremely slowly. Some considered this meaningless, as the census for non-sixteens was casual at best, particularly for the new humans and the ecological originals, but estimates were obtained and used.

Luna did not have that problem. The census for seventeens was exact, and verified by a dozen different sources. the population could easily be controlled and by tapering the gestation rate, there would never be a year in which there would be no cohorts of new seventeens, meaning less disruption in work assignments related to new seventeens. Centaurus' choice meant that the majority of the remaining growth in population would be happening on the other mines. This growth was going to be slow. The four next largest mines had reasonable populations and were growing, but the four smallest were not pressing the population button very hard. They were having only one or two cohorts a year, with the cohorts being small, so only of the order of a hundred new seventeens a year were being added to the total lunar population from these four mines.

Forrester was the exception, but not for overall number, but for the process. Forrester was producing one cohort every three tendays on the average, with a cohort size of – one. Every seventeen on Forrester was raised at least partially separately, like an only child from the old days of Earth. Forrester gestation chiefs had not gotten this plan from Earth, as no arcology had initiated anything like this. It was only appropriate for a tiny mine like Forrester. Naturally, for socialization, Forrester seventeens interacted with others a few tendays different in age, and the effect of this was somewhat uncertain. Earth didn't have any experience to draw on, except from the very earliest days of industrial gestation, where new originals were produced one at a time. Decision-making on Forrester was just as decentralized as on other mines, so it was actually the choice of one person at a time what size cohorts to have. Once this plan was started, apparently the successive gestation chiefs simply kept it up. No ill effects have been noted so far.

Perhaps having BBS and Forrester completed quickly and not far apart in time exhausted the sentiment for building new mines, for none were started for fifty six more years. Finally, it was Centaurus again who sounded the bell for a new mine. The next site chosen was even farther west than Forrester, and in fact, it was across Oceanus Procellarum. This was the best site for rare earth ores so far discovered on the moon. Just as on Earth, rare earths are not uniformly distributed, but appear in concentrated areas. Surely there would be more, but this new site was a good one. Centaurus did the route selection, and instead of staying on Oceanus Procellarum, and heading south around Eddington Crater, they chose to go through Russell Crater and then west. The route was almost a straight line from Forrester.

Forrester was far too small to take on the responsibility for starting a new mine, and could only contribute a volunteer or two to the process. Shortly after the choice of the site, the two largest mines on Luna, Centaurus and Ague-Tuilet, decided to handle the management of the startup operations at Ague-Tuilet, just as with Forrester. Centaurus committed many volunteers to the new mine, so that the committee managing the startup was not wholly seventeens from Ague-Tuilet, but as with Forrester, partially Centaurus seventeens. Nonetheless, the same formula for organizing the startup was going to be followed, and as with Forrester, Nobel was asked to run the exploration on the surface in the vicinity of the known rare earth ores. The new site had a sufficient share of the other critical ores nearby, such as nitrates, carbonates, and the rest, just as the other mines did, and they needed to be mapped out so the layout of the initial drifts could be done efficiently. Nobel started immediately with the preparations, waiting for the completion of the solar shield structures to signal that initiation was possible.

Nobel's exploration work went on simultaneously with the sinking of the main shaft, but it might have been better to slow down the main shaft. The detailed exploration work showed that there were indeed rich ores nearby, halide and hydroxide ores, along with some rich metal ores, chromium and manganese ores in particular, as well as others in lower concentration. But the ore bodies in the area around the main shaft in the rare earth ore region did not extend in all directions, but extended almost entirely to the south southwest. A bit of halide was to the southeast and some thorium to the northwest, but the large majority was to the south southwest. Ague-Tuilet and Centaurus decided not to sink a second main shaft in that direction and instead go with the single main shaft. This mine would have something of the longitudinal pattern that Gautama had, but it would be different in that Gautama was governed by a line between the two main shafts, where this new mine would be more of a network reaching mostly in one direction.

Forrester was swept into the new mine planning, scheduling, and organizing effort, even more than providing a volunteer or two. They were asked to come up with a name, which was possibly given like a token of appreciation for the hosting they had to do for all the convoys heading from Ague-Tuilet to the new site. Every one stopped at Forrester, the only mine along the route. Hosting is usually a pleasurable task for the residents of the mine that is visited, but Forrester is tiny, and the number of convoys was large, especially after the main shaft was dug and the stations laid out.

Three seventeens from Forrester wanted to be involved in choosing the name, and they were given free rein as to what it would be called. They chose Sirius, after the brightest star in Earth's sky. Some groups working on the new site had been calling it Balboa, after the nearest large crater. Nobel's exploration team referred to it as Forrester Two. One other group had called it Eddington, after an even larger crater, not as close as Balboa. Sirius stuck and replaced the others immediately.

Now Luna would continue its tradition of having no tradition at all for the names of its mines. Sirius was the first star name to be used for this purpose. One of the seventeens from Forrester who was on the naming committee said that they wanted something unique, from humanity's history, and since Sirius was so prominent in the night sky and used by all cultures on ancient Earth, they chose it. There was only one meeting of the naming committee, so it must have been an easy decision.

Sirius moved at the same pace as Forrester, and the initial underground habitation date, the inauguration of the new mine, happened in Nobel year 347. The exploration of the Sirius site had not completed by then, although much had been done, and Nobel continued to contribute volunteers and equipment. The inauguration date, while very significant for those working at Sirius, was not so important to the other mines, as any contributions they were making would continue for the decades to follow, as Sirius moved toward being a self-sufficient mine. However, Nobel year 347 was significant for another reason.

Long before, seventeens from Gautama and Gagarin had talked about a highway connecting the two mines. Now, to go from one to another meant going through Nobel, Ague-Tuilet and Centaurus, a long distance compared to the great circle route connecting the two. These two mines were still too small to build a connecting highway, or at least they considered that they were, and Nobel was asked to provide assistance in setting up the GG Highway. The GG Highway would have to travel almost exclusively through rough terrain, as the only flat section was a short piece through Mare Nectaris. If there had been a mare stretching between the two mines, maybe they could have stretched their capabilities a bit and done it themselves. Instead, it was going to involve a sinuous path, weaving around all the geographical features that the moon has. There were no huge craters with high walls on the route, but there were enough smaller ones that the highway would be far more interesting to travel than a great circle across a mare.

Gagarin and Nobel tended to interact with one another quite a bit, and Nobel easily found some seventeens, along with some equipment useful for highway construction that had not been consumed by the work for Sirius. Nobel, together with Gautama and Gagarin, started the highway in Nobel year 341, and it finished in 347. After the completion,

Gagarin hosted a small celebration to thank Nobel, and it was centered on some new dining experiences that nobelites, along with some guests from Gautama, came to enjoy. Gagarin had pioneered what one nobelite referred to as "eating in the dark." They had used an excavated chamber as a auxiliary commons area, but for certain occasions, they used tables that lit up, along with ceiling lighting, much of it in infrared, that only seventeens could appreciate in full. The light show lasted for the whole time of the meal, and the nobelites who attended left very impressed with what could be done by combining senses in this way.

Since planning for the three-and-a-half centennial had already started at Nobel, some of those who had been at the Gagarin celebration for the highway completion wanted to do the same thing at Nobel for their anniversary. There is no licensing of ideas possible on the moon, but the new centenary committee thought it would be much better to ask the Gagarin team, which worked out how to do the light show dinner spectacle, to do one at Nobel, and, in fact, to do it over and over again so those who came to the centennial for only a tenday or two could experience it. This was too much, and that Gagarin team offered to do it once every three tendays, which was still a large contribution. However, a facility would have to be found. At Gagarin, the spectacle was held in a chamber with twenty-four meter ceilings, enterable only through a normal-sized drift. Nothing like that existed in Nobel, and there was no point in building something so large to use only a few times in one single year.

Gagarin's team came to Nobel in 348, and scoured every square meter of useful space in Nobel, and found nothing even closely similar in geometry to their commons facility. At the end of their trip, they stated that there was a long, largely unused drift, only four meters high and five meters wide, that they wanted to appropriate. The Gagarin team said they would compose a brand new spectacle to match the facility before the centennial celebrations started, and the Nobel centennial committee was more than happy to have this happen. The show would be much more linear in extent, as the drift went on longer than was practical to use. As a result of this, Gagarin and Nobel formed an even closer bond, building on top of their racing history, which was still going on every half-year.

Gautama was also benefiting from the GG Highway that Nobel had contributed to, and their talk group records show it was appreciated there as much as in Gagarin. But Gautama was different in one way. By an accident of ore distribution, Gautama was built in a unique way, and that was taken as the Gautama way in every expansion of their mine that they did. At the time of the Nobel 350-year celebration, there were only two and a half thousand people living in Gautama, but the residential and living space there was more than twice as large per capita that in other mines, on the average. They were proud, as much as seventeens expressed that emotion, of their mine in that particular direction, but being so far away from the majority of the population of Luna, few came by to appreciate it. The GG Highway was meant to serve as an antidote to that isolation.

Gautama wanted to use it to full advantage. They contacted the Nobel celebration committee and suggested another road race be conducted, in addition to a Luna-wide competition on the Nobel-Gagarin loop. They proposed a race around the giant loop, Nobel to Gagarin to Gautama to Centaurus to Ague-Tuilet and back to Nobel, using similar rules. This was not meant to be a test of who could survive exhaustion, as traveling on many parts of the loop, especially the GG Highway leg, would involve multiple turns and climbs, so sleeping soundly would be difficult. Gautama proposed that each leg be run separately, with times collected for each and added up at the end. The team doing the racing would have a three-day break at each of the five mines on the loop. That would be more than enough time to tour Gautama, which they would surely want to do, complete with making 3vids of the teams on their tours. Each of the teams would need support staff at each of the stopovers, which Gautama would be happy to host in their finest roundabout lodging.

The Nobel committee looked at the proposal, not as something to do with any mine in particular, but as something that would set apart their centennial as a high point in any visitor's experience. No mine had anything comparable to the Nobel celebration every fifty years. And because there was nothing similar, all the mines wanted to be involved in some way. Tiny Armstrong wanted to participate on a regular basis. Armstrong had been busy for the last century in establishing themselves not only as a self-sufficient mine, but also as the home of Luna's only asteroid detection apparatus. They had achieve a bit of notoriety with their first discovery, some hours in advance of Earth, of a rogue asteroid back in Nobel year 267, but since then, nothing. Armstrong did contribute, way out of proportion to its size, volunteers for the K-scope project at the Saturnian Lagrange point, following Saturn around in its orbit. In a sense, the K-scope project had some similarities to Armstrong's search for asteroids, in that they both involved large detectors and very long periods of time.

Armstrong's first volunteer had left for the K-scope project even before the main trusses for the K-scope were in place, and the latest was there during the centennial. Armstrong wanted to be the spokesman on Luna for the K-scope project for the three-and-a-half centennial, through the persons of those who had been there and the other seventeens from Armstrong who had interacted with K-scope project managers on the GEO. All this interaction and experience was going to be focused on some 3vid presentations on one of the large screens in a commons area in Nobel, and then some discussion led by Armstrong volunteers from the project. Seventeens are, of course, routinely very intelligent, so discussions are interesting for everyone, which is why talk groups predominate in activities that mines support. Many come quite well prepared, time permitting, and there are seldom instances when discussions wander off into inconsequential details. Armstrong talk groups seemed to gobble up the data flowing out of the K-scope project and to interact with their own people out on the K-scope habitat. There was no interaction in a normal sense because of the long delays in communication time out to Saturn's orbit and back, but Armstrong was very used to a style of communicating that included gaps of about an hour and a half.

Armstrong had come early with their request, and their use of a large screen in a commons room was easily incorporated. They did the presentation three times, and discussions went on for hours following them, almost until exhaustion or schedules interfered. The concept of the K-scope, which finds new Earths by directly observing them with a giant observatory, was enough to motivate many seventeens to prepare well. Every seventeen was trained in astronomy by their mentors, and that was often enough to spark a permanent interest. Astronomy was a data-rich field, meaning that while the physics of astronomical bodies was well understood, and could be predicted, knowing just which was which took observation time, which was limited. So it could stay interesting.

Armstrong's presentation was upbeat in that the concept of the K-scope had been proven and some of the dishes were operating successfully, more or less at predicted resolutions. Planets with oceans had been discovered, making the hunt partially successful. However, the environments were uninhabitable, particularly, the atmospheres. No signatures of surface life had yet been detected at all, to say nothing of another civilization. Earth seemed to have no nearby neighbors, but finding one was a matter of intense interest on Earth, as well as on the outposts. So, the search would go on, and the K-scope project would continue building out to the full complement of twenty large dishes.

There was another reason why Armstrong's presentation would be so well attended and received. The K-scope project was like the moon-squared. Just as Luna was, so far, the only self-sustaining outpost of man beyond Earth, the K-scope project was trying to find some planet in another solar system that could be eventually self-sustaining. It would be quite expensive for Earth to have to supply Luna with everything they consumed, and insanely impossible to supply an exoplanet with anything at all. So, if mankind was ever to venture beyond the confines of its own solar system, it needed to find a place where humans could live with no assistance, and little in starting materials as well. So far, none had been found, but the search was going on. The K-scope project was expensive for Earth, but to this date, support has been found. Luna was too tiny to do more than supply some interested volunteers, and everything fell on Earth to supply the project. And it did.

Since Earth ran the K-scope project, the concentration was on finding another Earth. If Luna had been running it, the concentration might have been on finding another Luna, which could have been much, much easier. The basis for the preference was the expectation that colonizing a new Luna would be a much harder problem than colonizing a new Earth.

Unlike the K-scope, the Jupiter wheel had no mine that showed a great deal of interest in it, or even any interest at all. It is an generous assessment to say that not many Luna volunteers went to the Jupiter wheel. It was seen as a competitor to Luna, being devoted to figuring out how to develop a self-sustaining artificial habitat in orbit around Jupiter. Much of the funding went toward determining how to obtain energy from Jupiter, as lithium and thorium supplies were hard to find and hard to get from Jupiter's satellites, especially considering the intense radiation environment that surrounded them. So, the Jupiter wheel was trying methods of finding power from the magnetosphere or some other strange sources. It was far from a success, but again, funds from Earth continued to flow.

The Nobel 350-year anniversary celebration might be seen as just another attempt by seventeens to show that life on the moon was not dreary but could be interesting and enjoyable. Nobel's common spaces were packed for all the tendays of the year, with all the mines except the three smallest, BBS, Orion, and Forrester, taking up some time and making some contribution. Even the smallest three did have some visitors, and even some competitive teams in the different sports that enlivened Nobel for the whole year. BBS had grown fast, and was larger than Orion, even though Orion had been inaugurated many years before BBS had. The sports subcommittee of the Nobel celebration committee waived the rule that teams had to be all from one mine for these three small mines. A three person team for, say, wall-jumping, could have one seventeen from BBS, another from Orion, and the catcher from Forrester. Records from the various sports do not show any three-mine teams in any of the sports, but there were several with two of the mines combining to form a team. A team from BBS and Forrester did take second place in the ladder gymnastics competition.

The grand tour road race, around the loop formed when the GG Highway was completed, was entered by six mines plus one team from Armstrong and their neighboring mine, Orion. Armstrong was hardly larger in population than the other three small mines, but they had not requested permission to join the sports teams in combination with other mines. There were some Armstrong individuals who competed on their own, and a few did well, but they came to the race committee with a proposal to have their chief driver come from Orion. It was granted, along with blanket permission to include anyone from the other two smallest mines that they wanted.

No other drivers were included from these small mines, but some seventeens from both of the other two helped with the support teams located at each of the five stops. The value of this Orion driver became apparent, when the Armstrong-Orion team had the best time for two of the first three legs. Gagarin bested them, but by a small margin, and the combined team had the second best time. It was not simply driving that was better, it was the setting of controls within the vehicles that made a difference. Armstrong-Orion's settings were made common knowledge after the race, and their modifications were clearly highly original. Treads, spoke flexibility, and chassis weight were part of the tradeoffs they utilized. After that was available for comparison, it was wondered why Gagarin won, but that was explained by Gagarin's different tweaks to the vehicle and experience in racing.

The Nobel-Gagarin round race was held between three pairs of competitors, and then in the last tenday of the centennial year, between the three winners of the previous competitions. Gagarin won this as well, and Armstrong-Orion did not even win the first competition, owing to an incorrect turn made when the human driver overruled the autonomous one. Centaurus came in second, and Ague-Tuilet came in third. They had all been participating in races for many years. Nobel, despite being the host or at least the half-host of the race since its founding, lost to Centaurus.

3vids and other records of the Nobel celebration were made available, which means anyone in the solar system could access them. They were impressive, ranging from flying competitions, to acrobatics of seven different styles, sportsball of six types, and the finishes of the road races. It is true that these finishes showed a car crossing a line with rigid flags, but the spirit was there. Congratulations came from many origins, many places and individuals on Earth, some on Mars, and further out. One from Mars, the only mine there, was unusual in that it indicated that martians might want to return to Nobel. This meant many tendays hibernating in space for a short visit, and made little sense. Hibernation is not necessarily a bad thing because it extends lifespan, but what is the of such a trip?

About thirty tendays later, in Nobel year 351, the seventeen who had the role of managing external contacts in Nobel received a communication asking to start arrangements for a team of six martians to come to Nobel. It said it was part of a trip to Luna, so presumably other mines would be involved. Centaurus would have to be involved, as the only spaceport on the lunar surface was outside of Centaurus. From Centaurus, they could go either way on the grand tour, the old route, or using the GG Highway, but this meant one or two other mines would be involved at the very least. If for some reason, they wanted to see all of the mines, this would be a long trip. With Sirius, there were eleven mines on Luna.

So preparations began, mostly through communications, with the martians planning to start their trip in Nobel year 352, arriving on Luna in 353. Mars had never achieved total self-sustaining capability, although they were on the verge to doing so. The gap had been very gradually closing with time. The biggest boost came when they installed ore processing equipment near their largest mines, lowering transportation costs, but increasing the cost of maintaining these distant plants.

Their agenda was finalized before they boarded the shuttle to take them up to the Mars Orbiter, where they would catch the cycler to one of Earth's LEOs. Once on Luna, they would take the grand tour, hitting five mines, Centaurus first and last for the spaceport, Gautama, Gagarin, Nobel, and Ague-Tuilet. It was a clue that the two smaller mines would be toured before the second largest, Ague-Tuilet. This indicated that if time needed to be cut from the trip, they would be sure to have seen the smaller mines, and could speed through Ague-Tuilet if needed. They wanted to see the layouts at Gautama and discuss vehicles at Gagarin and Nobel. Their struggle for self-sustainability might be aided if they sacrificed some reliability for speed, without losing too much in energy costs to do it. Perhaps some approach taken here on Luna could be useful.

The travel from Mars orbit to Earth orbit could be slept through, with the usual one day per ten tendays wakeup for replenishment and health checks, plus some very mild and controlled exercise. It was the Earth area where travel could be exhausting. There was a possibility of normal sleep, while weightless, during the trip, but many could not sleep well. The Mars team was mostly in that latter category. They marched through their time in Centaurus without full alertness. The road trip to Gautama was mostly a restful one, so by the time they reached Gautama, there had been some recovery. The 3vids of their tours there confirmed this.

The Mars underground habitat was much smaller in relation to the population than here on Luna, as they had large areas on the surface that were used for living space. It does appear from time and expense records that, for Mars, it is more expensive to build and maintain surface facilities than to dig the same area underground. Mars has good rock, so there is no reason not to use it, except for the glorious legacy of mankind's hopes, that they would be living on the surface of a new planet, staring up at the sun and imitating Earth in as many ways as they could. Luna was usually ignored on Mars, as lunites were forced underground by their harsh environment. This is not exactly true, the original concept for Luna was life on the surface, but resources needed to be dug out of a mine, and minerals were very nicely concentrated here. Some earthlings on lunar work tours simply decided to live underground, found it more efficient for mining, and one thing led to another. Centaurus gradually moved completely beneath the surface.

Mars doesn't have the corresponding advantage of concentrated mineral bodies near one another, but the efficiency of a single shaft with airlocks, and everything else accessible in the inhabited spaces, plus the ease of sealing these spaces for pressurization, would translate to Mars. Did this meeting provide a push for the martians to go underground and do less surface dome construction? Maybe, but they did not record any such inspiration happening on the trip or during their reports back on Mars.

They did go deeply over the vehicle design changes, not particularly the published ones that showed each vehicle's configuration in each race, but the ones that were done and remained covert, either because they would be used in a future race, or because they had some problems. Most of their vehicle time was spent on Gagarin, but Nobel got a share of the interest in this topic. Regrettably, Ague-Tuilet had little to offer, except an indication of how a large mine might be laid out, and how the citizens interacted with the facilities. The martian travelers returned to Centaurus, ready to sleep their way back home, but lunites hoped that what they heard on the trip would improve their luck.

DIARY ENTRY (AGE 269, DAY 264)

I have just had my first meal and completed my first exercise after the first wake-up on the Saturn cycler. Our first sleep was twelve tendays and three days long, and there will be 26 of these. We wake up because it is healthier than hibernating for the whole trip. There is nothing interesting to see here from the cameras on the outside, except points of light and the sun. that will be the case for the whole duration of the journey. There are good comms from Luna to here, at least now, so I can send messages to my friends on Luna. Too many came to my going away party, so I need to be selective. we stay up for two days but the awake hours shrink as the trip goes on. The whole team going out to the K-scope wakes up at the same time, meaning there is not too much space. it is more than enough for what we need to do — that's one of the design considerations of the cycler — but because of the small space, we mingle a lot, just like back on Luna.

Most of the passengers are from Earth. Only two of the fourteen making the trek to the K-scope are lunites, one from Centaurus and myself. I have not met so many earthlings at once before, even on the GEO. Being in close quarters here on the cycler will give me plenty of chances to get to know them all, and then we will work together for five years before the trip back to the Earth and Luna. I don't know if anyone from Mars ever does duty on the K-scope, because the travel is even worse than from Earth. There is no cycler from Mars to Saturn, and there never will be. Potential traffic is too tiny.

At the first meal I met two sixteens from Earth, one a little older than I am, and another much younger. They were both from an arcology on the mainland of Eurasia near where a large river of water flowed into one of their oceans. The younger one surprisingly talked a lot about the beauty of the views from high up in the arcology, or down low near the ocean. That is not something sixteens talk about with seventeens very much. People at his arcology spend a lot of their leisure time walking in nature outside the arcology. There are lots of opportunities for walking in gaps of the arcology, which is made up of large towers connected by bridges at different levels. I understand these concepts and the geometry of them from seeing them so many times on 3vids, even of this arcology itself. The younger one talked about being able to walk in any direction from the arcology, and run into interesting parts of nature. I never react negatively to the sights that sixteens can see on their home planet, but just feel happy for them. We have our own lives. Instead, I am simply curious to hear how ordinary sixteens react to their home environment.

The older one was more reserved until he appreciated that I was happy, not upset, hearing about things I would never be able to see in person, and then he began to share his experiences as well. They swim there. There are pools of water in their arcology in many places, and they can also swim in the ocean and in the river. I asked them about going into one and swimming to the other, but the distances are too great. If I had considered that for a moment that would have been obvious. They both talked about water vehicles that made the trip in both directions. While talking about it, their expressions were very animated and happy, so I would suppose this is quite stimulating for sixteens.

I didn't share too much with them, as they were talking during the whole meal. They pay attention to many details of their own arcology and those of others located around Earth, and discuss these details quite openly and without having to be asked. But not once did they bring up Luna or ask me about life there, even in comparison with their own experiences on Earth. It was a strange aspect of our conversation, as if my home did not exist for them. Why do earthlings not care about what happens on Luna? Yes, they have a beautiful planet and it is true that their arcologies are quite different from inside the drifts on Luna, but why exactly do they pay no attention to Luna when they do pay attention to happenings on the other side of their own planet?

While exercising, I was thinking how fortunate it is for humanity that the geneticists were able to lengthen our lifetimes to five or more times as long as any of the originals could live. It was worth inventing a new species, or many new species, in fact, to accomplish this. Otherwise the trip to Saturn would be too long in comparison to the lifetimes of people we know. When I return, my friends will be fifteen years older, as I will be chronologically but not in experienced time, because of the hibernation. Fifteen years is not much of a lifetime of five hundred years, but it would be much more if lifetimes were still only eighty years. Originals will not be working on the K-scope. There were some originals who made one-way trips to the Jupiter wheel, but that wasn't an option for the K-scope. So, if a seventeen wants to meet originals, it will have to be on the GEO.

DIARY ENTRY (AGE 278, DAY 308)

This is about my first day in the shack. Somehow I misunderstood when I would be awakened near the K-scope. I thought it would be on the ship, before it docked with what they call the shack, so I could see the approach to the wheel where I would be living for the next four and a half years. I remember more than a century ago seeing the approach to the GEO, and it was something etched in my memory forever. But I was inside the wheel when I was awakened, feeling the same gravity as on Luna. There was disorientation, as always happens when someone comes out of hibernation, and the brain needs to start circulating its fluids normally again. Nine years in space, and for some reason, I kept thinking I would see the approach. Disappointment.

The shack is less than half the diameter of the GEO, but it looks as impressive in the 3vids, except there is only one wheel around the central cylinder. My first impulse was to try to walk, and that took a bit of effort, mainly because of balance. Then I ate the mixture that the hosts gave me, for revitalization. Despite the obvious idea that since I had slept for nine years, on and off, I would be completely fresh when I awoke, I was not. I wanted to sleep. The host closest to me told me that normal sleep did more to restore my capabilities than staying awake. So I let them lead me to my new cubicle and I fell asleep. Real sleep!

I had not even looked out the portal in my cubicle before I fell asleep. But when I awoke from my normal sleep, I looked out of the floor through the portal and saw simply stars. It looked the same as from the spacecraft portholes. I never went vacuum walking on the moon to see the stars, and I didn't find them any more interesting here. But I stood over the portal as the wheel rotated. First, there was the sun. It was brighter than the other stars, but small. Then the wheel turned again, more stars, and finally, the icosahedron came into view. With sides almost two kilometers in length, it was impressive, more so because the sides were so faint as to be hard to see.

Already there were fourteen dishes on different sides, each greater than a kilometer in diameter, with focal lengths of five kilometers. It was hard to see the secondary mirrors or even their locations as they were so far away. I already knew all fourteen were busy taking data, and that the fifteenth dish would be coming up soon. My spacecraft had carried some parts for it, and so would the next ones, arriving approximately every twelve tendays. As I watched, the icosahedron or K-scope drifted out of sight, leaving only the stars to look at. There was no hope of seeing Saturn up close, as we were at the Lagrangian point of Saturn's orbit, following the planet around its orbit, with the same eccentricity and inclination as the planet itself. People on the Jupiter wheel would be observing Jupiter and its satellites, but here, we observed the rest of the universe, outside our solar system. Eventually, all twenty dishes would be scanning simultaneously.

After staring out of the portal for a while more, and seeing the K-scope again, I left the cubicle and moved into the hallway outside the door. With a three quarters kilometer radius, it was possible to see the curve of the floor. The symbol for reconstitution was on the cubicle next to mine, so I now knew where that was. Going around the loop I saw facilities for everything that we had in Nobel, cleaning, manufacturing, recycling, air purification, and all the rest. But there was no one else walking, at least until I heard a door open behind me and turned to see another traveler from the cycler ease himself out to the pathway. I went over to him, and we together set off to explore the wheel. The nutritional area was just ahead, and there were two others there, taking food items from the cabinets and sitting down to consume them. My walking partner and I started to do the same. We all knew each other's names, so we just nodded in greeting.

I recognized immediately that with only eighty people on the wheel, there was going to be a lot of time alone. With two shifts of twelve hours and one fiveday on and another off meant there would be nominally twenty people working at any time. After eating something, all four of us walked a bit further and found the work area, where there were, yes, about twenty people monitoring the unpacking of the cycler's cargo and what the dishes were seeing. We just milled about, looking at things, with no one guiding us. My strangest memory is looking at one of the screens showing the instantaneous data from one of the fourteen dishes. It was another world, unlike those in our solar system. It was blurry, but I could make out blue and brown colors. The operator closest to the screen told me it was about a hundred and ten light years away. The blue was supposed to be an ocean and the brown, some continents. The other passengers from the cycler came in, and then we received our orientation. Just lunar gravity plus 15%. I could easily handle it.

I had not realized it before, but when I was admiring the icosahedron with its dishes, it was with both eyes and otay sense, as it was so dark at Saturn's radius. Perhaps that is one feature that makes the very unusual work assignment attractive to seventeens. Sixteens do not have the dark vision that we do, but more color receptors in their eyes, and they have no otays to see infrared. I have been thinking through this, and discussing it with other seventeens, since I have been here. There are twenty-two seventeens and fifty-eight sixteens. Another feature is that the gravity in the shack, which is what they call their wheel, is close to lunar. Earthlings can certainly cope with it and have since the first man, Armstrong, stepped onto the moon. But it is home gravity for seventeens. We are born feeling this strength of the pull downward, and learn all our motions in it. It is awkward for sixteens, at least at first. They don't know the gaits or the leaps or how to move themselves gracefully using grips. This gets learned, but perhaps even after a four and a half year work tour, they still can't move a fluidly as a seventeen. I can look along the wheel, and even at the farthest distance I can tell a seventeen from a sixteen by how they walk.

The cycler that brought me and the other new staff to the K-scope also brought beams for the fifteenth dish. Because it had much less mass to bring back than to bring out, there had to be a shuttle engine as part of the payload, used to bring the velocity down to match that of the K-scope centroid. The engines go back empty, adding to the mass discrepancy. The next cycler will bring more staff in rotation and more beams, but in the interim, I am assigned to the task of monitoring the assembly of the fifteenth dish. The struts out to the focal point will come in later shipments. I work next to two other seventeens on my shift who have put other dishes together, and after I used the simulator to learn interaction with the robots, work began. The dish will be assembled before the reflector is put on. To keep mass down, the icosahedron and the telescopes are all as flimsy as possible; a little bit of gravity would destroy them. They need to be assembled out of small pieces that can travel easily. I am monitoring the robot doing the preliminary assembly, as are the others. Then they will move on to monitoring the jockeying around of these delicate parts so the next larger stage of assembly can proceed.

The other portion of my work here is on the monitoring of the data collection from the working dishes. They each monitor one exoplanet for hours, and then in a coordinated manner, move the photon collector so another is in view. Rotating the icosahedron takes place only rarely, almost never. We do not really work a fiveday on and a fiveday off, as is done on Earth and on the moon. There is so little else to do here that it is not objectionable to work eight days out of ten. At first the assembly work was far more interesting than the data collection, but as I learn more about what I am seeing, that is changing. The K-scope is observing planets out to almost a thousand light years, but most of them are closer, under two hundred. There are a million and a half known planets in the planetary catalog with orbits precisely enough known to allow the detailed scrutiny of the K-scope. Here we do no searching for new planets.

Almost all of them were discovered with the Earth Lagrangian Observatory, which has been in operation for two centuries in the current form of three telescopes of a hundred and forty meters aperture. Seventeens do not serve on the ELO, as the wheel there has forty percent earth gravity, too much for us. The staff is very small. There is really no need for seventeens to participate in anything as our numbers are tiny compared to Earth's. We only contribute as a token for everything, especially the Jupiter wheel, but here at Saturn's orbit, we play a role far in excess of our population size. It takes so much energy to get out here that having a stronger wheel would not make sense. And lunites somehow took to the task quite well, with sufficient volunteers, even though it is probably the most onerous task in the solar system, what with seven to thirteen years of hibernation to get out here, and no interactive communication with anything at home.

The sixteens on the station are much more open and communicative than those I met on the GEO. They mingle with us indiscriminately. Perhaps that is because there are so few humans here, that each person is a major relief from the loneliness, or perhaps it is because we seventeens are doing a major part of the project.

The K-scope project is a tangled mixture of sadness and hope. Someday, one of these exoplanets might be a new home for mankind, tens or hundreds of millennia from now, but what we all hope for was to find another advanced civilization in our part of the Milky Way. There was sadness because none of the exo-planets being deeply monitored has shown signs of even surface life, much less civilization. Hope remains because there are so many more planets to examine. Mankind has been isolated in the universe up until now, and can live this way till the end of our existence, but it would feel so good to know that there was another Earth full of some sort of people somewhere in the galaxy near us. We seventeens feel it too. We cannot even go to Earth, but we are still throwing ourselves into the task of finding some equivalent out there. It is beyond ridiculous to think life could originate on a rocky world like the moon, and we all know that it is a lucky combination of events that allowed humans to make self-sustaining outposts there. But there could be another Earth somewhere with culture, music, and language, and tomorrow I will continue working on the hunt for it.

16

AGING ON LUNA

Following the martian's departure, life at Nobel settled down and simply grew very slowly, with no major disturbances. There were no serious moon-quakes, not in Nobel and not in any other mine. No new asteroids were discovered hurtling toward a target on the moon, and none of the well known and well charted ones changed their orbits enough during this interval to pose a danger. Armstrong tried hard, but no rogue asteroids from beyond the solar system were found in Earth's vicinity, although surely there must have been some in the outer solar system, just based on statistics.

The population of Nobel continued its steady, planned progression upward, with about 70 new seventeens gestated every year, pretty much with a cohort coming every three tendays. This meant that a large fraction of the work time would continue to go to gestating, nurturing and mentoring the new ones. It also meant that about 70 new habitats would be excavated each year, for the seventeens that finished their training and took up their own locations while they proceeded through mentoring and gradually took on work assignments. Mentoring had long ago been extended last for 30 years, as was done almost everywhere on Earth, and in Centaurus and the other larger mines, and this just added to the work hours consumed for the later generations of seventeens.

In Nobel year 376, a new stope became available, and was turned into a commons area, being divided into a dining area, some new space for the vegetation enthusiasts to put a plot, another pool, and multiple other uses. This meant that other facilities would be moved, as a nurturing facility swapped places with a commons dining area, giving them more space and transferring some meals to the new dining area in the new stope. And restitution spaces were increased by moving them to a former recycling facility, which had split into two, and so on. The moving around took two years to wind down.

The most boring part of Nobel, the spoils pile, now covers a sizable area on the lunar surface, starting near the central shaft entrance to

Nobel. It covered approximately 84 square kilometers up to a height of 4 meters, and was easily visible from Earth. New excavation added close to a half square kilometer to the area. The spoils pile was largely useless, except that it provided a means of shielding everything from the radiation from the small residual collection of radioactive materials that could not be used for any practical purpose. Since both the fusion and fission reactors were designed with isotopic materials designed to minimize lingering radiation, the amount was small, but it still had to be handled and stored with the same level of extreme safety that characterized anything done on the moon. The waste was buried just ahead of the spoil pile's leading edge, and it was soon covered permanently.

The same steady progress happened in the area of new mines. In Nobel year 381, a new luna-wide meeting was held, located in Centaurus, on the subject of another new mine. This would be the twelfth, and each of the first eleven would play some role in setting it up. Centaurus had a work group formed to recommend a location to the convocation, and they suggested three sites. All three were on the back side of the moon, to the east of BBS, with one staying in the northern hemisphere, as BBS and Armstrong were, another just south of the lunar equator, and a third even farther south. There was no suggestion recorded that any other sites be examined, even though all three of these stretched the transportation lines even thinner than they were with BBS, as the backside of the moon seemed to have even richer ores than the highlands on the Earth side. Routes to all three of these would travel through the lunar highlands, going left and right to avoid large and small craters and other lunar features. There was only preliminary mineralogical data available, and the group decided to put off making a selection until some more exploration had been done. This was turned over to Nobel, with Armstrong and BBS both providing some additional personnel.

The Nobel team dealt with these sites, one at a time, but it was considered by many within Nobel as excessive. A team from Centaurus and Ague-Tuilet went out on the surface to make the routes to the three sites clear and safe, and then to build solar shields at the center of each drilling area. Since all three sites looked like excellent locations for mines, this additional construction might be used later for future mines, and the initial exploration would confirm this. As soon as the northern site had its solar shield in place, when the Centaurus/Ague-Tuilet team was heading back to BBS for a break before proceeding to the second site, the Nobel drilling team was there, having passed the other convoy en-route.

The plan was to sink sixty deep holes centered around the vicinity of the initial drilling site, where only six had been put in. The first hole, a kilometer and a quarter to the north, found tungsten ore near the surface, and four hundred and thirty meters down, a composite of manganese ores with some cobalt included. The sixteenth hole, to the west, found a particularly rich vein of multiple halide minerals, and the eighteenth, not far away, found carbonates, with sodium, zinc and lead. In a few of the others there were worthwhile ores, but the site was not quite up to the level of the eleven mines already started. It's possible that the choice of drill sites was simply unlucky, but the site was left to be investigated later.

The second drilling site had been constructed, with solar shields, before the first site's drilling had gotten far, and as soon as the Nobel team returned to BBS from the first site and had rested, they headed for the second. Again, the plan was for sixty holes. A large cache of ores was found, all to the east of the site, with nothing very rich in the other three directions. It would be quite possible to put the main shaft to the east of the original position that Centaurus had guessed would be good, and have a successful mine here, as far as the initial exploration that Nobel had done would tell.

The third drilling site was also explored shortly after the second was completed, in Nobel year 383. This site was better than the second, with carbonates, halides, oxides, hydroxyls, and nitrates all available in good quantities and high concentrations. The whole periodic table of elements was present in an area fourteen kilometers around the initially chosen site. Much of the riches were further out than the initial exploration had checked, so this mine would be wider than some of the others, but that was not a sufficient stumbling block. Even before the Nobel team had returned to BBS, they understood what would be the choice of the design team for a twelfth mine location. It was, of course, and the eleven mines had a second meeting in Nobel year 384 to plan who would take on what role. Nobel did not anticipate any work tasking, as they had contributed the exploration drilling, and at three times the usual rate. This is what happened, and Nobel did not play much of a role in the next decade's work in starting up the twelfth mine, except for some almost honorary positions, such as on the naming committee.

There were eleven names proposed. It is not recorded who suggested which name initially, and it may have been done in secret, to prevent any influence of origin on the choice of name. For some reason, naming this mine took on greater importance than naming some of the previous ones, probably due to the personalities of the members of the naming committee. The name finally selected was Andromeda, after the nearest giant galaxy, the one most visible in the heavens over the moon. Andromeda was to be located just to the west of Joffe crater. The main shaft of Andromeda was dug by Nobel year 387, and useful ore was reached in the next year. Habitation areas were excavated along with stations for ore processing and power, and the first airlock was put in on the first station level in Nobel year 394, but first habitation did not take place until Nobel year 396.

In the same year that the initial convocation on the twelfth mine had happened, Nobel year 381, something on Earth happened to change the allocation of work on the moon, particularly Centaurus, and also to change the atmosphere there. A sixteen died from old age. The individual involved was from the first cohort of sixteens gestated on Earth, five hundred and ten years before. This was expected to happen, but the timing was uncertain by a decade or so. Since Nobel year 371, ten years before, there had been an informal 'Death Watch', in which the first few cohorts of sixteens were monitored to assess their condition.

Geneticists had pushed the limits of longevity as much as they could, back in the early days before sixteens and seventeens had been designed. Originals and species up to sixes still had cellular death programmed into them, into each cell in their bodies, and the cells themselves had a timing mechanism. It could only be stretched up to a hundred and thirty years, and to overcome this limitation, sevens had no such cellular death mechanism, but had instead a timing mechanism in the base of the skull, only a tiny clump of cells, that would lead to heart death at a predetermined time, which was a hundred and fifty for sevens, but had risen to five hundred by the time sixteens were invented. All cellular genetic mechanisms were bound to fail at some time, and so to avoid catastrophic failure and to control the process of death, the heart termination cells were invented and included in the genetic code for all human species starting with the sevens. There would probably be some cellular failure occurring in the last years of the timing period, but probably not complete organ failure. This meant a weakening and slowing of functions would happen before death, but in general, the death of sixteens would be gentle and kind.

There was some variation, individual to individual, in the timing mechanism, but it was fairly precise, and all the members of the first few cohorts of sixteens knew, when the first one died, that their horizon was limited to only a few years at the most. Fifteens had all passed away by this time, as had the earlier species, down to the eights, who still had breeding potential. A small number of them, living in just two arcologies, still preserved their species in the same way the originals did.

Seventeens were not exactly like sixteens in this regard, despite the fact that most of their genetics were identical. The moon was such a benign environment, with no microbes, no seasons, little background radiation, perfectly balanced nutrition, and especially lower gravity, that they had been programmed with a longer-lived calendar in their brain stems, and the estimate was thirty years more for seventeens than sixteens. The death of the sixteen from the first cohort in Nobel year 381 meant that around Nobel year 416, the same should start with the seventeens, as the first cohort of seventeens was gestated on the moon five years after the first cohort of sixteens on Earth. Luna's own Death Watch would therefore start in Nobel year 406.

Every seventeen on the moon understood very well that they were not immortals, despite the fact that there was no one dying on the moon. Mentoring on the subject of death was mandatory for all, and everyone going through that part of mentoring realized that after five hundred years or so, their bodies would increasingly weaken over a few years and then their hearts would stop. The weakening would serve as a sign to themselves and to others that their end was coming shortly, and anything they wanted to do before death should be done promptly. There was no way to prolong life further, as protein copying in cells in inherently imperfect, and would continue to build up, leading to a less pleasant way of dying. There would be no blindness, no deafness, no loss of usage for any organs, no major pains, no crippling, and none of the other ills that plague originals and earlier species. The designers of sixteens and seventeens had managed to build in good health for a period exceeding five hundred years, with a sixteen of four hundred able to be almost as active as one of a hundred. They had crowned their achievement with the development of this soft procedure for death, and by and large, this achievement was appreciated. It was not that sixteens and seventeens longed for death, by any means, but it was accepted and the mentoring on this subject reinforced that.

Despite the inevitability of the Death Watch, and the clear knowledge of when it would start within a few decades, very little had been done on Earth prior to Nobel year 381 to prepare for the onset of the sixteens dying. The same was true for Luna. There were good reasons for this. The most basic reason was that with the timing known, there was simply no point to spend any time planning for this event well in advance. Nothing in a mine was designed in such a way that major rebuilding or other changes would be required when the Death Watch began. Another is that death should occur in the order of gestation, so individuals would themselves know their own time, approximately, and could make their own preparations if they chose to. A third is that the population of sixteens was tiny at the time of the first cohort of seventeens, and so death would start in a very small number, which would increase only gradually over the following centuries. There would be little disruption of work schedules or anything else when the Death Watch started, and in fact, very little of anything except for those who were close to the seventeens in the earliest cohorts.

No physical or organizational changes were made between Nobel year 381 and Nobel year 405, a year before the Death Watch would start, taking advantage of the differential between sixteens and seventeens. There were psychological changes. Talk groups in Nobel, and in other mines as well, were noted to have death as a topic for many meetings, and in some, for a series of continuous meetings. There was only one seventeen in Nobel from the first cohort on Luna, and a few from the rest of the first year, out of a total population of about fifteen thousand. Few knew someone affected, but many wanted to discuss it, far out of proportion to the potential effect.

There would be no need within Nobel to organize anything related to the deaths of seventeens, as the talk groups had figured out options ten times over. How should a seventeen on the verge of death prepare? Should restrictions on activities be imposed for safety reasons? Should near-death seventeens relocate to be near a restitution center, or anywhere else? What ceremonies should be held to say farewell to the seventeens on the cusp? Should there be a ceremony after passing? Does there need to be new work assignments connected with the final years of the seventeens' lives, devoted to assisting them? What would be expected in terms of physical changes and appearance? Should gestation be ramped up to compensate for any population loss through death?

Recycling was such a universal process on Luna, even more so than in Earth arcologies, that there was no expectation that anything would be done with the body of a former seventeen, now deceased, other than it being turned over to recycling. Earth had long ago ceased preserving bodies, and Luna was not about to start it. Aside from making no sense, there was nowhere in a mine to do an old-time burial, and, while the lunar surface was vast and empty, burying them somewhere in a maria or inside a crater wall would be a waste of effort and resources. But the human brain, in seventeens just as in all previous species, doesn't do parting very well. Ceremonies are performed to alleviate the grief caused by having a mental empty space once occupied by a person. Many kinds of ceremonies were devised, long before they were needed.

There had literally been no deaths on the moon since the catastrophe of the second return, some six centuries ago. Initially earthlings came and left, to be supplanted by the home-grown seventeen population. There was no disease, and none had been brought from Earth. Even so, seventeens had immune systems able to handle any accidental contamination. There were few accidents, and no fatal ones. Safety practices were taught as the first mentoring subject, according to the earliest records, and in Nobel's fourth century, they occupied almost ten percent of the mentoring subject list. Little seventeens practiced doing simple tasks safely. There was no crime here, as on Earth, and especially no violent crime that might have led to a death. Thus, no one was familiar with death. No one had been involved with a person who had died. There was simply a void of experience on the subject of death, and soon everyone on the moon would have to become accustomed to it, and adapt appropriately. The talk groups spoke about modifications to the mentoring subjects that touched on death, specifically in the biological, psychological, and cultural areas.

The talk groups also had discussions about the preservation of items left behind by those who died, such as some of the original art that decorated passageways in the mine. One of the more useful ideas was to ban removing such art for a period after the death of the creator, and then donate it to anyone wanting to use it personally in their habitation.

Any sentience who compiled all the resolutions from the talk groups discussing various aspects of death would be able to put together a methodology for handling it. Many people had their sentiences do that, and they were mostly identical. No one at this time in Nobel was assigned any responsibility relating to death, so there was no one to present these methodologies to. The furor of the topic died out within a year and a half of the news of the first sixteen death, but since no data is lost on Luna, the methodologies, along with much other detail, were preserved for a future time, a couple of decades into the future, when they would be quite necessary.

Three of the talk groups focused on topics that were related to a change in attitude among residents of Nobel. The original view of anyone in Nobel was that death was not something that was ever thought of. It didn't exist in Nobel or anywhere else a seventeen might go. The concept was theoretically there, having been planted there in mentoring, but it simply did not come up in thinking. Then, after the death on Earth, and the hubbub it had created within the mine, it came up all the time. When walking down a corridor and passing someone, instead of thinking about greeting them and remembering their personal details, the thought was, "Are they older than I and will they die first?" Apparently some seventeens were strongly affected by this change of attitude. The emphasis on death did seem to fade over the next year or two, as evidenced by a decrease in any mention of it in talk groups and public discussions.

The interest in death planning resurged a bit, if only for a short time, when Earth made an inquiry to each of the mines to ask what they were doing concerning the imminent onset of resident deaths. Apparently, one of the arcologies was run by someone enchanted with the idea of completeness, and so, in addition to seeking plans from each of Earth's arcologies, all the mines were asked as well. At this point in the history of Luna, there was almost no formal contact between Earth and Luna. Informal contact was minimal as well. Seventeens on Luna didn't usually maintain contact with earthlings, even if friends were made on the GEO or somewhere else where the two species mingled together. Life is quite different in these two places, and the novelty of interacting with someone in a different world wears off quickly. Thus, when the individual on Earth made his request, it was unusual and caught the interest of several talk groups. The common response was that Nobel should respond, even if in the negative, and ask for the results of the compilation. Inevitably, they would be sitting somewhere available and could easily be accessed, but politeness called for Nobel to show interest in the subject, having been asked for a contribution.

The compilation did come back a quarter year later, causing another uproar in the talk groups, and essentially said much the same things as the methodology pulled together by the talk groups in Nobel. Earth was already in the process of dealing with the deaths of sixteens, and had progressed past the talking and planning stages some time ago. They were dealing with much larger numbers there, and had set up facilities for sixteens in the last parts of the weakness phase, as well as facilities to handle the bodies. Luna only had recycling facilities, but that would do. One arcology had commissioned some audio, non-rhythmic music interspersed with rhythmic voices, that they offered for use at ceremonies for farewells to sixteens nearing their last days. It apparently spread to other arcologies almost instantly. They had also set up a way to monitor the health of the oldest sixteens so that intervention would be possible. Apparently all this resulted in a smoother demise for sixteens, but had the opposite effect, increasing the sadness of friends. It was a trade-off.

The concentration on the upcoming Death Watch was minimal in comparison to the concentration on Nobel's fourth centennial celebration, again lasting the whole year. Other mines had so far been willing to allow Nobel to reap all the credit for having a giant celebration, as no other mine did anything nearly as complete and complex as Nobel, nor anything as extenuating. There was a four year planning process, and all those who had participated in the previous centennials as planners and organizers were formed into an advisory committee, which did not meet in person, but was charged with responding to inquiries from the fourth centennial committee.

Almost everything that had been exhibited, performed, played, or competed in for the last three centennials as well as the half-centennials was to be included in the Nobel year 400 celebration. Surface road races, on the round trip from Nobel to Gagarin, were organized early in the centennial year. The long loop through five mines, including Gautama, was held near the middle of the year. A trio of three seventeens, all fascinated by vehicle design, took on the job of deciding if any rule changes would be made for this race. Both had been run on a regular basis, but the two runs chosen by the Nobel centennial committee received special attention. Nobel was looking to have eight vehicles in the round trip race and five in the long loop.

The acrobatic flying competitions would be held between individuals, rather than between the mines' champions. Nobel very graciously made the use of its flying space available to anyone from any mine who visited Nobel for that purpose. These practices would run for the two years prior to the centennial, and then a third of the way into the centennial year. That would give visitors and residents both the chance to watch the competitors try new maneuvers. After a practice period of another third of a year, individuals would have one single chance to gain a place in the finals, where four competitors would show off their skills before judges.

More than twenty years before, Nobel's sports enthusiasts had completed a large set of small platforms anchored in the sides of the stope, which were large enough for a flyer to land on. These perches were part of the competition, with three long series of required maneuvers to be done, followed by a six-minute exhibition of whatever maneuvers the contestant wanted to display. the judging was to be done by a panel of eight judges, who would be stationed roughly in the eight compass directions, so the flights could be observed from every angle.

Acrobatics without wingsuits was not restricted to the ground. There were trapeze systems set up with twelve different levels in two alternating series, facing one another. This system of acrobatics had been derived from the previous, still utilized, system of acrobatics with oversized ladders, allowing the acrobat to move up and down during the movements. It had also spawned acrobatics on a series of hoops, which were simply ladders in circular form, giving a different type of three-dimensional motion to the movements. All three of these had formal contests and judging, with both a required series of movements and one free-form series.

Ground-based acrobatics had split into two separate competitions before the centennial as well. There were movements done on a mat as well as movements done on poles. Up until Nobel year 391, the pole-based acrobatics system involved one pole, but those who were most involved with the sport introduced a second set of movements using two inverted-U-shaped loops, facing one another. There was a debate within the Nobel committee managing the centennial as to whether to introduce it or not, and the final decision was that there were so far too few individuals involved with the loop acrobatics to have a good competition. There were these loop structures in several mines, and some informal competitions were held, but it was simply not sufficiently popular to be a centennial event. The organizers simply did not want the centennial to be the place for the promotion of new sports, but rather for contests among well-established ones.

The acrobatics competitions were set up so that three tendays was devoted to each one. This was to start in the tenth tenday of the centennial, and continue for fifteen tendays. The next nine tendays were given over to rhythmic acrobatics, in which ground acrobatics were done in a tempo matching that of some particular rhythmic music. Participants in this type of acrobatics competed in pairs or quartets, and did a series of movements of their own choosing in time to the rhythm of the music. This type of activity had been done as demonstrations in the third centennial and the half-centennial that followed, but over the decades that followed these, it had become a competitive sport. Five different rhythms were prevalent enough to have been introduced into the competition, and the first large display of competitive rhythmic acrobatics had happened in Nobel year 372, in Ague-Tuilet, with about one or two a year following that in different mines. Since there was no need for any high spaces or any equipment other than a large flat surface, virtually every mine had participants, even the ones with still tiny populations. Rule changes in Nobel years 374, 378, 385, and 388 led to the performances being more interesting and easier for spectators to follow.

Nobel would be running a competition similar to those held elsewhere, and for those nine tendays, other mines held off on organizing any similar events. The centennial celebrations on Nobel were so appreciated in other mines, that this type of coordination was almost universal. No one wanted to compete with the Nobel centennial for spectators.

Ball-based competitions were also coordinated in Nobel, with three sports chosen for centennial contests, out of the fifteen or more that were played in at least two mines on Luna. By far the most popular one was based on getting a ball to pass through the other sides' hoops, suspended off the ground, only using knees, hips and elbows to move it around. The game was so intriguing because it was so complex and appealed to the inherent intelligence of the population of seventeens on Luna. There were four teams, each with a hoop they defended, and much of the strategy involved knowing which opposing teams to most strongly oppose.

Actual coordination between different teams was forbidden, and the scoring rules were designed to eliminate the utility of coordination, even partially. That meant favoring other teams had to be decided on the spot, during the intensity of the game, and then coordinated between players on one team. The game was too fast to allow any communication other than by actions, so spectators for the games often sat in huddles to allow them to share their interpretations of how the game was going with each other. The competition for this game involved six teams, chosen by the committee and invited to participate, with fifteen matches, each with two teams not involved and four on the floor. Determining the winner involved a complex formula, so coming in second in an individual match was better than being third or fourth, which were non-counting end positions.

This type of ball game occupied much more time in talk groups than other sports, or in fact, more than almost anything else. Sports as a grand category did take up much of the topic choices, but because this game had only been around for some forty-plus years at the time of the centennial, no one had yet developed a master theory on how to most effectively play the game. Said another way, there were dozens of 'master theories' on how different teams should play in order to win, but none had achieved any prominence.

There were only four players on the floor for each team, with two substitutes waiting outside the bounds, fully equipped with elbow, hip, and knee protectors. The Nobel committee had announced their choice to include a large tournament for hoop ball, and some of the smaller mines began increasing their participation rate in games held in other mines, with the idea that they might make the selection threshold and be one of the six teams to star at Nobel. Centaurus had six teams of their own that played and could be chosen, as the Nobel committee did not mention that only one team could come from one mine. Since the Mayan Empire, this game had not had any close equivalent on Earth.

The second ball game selected by the Nobel committee for competitive performance involved teams of two players with rackets hitting a flexible ball against a wall, as close to the center of a target as possible. The opposing players had to hit the ball after zero or one bounce back to the reflecting wall. Because points were scored only from the impact location, volleys could theoretically go on for a long time, but they rarely did because the rackets' heads had curvature, which put spin on the ball. The spin resulted in a veering off from the impact point. This again is a game with a large strategy component, which seems to have been a factor in the choices made by the Nobel game subcommittee. Sometimes in other mines, this game was played with four competitors per teams, but the Nobel group decided against including this variant and stuck with the two player version only. Nobel's subcommittee followed the same ritual as with hoop ball, and announced they would choose six teams to play in the four tendays preceding the centennial year.

The third ball game that Nobel chose to include involved rolling balls from outside a circle, attempting to place them when they stopped close to the center. One ball could be used to move a second ball already in the circle, and the competition usually involved a combination of rapid rolls and very slow rolls. Each team had three members, and each member threw three balls per round, so one of the strategic choices was a direction to roll from, and another was about how many balls to sacrifice to clear a path, which might be used by the other team as well. Throwing was an immediate disqualification for a round. Once again,

Nobel's subcommittee would select the teams, but for this competition, they were allowing twelve teams. This game was clearly one that small mines could excel at, and they attempted to do just that.

Any sentience could do the physics of this game, and players were not prohibited from using them in competitions to advise on what strategic choices to make. This, however, did not reduce the game play to a question of how accurately the balls were started rolling. The use of a sentience is like the use of any other complicated apparatus, and it can be done with more or less skill, producing more or less exacting results. This game, including the simulation of it, was again a common thread in talk groups. Furthermore, there was a large amount of computational energy that went into simulating games, which could be shown on any large screen. Some seventeens even played in simulated competitions, but since this removed the physical element, the results were too simplified to appeal to most lunites.

Competitions were only one part of the centennial celebration. Following the tradition of previous ones, food presentations by different groups were encouraged, and so many different groups chose to volunteer, there had to be a severe restriction of the number of people who could be allowed. Each group selected was confined to what they could do, in order to make dining during the centennial as organized as possible. Each group would have only four meals to prepare, each to serve eighteen people, and the timing was spaced so that different shifts would all be included. Nobel's food preparation facilities would be overwhelmed if used by everyone, so each mine had to bring apparatus for completing their meals with them.

Three venues were set up for music presentations, and two for large-screen showings of 3vid performances. One loss of tradition was that silhouette shows were no longer done anywhere on Luna, so this would be missing from the 400-year celebration. There was no point in showing previous ones, as they had been seen by everyone, even multiple times.

In the second to last tenday, there was a costume parade moving from one side of Nobel to the other during the first half of the second tenday, and then another, likely with mostly different people, during the second half of that same tenday. The committee organized the parade by providing dressing rooms, line numbers, and organizers to control the speed of the walk. They had rules about staying in line, with no jumping, no ricocheting off walls, no food, and many more.

All in all, Nobel put together so many rules that the compilation of them was quite impressive to anyone considering attending. At this time, Nobel had about sixteen thousand people, but they expected to host between one and two hundred thousand visitors from all the other mines. Temporary housing was a large undertaking, and Nobel actually had adapted its excavations to a degree, for over a century, with the idea of hosting Luna's grandest celebrations. Most visits would be for a short period, so there were four thousand spots for visitors, plus twice that many in the habitations of residents, restricted to friends. It is quite clear why Nobel has no competition on Luna for celebrations.

I remember one of my mentors explaining to me how the work lottery was done, but I don't remember the process. All I needed to know was how to apply for work tasks I was most interested in, and avoid those I didn't want to be involved with. Work tours start quarterly, so there are a lot of entries coming into the lottery simultaneously. The average duration is three years, but some are two, and many others go up to five. There is a preference for those who wish to stay in the same work task for a second or third tour, except in some tasks, where rotation is mandatory. Residents and those from other mines here for work tours have to compete in the same way. The same process is used for people seeking work breaks for one or two quarters.

My current assignment is management, and for this six half year I am monitoring the residential allocations, but for the current period of two tendays I am overseeing the lottery. I have learned all the details of how it works. The algorithm runs in a prestage and then three stages. The prestage simply eliminates those who seek a work break, tentatively, and keeps them separate from the rest of the applicants. Then the three stages start.

First come those who want to return to the same work task for another period. Spoils can't be done twice in a row and neither can surface transportation. They also don't alternate with each other Nurturing is a one time duration, as is training, and they don't alternate with each other. Power can't be done twice in a row. Other than these, and maybe one or two more, returns get a priority, so almost all requests are granted. Three in a row is possible for about half of the categories, but after that, switching is mandatory. Management can be double-tasked, but not triple-tasked. The only issue with multiple tasking occurs when there is a downsizing and slots disappear.

Once the returns are dealt with, everyone goes into a big pot for selection. Random selection pulls each applicant out in some order, and they get their first choice, or if it is filled, their second, third, or as far down as they have listed, up to fifth, if there is congestion in their upper choices. Anyone who cannot be matched to a preferred spot goes into the second pot.

If anyone is in the second pot, the third part of the algorithm finds open slots and picks someone, by random priority, who does not have it included on his avoidance list. Up to five choices can be made. If nothing matches, the unlucky person goes into the third pot. There, anyone who can be assigned to an avoid list work task in their fifth entry is assigned to that, and if there are multiple, a random selection occurs. Then, the fourth entry is eligible for assignment, followed by the third and second. Only the unluckiest of individuals would be assigned to his most undesired work assignment. It never happens.

If the number of individuals seeking work is greater than the number of slots available, the last to be assigned will have to take a one quarter work break. If it goes the other way, and some work slot is left unfilled, the last person to be given a work break in the prestage loses it, and gets to take the work slot. Since empty slots are empty because someone's work term is ending, there is usually a close match. There has to be an increase in the number of slots because of the growth in population. Growth in population comes from when immigration exceeds emigration, combined with new cohorts coming of age, and eventually we will have to take account of seventeens reaching the end of their lifespan.

The trickiest part of this balancing act is deciding which areas of work will see growth. Some increase and some decrease, but a growing population should have growing numbers of work slots. Exactly where is the trick.

On the first day of the two tenday lottery period, all the algorithmic computations happen in a millisecond. Then there are algorithms that compute the number of new slots which can be put into any area, and the master plan for the mine is examined to see where they would be best used. My management job will be to monitor the algorithm operation, which is almost never in error, and then to listen to special requests or complaints, and try to find another applicant who would want to negotiate a change that could make both of them happier. Sometimes I am able to find a triangle of changes that improves the situation. Some people do not come forward with their complaints, and I have my sentience look through the results for some swaps that might be better, and contact the two people involved. My success rate is high.

I use some rules for finding swaps that the previous holder of the work slot transferred to me, sentience to sentience. They probably date back to pre-lunar Earth, as almost nothing new can be invented now, after so many centuries of experimentation and development. I will be doing this task every quarter for the next three years, which is good, as I really enjoy the negotiation process.

DIARY ENTRY (AGE 309, DAY 210)

When I returned from my duty at the food production center today, I couldn't help but think about Forrester, not the newest lunar mine, but the man after whom that mine was named. I know who he was very well, and I remember hearing about him in the last years of my training, to say nothing of multiple mentoring lessons. Not many individuals are singled out during training, so I knew even then he was special. One of the avatars was training me in visual perception when he showed a picture of humans and robots together. I asked if robots ever worked alone without human guidance, and it replied that they had not, since Forrester. We diverted to a discussion of who he was. I remember it being only a capsule history, of how Forrester had invented an even smarter type of robot, actually a robotic manufacturing plant, and the robot started making components for itself.

My avatar explained that it had started by giving orders to other robotic components nearby, including ordering parts, and installing more power lines, communications channels, and means of isolating itself. Forrester was supposed to be monitoring what the new robot was doing, but it sent false reports and he and his associates were all fooled. Within three Earth months, the robot was building another factory, identical to itself, in a building it had deceptively emptied. Forrester finally caught on, and began the long struggle to depower the robot. He finally succeeded, and he spent the next years figuring out how to build in controls so that robots would never operate without human guidance and full transparency. Since then, there have been no more attempts at robotic independence.

I remember this making sense to me, as there were always humans present in the nurturing and training centers, even though the avatars, a very human-looking robot, and some specialist robots were doing all the physical work, the communicating, and everything else. Humans had to be present and involved, or the avatars couldn't function. That was their programming, after Forrester. I had no serious sentience available to me back in early training, so the topic was forgotten until I was in mentoring and then I could dig deeper on my own. I remember that it was one of my earliest mentors,

Balak, who led me to understand the programmatic structure of various types of robot intelligence, and how they all had a keystone component named the Forrester module, which served as both a monitor of internal activity and a filter for output. Most of the module was isolated from the learning mechanisms, which change program details. I remember missing the importance of that point until Balak hammered me on it.

Forrester and his module came up over and over again during the course of mentoring. I can remember dissecting the module, and seeing how its self-protections worked, and how it was positioned to have the final say in proceeding with any activity. I can remember other things my mentors stressed and things I learned on my own, working with my own sentience. I remember how Forrester inspired geneticists designing brains for various creatures to be used as pets on Earth so they would be docile with humans. The genetic equivalent of a Forrester module was nothing like a Forrester module in robots, but instead involved the neurochemical synapses that would inhibit aggression. And I remember lying awake in my chamber, wondering if sixteens and seventeens had the same inhibition mechanism inside them, and realizing that we couldn't, because humans couldn't be effective leaders or innovators, and take on all the tasks of building a new world.

What bothered me today was if some type of damage to a robotic brain could disable the Forrester module, and allow the affected robot to act independently and in its own interest. The food robots I interact with daily might have that happen, and then could they do damage to the food production line? Could they add poison or something else into one of the main food streams, leading to a depopulation of Nobel? Do they have access to the sentience network that would allow them to get the data necessary to plan such an attack? It doesn't make sense that after centuries of robots interacting with humans when nothing like this has happened, it could suddenly happen here on Nobel. There are tens of thousands more nutrition production sites on Earth, and it would almost certainly have happened there first. My sentience couldn't come up with any reports of such behavior happening, even after I requested a second and third deeper digs into old news. Nothing, and so I am recording in my diary, instead of sleeping, that this is something to investigate further.

17

BEGINNING THE FIFTH CENTURY ON NOBEL

Right in the middle of the planning period for Nobel's 400 year cele-bration, there was another, much, much smaller celebration. There were always small celebrations going on within Nobel and the other mines, such as the anniversary of the gestation of some cohort, where they would all get together with friends and reminisce about their train-ing and mentoring, and share stories of their more recent activities. Seventeens who had all migrated from a different mine might like to get together to celebrate events there. There were celebrations for the completion of a sizable project as well as celebrations to inaugurate one. New space being made available was a cause for celebration. This one was a bit different.

Hamer Govoz Bishek, a seventeen born on Nobel in Nobel year 197, had decided to go to Ceres on a work assignment. Hamer would be the first from Nobel ever to do that, and the first from Luna. Ceres was populated by eighteens, gestated on Mars, who had traveled to Ceres for a five-year duty tour. There always was an open invitation to lunites to join them, but, none had so far. Ceres only had a population of 230, which was the size of the smallest mines on Luna, but larger than Vesta's population, which was only 80, and larger than the popu-lation on the Saturn K-scope. Even the Jupiter wheel had more people than Ceres. Hamer would be separated from all other seventeens, but eighteens had never shown any discrimination against lunites, so that should be no problem.

Hamer certainly had his own reasons for deciding to go to Ceres, but the general attitude toward Ceres within Nobel was that it was a venture done by and supported by Earth, using Mars as a go-between, just to put another human outpost somewhere in the solar system. Ceres apparently lacked the mineral wealth to become self-sustaining, and depended on incoming shipments even more than Mars did. It did have what was less common on Luna, in particular hydroxyl compounds, but it did not have heavy elements in sufficient concentration to provide sustenance at a low enough energy expenditure.

It is not widely recognized that Luna's one-sixth Earth gravity made mining easier. Ceres' negligible gravity, less than 3% Earth gravity, meant that any excavation left the removed material scattering in all directions. As a mined area became larger, this phenomenon led to collection problems. Ceres was mined behind nets, but this nuisance added to the cost, putting self-sustenance even further out of the picture. Ceres had lithium for fusion fuel, but there was not so much concentration of single minerals on Ceres, so processing was less efficient. Then, there was all the waste rock, the useless light carbonates that comprised much of the surface. Earth supported Ceres, and the surface was still being explored, but prospects were miserable for being self-sustaining.

Ceres had a single underground habitat where Hamer would live. Everything had to be done differently because of the low gravity. Something simple on Luna, like food processing, was more difficult there. Luna's gravity kept things in place, even though much more care had to be taken with liquids, powders, and slurries. Hamer would have to keep everything in a container, and fasten these containers inside his habitat. Some things would be similar, such as the way rock walls were sealed and how airlocks were attached. But even going through an airlock would be different, to avoid a slow bounce off its ceiling.

There were countless 3vids available of living inside the habitation on Ceres, as well as of the exploration activities outside, so Hamer had every opportunity to understand how he would be living on Ceres long before making a decision to go there. He would understand the difficulty of moving and using heavy equipment on the surface of Ceres, and how exploratory mining had to be done, in order to drill deep enough to collect complete data. He would understand how to simply move on Ceres, and why surface vehicles did not work, so rocket packs had to be used. They could be small, and of high endurance, but nonetheless, that was how people had to move on the surface of Ceres. All of this simply added to the resource and energy costs of life on Ceres.

Some of the 3vids from Ceres clearly attempted to show that, after adapting, there was a certain amount of amusement to be gained from life in very low gravity. Some of the 3vids showed people jumping, under human power only, up from the surface. This was not the closest humans could come to putting themselves in orbit, but the obvious exhilaration shown during the jump, presumably after the person had grown accustomed to being isolated and very high off the surface, about 20 meters, indicates that it served as a sport on Ceres. This was more than five times the highest recorded standing jump of a seventeen on Luna, almost four meters. Other 3vids showed some residents in Ceres navigating over the surface in a floating car, powered by its own small rockets, with directional nozzles. Most of the faces shown seem to be more excited than the equivalent here on Luna, which would be traveling in a surface vehicle at about 25 km/hr.

The celebration for Hamar was not about Ceres, but about his contacts here and the imminent loss of them. Ceres communicated to Luna when it wanted to, but only with a fifteen to thirty minute delay in response, leaving communication awkward, much worse than with Earth. Many of his co-workers from the work task he had just completed, ore processing monitors, were in the group that gathered to say farewell to him. There was no indication that Hamar would necessarily return after his five year tour there, as extensions for such service are almost automatic to conserve resources, namely, spaceship travel. Someone could go out to the K-scope shack for life, if they wanted to. The K-scope was full of seventeens, but almost none stayed for a second tour. Perhaps Ceres would be different.

Hamar's speech at the celebration was recorded like all other speeches, and there is no indication there he was inviting others to follow him. He does not say exactly why he chose to go, other than for the adventure of it, so that would remain unknown until he returned.

Small celebrations such as the one commemorating Hamar's departure for Ceres would continue to go on, with one difficulty. During the centennial year, most public spaces were spoken for, and there would be nothing left for a small group. Gestation had gone on at the same rate during the previous centennials, meaning there were cohorts celebrating their hundredth or two-hundredth year, or even higher. Others might want to celebrate a quarter century or something else. Work projects would continue to end and commence, and people's work tours were even celebrated when they finished. There was nowhere left, as all the usual spots had been noticed by the 400th year committee and swept into their planning.

The anniversary cohorts for higher centennials had gotten used to this. Some cohort celebrating their 300th year since gestation would have celebrated their 200th year during the 300 year centennial, and their 100th year during the 200 year centennial. This was the origin of the habitat and street celebration ritual, which had spread far beyond its use in avoiding the congestion of a centennial celebration. Preferred locations are cul-de-sacs of residences, where someone's habitat can be opened as a gathering and preparation space, and the corridor screened off or otherwise closed off. It is not too unusual for a seventeen to be returning home and to find a small party going on along his way home. Tradition on Nobel, not always observed, is to invite such inconvenienced people in to taste the menu.

Nobel's 400 year celebration went off mostly as planned. Anything this complicated would have some problems, and so, having a rolling ball team cancel shortly before the game due to transportation limitations, mostly a sentience communication error, simply led to a Nobel team being called on to fill out the tournament competitors. They actually did not come in last. The flying competitions were mostly won by Centaurus seventeens, but acrobatics awards spanned almost all of Luna. Rhythmic acrobatics was won by a team from Ague-Tuilet, a team from BBS and Armstrong, and a team from Gautama. Some seventeens from Nobel, not part of the Nobel centennial committee or even the advisory committee, decided to take a poll on whose food was the most provocative, unusual, and flavorful, and managed to get the poll to Nobel seventeens. People on Nobel could partake of most of the offered meals, while visitors coming for a two tenday stay, for example in connection with the round trip vehicle race, would only get to try a few of the culinary innovations, and therefore could hardly be expected to have any competent opinion on what was best. The top three winners were all from Gagarin. It is hard to know if all the poll contributors were objective, or whether Gagarin's reputation as the place to find the best food simply spilled over into the Nobel presentations. Nonetheless, Gagarin did it again.

Nobel came in second in the round trip road race, despite having contestants who had raced fifty times already. Armstrong won. Armstrong had one vehicle that simply outperformed all the others. They did not use this vehicle on the large loop competition, but Nobel did not fill in the gap. The best Nobel time was seventh, with Boötes taking first and second, quite unexpectedly. Sentience investigation of their vehicle, after the race, indicated about a dozen changes had been made, each of which added microscopically to their average speed.

Some last minute changes were made to the celebration schedule, where "last minute" in Nobel means with less than a half year warning. During the loose days at the end of the year, the two parades were combined and repeated, with a longer route, actually with some doubling back so the paraders could all observe one another. Costumes from Nobel, and other groups from other mines that participated, were just as outlandish as some worn at the more festive celebrations.

Over a thousand marchers had shown up. In place of the usual tunic and trousers worn everywhere on Luna, there was everything from old Earth dress such as togas and saris to special creations by seventeens who did little else, not counting their work assignments, than design costumes. A large group from Boötes had animal costumes, which were expected. Some BBS seventeens, five to be exact, came as parts of old sentience and pre-sentience equipment. Nobel's designers concentrated on hats, and it was almost the standard answer to ask someone where their hat came from, and hear that it was from here in Nobel. Some of the hats revealed the otay senses, and others covered them up. Ague-Tuilet visitors included people who dressed in masks resembling those of old Earth. There were reflective materials, reflecting in different parts of the spectrum, in many costumes. Some had stiffeners that made the person wearing it look like a balloon or an hourglass. Several from other mines brought shoes and boots widened to absurdity. This served as a splendid finale for the centennial celebration.

On the first tenday of the next year, a talk group took up the topic of why, after witnessing how jovial, amusing, and entertaining life on the moon was, did Earth still regard Luna's mines with disdain, or rather simply didn't pay attention to Luna at all. Four hundred years ago, when Nobel was founded, there were many earthlings still on Luna, and work tours to Centaurus were common. Now, virtually no one comes. The discussion of the talk group is quite interesting, and worth repeating, as it bears on how the two worlds simply don't pay any attention to each other. It was true that Luna could not send visitors to Earth, and that may contribute to the lack of interest in Luna's people, traditions, and activities. The recordings of the ball competitions, to take an example, were watched over and over again by seventeens, alone and in groups, according to the records of the communications system. Only a few were even transferred to Earth databases, and a seventeen in the talk group asked his sentience to find out how many times they had been watched by earthlings, at least as measured by their being transferred. Usually once.

The talk group noted that Earth had its own ball sports, actually hundreds of variations, many common across the arcologies and some restricted to only the one where they originated. So why would they need to watch Luna's? The same seventeen had discovered through his sentience that there had been over fifty billion views of ball sports recordings on Earth during the last year. Fifty billion is where the sentience stopped counting. It was the same with vehicle races, acrobatics competitions, and everything else that Nobel had done. No Earth interest. Luna and Earth shared the same orbit around the sun, and their residents still collaborated on the GEO and a few other things, but they didn't do much else together. It was now actually mentioned in the mentoring of all seventeens on Luna that Earth regarded the lunar mines as analogous to prisons, but that term was growing anachronistic, as there were no prisons left on Earth. Perhaps earthlings' study of their own history gave them the impression that confinement is disgraceful and those involved in it should be avoided.

Perhaps it is because Luna is developing so methodically and gradually, even routinely, that the news from Mars, Jupiter, or Venus is more than enough to capture the attention of those on Earth who are interested in space. Luna might just be boring in comparison.

The talk group came to no specific consensus conclusion about it, but what was interesting was that everyone in the talk group regarded it as an interesting question, well worth investigating, but no one saw it as anything worth doing something about. In other words, as far as this small sample of lunites went, no one cared about interacting with Earth. The equivalent question of why lunites aren't interested in Earth, except as a discussion topic, wasn't asked in the talk group. There is extensive knowledge in each and every seventeen about Earth, gained during their mentoring, as well as a small amount that seeped down into the training years. Perhaps there is something about the mentoring guidelines concerning Earth that leaves seventeens with this lack of interest.

Perhaps the lack of interest in Earth is simply the response of a neglected or abandoned group of humans toward those who choose not to associate with or be involved with them. Alternatively, perhaps lunites have accepted their role as those who are confined and therefore ignorable. It's even possible that the fact that lunites are all seventeens and earthlings are mostly sixteens means that, being different species, they'll naturally drift apart – the psychological impact of being different having a deep subconscious impact. Whatever the reason, there are clear disadvantages to these two worlds following separate paths.

Life on Nobel after a centennial sinks into routine, just for reasons of exhaustion, not physical or mental, but organizational. For several years after it completed, Nobel continued to increase in population, extent, and activities. Everything functioned as before, as if planned to the smallest detail. Work assignments continued to be swapped, talk groups formed and broke up, people moved their habitats, all the utilities kept serving properly, and basically, not much happened.

The same could be said for the other mines, with one exception. Even before Andromeda had its inauguration as a mine, with twenty-nine seventeens spending the first night underground in Nobel year 396, Centaurus had been preparing for another one-two punch in the same way that they had pushed for BBS and Forrester to be completed close together, with the teams transferring from one to another with as little loss of time as possible. Andromeda was planned to have a partner mine, started after itself, but not much later. The committee that Centaurus had assembled still met, every year or so, but with the inevitable ending of work task periods, none of the same people on the Andromeda startup plan were still on the committee. All the records were there, and the sentiences could easily mimic the sequence of work, but some choice had to be made as to location.

The two spare locations examined by the Nobel exploratory team were looked at again, and were again put on the list of future mines, but not the next mine. Instead the committee wanted to look beyond Sirius, even further to the west, and quite a bit further. The Nobel team was asked to do the exploratory drilling for the next mine, mine number 13, beyond Sirius across some of the roughest highlands on the lunar surface. The exploratory team for Andromeda had disbanded after fulfilling its mission, and there were not enough volunteers within Nobel to complete the staffing, so two more seventeens were picked up on the trip to Sirius, one from Ague-Tuilet and the other from Armstrong. There was only one site on the list, so this round of exploratory drilling would be much quicker than the one for Andromeda.

A combined team was first put together to blaze the trail from Sirius to the new site. The team was mostly Centaurus residents, but also had volunteers from Ague-Tuilet and Gautama. The pathway found was very sinuous, avoiding the steepest regions between the two end-points as well as large and small craters. It was marked, and the progress was slow, with the marking team returning to Sirius six times to meet with supply convoys coming over from Centaurus. As soon as the route was finished, the solar shield group gathered itself at Ague-Tuilet to make its way over to Sirius for its last stop before leaving for the work site. This group would have crossed paths with the marking group returning along the same route, the only route, and could have stopped together for a break, except for one thing. The marking team was asked to go further.

Every mine put into the lunar surface had been connected by a single pathway from an existing mine, except, of course, for Centaurus, which was located close to the landing site for the many landings that were used almost six hundred years ago to establish the first mine. The new thirteenth mine committee had decided that for this mine, there would be two roads. The marking team was asked to continue their arduous task of stretching the road from Sirius even further, until they reached Andromeda.

The task was even more onerous than doing the first road, as the new mine committee asked that the road pass through another proposed site between the new mine and Andromeda, which would require deviating from the main path. There is little recorded dissension from the marking team members, as everyone knew what this additional link represented. There would be a highway completely around Luna. One of the team members who had a great interest in Earth history compared it with the railroad crossing of the northern part of the second-largest land mass a century before space flight was attempted, or the crossing of the eastern part of the largest land mass fifty years after that, on a northern route, followed by a southern road crossing the same distance in the century after space flight, or even the north-south railroad on the third-largest land mass, which was incidentally of unmeasurable importance in the building of the Earth Spaceport at Alice Springs. His depiction of how important this would be completely convinced the team members to push onward.

While the marking team was busy finding a path through another thousand kilometers of lunar landscape, erecting transitory solar shelters, and ensuring there were no dangerous formations, they argued about what recommendation to make for the name of this segment of the road. One of the two choices was to call it another piece of the Armstrong Road, and, in fact, to designate the entire road around Luna the Armstrong Highway. Another choice was to name each segment differently, and let this one be called the Alice Highway, after the spaceport which was used in the founding of Centaurus and indeed, which led to establishment of all the mines on the moon.

The last segment of the circumlunar highway was not completed until Nobel year 408, owing to the need to refurbish some of the convoy vehicles during the period, and the long time needed to return for supplies to Sirius. It might have been more expedient to cease work halfway, and then go around the entire satellite to Andromeda, starting out there to join up with the stopping point. This was not done. Instead, the team simply pushed onward until they reached Andromeda from the east. Unfortunately, there were some steep crossings that could not be easily avoided in the first part of this route, but the second half was easier and went faster.

During the last year of road location and navigation, two things happened. An individual from Gagarin was assigned to the team with the principal responsibility of recording more details of the work, and making them available to all on Luna. There was widespread interest in the completion, and some mines showed 3vids of the routing on their large screens during off-times, when there was nothing else being shown live and no public interest items were scheduled.

After the routing was completed, the routing team chose to return home via the eastern direction, meaning that they would have circumnavigated Luna for the first time. While this was an honor for each of the members, it was decided nine tendays before the expected completion date that a convoy would make the trip, with members from every mine, stopping at all nine working mines along the route, meaning Centaurus, Boötes, Orion, Armstrong, BBS, Andromeda, Sirius, Forrester, and Ague-Tuilet, as well as the work site for mine 13. To make the trip across the new expanse of lunar surface, the convoy had to have hydrogen and oxygen tankers accompany it.

At each of the nine mines, there was a celebration, informal at the smaller ones, but with large public gatherings at the last one. There were actually two on Centaurus, one to send off the convoy and one to greet it upon its return. Of the many public speeches made during the convoy stopovers, one at Boötes was viewed much more than most. The speaker, Granin Topil Rimes, pointed out that it was not so much a great achievement that was being celebrated, which is was, but the fact that the back side of the moon was now opened up much further for exploration and colonization, and that the whole satellite was now unified in a tighter way. He praised the combined team that had done the path marking, and saying that this was like lighting a fire which would eventually spread all over the moon, with someday a large network of highways connected to and surrounding the Armstrong Circumlunar Highway. More was said about the location of new mines on the Earth side and the back side of the moon, but this speech seemed to have forced the choice of naming the road. It was widely known from the 3vid recordings of the work in progress that it might be divided into segments for nomenclature, with one being the Alice Highway, but that possibility seemed to vanish with Granin's speech, memorable as it was.

The Nobel team, plus associates, that did the exploratory drilling around the 13th site, was asked to go to the site further out the highway, which the road marking team was asked to cross through, and the combined team doing the solar shields at the 13th mine was asked to go to this site as well, but since there was no planning for it, it would be clear that the mine would be decades away. The solar shield team and the Nobel team felt there was no need to do this work so far in advance and instead opted to simply go home.

While they were working on the site, the solar shield team had been calling it the Shamrock mine, as one of the team members had learned about ancient Earth superstitions, meaning 13 was unlucky for anything and finding a shamrock, a kind of Earth plant, was lucky. The team humorously continued with the name, and, during the time both were on site, it spread to the Nobel team as well. It appeared in all the reports of both teams, made daily, showing the progress each had done during their separate periods. It did not spread to the planning committee. They called it the 13th mine, and put together a group of nine seventeens, to come up with the real name. Shamrock was almost preferred, but Glasov won out. Glasov, the first human to set foot on Mars, was not as important to lunar history as Armstrong, but the Mars colonization that started with Glasov and his colleagues never halted or slowed down, until there was permanent residents on Mars, or at least residents with shelters to live in. No one stayed on Mars in the early days, just as no earthlings stayed on Luna for too long, when they were the only humans on the moon. Glasov symbolized not just a new planet being conquered, but also human persistence.

Outside of their participation in the Glasov new mine, what did happen in Nobel during the next two decades or more following the four hundred year centennial was seemingly minor. In a public meeting relating to expanding some residential area in Nobel year 407, the attendees seemingly insisted on a vote. There were six choices that the design squad had come up with, all feasible and not too different in cost and time to complete. There was a vote, and all six received sizable numbers. However, after the numbers were announced, one seventeen stood up and asked to change his vote to the choice that had received the higher amount. There were unrecognized voices all around him saying the same thing. The seventeen running the meeting asked if that choice should be taken as the consensus, and there was almost complete assent. No one dissented, just like in almost all the previous public meetings where some choice had to be made. The experiment with voting worked, but seemed very ephemeral.

In Nobel year 416, there was a change in mentoring scheduling, as in a public discussion the resolution was accepted that no more single year mentoring would be done. The shortest term would be a year and a half, and scheduling was reassembled to accommodate that. It was two years in most mines, and in most arcologies on Earth.

In Nobel year 420, Centaurus asked for a Luna-wide meeting, with representatives from every mine, to discuss the possibility of adding a second spaceport to Luna. The meeting was to be held in Centaurus, and in the quarter year prior to the meeting, each mine would have public discussions of their response, and, if it was positive, or even negative, what role they might like to contribute to. This seemingly simple question split the lunite population quite significantly. Sentience estimates of the support indicated that Centaurus favored it fairly heavily, perhaps because the burden of space travel fell disproportionately on them, and other mines, except for tiny Armstrong and BBS, responded more or less negatively. Some of those busy excavating the new mine, Glasov, chimed in with comments that it could be delayed. Armstrong and BBS had public meetings, as requested, and the consensus in these two mines was that it should be done soon.

At the all-mine meeting in Centaurus, representatives from each mine came with a synopsis of their population's sentiments about a new spaceport, and there was so little support for a new spaceport that Centaurus knew they would continue to be responsible for all the fuel and refurbishment costs for the near future, as they had been for five centuries. Nobel's response was that the spaceport, if built, should be on the backside of the moon, to further eliminate any chance of a catastrophe taking out both of them. Ague-Tuilet has always been the second largest mine, but they are also closest to Centaurus, so the common risk factor might keep them from being contenders for a spaceport, if it was ever decided on. BBS and Armstrong had collaborated, and felt that whenever it was built, having it along the Armstrong Circumlunar Highway, midway between their two mines, meant that they could share the burden of managing it. They had prepared some estimates of the flights they would have there, considering that almost all of them would still go to Centaurus. It would be tolerable after their populations exceeded twenty thousand each, which was still in the distant future as both mines had populations under a thousand.

In Nobel year 422, Glasov had an occupied habitat underground, which qualified it as being an official mine and not simply a work site. It would take the next several decades before it achieved full and complete self-sustainability. Now there were thirteen mines operating on Luna. In

Nobel year 424, Glasov became the first mine to discover a cave on the moon. While boring a drift from the central shaft to an ore body, the tunneling machine came upon a curved crack in the underground surface. At its widest, it was 0.8 m across, and extended 11 meters vertically and 80 meters horizontally. Since this crack was in a mining drift, that would not be not be pressurized until some distant future date, there were no operational consequences except that a very unique bridge had to be built for the mining equipment to cross. The edges of the crack, nicknamed Glasov cavern, were quite strong and the crack was simply left alone. If it had not shattered when the tunneling equipment first contacted it, it was considered a permanent feature. Nevertheless, the bridge was over 20 meters long and spanned the entire drift, for safety reasons.

In Nobel year 427, some seventeens living in the Gagarin mine finished constructing a vehicle modeled on the ones used on Ceres to travel over the surface. It had eight rocket nozzles, organized in four pairs at the ends of four struts forming the diagonal lines of a square. There were hydrogen and oxygen tanks near the center, along with controller equipment. After some experimentation, it was successful, but the range of the vehicle was much too short to be useful for inter-mine travel. The originators did find it highly amusing to travel up above the surface for a view. There was sufficient thrust in the nozzles so that if one failed, the other in the same corner could compensate sufficiently for a safe landing. Even so, the altitudes involved in the test did not exceed eleven meters.

One of the seventeens involved was Hamer Govoz Bishek, who had been the first lunite to go to Ceres. Hamer had spent two five-year terms there, before returning to Nobel in Nobel year 408. He emigrated to Gagarin in Nobel year 410. On Ceres, Hamer had spent some time using the Ceres vehicles, which had a much longer range, and were dangerous in a different way. They could go into orbit. Ceres vehicles had reversible nozzles to deal with this possibility. Hamer's 3vids of vehicle operations were widely seen around Nobel, and in other mines as well. He left Nobel after a two-year work term in the power stations, during which time he was mentoring three other young Nobel residents as well.

Almost simultaneous with Hamer's departure for Gagarin, two other seventeens, much younger than Hamer, left for Ceres on the typical five-year work tour. Their departure was no less celebrated than Hamer's, even though they were not the first to leave Nobel for service on Ceres. A half year later, there was a pair of seventeens who left for the K-scope project, although nobelites and other mines had been providing volunteers for this project for most of the hundred years that it had been progressing. The Jupiter wheel did not benefit from the increased interest in interplanetary volunteers, and the inner wheel there was still only occupied by Martians, if at all. The experimental stations orbiting Venus and the Mercury orbiter and ground station had no attraction either. There were more than enough volunteers from Earth, and in fact, the lotteries for slots sometimes had a hundred earthlings vying for a single opening. Neither the Venus orbiters or the Mercury orbiter had a wheel with lunar gravity, and Mercury itself had the same gravity, approximately, as Mars did, so it was quite reasonable to see an absence of contributions from Luna.

The Uranus wheel that Earth was constructing in geosynchronous orbit did not even have an inner wheel with lower gravity, and no one on the moon was noted as having raised an objection to that aspect of the design. It was about half way through its twenty-six year construction schedule, and after construction was finished, there would be a hundred and fifty-four year journey out to an orbit around Uranus. The wheel would be unoccupied when in transit, just as the Venus and Mercury wheels had been. People would begin arriving shortly thereafter. It would require hibernation for about a century, but Earth's planners estimated that there would be sufficient volunteers. Since the human calendar did not move forward in hibernation, there was no loss of personal longevity that came from hibernation, except perhaps for the 2 to 3 percent uptime that hibernation required for long voyages. It would be a little strange when the cohorts that provided Saturn volunteers came to the end of their lifetimes, those who had made the trip to Saturn and back would be around for an additional twenty-oddyears, on average.

18

THE COMPLETION OF LIFE ON LUNA

For seventeens, the Death Watch began in Nobel year 431. This was the beginning of a ten year interval before the prediction of death date for the first cohorts of seventeens born on Luna. It was plenty of time to get ready to readjust society to the fact that no one was immortal, and death was an inevitable final stop for everyone. The announcement was made, in an off-handed way, by means of one of the leaders in Centaurus saying that several new work tasks would be opening up, for dealing with seventeens in the end-of-life processes, and that some task revisions would be made for existing positions.

Centaurus leaders had thought everything out, but it was all obvious anyway. Reconstitution centers would be the places where monitoring was arranged for. Even though that was not expected, some space changes within the centers might be necessary to create a resting place for seventeens who lost mobility before their final days. Housing near the reconstitution center would be gradually vacated and re-used as hostel space for seventeens in their final tendays. A slight juggling of nutrition output would be necessary. Some work tasks related to providing any additional assistance a last-days seventeen would need were created, and volunteers were not scarce to be in the lottery for this task selection. Reconstitution teams would have the additional task, which is actually already included in their tasks, of picking up the bodies of a seventeen who died away from the reconstitution area, and bringing them to a temporary holding place, a former habitat, before they would be brought to recycling, in a special vehicle marked for that purpose.

Seventeens from the first year's worth of cohorts in Centaurus seemed to have developed differently than later seventeens. Many of them were excellent at public speaking, and 3vids created by these lunites were recorded and watched frequently. One noteworthy one talked about how, when he finished his training at age 15 on Centaurus, he entered life in the mine, while participating in mentoring. It was like being a strange animal, wandering among all the earthlings in Centaurus at that time, looking quite different from any of them, and watching them watch him. That was the case for the first several decades, before the numbers of seventeens in the corridors began to be significant. The earliest seventeens were drawn together, not because they were ostracized by the earthlings, but because they were special objects of attention. He did not feel the same way in training, because, although there were always earthlings around, most of the training was done by avatars. These avatars were completely different from him; he claimed that he had become aware of that very young, but there were other seventeens around all the time and the idea of being a tiny minority did not sink in. But once training ended and he left the school residential area to began mentoring, exclusively with earthlings, he was overcome with feelings of isolation and separation.

Other first- and second-cohort seventeens talked about being the first seventeen to work in the nutrition facility, in the power facilities, in the recycling facilities, or in mining or ore processing, and how good it felt when a second seventeen joined him there. Always the isolation, always the uniqueness, always the disconnect from the rest of the population. This certainly affected how the seventeens from the early cohorts developed. Many became lifelong innovators, ready to be the first to try anything new, whether it was a new sport or a new culinary concoction. Others developed a strong bond with other early seventeens, and even a reluctance to be with earthlings.

Another early cohort seventeen made a speech, summarizing the events in his life, and concluded that being the first seventeen in different things was actually a thrill for him, but until recently he had not realized, or at least not thought about, that he would be one of the first seventeens to die. With no deaths on Luna for this long period of five hundred plus years, it was easy for seventeens to forget about their mortality, and speeches like this were like an emergency alarm, grabbing everyone's attention. Life on Luna was all enjoyable and interesting work tasks, good living conditions, all manner of facilities for sports or other athletics, large numbers of people to talk to and discuss all manner of topics, and more. But now it also was a place to die. Other older seventeens began to mention in their talk groups that they were thinking about how to spend their last years, how these years would somehow be special for them. They discussed what they wanted to work on, whether is was to mentor some particular subject or something else. The subtle start of the Death Watch changed the tone of life on Luna, at least until the novelty of it wore off.

The first year of cohorts of seventeens had not all stayed in Centaurus, and in fact, almost exactly half of them had moved elsewhere, some several times. A few had experienced six or even eight different mines. When the initial announcement about new tasks came out in Centaurus, it was repeated everywhere as the signal of a new era. People in smaller mines responded quite differently, as they did not have the resources to provide care for near-terminating seventeens. There were public meetings in each mine to discuss options for their own Death Watch. The largest five mines besides Centaurus came up with plans similar to Centaurus' plan, but the rest, from Armstrong down to Glasov, had little they could do. There was a large gulf in population between Gautama, the smallest of the big six, which had over five thousand people, and Armstrong, the biggest of the rest, with just over one thousand. There were first-year cohort seventeens almost everywhere, but the problem solved itself.

First-cohort seventeens living in the smaller mines almost universally decided to return to a large mine. Many chose Centaurus. A sprinkling chose other large mines. One seventeen in this group who was living in Glasov announced to his talk group that he was returning to Nobel, having spent most of his years there. He had left to help sink the main shaft at Armstrong, and stayed there for decades after it became a mine, bringing it close to self-sustaining capability, then spent time at Boötes before leaving to help sink the main shaft at Glasov, working out of Sirius, and then stayed there at Glasov to build out the facilities. There were some seventeens who really enjoyed the new mine environment, or even the pre-mine surface work, and then there were some who preferred living in a small population. This would come to an end as the affected seventeens returned to a larger mine where care for them would be better.

On Luna, there is a tradition that people can live wherever they want to, although there might be a wait while spaces become available. No one ordered the early cohort seventeens to go to the larger mines, but seventeens are all practical, having been grown and raised to be that way. Foolish choices simply weren't made. So, the return migration started, shortly after the Centaurus announcement. The migration affected not only the oldest cohort seventeens, but also many other cohorts, stretching back decades. Census numbers indicated a gradual flow of older seventeens back to their mine of origin or some other mine where the population was high and facilities were more complete.

The first death of a seventeen occurred, right on schedule, in Nobel year 441. It was in Centaurus, and if the Death Watch announcement and the significant facility changes were not sufficient to change the tone on Luna, this was. Many talk groups canceled their meetings, not only in Centaurus but also in other mines, during the tenday following the death, even in cases where the individual was not known to anyone in the group. There were no public meetings held in the next few tendays. The first death was from the third cohort to be gestated in Centaurus, and more deaths followed in succession in that year, totaling 27 in all. The next year had a total of over a hundred, which was just slightly more than the number gestated in the first year of seventeens. Some were from the second year. Deaths of seventeens became commonplace and Centaurus gradually relaxed back into normal operations, with death vehicles a common sight near the largest reconstitution center. The false lull was over, and work continued.

For Nobel, the experience was somewhat different, due to the low numbers of early-cohort seventeens that lived there. Deaths were still unusual, and it took some years for the rate to grow frequent enough that the special vehicle became a common and unremarkable sight. Population counts were hardly affected until well after the next half-centennial.

Earth started acting up in Nobel year 443. Earth was mostly composed of arcologies, some three hundred or so of them, each one more or less independent, with frequent trading and travel between them. A typical population would be between five and twenty million. Thus, when the leaders of three of the arcologies got together to do something regarding Luna, it was not that important. However, the three involved were among the largest and most influential, so the contact could not be ignored.

These three leaders had noticed, among the vast amount of other news that must flow by them every day, that Luna was almost not interacting with Earth. The main interaction was aboard the GEO, and at this time, only seven lunites were living there on work assignments. There was space for thirty without the least bit of crowding. There were a few lunites out on the K-scope, as there always had been, but none of the other of Earth's outposts had any volunteers. The contact with Ceres had dried up after the pair of seventeens had returned after a five year work cycle. These leaders were sixteens, with a psychology much like that of seventeens, and they recognized that there was a problem that needed to be fixed. They had remote discussions about it, which were recorded as usual, and the point they made was that humanity may be divided into different species, but they were still all humanity, with many similarities, and should not be drifting apart into separate communities.

Their first step was to invite Luna to send more volunteers to the various projects, in particular the GEO. The GEO was where all the space operations were coordinated, where different projects were designed and managed, where unique apparatus was built for space use, and where transport between Luna and Earth, as well as out to all the outposts, was controlled. If more seventeens became involved with project planning and everything else on the GEO, they might spark some more interest at home when they returned, or even in their communications with associates and friends still on Luna.

No one spoke for all of Luna. The mines were just as independent as the arcologies on Earth were, so the three leaders on Earth sent suggestions, or perhaps requests might be better, that Luna's mines consider making more personnel contributions to the GEO. All task assignments on Luna were voluntary, and not having one on Luna was so onerous, in fact downright boring, that there was never much need to make second or third calls for volunteers. The number of tasks was less than the number of seventeens in each of the mines, but the reason was not that someone wanted to be idle. Everyone was busy, and even during a work gap, a seventeen would be occupied with something. The sentiences arranged schedules, through the work lottery, so that most individuals would only have a quarter year gap with nothing to do. Slots were always filled because seventeens were designed to be uncomfortable to be idle. There was nothing like a low-status job in any of the mines. An individual might not like a position, but that would be the preference of that person alone.

Interplanetary work, and work on the GEO, were exceptions. Filling these was not mandatory for the work lottery, and those slots stayed unfilled, even when there was someone who had been idle for ten or twenty tendays. It was the same in all the mines. Working outside transporting materials from one mine to another appealed to some seventeens. Monitoring the gestation of new seventeens appealed to others. Managing specialty plants appealed to some subset as well. And so on with the other assignments, excluding work on the GEO. For some reason, that had appealed to very few for a very long time. It made no difference which mine was asked. The mines were quite different in some regards, but not in this one. The psychology was not quite transparent as to why this was so, but it was. And the request from three important positions on Earth did not immediately reverse a century-old attitude. A few more seventeens, six to be exact, volunteered to be flown up to the GEO and to do a two-year work term there. This would make thirteen all together. The important personages on Earth could claim some success, while life on Luna hardly changed. For a few work terms, numbers on GEO stayed where they had gotten to after the request, so that was more success.

In Nobel year 446, the inevitable committee to manage a half-centennial celebration was formed. Once again, Nobel was going to entertain the rest of Luna in a thoroughly unique way. The committee proceeded by getting out all the records from the 400th year celebrations, and attempting to see if it could all be done over again. Mostly it could, as each of the various things included continued with a life of their own. There were competitions around Luna in all of the events that became concentrated in Nobel during one of these celebrations. The Nobel competitions were a bit more orchestrated with a few more flourishes, and so there was no reluctance for, say, the organization that organized ball tournaments of different kinds to structure their next four years around bringing the best teams and individuals to Nobel during the celebration. Nothing happened for the tournaments in Nobel that would not have happened otherwise. A hoop ball team's star player might migrate to the opposite side of the moon, crushing someone's hopes of a spectacular competition. A flyer might just decide enough was enough and retire to become a racing contributor. These types of events always caused changes in the planning but never forced an event to be canceled.

While all the usual planning was underway, which involved over two thousand individuals, most in Nobel, an unusual twist came about. Earth, specifically the three arcologies that had been in contact with Luna about GEO slots, asked to send observers to the centennial. It was not hard for any talk group at all to realize this was step two in trying to build better bonds between Luna and Earth. It was unexpected, and, to many, unwelcome. Hospitality is written into the psyche of seventeens, but so is much else. Luna was a clean place. Earth was not, as there were microbes everywhere. Bringing earthlings into Nobel would run the risk of contamination. The risk was small, as there was little media for microbes to live on, but it was non-zero.

Noble had three public meetings in quick succession, and one was with the centennial committee, resulting in no reason arising from the centennial itself to ban these visitors. Two more were held with a remote connection to a group in Centaurus, who had the responsibility of dealing with off-world visitors. All that was needed was a sterilization chamber and a quarantine period. Sixteens were no different from seventeens in that they had no need to have microbes interact with them symbiotically. A sterilized sixteen was a healthy sixteen. A visible solution was right in front of everyone, until someone from Nobel asked about what would happen if Earth wanted to send some originals. Everyone who had completed mentoring knew that you couldn't sterilize originals.

Why would Earth want to send originals? At the time of the meeting, Earth still had a large population of originals, two hundred million out of four billion. The solution would be to inform the arcologies of the need for sterilization, and that would ensure no originals were included in the visitor group. So, quite quickly, agreement was made, and Nobel began arranging for what was needed to have Earth sixteens present in the mine, anywhere at all. This was more work for Nobel at the busiest time possible, but it could be done, and was done. About nine tendays before the beginning of the celebration in Nobel year 450, the three arcologies' leaders, actually two plus the replacement of the third, sent a list of visitors. Eight groups of twenty each. Nobel planners had assumed it would be one group for the final tenday of the year, with maybe five or six visitors. This meant evictions of residents or cancellations of visit arrangements, not many, but it was uncomfortable for the Nobel centennial subcommittee to have to do this. Centaurus was going to have to find fuel for the large number of ships that would be traveling from GEO to LPO and then to their landing pad so they could be fueled for the return flights. Centaurus would have a great deal of work to do, simply to support the Nobel half-centennial and its Earth visitors. There was, for the period of this half-centennial, a lack of appreciation among several different groups. Nonetheless, everything happened as planned.

Or not quite as planned. When the first earthling group was here, during the period of one of the flight competitions, they did not stay together. Nobel had appointed two hosts to steer them to dinner, around on tours of the mine, to presentations on the screens, to the stages of competition, and they were totally prepared to answer questions and resolve petty issues. This was actually set up as a work task for the pair. Unfortunately, the visitor group did not stay together past the first hour of their visit. The leaders of the three arcologies must have combed their populations to find the most extroverted, most gregarious, most polite, and most unassuming sixteens, and gathered them all together for the trip to Nobel. They spread out as if on command, and began to join other groups of spectators, sit down with separate individuals for small or large meals, mixing and mingling continuously and as smoothly as any human could hope to do.

The tour leader pair informed those who were filling decision-making positions in Nobel, including the centennial organizers, of what was going on, and they immediately recognized that they had not had any idea what the purpose of the visitors was. That became more obvious day by day. It was not possible to interact with the earthlings and not realize that earthlings were incredibly nice people to associate with. Some lunites began to wonder why lunites couldn't be more sociable, agreeable, and so on. There was nothing to be done but to host the eight groups during the year.

The half-centennial was a success for some and not for others. Gagarin's vehicles were disqualified from the large loop race, and did not come in the top three for the round trip. They somewhat redeemed themselves when a different group displayed the Ceres vehicle on the surface. Boötes had developed over twenty novel living things on a small scale, a few centimeters each, and had brought them for display, resulting in great attention. Gautama had large animals to show, and Orion had a snake-like creature. Nobel's vegetation showed the results of much attention, with the mine's name spelled out in colors on the plots. This would not have been so impressive, except that the colors changed, synchronously, every few days.

The other mines had recognized the level of effort that Nobel put into their celebrations, and were both impressed and appreciative, and knew that it would be better if Nobel were not asked to divert its attention from planning the centennial to planning a new mine. Ague-Tuilet took the lead in setting up the process to build a new mine along the Armstrong Highway, at the place previously determined and used as a passageway by the highway marking team. In Nobel year 448, Ague-Tuilet kicked off the work on that site, with Gautama doing the exploratory drilling instead of Nobel. A composite team worked on building the solar shields at the site. There was no need for any road marking at all. During the centennial, a second composite team began the task of sinking the main shaft.

Even after the celebration continued and the Earth visitors had all been shipped home, the 14th mine team did not draw Nobel into the work crews that were finishing the main shaft, building the stations and the head frame, and excavating the first drifts. Nobel contributed less to this mine than to any mine since it was itself inaugurated and became self-sustaining. They were invited to contribute suggestions to the naming committee, but that would have been self-defeating, as the name Alice had already begun to be used, even in the committee's planning. Alice was the name chosen in a perfunctory video session by the committee. Ostensibly, this was to commemorate Alice Springs, the Earth spaceport that was responsible for getting the first mine started. It didn't stay that way, however.

Actual physical pictures of an Earth girl, an original, had been put up in the interior of the solar shields around the site when the head frame was being delivered in components and erected on site. They stayed up and multiplied over time. When the upper stations were being excavated, someone in a suit put up a much larger one in the hoist cage, on the outside of the screen facing inward. When 3vids of the picture circulated, most seventeens knew from early training it was Alice from

Alice in Wonderland, a book from before the space era. Alice from Alice in Wonderland seemed to be stealing the name of the latest mine from Earth's spaceport.

Habitation underground at Alice happened in Nobel year 460. A Nobel seventeen had been lucky enough to have won the lottery to both be on the habitat construction team at Alice and to be one of the group of eight to go to sleep underground and wake up on the first day of the new mine's formal existence. He was in frequent communication with a former talk group back on Nobel, and let them know that there was music from Earth, with the Alice in Wonderland theme, playing that evening and again in the morning. One of Earth's Alices had displaced the other.

Nobel year 460 was also the year when Nobel began to question itself. Since Centaurus' first day, all the mines had been growing in population, with no exceptions. There were fluctuations in the growth rate, but never any downward trends. Since the half-centennial, and to a lesser extent before that, Nobel had been experiencing heavy rates of emigration. There was still only a small death rate, which hardly affected the population. Instead, almost as many seventeens were emigrating as were gestated each year, meaning the population was only very slightly growing. This meant that not much excavation was needed for new housing, nor were any facilities, nor anything at all. It was an unusual situation, and the lack of expansion was noticeable.

When someone emigrates, they need to coordinate it with the destination mine. Emigrants from Nobel were not going to the largest mines, Centaurus and Ague-Tuilet, but to Gagarin, Gautama, Böotes, and BBS mostly, with some smaller numbers going to other small mines. The reason for the request was often given in terms of the destination mine. For Gautama, it was to experience the design of a mine laid out with totally different rules. For Böotes, it was to experience animal design, creation, and husbandry. For Gagarin, it was to learn to be creative in nutrition preparation. For BBS, to be in a smaller mine where life was less impersonal. These were almost all formulaic answers with no originality, but also nothing related to avoiding something in the departure mine, Nobel.

Centaurus was also experiencing low growth, but that was due to their decision to cap their population at a hundred twenty five thousand, and to taper off gestation to achieve that smoothly. Ague-Tuilet was also experiencing low growth, not from any caps, but from emigration as well, but not as severely as Nobel. Some talk groups on Nobel took up the challenge of deducing the hidden reason behind the dwindling of Nobel's permanent population. Comparison with other mines showed almost all had high rates of emigration, and the problem was not emigration, but the lack of compensating immigration specifically to Nobel. Few were seeking to come to Nobel, and certainly nowhere near enough to balance out the emigration. Instead of focusing on the emigrants, the hidden reason needed to be sought in the other mines, asking why so few who lived there thought of migrating to Nobel.

Three talk groups decided to merge their get-togethers in Nobel year 461 to try and decipher the low immigration problem. One suggestion was that some people did not like to be around celebrations as large as Nobel's centennial ones. However, since this only happened every fifty years, it couldn't be the reason for low immigration now. Another suggestion reminded everyone that Nobel was the only mine to have experienced a moonquake which tripped the sensors. Anyone who was extremely concerned about personal safety might regard this as a deterrent to immigration. A third suggestion was that those other mines that had features that attracted emigrants also might be holding on to residents, as they found they actually greatly enjoyed the feature. Another suggestion, more subtle, was that Nobel was seen as a luxury mine, with the centennials, pools, vegetation, flying stope, and perhaps other features that left those seventeens in other mines thinking they did not want to be so special, but stay in a more ordinary mine. A further suggestion was that Nobel did not encourage a sense of identity that other mines did. The hypothesis was that seventeens in Nobel thought of themselves as lunites, whereas those in other mines felt they were Armstrong guys, or BBSers, or Gautamians, and so on.

The leader of Nobel, shift one, which was the senior one, was a member of this merged talk group, and would be the one to try to do something about the problem. He spoke during one of the sessions of the merged group on this, asking them to continue to investigate causes, because he did not see any clear way to resolve it. The merged talk group did continue to meet for some time.

While Nobel was involved with its own issues, Earth had not been leaving Luna alone. The visitor effort to Nobel's half-centennial did have an effect on the seventeen population on the GEO. It rose from thirteen to twenty four in the three years following the celebration, and crept up to twenty-five the year after that, almost to capacity. The same three arcologies asked Böotes if they would like to host a delegation from the large genetics group in the largest of the three arcologies. The number of people involved with this genetics organization in the arcology was larger than the entire population of Böotes, so the request was met with apprehension. On Earth, genetics was a huge occupation, and played a large role in their economy. On Luna, it was a hobby for amusement. What was the point of the delegation? Böotes declined the offer, but after discussion back and forth, they accepted the visit of two earthlings for an informal visit.

Next, Earth suggested that Luna send some seventeens to the Mercury wheel, to work on the mineralogical exploration of that planet's surface. The wheel had only been in Mercury orbit since Nobel year 439, and surface exploration had only been going on since 441. There was a tremendous amount to do, according to the Earth suggestion, and there was not a whole inner wheel of lower gravity, but two large chambers on opposing sides of the central cylinder, where a seventeen could live with some restrictions. There was someone in Ague-Tuilet who signed up for it on the condition that another volunteer be found, and one was, from Gautama. They left in Nobel year 457 for a two year hibernation cruise and a five year work assignment. So, Earth's quest to involve Luna in more joint activity was microscopically successful.

Their success with Mercury may have encouraged them to take on a more difficult persuasion task. After the two seventeens had reached Mercury, and were involved with communicating back to Luna, Earth's three arcologies, the ones that continued to have a interest in involving Luna, suggested that Luna's mines try and find some volunteers for the Jupiter wheel.

Earth had started the Jupiter wheel very long ago, with the first residents there arriving in Nobel year 276. For a hundred and eighty years, the wheel had served as the location for research on Jupiter itself, on the four Galilean satellites, and on the magnetosphere surrounding the giant planet. There had been multiple landings on the satellites, various clever devices dropped into the Jupiter atmosphere, and particles captured and tracked, amounting to perhaps a hundred different experiments. The Jupiter wheel was something that Earth was proud of, and was not even considering terminating, but it had not succeeded in the one task that would have made a difference. It had not found a way to turn the gas giant into something useful for humanity.

There was no way to extract energy from the magnetosphere, despite the massive amounts of energy within it, even more than Earth's annual consumption. Capturing hydrogen from the top of the atmosphere was simply too costly in terms of getting it out of the potential well. The four satellites were even less valuable for minerals than Ceres. There were some there, but too highly mixed with overly common elements. Samples could be retrieved from any one of the satellites, or from any point on any of the satellites, but there was no place there which would provide a great benefit to those in the wheel or those on Earth. Did some people on Earth think a couple of seventeens from Luna could provide the missing idea? Earth was no more successful with their suggestion for working on the wheel than were all the previous requests for assistance there.

DIARY ENTRY (AGE 317, DAY 3)

Today was spent watching 3vids from Earth, which I almost never do. They might be interesting in the sense I have never seen anything like them before, but they are disconnected from my life. Today I just got interested in them, and watched them while eating small meals for the whole waking day.

Of the millions of possibilities, I was watching mostly synthetic ecologies. There are few plants here on Luna, few animals, and few microbes as well. But on Earth there are countless numbers of them. Since genetics became well understood, five or six hundred years ago, earthlings have been adding to the number every year. I was watching the winners of the genetic ecology competitions for the last century or so, selecting the best of the best to view. The one that spurred me to write a diary note was one from seventy four years ago made in an arcology in the center of an archipelago between the Indian and Pacific oceans. Each contestant team was given a five-kilometers-square area to create their ecology. The one that won had made dragons, which is their word for animals exhaling flame. It was quite clever genetic engineering. The dragons had a sac that was filled with alcohol made in glands, isolated from the rest of the body, with an openable restriction to the throat above the lungs. Muscles in the sac would push some alcohol into a forceful exhalation of air, and the teeth at the front of the jaw had precipitated metals which would spark. The flame wasn't hot enough to burn anything, but it was impressive enough to win that year's competition.

The engineering of the animal was quite comprehensive, in that there could be no significant absorption of alcohol in the throat, so they had to design a new surface there. There were other metabolic changes as well, to be able to grow the new organs. There were four of these animal types, as well as all the vegetation they needed to eat to grow from embryos. The animals were bisexual, and the flames were used in mating displays. Each of the vegetation types was also interesting, but that is standard in these genetic ecological competitions. There were flowers, hanging vines, large leaves, and ground cover, and all the plants were viable, living on soil and solar photons. That was a rule of the ecology competition. It is more than a collection of interesting life forms, some of which ate other ones. It is an actual symbiotic set of organisms that would last for decades, if untouched by humans or other life forms from nature or other synthetic ecologies. Humans were shown taking tours of the region, quite cautiously so as not to disturb anything.

I must have watched six of these 3vids, each going into the genetic inventions, the formation of the area and startup of the ecology, the endurance trials, and the judging. These were overviews, and I looked at only three in detail to see more of the design choices the genetic inventors made. It took all day, without any interruption except to go and fetch small meals.

Earth knows what it is, a biological planet. Luna does as well. We are a mechanical planet, or rather, a satellite. Mars is confused about it. This might be another reason there is some deep psychological rejection of other worlds. Somehow today this reaction was overcome, and I was truly fascinated by what I saw. I think I will spend the whole fiveday off-shift looking at synthetic ecology 3vids. One day has not made me wish I was an earthling, far from it. It is more like they are just one more subject of education. It will be interesting if I mention any of this in my next talk group meeting. Over the years, some people in talk groups have mentioned earth and 3vids from there, and their reactions and so on. No one seemed to react much to it, however, so perhaps I will just participate in the host's topic only.

19

NOBEL POSES A CHALLENGE

The merged talk groups continued to meet on the problem of encouraging immigration into Nobel, and one speech from Nobel year 464 stands out. The speaker pointed out that lunites cannot be bribed. What can they possibly be offered? They already have the food they need, and by taking time to seek out specialty delicacies and have them prepared, they can dine at whatever level they want. Is there some amusement that might be sufficiently appealing? For athletics, Nobel offered any opportunity that was desired, and a seventeen could exhaust himself in a large variety of different ways. There were friends to be made here, and the population was large enough so that finding an interesting person was not difficult. Health was well taken care of, as genetically, seventeens are resistant to almost everything. Reconstitution centers fix anything short of brain destruction. Life can't be prolonged, so no promises are possible. A seventeen's life will end at the appointed time, give or take a few years, barring brain destruction in some horrible accident. There is nowhere to go on the moon that a seventeen cannot request to go visit, and stay for a period long enough to get to know it. Intellectual stimulation is like a flood on Luna, with information on anything available from one's own sentience, and smart people gather together in talk groups continually.

In short, there is nothing to offer a seventeen with one exception. A challenge. Seventeens are raised to gravitate toward something that would be difficult to do, but possible. The speaker ended by saying that to improve the attractiveness of Nobel, it would have to find some challenges.

Earth could learn from that speech. Their attempts to entice lunites into common projects were centered on a process, not on a challenge. The goals of the various outposts seemed to be lost beneath the things that needed to be done, activities, reports, transfers, supplies, and more. If there was a goal, such as starting a new mine in the middle of a barren lunar landscape, their offers might have been more readily accepted.

Nobel wasn't offered any new challenges as a result of this speech. The population problem the nobelites were facing did not grow any worse, and the population never decreased year-to-year, but neither did it resume its upward growth. The death rate from Centaurus seventeens who had migrated into Nobel gradually increased, and was compensated for by an increase in the gestation rate. Still, emigration outweighed immigration considerably. This condition did not spread to other mines, however, so the problem was unique in its magnitude to Nobel.

Other large mines did find some challenges to take on. In Nobel year 471, Gautama finished their Mars dome. Gautama had taken a large secondary shaft, stretching down to a residence level at 180 meters depth, and sealed the circular wall surface for pressurization. There was the usual two-way spiral staircase stretching up to the lunar surface, and the gautamians had removed the building covering the shaft, and replaced it with a 11 m wide transparent dome, made of the same extremely strong and tough material that was used for the Mars domes. The dome was pressurized, and even more, next to the airlock 180 meters down, there was a large ventilation system that circulated air upwards.

As on Mars, the dome material was made of multiple thin invisible layers, which together had a very low heat conduction coefficient, meaning those who sat around in the dome could do so at the same temperature as was ambient in the mine, plus or minus two degrees. It was not designed for any utilitarian project, such as an Earth observation telescope, but for simply the enjoyment of gautamians, who could bring small meals up to the surface and enjoy looking at Earth while they ate. The dome material blocked ultraviolet, so the sun posed no threat at all to the diners.

Walking up or down 180 meters is nothing for a lunite, unless they are on death watch, and the dome has been scheduled to saturation since the day it was completed and made available. Some time was blocked out for those who stopped over in Gautama on their way to another mine, as a measure of the hospitality that Gautama had for everyone else. Even with the thickness of the dome material, and its resilience to thermal stresses and micrometeorite impact, safety precautions were taken. The original airlock was left in place, and the ventilation system would snap shut if air pressure in the dome dropped suddenly. There were suit cabinets inside the dome, and more cabinets with breathing helmets along the shaft. Using them was part of the drills that happened in Gautama, and other mines as well. Visitors could be expected to be prepared for the worst, even though it was an extremely low probability.

The dome was called Phobos within Gautama, and perhaps there was a plan to build another called Deimos sometime in the future, when Gautama grew larger. The other mines seemed to call it the Mars Dome. For some reason, perhaps known only to gautamians, it became a tradition to have a certain specialty dish when eating up in the dome, and the nearest nutrition facility to the dome entrance started ensuring it was always available. The dome was occupied fully and continuously. Nobelites did visit Gautama for various reasons, and those with planned visits always included dining in Phobos as guests of their gautamian hosts. Talk groups on Nobel often raised the topic of having one, but no plans were ever made for it. It would most likely have included sinking another secondary shaft, as the one used in Gautama was much wider than the usual shaft. It was currently on the edge of residential areas in Gautama, but plans for expansion were concentrated around the novelty. Another circular residential island was being planned, similar to the ones on the path between the two main shafts there, but away from this line.

In Nobel year 472, Sirius surprised the residents of Forrester with a vehicle-load of rare-earth metals, distributed not according to their prevalence in the very rich ore deposits that led to the Sirius site choice, but according to the prevalence of usage at the large mines. Forrester and the other small mines had rare earths, combined with other metals, and could refine them out, but it was often more efficient to use substitutes and accept the diminution in performance of whatever equipment was being built, whether it was recycling catalysts, semiconductors, or whatever. Sirius, without asking in advance, simply took what it had in great abundance and started to share it. Forrester had done a great deal in the founding of Sirius, and it was chosen as the first recipient. There was enough in the vehicle load to last for many years at a tiny mine like Forrester.

In the same tenday of the next year, Sirius did it again, but with Orion, another notable contributor to Sirius' founding, whose volunteers concentrated especially on the head frame and hoist apparatus. It seems to be a luna-wide pattern that volunteers for large tasks, like setting up a new mine, to gather into bunches from one mine, a group of friends and acquaintances taking on a task where they can continue to be together. Sometimes, though rarely, a whole talk group has gone off together. Sirius provided their vehicle of rare earth metals to Orion, which was almost identical to the one that had been provided to Forrester. Orion was the next largest mine in population to Forrester, as BBS, which started after Orion, had grown much faster and now exceeded Orion's population by ten percent or more. Some small mines seem to be more attractive for some reason than others, and population figures reflect this.

Sirius chose to make their gift of rare earths an annual thing, and each year one mine was the recipient of the wagon-load of rare earths. Each of the small mines other than Sirius received a shipment, one per year, always on the same tenday, and it was noted, Sirius had timed their departures so that the arrival was in the same tenday of each year. Sirius did not make any announcements of why they were doing this, and there were no refusals or suggestions to take the vehicle somewhere other than its intended destination. Nor was their recipient announced in advance, but by the third year, when Armstrong got the gift, the departure of a vehicle convoy from Sirius at about the right time was used to accurately figure out where they were going with their present. It was a major clue as to whether the convoy would go east or west on the Armstrong Circumlunar Highway, as that allowed the timing calculation to fix which mine the convoy would arrive at during the tenday that was being called the Gift tenday.

The following year, at the appropriate time, there were two convoys on the Armstrong Circumlunar Highway looking to arrive somewhere during the Gift tenday. One had left Sirius, and sentiences had been monitoring the vehicle departure schedule at Sirius to find out in advance where it was going. The idea of a surprise simply did not work on Luna. Sirius' leadership was under no obligation to propagate this vehicle schedule in advance, and so it was completed and allowed loose in the communication channels two minutes before the convoy started their engines and left. Sirius obviously would have preferred to have a surprise, and this was the closest that they could come to it. No convoy showed up at the main shaft of a mine unannounced.

The other convoy left Armstrong, and was of no interest to anyone on Luna, as the number of convoys on the Armstrong Circumlunar Highway was large, as well as on the Grand Loop through Gautama. The convoy from Armstrong arrived at Sirius within 30 minutes of the convoy from Sirius arriving at BBS. The Armstrong convoy contained a vehicle load of rhenium, as a gift to Sirius. Armstrong had two very large and rich veins which that rhenium with molybdenum and rhenium with copper. The two associated metals were easily found everywhere, but rhenium was not. So Armstrong decided to return their gift and sent Sirius enough rhenium to last them several decades. It should be noted that no communications between Sirius and Armstrong ever mentioned the idea of a trade or barter. According to the records, this was a pair of gifts.

This went on for some time, with no mine asking for a gift of rare earth elements, or rhenium, or anything else, but both Sirius and Armstrong continued making their annual donations to different mines. Sirius was going through a second round for the small mines, when, in Nobel year 483, they gave their rare earths to Boötes, one of the larger mines. Boötes had not had any of the immigration deficiencies that Nobel had, and was, in fact, almost as large in population as Nobel, with the trends clearly showing they would pass Nobel in the near future if Nobel did not figure out its problem and solve it. Boötes was refining its own rare earths, from ores that had them as contaminants, so they did not need rare earths from Sirius to deal with a substitution situation. Nevertheless, the efficiency of the gift was very obvious. Sirius could refine rare earths and transport them to Boötes for a small fraction of the cost in energy that it took Boötes itself to produce them, so from a combined economy viewpoint, it was useful. From a self-sustenance viewpoint, not so much.

Every time the Sirius convoy arrived on the Gift tenday, speeches were given. At Boötes, the speeches by the sirians emphasized the contributions of Boötes volunteers to the air purification systems within the Sirius habitats and the recycling facility. They even mentioned the gift of a self-contained habitat with one of their tiny living creatures, even though it had already died. The Armstrong people who accompanied their gifts of rhenium never talked about any gratitude for the founding of Armstrong, but instead just spoke briefly about the good relations that existed between all mines, and how it should continue.

The next year, in Nobel year 484, not only the small mines were watching the schedules of convoys leaving Sirius, but the large ones as well. The gift went to Nobel. To be honest, this amount of rare earths was a nice contribution, but the energy saved was only a small part of Nobel's energy consumption. Nevertheless, the Sirius delegation was warmly received, treated to the finest residences for visitors in Nobel, and feted with meetings from all of those in important slots.

While these words of gratitude were being offered to many different mines, they were also being earned. In Nobel year 475, Ague-Tuilet's leaders had called a conference on starting the next mine, and Centaurus asked to be excluded, for the first time in the history of Luna. They had started, or shared the starting of 13 mines so far, and had simply decided to let other mines have all the fun. They would provide volunteers, but no leadership of any task teams. This may not have been completely agreeable to everyone on Centaurus, but the public meeting held in response to the call from Ague-Tuilet resolved this, and everyone came to a consensus on it.

The first step in Ague-Tuilet's plan was to decide on a site, and there was to be no hasty decision. The mines, all except Centaurus, submitted suggestions, and a 3vid conference was convened to narrow that down to four. The list of good sites from LPO exploration and some other early exploration was growing thin, and it was time to add to the list. Of the four, none were along the Armstrong Highway. The first one agreed upon was south of Gagarin, and the second one was south of the highway, but for a direct path, west of BBS. A third one was fairly close to Andromeda, to the southwest, and the only one north of the Armstrong Highway was northeast of Armstrong mine, midway between the Jackson and Morse craters.

Nobel had come back to life with respect to new mine contributions, and volunteered to do the exploratory drilling in the four sites. So did Gautama. The result was that each would do two, cutting the time in half. A chance draw had Nobel get the first two, and Gautama the others. Ague-Tuilet would handle the road locations to these sites, all of which might become future mines if the exploratory drilling proved to be very positive. Gagarin would assist with volunteers. Boötes would handle the solar shields the drilling teams needed, with help from Armstrong,

Andromeda, BBS, and even Sirius and Glasov by way of volunteers. By Nobel year 478, Nobel teams were out on the surface, plunging the standard sixty drill holes very deep into the lunar surface. The first site was the richest in general, plus it had an ore body rich in tungsten, another in gold flecks, and a third in mercury. The second site was worth later investment as it also had rich ore bodies, with potassium and phosphorus higher than in most other places. Gautama did not do as well, and the two sites they investigated had ores, but one was not extensive and the other was not as concentrated.

Ague-Tuilet's leaders, those in charge of the new mine program, did not like in-person meetings, so everything was conducted by 3vid conference. The choice was made to go with the site south of Gagarin, who would be preparing to host all the teams going there for the next two decades. They could handle this. Gagarin's situation was the polar opposite situation of Nobel's, as it had been experiencing significant immigration for the last two decades. Their population in Nobel year 481, when the main shaft work began, was already larger than Nobel's, and they had exceeded Boötes more than a decade before that.

The naming subcommittee, with eight members from eight mines, had picked names and had chosen to name it after the two astronauts who died on the surface of Luna during the second return. There was such a negative reaction from the team members who were working on the mine that this suggestion was withdrawn. It was not that the brave astronauts who were the first to die on the lunar surface should not be remembered, but they should not be the namesakes of an active mine. Their names were already given to craters on the moon. One seventeen on the head frame team suggested Phoenix, which was something positive, being a mythical bird from Earth who regenerated after some catastrophe. Phoenix would symbolize the restart of progress toward settling Luna after the abandonment and failures that had started the program. It would be a first on the moon, having a bird as a mine name, but it caught the attention of the teams on the surface and down in the hole, so the naming subcommittee simply gave into the request. Phoenix it was.

The Phoenix mine was also unusual in that the habitation was done out of the usual order, leading to an early start to the mine, in Nobel year 485. This meant it would take much longer to achieve self-sustenance, but that was the new order of things as seen by the leaders in Ague-Tuilet. The habitation section was built large, holding two hundred people from the outset. All the downhole teams lived there, instead of on the surface.

In Nobel year 486, Nobel sent some volunteer seventeens, long-term residents of Nobel, who were not involved in a work assignment, to Gagarin for three tendays, in order to see if they could understand why Gagarin was growing so fast, via immigration from everywhere, and Nobel was just scraping by. There were six in the group, and Gagarin was able to host them, even with all the coming and going of Phoenix work teams. They came back with a conclusion, which was required, but it seemed unsubstantial. They reported that there was a mood at Gagarin, unlike that at Nobel.

Seventeens there seemed more lively, more enthusiastic about what they were doing, and more optimistic about everything they attempted. Seventeens are not prone to depression or pessimism, so this was just a comment about the degree of enthusiasm there, and the investigation team admitted that there was nothing physical that they noted that would account for the immigration differential. the food was a little better, and gagarinites seemed to be more enthusiastic about sharing meals with the visiting team than they had expected. The facilities were not as good as Nobel's, but they were more than adequate. Nobel's special features, such as the wading pools, had not been copied in Gagarin. They didn't have vegetation plots. They were just full of energy, in an intangible way. This was no direct help to those in Nobel who were concerned that the population might actually start dropping if no changes were made.

One nonsensical opinion was that Nobel was suffering because they were not on the Armstrong Circumlunar Highway, but that was obviously not the case, as Gagarin was even further from the highway than Nobel was. It was true that it was easier to travel to other mines for those who lived on the Armstrong Circumlunar Highway, and the highway had been contributing to an increase in travel, for visitation, temporary work assignments, and migration. In Nobel year 484, there was a public discussion, arising from some talk groups, about having scheduled circumlunar transportation. Once every two tendays, for example, a convoy of passenger vehicles could set out, stopping at the eleven mines along the highway to let off or take on passengers, for their final destination, or to take a break for sleeping. It would take two trips around to ensure all possible combinations of origins and destinations were included. This would eliminate many of the trips now being made, and eliminate the trips with empty vehicles returning to their source point. No action was taken, but talk groups in other mines noted the discussion, and fed back to the meeting point of contact that some of the mines had very little space for visitors who wanted to stop there, and that should be addressed before any highway transportation was scheduled.

Nobel was not on the Armstrong Circumlunar Highway, so it would not be a contributor to this new venture, but a talk group within the mine thought a better idea would be to have scheduled transportation around the Grand Loop, as it was now called, with five well-developed mines on it. The Grand Loop mines had the majority of the transportation between lunar mines, and it only made sense to put the first transportation there. The Armstrong Circumlunar Highway was much more attention getting than a simple loop on the earthside face of the moon, but the arguments were quite valid. Later in that year, Nobel put a tentative plan together for this scheduled transportation, with a convoy going not once every thirty days, but continuously around the loop, about once every tenday not counting stopover time.

Gautama, Ague-Tuilet, and Centaurus immediately agreed that this would be a resource saving activity, and were in agreement with the plan and the schedule. Gagarin was not. They had a public meeting, attended by those most interested in the topic, and they wanted a special vehicle to be designed for this, with a higher top speed. In fact, they had such a design, or at least the basics for one. There would be three vehicles in the convoy, so in case of the coincidence of a vehicle breakdown, which actually never happened on the lunar surface because of the intense care for both the vehicles and the route choice, and a solar flare warning. All the passengers could get into the two remaining buses and get to the nearest solar flare waystation, and crowd into the shielded area.

Since the flare danger was mostly one to as much as three hours, the crowding meant that the capacity of the vehicles could be large, and all five mines had more than ample space for as many visitors as could fit on three vehicles. Some had very nice special spaces reserved for visitors, e.g., Gautama. These mines had most of the unique features of mines on the moon as well, meaning visitors staying between convoy passages would not be completely bored. There was, however, talk of having two convoys go simultaneously, either in the same direction or in opposite directions. That was left for later, and Nobel became the coordinating center for the transportation, which began in Nobel year 486.

One group of Nobel seventeens, who had developed a strong interest in the early Earth moonshots, was quite interested in having counter-traveling vehicles, as that would allow them to bring visitors to a secondary stop along the Centaurus-Gautama leg of the Grand Loop, which ran quite close to the remains of Luna 21 and Lunakhod 2. Centaurus had often discussed whether these should be collected and housed in a museum inside Centaurus, but it was never done, and they now lie almost pristine on the lunar surface. Centaurus sometimes took visitors to see them. This Nobel group wanted to build a site on the Grand Loop, with a solar shield and a vehicle to travel from the highway out to the artifacts. It was put off until later, when the transportation system was more developed. Along these lines, Boötes began discussing a out-and-back addition to Nobel's Grand Loop route. This would connect with the Grand Loop schedule and take passengers to Boötes and back from Centaurus. Boötes was the only large mine not included in the Grand Loop, and seventeens there thought that was certainly not a good idea, efficiency-wise, and so on. Their next step was to work with Gagarin on producing more of their faster vehicles.

Nobel year 488 was the year that Earth finally won its persuasive game with Luna. It was done by persistence. Earth had started with their visit to the Nobel half-centennial, which was the way that Earth got its foot in the door. Their next step was to set up visits to Boötes by some sixteens interested in genetics from one of the largest arcologies on Earth, located on the east coast of the Baltic Sea. It was one trip at first, in Nobel year 455, and again the visitors must have been winners of a sociability contest. The trip was repeated two years later and began to be a ritual. By Nobel year 459, there were trips beginning from Earth, actually from a different arcology located on one of a series of huge lakes in North America, to the smaller mines on the subject of mining equipment. Underground mining equipment reached its peak in technology before Centaurus was established, and not much had changed since then over the centuries that had passed, but there were some things that could be shared.

In Nobel year 468, some Mars visitors, with Earth participants from an arcology on the mouth of the largest river in South America accompanying them, went on tours of Centaurus and Ague-Tuilet, which were examples of successful large mines for Mars' single large mine. Gestation specialists started visiting in 473, and like all of the previous ones, this turned into a series of repeat visits, not every year but every few years. The gestation teams visited several mines, but different ones each trip. People who grew specialty foods on Earth started visiting in 480. There were a total of five arcologies involved with visiting the moon, the three original ones plus two more, both on archipelagos. More trips, one each for recycling facilities and the processing of halide ores, happened in the early 80's, and this led to return visits, with the expansion to cadmium and tellurium processing. The Earth visitors were all of the same ilk. They were quiet but friendly, good at absorbing information and not forceful in the least. No one seemed to mind talking to them, and the only difficulty was that, beyond the sterilization equipment requirements in Centaurus was the costs in fuel and ship supplies, mostly borne by Centaurus itself, with assistance from Nobel and Gautama.

Tn Nobel year 485, a tipping point occurred. This was the speech made at a public assembly welcoming one of the Earth teams to Nobel, by Gricen Sator Nibet, a young seventeen gestated and raised in Andromeda, who had emigrated to Nobel twenty years before. Gricen talked about how the mines on Luna were marginal. There were so many factors that had allowed Centaurus and the successive mines to become self-sustaining, and the one that was so commonly referred to, the richness and diversity of ore deposits on the crust of the moon, was certainly one. But he spoke of the technologies that Earth itself had pushed to its limits, in many areas, all of which were crucial in making life on the moon a net positive balance.

The energy needed to do everything needed for life was costly in that everything had to be mined, and the amount of energy needed for all the mining was much less than that needed to support the mines by a significant multiple. But the multiple was high only because Earth had developed recycling and reuse technologies and techniques, that were remarkably efficient and convenient for a population living close together to use. The multiple was high also because of Earth's development of successively more efficient ways to process ores, separate materials, and process them into components needed in manufacturing, which in itself was made very efficient by Earth, long ago before Centaurus was founded. The same was true for nutrition, and the biological and physical processes needed for it were the result of Earth's brilliant technological progress, as were air purification, fuel processing and delivery, transport, lighting, and every single aspect of life on Luna.

If Earth had failed in any of these areas, for example if power generation had been less efficient over its whole life cycle or required more materials, or if it did not have the reliability or longevity that it did, there would be no energy left over to provide a pleasant existence for lunites. Gricen said he could go on and on about the accomplishments of Earth's technologists and how so many of them were absolutely mandatory to sustaining life on the moon, but he stated that Luna owed an unmeasurable debt to Earth and especially its technologists for what they had done. He concluded by saying that lunites needed to step up and contribute to this process. The speech was so lavish it likely embarrassed the Earth guests, but they accepted it cordially. It was recorded and transmitted everywhere, and somehow it was raised to being one of the best speeches given on Luna.

It resulted in two things. One was the chatter in talk groups about participating in research and development, at least in the largest mines. The second was what Earth had been silently working toward: participation in Earth's projects. Over the next three years, as work terms came to an end, volunteers came forward to return to Ceres and to go to Mercury to work inside the wheel on their remote mining ventures on the Mercury surface. In 488, the jackpot came, and seven seventeens volunteered for the Jupiter wheel. All the plans that Earth made for Luna's contribution were fulfilled. Again, the only problem was that it meant much higher costs for Centaurus, which managed the spaceport.

This spate of volunteering did not disappear but appeared to continue. Even before the Ceres pair had finished their tour, more were on the way there. Jupiter received three more, who left Luna in 491. The Earth visits continued, and something like a good relationship between Luna and Earth was underway.

The planning for the next centennial, a big one for 500 years, began five years in advance, in Nobel year 494. Nobel had done such a good job of managing it for the previous half-centennial, that the same pattern would be followed with some additions. One involved Gagarin.

After the last celebration in Nobel year 450, when Gagarin people had brought a demonstration Ceres vehicle over to Nobel, interest in it faded away, or rather was replaced by different interests. Gagarin's more vehicle-interested seventeens had switched from a surface flying vehicle to an indoor flying vehicle, of course much smaller. A different group had decided on a different leisure project, and had produced, by Nobel year 460, an automaton like a snake that was crawling in the corridors of Gagarin. There was no new technology involved, just some hobby activity. The robotics projects seemed to lapse for some time, but again in Nobel year 479, more automatons were seen, snakes of two sizes, one two meters long and another stretching three and a half meters. There were also flying objects both with movable wings and encased propellers, and jumping objects. They were entertaining to watch, and visitors returned to their own mines with the idea to invite gagarinites to bring them for celebrations there.

In Nobel year 480, the automatons were brought to Gautama for the opening of a new residential plaza, and were some of the more interesting objects there. In 481, they were brought to Boötes to celebrate some visitors from Ceres, and later that year to Armstrong for the opening of a new panel of their arrays. Two to five trips a year happened from then onward, and in 483 they were invited, among other trips, to Orion's 250 year commemorative celebration happening in the last quarter of the next year. By that time, there was a new star of their show, a rolling object with eyes on the axles, able to flex and right itself if it tipped over. Orion had someone on their half-centennial committee who had been to the last Nobel half-centennial and had ridden in the surface Ceres vehicle. Orion politely asked if that could be along brought as well.

The Ceres vehicle had long ago been committed to recycling, and there was nothing left of it. But gagarinites loved a challenge and agreed to do it. They built another flying vehicle, able to hold four riders, with more power, twelve nozzles, four large non-movable ones and eight directable ones. The fuel tanks were much larger, and the vehicle was completed and fully tested, including safety concerns, before it was due to leave for Orion.

Over the next decade, Gagarin seemed to show such overwhelming energy that they had produced twice as many varieties of automatons, and had included better sentience in some of them, so they could navigate a whole mine. The snakes could climb stairs, go up poles, and even move upwards in one place on Gagarin where there were two parallel walls a quarter meter apart. The other automatons had gained capability as well. The automatons were divided into separate groups, and were getting familiar with many mines other than Gagarin. They had also improved the Ceres vehicle. In Nobel year 494, just after the 500 year centennial committee was formed, they sent in an early request to Gagarin to bring all their toys to Nobel, spaced out over the year.

One of the other novelties for the 500th anniversary was going to be a music contest, of three types of music but supposedly only that specifically written to commemorate Nobel's half millennium of growth. It was accompanied by a poetry contest, also of three types, in the three dialects of Dorn. The poetry could be of any type, as long as it celebrated the half millennium event. Lastly, they announced a history contest, a competition between any of the seventeens in Nobel who would write a history of the mine, from year 0 to year 499.

This was in addition to the complete schedule of activities that had appeared in the half centennial fifty years ago. Some of the competitions in sports and athletics were expanded in terms of the numbers of contestants, and Nobel allowed the all-Luna committees on the different sports to include all the rule changes that had happened since year 450. Some talented individual in Andromeda had picked up making silhouette theater presentations, and he was invited to give a series of shows during the celebration. The next four years were spent in planning the details of the schedule, the logistics, and the housing for visitors. This led to few surprises. No moon-quake happened. Earth was invited to send visitors, and they responded almost immediately with an determination of how many would come and when, since they had the tentative schedule in hand by this time. By the loose days of Nobel year 499, everything was in hand, and on the first day of 500, the history competitors submitted their versions.

DIARY ENTRY (AGE 399, DAY 266)

How I enjoy sleep. Last night was another ideal night. How many diary en-tries do I have now about sleeping? Enough. No point in writing another one now.

Instead, today I am writing in my diary about what I found in the com-mline this morning. It is the biggest thing for me in years. There was an announcement sent to everyone but really meant for me. A writing contest has been announced in Nobel.

I feel I can take this on and finally show off my abilities. I may be the best possible contestant. No one I know keeps a diary but me — I write in it frequently. Nobody I know cares as much about Dorn grammar and vo-cabulary, at least, no one ever talks much about it. The competition is to write a history of Nobel on the occasion of its five hundredth anniversary. Since I am one of the older people here, 399 years old, I have lived through almost all of the history. I know the history like my own life, and I can write it well. I have been everywhere and done everything in Nobel, and the city holds no secrets for me. I have participated in its great events, although mostly as a spectator. Now is my chance to leap from being a spectator to being a contributor.

I will use my diary to plan my victory in that contest. First things first. I must have a schedule. They give the contestants one hundred and twenty tendays to write their entries. I could do in half that time, but the full du-ration will give me time to be fully organized. Three hours a day — no need to burn out — instead, stay creative. To make the time, I'll have to reschedule my time with friends and partners, my sports time, my relaxation time, my meditation breaks, my social commitments like meal organizing for the neighborhood, wall checking, my work time in the recycling units, and maybe even my talk groups. Today I will attack my calendar and begin the re-organizing. I am on my way!

DIARY ENTRY (AGE 399, DAY 269)

What happened to my enthusiasm and excitement about trying to win the history writing contest? Yesterday, as soon as I read the commline announcement, I thought I would try and I felt I could win. But now, I'm not so sure. It is open to all of Nobel's eighteen thousand inhabitants. I know a lot of people, but nothing like even 10 percent of them. There are probably tremendously good writers who do more than keep diaries. Just because I don't know them doesn't mean Nobel isn't crawling with them. How many hundred competitors will there be?

I was about to disrupt my whole life for a hundred and twenty tendays or more, and what if it was just a waste of time? My life is full of interesting activities. Why should I shut that off, just to compete? Maybe I could just spend one or two days each tenday, doing something short but very clever. I could probably find three or six hours somewhere each tenday, without changing anything in my schedule. Since I'm older than most people here, I'm probably better at finding something unique and interesting to write about. Maybe I could write about the interaction with Earth that has been accelerating for the last fifty years. Or about some of the public assemblies we've held to discuss our future plans or celebrate the results. Or about the centennial and half-centennial events that make Nobel a unique mine, at least for a year every fifty. Or maybe that's not such a good idea, because so many people all over Luna listened to the talks and participated in the celebrations. Maybe something less popular and well-attended would be better.

Tomorrow, I will read the detailed contest rules. There is no need to be hasty about this; I need quiet time to think up a good strategy. Maybe I have a chance, without too much effort and disruption.

DIARY ENTRY (AGE 399, DAY 298)

I was not going to say anything about competing in the history of Nobel contest, because I didn't want anyone bothering me about how I was doing. Especially since I might find it too difficult and give up early. But I slipped and talked to my friend, Balat, who caught the mention and started prying into my choices. Now I'm committed. He'll tell everyone we know.

Worse yet, I read the contest rules, and they say the history has to cover the whole 500 year history of the mine. Not a single incident but the entire thing. That means effort, and a lot of it. So do I do a quick thing, and then everyone will think I'm not really trying, and joke about me. Nobel people joke about everything and everyone. Four hundred years of living here, and I haven't gotten a thick enough skin yet that I can ignore it.

A hundred and twenty tendays is a pretty long time to put up with a disruption. I have spent twenty-nine years on the work trip to the K-scope at Saturn orbit, nine out and fifteen back, with five in the shack, and that was nothing like living here on Nobel. I put up with it, did my duty, and came back with no psychological trauma. there were only fourteen people to interact with on the ship during hibernation breaks for the twelve years on the cycler, and the same when I returned, so not much opportunity for involvement. The avatar crew tried to keep things interesting. That was over a hundred years ago, but I haven't changed much. So I can stand some separation from normal life for a hundred and twenty tendays. Tomorrow I should make the application.

DIARY ENTRY (AGE 399, DAY 301)

So I filled out the application. It didn't say if I was number one or one hundred. Probably, number one thousand. But I'm in, and Balat will be asking me about it when we meet at the dayfive talk group tonight. I'm not canceling talk groups, because I can get some of the members to listen to my chapters and comment. The rules say no sentience help and that nobody can help me write, but somebody can read it and comment. There's a fine line there, I suppose. It doesn't say you can't have fifty people read it and comment, so I'm going to use that rule to its fullest extent.

I'm not going to meditation tomorrow. It's good for calming and clarifying thoughts, so maybe I should keep going to the dayone sessions and only ditch the daysix one. I'll see how much I need it and miss it. Even on the Saturn cycler there was meditation.

Tomorrow, during my new free time, I will start writing. I don't see how I can start writing about Nobel's first year, which is where I probably have to start the history of Nobel, without any background. I need to say something about our founders, about the struggles they went through, the decision to start the mine, the planning they had to do, and the great difficulties they went through to get the resources together. I need at least one whole chapter on this. Conditions on Centaurus were so important they could not be ignored. Maybe I need two chapters, as Centaurus is huge and was even large 500 years ago. One chapter can be on the mine itself, and another on the founders who left there to form Nobel. There is a lot to write, both about Centaurus and also their experiences, and I got some very good mentoring lessons about it.

When I was young and in my mentoring phase, Nobel had only been around for a hundred years and didn't have all that much history yet. So the lessons were about Centaurus, and how they developed. I remember the lessons even now, and when news from Centaurus comes to us, it makes more sense to me, I suppose, because I know the history better. So, first thing, write one or two chapters about Centaurus, before Nobel was founded. I could even write something about Earth, as that was mentioned a bit in the lessons. Not too much, because lunites often find Earth history tedious.

Nobody can go there because our bones would break, nobody goes outside to look at it except for some vacuum walking exercise, or in the Mars Dome on Gautama, although we have good videos of it during the different solar phases taken from GEO. Once, we decided to ignore them when they stopped communicating with us, although the convocation was pretty divided. All convocations, whether neighborhood, region, mine-wide, or Luna-wide, are always pretty divided, though, so that's not saying anything.

I'll put a little in about Earth before Centaurus, but not enough to bore people. That would be a contest-loser. I could even go back to the first space activities there. Everyone knows about the Apollo program just from the comedy shows. I must have heard a hundred jokes about why the earthlings almost stopped coming to Luna after the program was successful: Everything from golf balls going too far to walk through ("The course would be the size of Aristarchus Crater") to the amount of dirt those travelers tracked into their lander ("Buzz, did you shake your boots off on the top step?"). This recurred after about two hundred years of getting Centaurus started, or whatever it was. We lunites almost universally feel Luna is the best place in the solar system, and anyone who had a chance to come and didn't is a perfect fool. I can't imagine seriously why they would quit, except maybe they had one of their wars (people wasting resources killing one another) or something else crazy. But, unlike seventeens or even the twelves, the original humans were not particularly bright to begin with. A few paragraphs should be enough. I certainly can't cover cavemen.

DIARY ENTRY (AGE 400, DAY 2)

One of the first questions I need to resolve for my contest competition is language. Dorn is the only language of the seventeens and all of the earthlings on Luna speak it well, or they would not have been sent here. It is universally known on Earth itself. All the other outposts use it. It is inevitable I would write using Dorn. My judges will be seventeens living in Nobel, but certainly my submission will be available to others, even back on Earth or out on the Jupiter wheel, so I should choose carefully. Which form?

I can choose based on ease of writing, clarity of content, likeliness of winning, or appreciation by a wider audience. Ease of writing might be a good choice because then I can write a longer submission with the same effort. But length is not necessarily something that will help with the other goals. Clarity is important because vagueness would be disliked by the judges and by other readers, but it should not come at the cost of making the submission tedious to read. That would be another negative for the judges, although the contest announcement did not provide any specifications as to what the judges might decide to favor. This makes the likelihood of winning a difficult measure to evaluate.

For a wider audience, should I include those who do not know Dorn? The three types are not equal in their ability for the sentiences to translate into one of the ancient languages. Dorn was created before the first mine on the moon was inhabited, as the best possible language for communicating precisely and quickly, as well as for the ability to remove ambiguity in discussing complex topics, such as some more abstruse science and engineering. The ancient languages are not as good receptacles for complex topics, but I will be writing about the simplest subject possible, history. So translating into ancient languages should be done easily, no matter what form of Dorn I use.

Should I really care about translating for people who have never learned Dorn? These are likely only originals, and I have met some originals in my life, on GEO during my tour there and while visiting Centaurus for meetings with earthlings, and none of them couldn't speak Dorn. Sentience tells me there are many millions back on Earth using only ancient languages, but

I suppose that it is certainly not worth the trouble to make a different choice of Dorn variant than I would otherwise.

The Dorn authors divided the language in three forms seven centuries ago so that ideas that fit the different forms could be expressed in the form which suits them best. The juxtaposed form is good for creativity and quick communication when deep understanding is already present. History is creative in that I will have to choose what to include and what to emphasize, so perhaps that is the best form. The short form is good for logical arguments and streamlining discussion, and it is what is used in most of the talk groups most of the time. I probably use it more than the other types, so perhaps I should stick with that. The long form is great for explicit statements, especially in mixed time concepts or clever relationships between ideas. History has a few intricacies, so there may be a reason to go for the long form, even though it is harder to write. It is poor form to write something with mixed form, but I could do that, perhaps in an organized way. It does degrade understanding to switch too much, but I am planning to write a long submission, so perhaps I can use two forms in different sections. But why, and wouldn't that be a negative for the judges?

The judges could actually read it in any form, with their sentiences translating for them if necessary. The authors of Dorn made sure that this could be done accurately, but the resulting translation is not what anyone would write if they were writing in that form. What goes on in the brain depends on which form you choose to write in.

I think I will go for maximum clarity in complexity, and use the long form of Dorn. This will allow me to write more explicitly. Nobel's history is not that complicated, but I want to be clear chronologically, which is best handled by the long form. After all, history is all about how events work out and how they are connected to one another.

DIARY ENTRY (AGE 400, DAY 43)

Writing is an exhausting occupation. Wringing words one by one out of the brain and recording them, only to revise them a few hours later, leaves that part of the brain depleted. Writing a diary entry after writing a thousand word or even less is like trying to jump up all six levels in Nobel in rapid succession. Energy just gives out. I have decided to sacrifice writing in my diary when I am in this state. After almost four hundred years of writing whenever I felt like it, I find myself in a new state of inability. In this state, I don't even think of writing anything personal. I don't even think about the diary that often.

Figuring out what facts to put into the history and what to leave out takes another burst of mental energy. Perhaps I now know why history writing is so rare.

I have finished a draft of the first chapter, perhaps the most boring for Nobel's judges. The idea of setting the stage for Nobel ran away with me, and the first chapter turned out to be mostly about Earth. I was going to write about Centaurus in the first chapter, but after a few paragraphs covering Earth's history, I just decided that there are too many antecedents in Earth's history that needed to be mentioned. I suppose it would even be possible to write a whole history, just about Earth. I can't imagine I would ever want to do it, or anyone would care to read it. The changes they went through, evolving from early humans to the new species, which includes us, could occupy a whole book. It certainly wouldn't be of much use for lunites, as only the last few centuries had much effect on us, and the effects are all that matters, not what the earthlings went through to create them. I'll think about thinning it out to the more essential items if time permits. Next, after I've gathered my strength, I'll start on the first part of the history of Centaurus. But no more diary entries for a while.

EPILOGUE

What does the future hold for Nobel? After compiling an exhaustive history of its first five hundred years, it is only reasonable to be curious about the next five hundred. There has been no indication whatsoever that Luna will not continue to expand its population, both at each current mine and at new mines. In five hundred more years, there may be twenty or thirty new mines, and more highways, even ones that are transformed so higher speeds can be safely accomplished. Resources will not be a constraint for perhaps a hundred thousand years, even with forty mines, as usage is so minimized.

Technology ran its course on Earth and finished itself off four hundred or more years ago, and nothing is left but applying it to some new situations. Nobel will not be changed in any way by technology, and in five hundred years it will look very similar to today, as far as utilities, mobility, activities, and everything else go. The same will be true for the other mines, and on Earth as well. Earth will inevitably continue its population decrease, which is gradual and well-planned, as there is no benefit to a huge population.

The most significant changes in the solar system will be happening at the outposts. Mars may figure out how to be self-sufficient completely, and Mercury, despite a later start, may do the same. But there is no indication now that anywhere else will be successful. The Uranus outpost will certainly help in developing the techniques needed for interstellar travel, if the Saturn K-scope ever finds somewhere to go. I am beginning to think that five hundred years is just a little bit of mankind's future history, and to understand mankind in the broadest scheme, one would have to be curious about the next fifty thousand years. If we spread through the galaxy, our little history that we have so far in this solar system will be like the first paragraph of our long-term history. The results from the K-scope will tell us, Earth and Luna and everywhere, what lies ahead of us for expansion beyond this solar system.

For millennia in the past, Earth regarded itself as a monumental and unique location, which it was and is. But when one considers how humanity is modifying itself and dispersing throughout the solar system, Earth no longer seems so important. The solar system is now the most important location, and that prominence will shrink if mankind makes the leap to interstellar colonization. Perhaps the history of the solar system will be a short note in the introductory chapter of the history of mankind written fifty thousand years from now.

With such a vision of mankind's future, I can only feel regret that the facts of genetics only allow lives to be extended to five hundred years. I would like to see the first interstellar ship launched, but it cannot happen. Thus, the writing of this history of Nobel has left me with a strange type of sadness, thinking about how the successful history of our great mine might be so overwhelmed by future successes that it is not appreciated by anyone alive at a far future date. An alternative view sometimes erases this sadness, when I realize I am contributing my atom to the building of the future. I have done my duty and can be proud of that.